Moondog's Academy of the Air and Other Disasters

Moondog's Academy of the Air and Other Disasters

Pete Fusco

Writers Club Press
New York   Bloomington

Moondog's Academy of the Air and Other Disasters

Copyright © 2000, 2010 by Peter J. Fusco

Published by Writers Club Press
an imprint of iUniverse, Inc.

iUniverse books may be ordered through booksellers or by contacting:

iUniverse
1663 Liberty Drive
Bloomington, IN 47403
www.iuniverse.com
1-800-Authors (1-800-288-4677)

Because of the dynamic nature of the Internet, any Web addresses or links contained in this book may have changed since publication and may no longer be valid. The views expressed in this work are solely those of the author and do not necessarily reflect the views of the publisher, and the publisher hereby disclaims any responsibility for them.

Cover art by Taylor Meier

ISBN: 978-0-595-09709-8 (sc)

Printed in the United States of America

iUniverse rev. date: 09/27/2010

Dedication

For Lynn and the kids. They put up with a lot of grief, including a swarm of locust, while I chased my flying dream.

Preface

I learned a great many things in the writing of this book. Mostly, I learned that books such as *Moondog's Academy of the Air and Other Disasters* don't just happen. They're fated.

In 1970 my first flying career, seemingly cursed from the start, came to a dead end. I left flying and changed careers. Through an unlikely set of circumstances too unbelievable to be included even in *this* book, I became a reporter for the Dayton (Ohio) Daily News.

In 1978, through yet another unlikely set of circumstances, I returned to flying, reasonably certain—but with no guarantee—that the playful aviation gods had forgotten about me. With any luck, they had found another patsy to torment. Surely, I had amused them enough during my first flying career.

At that point in my life I felt uniquely qualified to write a book about pilot misadventure and aviation's droll uncertainties—*especially* its droll uncertainties. My newspaper years had taught me how to take a very small detail and blow it wildly out of proportion, a skill essential to landing a story on Page One and, not coincidentally, the writing of humor. As for small details, I had become something of a living index of extraneous, disconnected flying story details.

The trick was to link them. It took a very long time. *Moondog's Academy of the Air and Other Disasters* remained a "work in progress" for a decade. It wasn't entirely my fault.

Each time I thought the story complete, I'd meet another pilot who'd contribute a gem so stupid or, in rare cases, so profound that I had no choice but to work it in somewhere. I'd tailor the new info to fit my needs and implant it into the manuscript. As often as not, the insertion would dictate the rewrite of at least a few paragraphs or pages, sometimes an entire chapter. It dragged on and on.

I might never have finished the book at all were it not for a dozen or so pilots whose faith in the project far exceeded my own. Over the years one of them would spot me on a ramp, airport terminal or bar and demand, "Is that book finished yet?" I'd squirm with guilt, gather my strength and resurrect the project.

Despite the encouragement, the chore often seemed impossible, the rewards uncertain, even if I did manage to finish the book and get it published. Why bother? What was I trying to prove? Writing, particularly the writing of humor, is a hell of a lot of work. One of the reasons I became a pilot in the first place was to avoid work.

Writing is also a sequestered, friendless lifestyle. During long hours staring at blank pages my only contact with other life was with Puffyrito, the somnolent, moody former alley cat officially licensed to the neighbors but who preferred my company, not to mention the fish-pond in my back yard. Puffyrito seemed to appreciate that a writer's life, like that of a cat, is a lonely, paranoid, superfluous existence. He tried hard, though seldom successfully, to stay awake as I ran dialogue, characterization and turn of phrase past him. Not surprisingly, the rejection letters pleased him most of all. Cats live for human failure.

While old Puffyrito sought fulfillment in sleeping and spooking the fish, I sought mine in writing. I pressed on, driven by the conviction that, while my own passing may be little lamented, it would be a crying shame to take so many good flying stories to the grave. I even convinced myself that there existed a *need* for a book that viewed aviation from an oblique angle, a book that celebrated pilot folly, botched opportunity and, of course, villainous employers.

As the pieces slowly came together, this book grew both in size and scope. Rather than my own story, it became the story of *all* pilots who ever chanced the long odds against making a living flying airplanes. For continuity I've written the book in the first person, as if I had lived all the experiences. In exchange for this license, I willingly take the heat for the indiscretions and idiocy of many other pilots.

Taking the heat for others wouldn't be so bad if I could also hog some of the glory. Alas, *Moondog's Academy of the Air and Other Disasters* is mercifully free of heroes and heroics. It's about working pilots, who are not heroes and don't want to be. Most are happy to just fly airplanes, avoid the weather, draw a paycheck and drink a little beer. Like me, they want only to be remembered as pilots whose lifelong number of landings equaled their number of takeoffs. Many heroes are far too willing to write their stories; stragglers like myself seldom bother.

This book is neither entirely fiction nor entirely non-fiction. Where truth and invention collided, entertainment alone decided the victor. The reader is forewarned not to attempt to separate the two. Such analysis would only ruin the fun and, besides, the reader would be wrong most of the time. Truth is not only stranger than fiction, it's a lot funnier. And if the truth is sometimes squeezed extra hard to extract the humor, make no mistake about one thing: Everything in *Moondog's Academy of the Air and Other Disasters* happened, not necessarily to me nor in the order or manner related, but *it all happened.* All of the characters are real, some disguised more thinly than others.

While I never rejected a worthy character, not every story made the cut. One pilot, for example, told me a great yarn about his days flying contraband televisions and the like from the Texas border into Mexico to sidestep high duties in that country. On one trip he was forced to dead stick his single-engine Cessna 205 onto a Mexican beach after the engine failed. His boss flew down to the beach, surveyed the situation and talked him into sitting inside the disabled Cessna while the boss *towed* it into the air and back to Texas with a second Cessna 205.

Frankly, I did not believe him. That is, until he showed me a *picture,* a clear 8-by-10 glossy, taken from the tow plane. That picture remains one of the most remarkable aviation images I've ever seen, the equal of the Wright Flyer on that thunderous day at Kill Devil Hill or the fiery end of the Hindenburg. I had a perfect spot for the towed-off-the-beach story but left it out of the book. It certainly met my standards for pilot brainlessness, but it was too far-fetched. No one would have ever believed it—with or without the picture.

Moondog's Academy of the Air and Other Disasters targets a variety of audiences:

1. Pilots as yet unborn, destined to inherit an aviation world sanitized of all fun by corporate and federal memo fairies.

They should know that there was a time when pilots who took themselves seriously were a hated minority.

2. Professional pilot hopefuls who see flying lessons as a ticket to easy street. For them this book is intended as a primer, a sobering glimpse into career prospects at the hands of unsympathetic, manipulative employers and the aforementioned mischievous gods of powered flight. Many valuable cautions are included at no additional charge.

3. Working pilots currently struggling to find a comfortable berth in aviation. They may gain encouragement in the fact that others have persevered and succeeded.

4. Pilots who have beaten the odds and are sitting pretty— temporarily at least. They will find a perverse validation of their indefatigable courtship of aviation.

5. Pilots who by some miracle never suffered on the way up. The lucky bastards will learn what they missed.

6. Anyone, pilot or otherwise, who enjoys a good laugh.

This book contains some pungent language. I can't remember how many times I took out the four-letter words only to replace them a day later. Working for pirates, slave drivers and con men such as Moondog McCutchinson, Ernie Gorotny and Three-fingered Hank drives one to such language. I've tried not to use it gratuitously and only in the interests of humor or, in some cases, history. Adversity may be the mother of humor, but belligerence is the uncle who shows up drunk at the family reunion with his girlfriend instead of his wife.

A fair warning: No one even remotely associated with the flying gig is spared in *Moondog's Academy of the Air and Other Disasters*. In the interests of fairness I've tried to scorch all equally and, because it's so richly deserved, no one more than myself.

The author

Acknowledgements

Captain John Palmer, one of the great chief pilots, who once gave a kid with no time and even less potential a shot at the Big Iron. It was the start of an airplane ride that would last a lifetime. Thanks!

Captain Mason Green, who stuck his neck out for me.

Captain Bill Angel, who also helped me get hired and who once bought Cleveland Hopkins a new taxiway light.

Captain Jimmy Ledbetter, whose flagrant disregard for historical accuracy proved invaluable in the writing of this book.

Captain Jack Morgan, an expert on Corrosion Corner and just about everything else.

Captain Bill "Firecan" Haddock, who tried to teach me the finer points.

Captain Ralph Queener, a big fan of this book. May he fly his B-24 in smooth air for eternity and never see another ME-109.

Captain Jim Piavis, who always waited until 2 a.m. to call in an idea.

Captains Bob Weir and Roger Perkins, who overlooked the fact that I had been flying a typewriter for seven years and took me back into the aviation fold.

Charlie Stough, who shared his editing expertise for the price of a box of good cigars.

Barney McIlvaine, who listened to every idea in this book at least ten times.

And to the hundreds of unnamed pilots who contributed to this book through comment, example, reputation or legend. I thank the good guys as well as the jerks. Both gave me a reason to write *Moondog's Academy of the Air and Other Disasters*.

Any flyin' job's better'n any non-flyin' job.

Lloyd Baker, pilot instructor

Prologue to Chapter One

In 1962 I would not have guessed that the lowly Piper Cub would ever be celebrated, much less someday hang from a museum ceiling. Yet there it was, a Piper J-3 Cub restored to factory new, its yellow paint job gleaming in the museum floodlights. I squinted to read the bronze plaque provided with the exhibit.

"The Piper J-3 'Cub' was built in great numbers during the 1940s. It is considered one of the finest training aircraft of all time. During its long career the Piper Cub introduced thousands of pilots to the wonders of flying. The museum's example is displayed as a typical training Cub might have looked in flight."

"Typical training Cub? They call this a typical training Cub?" I whined, to no one in particular. My comment annoyed another museum visitor standing close by.

"What's wrong with it? Looks like a beautiful Cub to me," he said.

"Nothing's wrong with it!" I snapped. "Absolutely nothing! That's the problem. Don't you see?"

"You crazy or sumpin,' buddy?" he said, before quickly moving to the next exhibit. He kept a wary eye on me. I couldn't blame him. Museums attract loonies.

Had he remained, I would have explained how the museum's Cub was clearly a charlatan, more hoax than history. The ship was too intact, too unblemished to warrant the title of "training Cub." I once slaved in genuine training Cubs during the larval stage of my flying career and felt betrayed, as if the museum had rewritten the past and invalidated my suffering. At the very least, this misrepresentation of a training Cub masked the cynicism of airport operators and the desperation of thousands of flight instructors who began their flying careers in such aircraft.

The museum should have consulted me if they seriously intended to convey the image of a Piper Cub doing hard time as a trainer. I imagined what I might do if the museum lowered the Cub to the floor and gave me a day or two to correct the mistakes.

The gleaming yellow paint would be my first challenge. Training Cubs didn't gleam; nor were they really yellow. They were more a faded shade of bile, streaked prop to tail with indelible grime, scorched oil and raw gasoline. After I remedied the bogus paint job, I'd fray the control cables, splinter the prop tips, loosen every bolt on the airplane a turn or two, scuff the windshield with cinders and tear holes in the fabric in places no flight instructor at old Brookside Airport would have ever bothered—or dared—to inspect. As a final touch, I'd round up a dozen rats, big ones with razor teeth, and turn them loose to gnaw at the tires and landing gear bungee cords at night in a darkened hangar.

Thus authentically abused, the museum could again dangle the finished product from the ceiling and know that posterity would be served the truth about "training Cubs."

The museum deception did not end with the condition of the airplane. The bronze plaque further explained:

"...The mannequin in the back seat is the student pilot. The mannequin in the front seat is his flight instructor."

Except that the flight instructor did not look the part. Not even close. Some idiot had dressed the impostor in a shirt and tie, leather jacket, military Raybans and wide-brimmed hat. Hell, the hat alone would have gotten him laughed off old Brookside Airport, maybe even beaten up. Adding to the insult, the instructor's smiling face glowed with contentment and job satisfaction. No doubt about it, I'm certain W.W. Storm, Hangardoor Herliwitz and I would have kicked his ass before we ran him and his shiny Piper Cub off the field.

An armed guard stood nearby or I would have used something sharp and proffered, in the name of historical accuracy, the following addendum to the bronze.

"Neither this fairytale Piper Cub nor the heavily tranquilized flight instructor with the silly-assed grin ever spent a single hour in the employ of Moondog McCutchinson, aviation outlaw."

The museum managed, probably by accident, to get one thing right: the student pilot, the bewildered skinny kid in the back seat of the Cub. I shuddered at the recollection, overwhelmed with guilt and shame even after four decades.

1

There wasn't much to recommend flying as a career in Cleveland, Ohio in 1962. When a desirable piloting job became available, it went to a guy with a square jaw, ten thousand hours flying time and a drawer full of air medals. Flight schools, charter operators and corporate chief pilots laughed in my face. They wouldn't even talk to a nineteen-year-old kid with a handful of new ratings and two hundred hours total flying time, half of which they suspected—correctly—were brazenly falsified.

Rejection spawned disillusion. Disillusion spawned despair. As my options dwindled, I began to doubt that I would ever break into the aviation dodge. Properly humbled and desperate, I was prepared to accept, unconditionally, the first harsh canon of professional aviation: No matter how bleak the market for flying jobs may appear, there always exists one position with pay so scant and working conditions so grievous that no pilot with any real qualifications would even consider it.

Which is how, for the record, I began my flying career working for an ex-biker named Moondog at a patch of toxic wasteland known as Brookside Airport.

A flight instructor friend told me about the opening, which he created himself when he quit Moondog after not quite one full morning on the job. I ignored his warnings and decided to apply. I drove my 1948 DeSoto to Brookside Airport, located in the sooty shadow of Cleveland's industrial flats.

Without leaving my car, I lit a cigarette and sized up the operation. It was not encouraging. The cinder runway had potholes the size of my DeSoto. The wooden hangar, a relic from an earlier aviation age, leaned hard to starboard. The roof was peeled back like a canned ham. Wrecked and nearly wrecked airplanes were everywhere; they fought for airport space with orphaned autos, rusty bathtub cores and disemboweled, flaccid mattresses that overflowed onto the airport in unchecked migration from an adjacent junkyard.

Amid the airport rubble were a half-dozen randomly scattered Piper Cubs caked with mud, sludge and all manner of organic deposits, including but not limited to bird droppings and the kaleidoscopic remains of untold generations of flying insects. Cubs at other airports were invariably a cheerful "Cub Yellow." Not these. Corrosive fallout from the nearby steel mills had chemically mutated the yellow paint into a color normally seen on the ground near roller coasters. Great patches of peeling paint made the Cubs appear to be in molt.

Could this be the training fleet? Did I really want a flying job this bad?

The sound of gunshots coming from behind the hangar aroused my curiosity. I got out of my car and, staying close to the hangar for cover, peeked around the corner.

The gunman was built like a length of concrete sewer pipe. He wore dark coveralls, a black leather motorcycle jacket and a biker cap. His left leg was twisted; the foot crabbed ninety degrees off course. In one hand he wielded a bazooka-sized pistol; he strangled a whiskey bottle in the other. The description matched the one I had been given of R.P "Moondog" McCutchinson, owner, operator and supreme commander of Brookside Airport. The description came with a caution to "approach the man carefully even if he isn't armed and drinking."

A guy in a suit, standing a few feet from Moondog, was trying to talk to him. Even at that early stage, I knew that anyone wearing a suit at an airport spelled trouble. He was either a fed or a banker. In either case, Moondog didn't seem to care. He ignored the man and reloaded. He took aim at the rusting core of an aircraft engine trying to hide in the weeds. The pistol barrel moved in drunken, elliptical orbits.

"Boom, boom, boom, boom, boom, twang!" Moondog's first five shots missed. The sixth shot ricocheted off the engine into the corner of the hangar just above my head, pruning away a couple rotted boards. I hit the deck. Splinters and wood ants showered down on me.

With the echo of pistol shots and the smell of gunpowder fresh in the air, I chanced another peek around the hangar as I picked biting ants off my neck.

Moondog probed the pockets of his coveralls and motorcycle jacket. He seemed to be looking for more ammunition but found none. It didn't please him. He took a swig from the whiskey bottle. It was empty, which pleased him even less. He threw the bottle over his shoulder and continued his ammunition search, rooting around in the dirt with his foot for live cartridges he might have dropped.

The man in the suit, taking advantage of the ceasefire, again tried to talk to Moondog. From my prone position, I cupped my ear and strained to hear what he had to say. There was a slim chance I would launch into aviation with this Moondog character and I sensed the information might prove vital.

"Uh, McCutchinson, our bank feels it has been extremely patient and generous with you...," the suit began.

The guy was a banker. Bad news. The Federal Aviation Administration likes to believe it controls the aviation game but banks hold the real power. The feds have never cost me a flying job. Bankers have pulled the plug on several.

Moondog continued to ignore the banker's presence.

The banker, a tall, slim man who walked with a giraffe-like cant, swallowed hard. "Fine, you don't have to talk to me, McCutchinson. Just as long as you understand that the terms of your note must be met in sixty days or we'll foreclose on this airport. That's final!"

His message delivered, the banker took out a notebook and began wading through the airport blight, presumably searching for anything that might bring a buck or two at auction. He then pushed his luck, speaking over his shoulder to Moondog. "Frankly, McCutchinson, we'll be doing the community a great service when we shut you down. This place is a disgrace. It looks like hell, like no other airport I ever saw in my life! I don't suppose it ever occurred to you to clean this pla..."

The banker stopped mid-word when he turned and saw that Moondog had the pistol pointed at him.

"Hey, McCutchinson, what do you think you're doing?" he said.

"Git offa muh fuckin' airport!" Moondog grunted. It was a fair warning, the kind a large predator might issue to clear a watering hole of lesser creatures in the afternoon heat.

"Hold on a minute, McCutchinson, this isn't exactly *your* airport," the banker said. The guy had balls.

Moondog, apparently not in the mood to argue minor ownership technicalities, clicked back the hammer on the pistol.

All I had planned to do was ask about a flight-instructing job; instead, I was about to witness a homicide. Did I really want to testify against this man?

I couldn't watch. I turned away.

When I heard no shots after a half-minute or so, I looked again on the confrontation.

The banker hurried toward his car, apparently unwilling to bet that Moondog was out of ammunition. No doubt disappointed that Moondog had not groveled, he would have to be content to wait for the day when he would have the intense satisfaction of putting another deadbeat airport operator out of the aviation business.

I also started to leave. Like the banker's inventory, my flying career could wait. My immediate objective was to get out of pistol range. This gun-toting lunatic didn't know who I was and I planned to keep it that way.

I climbed into my DeSoto and began the process of starting the engine, which took five minutes on a *good* day.

Moondog came around the hangar and spotted me. "Hey, you, wuddaya want?" he challenged. "Ya lookin' fer flyin' lessons?"

He jammed the pistol, still cocked, into his motorcycle jacket and started limping toward my car. Moondog's left foot, jutting out sideways from his corkscrew leg, made him appear to be traveling in two directions at once. He moved surprisingly fast for a big, drunken man with feet that fought against each other. The DeSoto's balky motor gave him time to catch up with me.

"I'll ask ya 'gain," Moondog said, nearing the car. "Ya lookin' fer flyin' lessons?" It was not a friendly inquiry.

"Naw, not really," I answered out the car window while I pumped the gas pedal and held the starter. I coaxed the engine with fiery curses. Sometimes it helped.

"Wudja call me?" Moondog said. "Didja jist call me a dirty bastard son of a bitch?" He made a move for the pistol.

"Oh, no, not you sir," I said contritely, wrenching my face. "My car, I just called my car a dirty bastard son of a bitch. Honest!"

"Oh yeah, the car. Geez, it *looks* like a dirty bastard son of a bitch." Moondog thumped his fist on the roof of the DeSoto. The roof changed shape but I didn't protest. He grabbed the doorpost and seemed intent on keeping the car from moving even if I succeeded in getting it started. Which I didn't.

Moondog studied me with eyes better suited to scanning tundra for food. His nostrils flared.

Don't show fear, I thought. I hoped he couldn't hear the valves in my heart clacking.

"So wuddaya want? Wutcha doin' here? This here's private property. Ya 'ware o' that?" Moondog's voice had an edge.

Moondog released his grip on the DeSoto. While he awaited my answer, he removed his biker cap. With a bear-like claw he scratched the outline of an S-shaped scar on top of his shaved head. Minus the cap the cylindrical, stocky Moondog looked less like a sewer pipe and more like an enormous artillery shell, the kind they used to haul around on railroad cars in World War One. Given the choice at that moment, I would have gladly taken my chances with the artillery shell.

"Ya ain't a' instructor by any chance, are ya?" Moondog grabbed the doorpost again and shook the DeSoto. He leaned through the open window into my face; his breath reeked of alcohol and menace. I heard his stomach rumble, as if it were digesting large chunks of raw meat and bone. An assortment of zippers, bits of chain and metal studs on his motorcycle jacket scratched what little paint remained on my car door. Again, I didn't mention it.

"I needs some goddamn instructors. You a' instructor or not?" Moondog asked again.

There are some faces into which it is not possible—nor recommended—to tell a lie. I quit cranking the engine and forced myself to look at Moondog. I came clean.

"To tell the truth, I *am* a flight instructor and was going to ask about a job but you look busy so I'll stop back later, sir. No problem at all. I just got my instructor ticket and you probably wouldn't be interested in hiring me anyhow, sir. I don't have near as much time as my logbook shows. Lots of Parker Pen time. Know what I mean? Heh, heh. Sorry to bother you, sir. As soon as I get my car running, I'll be leaving, sir."

I couldn't believe what I was saying. After two years of spending every cent I could lay my hands on to earn my pilot ratings, I was doing my best to convince this man—begging him actually—*not* to hire me.

"You're hired! Get your ass in the office. We're 'bout to have a pilot meeting," he said. Moondog pointed an imperious finger at a shack that served as the airport office. "I'll be over in a few minutes."

He hired me on the spot, despite my self-deprecation and admission of a spurious logbook! Aviation's like that. Sometimes 25,000 hours of flying time and a dozen lunar landings can't get you a flying job. Other times just showing up, not too drunk or high, with no outstanding warrants or recent crashes and a reasonably steady pulse, is sufficient.

Moondog's tone, not to mention the pistol, made it clear I had no right of refusal in this, my first aviation employment opportunity. As ordered, I got out of my DeSoto and walked toward the office shack, sidestepping numerous puddles of frothing black oil.

Thus did I join the ranks of professional pilots on that long-lost summer morning, not to the sound of cheers and popping champagne corks but to threats and the ring of pistol shots.

Moondog hollered across the field to two guys who had also watched the scene with the banker from a safe distance. He ordered them to the meeting.

When the two entered the office, I introduced myself. They were Hangardoor Herliwitz and W.W. Storm, Moondog's other flight instructors. I nervously asked for information about my new job and, in particular, my new boss. Hangardoor and W.W. bitched about the wretched conditions and pay but they confessed that they somehow enjoyed working for Moondog. He was, they explained, dangerous and unpredictable but always entertaining.

"There's two kinds of flying jobs, goods ones and fun ones," Hangardoor told me. "I don't like good flying jobs, too many assholes makin' too many rules."

How right he was.

While we waited for our boss to enter the office, the three of us speculated on what Moondog might have up his sleeve.

"I've never known Moondog to call a pilot meeting like this," W.W. said. "He ain't the meeting kind. Must be something big. Probably's gonna tell us this is the end of good ol' Brookside Airport."

"I'm not so sure," I said. "Why would he hire me?"

"That worries me even more," Hangardoor said. "It could mean he's cookin' up a way to keep the airport open. I was kinda hopin' he'd shut this place down. I could use a break."

Hangardoor, I soon learned, had little to lose if the airport folded. A dedicated cynic who saw no future in aviation, Hangardoor had already pretty much retired from flying at age 24. He instructed as little as possible, preferring to spend most of each day sleeping on a bed constructed from four oil drums and a door which had fallen off the hangar.

Aviation has a place for everyone.

"Maybe there's something to the rumor I heard 'bout some kind of new plan Moondog's got to save the airport?" W.W. said.

I listened eagerly. The fortunes of all pilots rise and fall on rumor.

"Yeah, just remember that the fiasco with the monkey started with a rumor about an airshow," Hangardoor said.

I knew about the monkey fiasco. In fact, most of northern Ohio knew about it. Earlier that summer Moondog had staged an airshow that featured, among other equally unforgettable acts, a monkey named Spikey. Moondog outfitted Spikey with a tiny parachute, which he tested by dropping the monkey off the hangar roof several times. The test drops were flawless.

On the day of the airshow, Moondog grabbed the reluctant primate and took off in a Piper Cub. He made a pass over the crowd and tossed an object that looked like a monkey out of the airplane. The parachute failed to open. The monkey fell to the cinder runway, striking the earth with a sickening squishing sound.

"'Splud!'" is how W.W., an eyewitness, remembered it.

The crowd screamed in horror. Moondog made a second pass. He held a frantic Spikey by the neck out the open door of the Cub for the crowd to behold. What had fallen to the ground was not Spikey but merely a monkey doll stuffed with a ripe cantaloupe.

The duped crowd cheered in joyous relief, unaware it had just watched a lurid dress rehearsal of Spikey's imminent demise.

On the third pass Moondog tossed the real Spikey out of the Cub, following a brief and bloody struggle audible from the ground. The parachute popped open. For a few brief moments Spikey was a star. The little chutist floated down softly amid wild applause. It appeared he would land directly in front of the crowd. It was a perfect jump, a credit to Moondog's genius as showman, not to mention Spikey's skydiving expertise.

Clearly, an airshow act to end all airshow acts.

But Spikey apparently grew apprehensive—or bored; no one will ever know for certain—as he neared the ground. He began climbing the parachute shrouds and grabbed at the canopy with his little monkey hands. The crowd thought it all part of the act and laughed at the darling Spikey.

Until the chute collapsed.

Witnesses, the few who could talk about it, grimly recalled a shrill death wail as Spikey, holding the bunched-up chute over his eyes, plunged to the heavily-traveled road in front of the airport. Whether or not Spikey survived the fall is still hotly debated wherever Brookside Airport alumni gather. A speeding truck, however, mooted the issue.

The humane society levied a stiff fine against Moondog. Harsh publicity from the unrelenting Cleveland media took an even greater toll. Moondog's cold, unrepentant comment to reporters on the day of the incident didn't help. "When's your number's up, it's up, even if you're a goddamn monkey," Moondog was quoted in the *Cleveland Plain Dealer.*

Brookside Airport seemed beyond salvation, condemned by Moondog's shameless schemes and unabated neglect. One by one, the students vital to the success of a small airport stopped coming for their flying lessons. All that remained were Brookside's loyal airport bums, a small contingent of apparently homeless pilots who hung around every day but seldom had even the few dollars it took to rent one of Moondog's time-ravaged Piper Cubs. Nothing short of a miracle could save Brookside Airport.

Such was the mood while the three of us waited for Moondog, whom we could hear relieving himself outside against the office shack, marking his territory.

Moondog entered and slammed the door behind him. I was about to learn that nothing good for a pilot ever comes out of a pilot meeting.

"What's the deal, Moondog?" W.W. asked before Moondog had a chance to say anything. "You shuttin' this place down or something? Do I have to go back to sellin' shoes? Christ, I hate selling shoes."

Many pilots in those days fell back on selling shoes with frightening regularity. Usually they made more money at it than they did at flying.

Moondog let the comment slide. He seemed to be in a pretty good mood, despite the banker's ultimatum. He had the look of a man with an idea. An idea, as it turned out, that would revolutionize pilot training in Cleveland, Ohio—for a few months at least.

"Now would I hire this new kid here if I was gonna shut down?" Moondog answered, pointing to me with his anvil chin.

In truth, it would not have been the first time a pilot was hired and laid off on the same day.

"In case you geniuses ain't figured it out yet, we're dyin' here, headed down the toilet," Moondog said. "If we don't git some new students pretty goddamn quick, there ain't gonna be no airport anymore. You guys is gonna be out of work, like you was when I found ya. The Polacks is gonna be growin' cabbages here."

Moondog sneered in the direction of the enemy, a poor but impeccably maintained Polish neighborhood that bordered the airport on two sides. Residents of the neighborhood had co-existed peacefully with Brookside Airport since the 1920s. Tensions began to build only after Moondog took over the year before. His midnight buzz jobs, impromptu low-level aerobatics and drunken three-day hangar parties were a dark side of aviation the airport's neighbors had never known. The old Polish ladies made daily reports of Brookside Airport activities to anyone who would listen including, of course, the FAA. Oddly enough, the feds seldom bothered Moondog. They seemed to regard his operation as a kind of aviation subspecies not entirely within their jurisdiction.

"I gotta plan to bring in new students that's gonna make us all happy," Moondog said, allowing the suspense to build while he adjusted the brim of his motorcycle cap. The cap, the leather jacket and his twisted leg were all that remained of Moondog's glorious biker days. The back of the jacket, which he seldom removed, sported a faded silkscreen of a naked infant with glowering eyes and a knife in its teeth. Above the infant's head appeared the legend, "God's Children, Cleveland, Ohio." It was the closest thing to a corporate logo we had at Brookside Airport.

"What I'm gonna do is start a guaranteed solo plan," Moondog said. "A forty-nine dollar and ninety-five cent guaranteed solo. We're gonna solo any asshole who strolls in here with a heartbeat and fifty bucks. Cash, of course. It'll be the biggest bargain around. No one's gonna be able to resist. Everyone in this stinkin' city's gonna be a pilot before I'm done."

He made the announcement like it was some kind of big deal. Frankly, I had expected more of Moondog, considering his reputation. A lot of airport operators offered guaranteed solo plans. The going rate was about one hundred dollars, *twice* what Moondog proposed. At best, guaranteed solos were a come-on, a way to snag new students, some of which would hopefully stick around after they soloed and spend more money renting airplanes. Even at a hundred dollars, operators were lucky to break even. Teaching people to fly for *half* that amount didn't strike me as inspired. I didn't yet know all the details, however.

Moondog read our minds. "You guys is probably wonderin' how we're gonna be able to teach people to fly for fifty bucks and still make money," he said, eyeing each of us, "but it's real simple. You're all gonna have to make sure everybody solos in four hours. Or less, preferably."

Just like that! Teach a person to fly in four hours. Or less! Most students did well to solo a Piper Cub in eight to ten hours.

W.W. Storm was the first to speak.

"What if they take a little longer than four hours, Moondog?" he asked in a voice far from oppositional. "Lotsa people do ya know."

"Not at my airport they ain't gonna!" Moondog snapped, way too confidently. "Not after ya hear 'bout the little incentive program I got worked out for you guys."

I should have figured that what Moondog had in mind wasn't an ordinary guaranteed solo plan. I braced myself.

He explained his "incentive program." "Let's face it, you instructors always dog it a little and stay with students a couple extra hours 'fore ya solo 'em to bleed money out of us airport operators," Moondog said self-pityingly.

I've heard the same line many times since in my career. It's always presented by some management prick who begins by accusing the pilots of sticking it to the company. The speech invariably precedes the new austerity plan, longer working hours and pay cut.

Moondog played with his leather cap again. The stall was meant to give us time to appreciate how lucky we were to have any flying job at all.

"Here's how it's gonna work," he continued. "You'll get your usual hourly rate, but for every student you solo in four hours or less I'll pay a five-dollar bonus!"

The boss suddenly enjoyed our rapt attention. In 1962 the going rate for flight instructors was under three dollars an hour. Needless to say, the five-dollar bonus was considerable inducement. I held my breath and waited for the catch I knew was coming.

"However, if ya takes more than four hours with a student I ain't gonna pay ya nuthin' for the extra time. I might even charge ya for the gas ya's burnin'."

Talk about inducement! Moondog hit us where we lived with that one. Flight instructors, generally considered the lowest form of flying professional, have worked for starvation wages since the Wright brothers. Instructing for peanuts was the norm and just barely acceptable; instructing for *free* was unthinkable. Not that we had much choice. It was either agree to Moondog's terms or get out of flying, a fear which nags all working pilots their entire lives.

"Take it or leave it," Moondog said. His eyes darted among the ranks, searching for signs of dissension.

I thought about the offer. What the hell, it wouldn't be all that tough to solo someone in four hours—or less—if I concentrated mostly on takeoffs and landings and skirted the finer points, most of which I didn't completely understand anyhow.

W.W. and Hangardoor felt the same. To a man, we accepted.

My budding aviation career became inextricably linked to an ex-biker named Moondog with a highly unfeasible guaranteed solo plan fraught with pitfalls for both student and instructor. Somewhere known only to them, the Gods of Aviation Misadventure, sipping nectar and smoking good cigars, must have smiled broadly.

"I guess ya know, Moondog, that the problem with these guaranteed solo plans is that there are some people who can't be taught to fly no matter how much time you give 'em," the veteran instructor Hangardoor said prophetically as the meeting broke up.

Moondog McCutchinson, champion of aviation in a difficult time, shrugged his shoulders. "If that happens, send the goofy bastard ta me. I'll take it from there," he said.

His tone chilled the room.

That same day W.W. and I made a sign out of a crippled Cub wing panel reclaimed from the drainage ditch that ran alongside the runway. We stuck it out on the road in front of the airport. Large red letters on the wing advertised to the passing public: "LEARN TO FLY! GUARANTEED SOLO ONLY FIFTY BUCKS! WOW! INQUIRE AT OFFICE."

I wrote the copy.

Reaction was immediate and better than anyone had imagined, even Moondog. People gladly overlooked Brookside's appearance, the condition of the airplanes and the ongoing *Plain Dealer* editorials about the exploited monkey. Eager applicants queued up with their fifty dollars to take advantage of the aviation bargain of a lifetime.

Within a month every unemployed flight instructor in the Cleveland area worked for Moondog. The fleet of six Piper Cubs stayed airborne from dawn to dusk. Brookside Airport became a pilot-training assembly line, equaled only by the efforts of an air force under wartime pressure.

Teaching a person to fly well enough to solo a Piper Cub in four hours proved surprisingly simple, even though it required skipping over most of the recommended tutelage in the first hundred or so pages of *The Flight Instructor's Handbook.*

New students received a short but sobering indoctrination ride, which included a couple spins and graveyard spirals to instill in them a fear of the more obvious dangers of powered flight. The next three hours were devoted to takeoffs and landings after which the student, understandably reluctant, was urged to solo. Some had to be shamed into it. A half-dozen student pilots, capable of a reasonably safe takeoff and landing but blissfully unaware of anything else about flying, soloed each day. On the ground, their cringing flight instructors stood with backs to the action, fingers crossed and eyes closed.

Moondog was delirious with joy over the success of his guaranteed solo plan. Some days his good moods lasted almost an hour. Ever the promoter and aviation innovator, he allowed newly soloed pilots to take their mother or girlfriend up for a quick hop around the patch. No charge.

No one dared mention it but every instructor on the field knew that the situation was ripe for disaster. We were on the constant alert for winos and drug addicts with fifty bucks and a sudden urge to learn to fly. But because life's really grand debacles give no warning, none of us thought twice about the skinny kid with the ready smile and shrunken T-shirt.

His name was Elwood and I was to be his flight instructor, the first of several.

"Hi, name's Pete," I said, holding out my hand. "Guess I'm gonna be your instructor. Be here 'bout seven-thirty in the morning and we'll get started." It was the standard opening line of flight instructors the world over.

I started to walk away before my new student could assail me with questions. I wasn't being paid enough to answer questions. Besides, I didn't have many answers, then or now.

"Before we start, I got something I think I ought to tell you," Elwood said meekly, almost in a whisper.

"What's that, Elwood?" I asked, not the slightest bit interested.

"I think you should know that I tried to learn to fly at a couple other airports and didn't do too good at it," he said. "In fact, my last two instructors told me I should never try to fly an airplane again as long as I lived. They said I might kill myself and maybe some other people."

"Ah, don't worry 'bout it," I said. "It ain't that hard to learn to fly. You probably just had shitty instructors."

They were brash words, words of the unseasoned and unwary, words that would ring loudly in my ears for weeks as Elwood painfully reshaped my belief that flying was an effortless pleasure meant for everyone.

I passed Moondog as I was leaving for the day.

"Hey, Fusco, that kid you got in the mornin' already has six or seven hours o' dual from somewhere else," he barked.

"That's right," I said. "So what?"

"So here's what: git the kid soloed in an hour."

"Or less!" I said, daring to ape Moondog to his face. "No problem. Couple times 'round the patch and I'll cut 'im loose."

"Make sure of it," Moondog said. "'Cause I got you scheduled for ten more students tomorrow."

Aviation is a table of feast or a desert of famine.

I arrived at the airport early next morning greeted by the usual heady aroma of hydrocarbons from the industrial flats. A row of open-hearth stacks towered over the airport like angry, semi-active volcanoes. Smoke from the stacks teamed up with the morning sun to create a blinding haze. It was a beautiful day by Brookside Airport standards.

Since I was the first to arrive, I entered the office shack to reheat the coffee from the day before. I inadvertently walked in on Moondog and his girlfriend Betty, engaged in what could only loosely be called a sex act. Betty, a redhead of enormous heft, lay sprawled over Moondog, eclipsing his own considerable mass. All I could see of Moondog was one arm and one foot, like the limbs of an earthquake victim protruding from the rubble. They were deeply submerged into the springs of a dark green velvet couch, the airport's only concession to comfort. Moondog grunted barnyard noises. I offered a lame apology and backed out of the office. I never sat on that couch again.

I decided to wake Al, our resident mechanic. Al lived in the back seat of his 1950 Buick, which hadn't moved in two years. His yellowed false teeth rested on top of the dashboard. The choppers stared blindly through the cracked windshield as if warding off evil spirits.

"C'mon Al, rise 'n shine," I yelled, lobbing a rock off the hood of the hulking Buick.

"Fuck you!" Al snarled. He tossed an empty wine bottle out the car window in my direction. Al was not a morning person.

Al had been a first-rate line mechanic for Pan American World Airways in the flying boat days before World War Two. He still wore his Pan Am mechanic's uniform, which once included a bow tie and a kind of pilot hat, both long lost. Among Al's few possessions was a faded photograph of him in younger, more sober days posing with a couple of gorgeous babes on the bow of a giant Pan Am flying boat in Miami's Biscayne Bay. Al grieved nonstop over the demise of the flying boats and aviation as it once existed in that idyllic photo. His curse was that of a man who had participated in a Golden Age but was not lucky enough to die with it. He was a mechanic of the Old School and, in keeping with the breed, hated all pilots indiscriminately.

"I used to work on real airplanes," went Al's tireless litany to the flight instructors on the field. "Them flyin' boats was like nuthin' any you assholes ever saw or is ever gonna see. They was bigger'n this whole fuckin' airport."

Unfortunately, there weren't any Pan Am flying boats at Brookside Airport and a lame Piper Cub seldom held Al's interest for more than ten minutes. A few days before, I had complained to him about an engine hemorrhaging so much oil it blackened the windshield of the Cub. Al didn't fix the oil leak. He did, however, offer a pragmatic solution.

"Wuddaya tellin' me 'bout some goddamn oil leak for?" he said. "Go git you a rag an' wipe the oil offa the windshield. Ya don't need ta be a mechanic to do that! Christ, are you stupid or sumpin'?"

Al was an early proponent of the four-day workweek. He'd walk away from the airport with his paycheck in hand every Friday afternoon, find a nearby bar and remain there until sometime Tuesday. He always returned. Be it ever so humble, Brookside Airport was his home.

Moondog kept Al around to work on the one airplane that received regular maintenance at the airport, a war-surplus B-25 Mitchell medium bomber. The previous owner had landed the B-25 with the gear up. He left the airplane for dead, just happy to have survived the crash.

A lesser person might have cut up the Mitchell for scrap but Moondog, a man beyond the call of ordinary transportation, hocked everything of value at the airport to get it flying again. He even sold his Harley.

When the Mitchell was ready for a test flight, Moondog commissioned an artist to paint a striking nude redhead, based on a picture of girlfriend Betty twenty years earlier and a few hundred pounds lighter, lying on her back on top of the fuselage. The babe's crimson locks cascaded over the nose; her wide-spread legs sensuously straddled the windshield, toes touching behind the cockpit. She was the *Big Red Momma Bomma,* the pride of Brookside Airport and the joy of Moondog's life.

Crawling out of the Buick slowly, Al squinted against the haze through bloodshot eyes. A cigarette dangling from the corner of his mouth suggested he smoked in his sleep. The threadbare, grotesquely stained Pan Am uniform hung on his bony frame like a curtain on a rod. The seat stretched to his ankles from years of being weighted down with wrenches and wine bottles. Exposure, nicotine and booze had partially mummified Al's skin, which was drawn tightly against the skull. His face was three-fourths jaw. He had the color and texture of those guys they dig up in peat bogs.

Al took a long, regenerative swig from a wine bottle—breakfast on the go—and walked toward the toilet in the hangar, sans teeth. He stopped at a crinkled Globe Swift fuselage pinned under a fallen tree. The fuselage was the daytime sleeping quarters of Pratt and Whitney, two extremely fierce and evil-natured airport cats. The cats' diet consisted chiefly of Brookside Airport's abundant hangar rats, whose diet consisted chiefly of Piper Cub landing gear rubber bungee cords. Everyone gave Pratt and Whitney a wide berth. Except Al.

"Goddamn cats kept me 'wake all night again with their fightin' an' fuckin' around," Al mumbled. "Now they thinks they's gonna sleep all day? Bullshit!"

He gave the aluminum fuselage a reverberating kick with his scuffed, steel-toed boot. From deep within the Globe Swift came a duet of howls, the cry of the damned awakened, the trumpeting of death on the march. Out walked Whitney, then Pratt, spitting, hissing, fur erect, claws sharp and glistening. The cats seemed ready and eager to retaliate.

I froze.

Anyone else would have been in serious trouble but when the cats saw Al they turned around and skulked back inside the fuselage. Somehow Pratt and Whitney must have suspected, as we all did, that Al's diet included an occasional airport cat.

A check of the airport fuel supply, a leaky war-surplus 200-gallon water tank on a trailer, showed it low. I hooked the trailer up to the airport pick-up truck, a relic of indeterminate age, color and manufacture, and drove to Smiley's Discount Gas Station.

"GET MORE MILEYS FROM SMILEY'S" avowed the sign over the gas pumps. Smiley was a drinking buddy of Moondog's and foolishly allowed the airport to put gas on the tab. I pumped a hundred and fifty gallons of Smiley's discount low-test, about thirty dollars worth, into the tank and drove back to the airport.

To give Moondog his credit, he was ahead of his time. The FAA did not approve automobile gas for use in aircraft for another 15 years.

I selected a Cub that promised the least resistance for the day's flying. It had only a six-inch rip in the rudder fabric. I found a scrap of cotton cloth and a can of dope.

As I performed the skin graft on the rudder, it would never have occurred to me that the Piper Cub would someday become a classic. As much as airport operators and student pilots abused them, it's a wonder that any Cubs survived long enough to even be considered for the honor. Nor does the Piper Cub seem to possess the attributes of greatness. Its uninspired barn door wings are abnormally, no, *clumsily,* large for its scrawny fuselage. The landing gear is too wide, too low. Cubs squat! The engine compartment, an odd afterthought of flimsy, exposed baffling, gives the airplane the appearance of a hooded, four-eyed insect. All in all, the Cub seemed to me a very homely airplane.

Alas, the Piper Cub proved to be a lot more airplane than the sum of its parts. In time its alchemic, magical proportions of wood, aluminum, steel and fabric even became beautiful. Don't ask me how.

I finished the rudder repair and filled the gas tank with some of Smiley's discount low-test. With any luck, it wouldn't contain quite as much water as the last batch. I sat down on a handy drum full of dope thinner, lit a cigarette and waited on my new student.

Elwood arrived right on time.

The first thing I noticed was that he didn't have the enthusiasm of most new students. He seemed to dread going up in an airplane. I attributed his uneasiness to the appearance of Moondog's fleet. I recognized the look and had a spiel prepared.

"Hey, don't worry too much about how this Cub looks," I said in an effort to calm my student. "Ya can't tell anything about the condition of an airplane by the way it looks." Of all the whoppers I've told in my life, that statement ranks among the least defensible.

I further attempted to allay Elwood's fears by demonstrating a Brookside Airport walk-around inspection. The procedure was never taken lightly, even by the most careless Brookside instructors since it involved making sure that Al had not borrowed an important airframe component for use on another airplane. Brookside flight instructors joked—nervously—that Moondog's fleet of six Piper Cubs was constructed from enough parts to build five.

Reasonably certain the Cub lacked nothing critical for flight, I proceeded to the left wing. I grabbed the wingtip and rocked the airplane violently.

"Wutcha doin'?" Elwood asked.

"Just checkin' the wing struts, Elwood," I lied. Actually, I was shaking out anything that might be under the seats, in particular the aforementioned *rattus hangarus.*

I spared Elwood the details, but the problem was that Moondog's instructors were seldom allowed to leave the airplane in the course of a typical twelve-hour day. This enabled Moondog, a shrewd if tyrannical efficiency expert, to schedule about two more students. At lunch and dinnertime Moondog tossed cold, soggy hamburgers or hot dogs into the cockpit, zookeeper-style. The hangar rats made nightly forays for the scraps of food that inevitably reached the cockpit floor. Now and then one would sleep off the feast under a seat.

A few days earlier an instructor named Bill Bates, better known as "Master Bates," and a student started their takeoff roll before they discovered a fat, frenzied and razor-toothed stowaway in the cockpit. The short-lived but fast-paced aborted takeoff amused everyone on the field except Master Bates, his student and the rat.

"Okay, Elwood, now remember that a Cub's a bear and a bear'll kill ya," I said, trying to sound like a veteran. I stole the line from

Pops Baker, a legend among local flight instructors. "Ya might also want to memorize the First Law of Aerodynamics."

"What's that?" Elwood asked. He got a stricken look on his face, as if he feared I might launch into a complicated explanation of aerodynamics. He had nothing to fear. To this day I remain stuck on page one of *Aerodynamics for Beginners* and fully intend to avoid such useless details of the flying game for the rest of my career. However, I knew well the First Law of Aerodynamics. And still do.

"The First Law of Aerodynamics," I said professorially, "is that toast always lands with the jelly side down. No matter how ya drop the damn thing, the jelly hits the floor first. Remember that!"

The wisdom about man-eating bears and falling toast was the only ground school a student received with the fifty-dollar plan.

Elwood, bewildered by the implications of bears and falling toast, walked toward the airplane. He paused and turned to me. "Remember what I told ya yesterday, Pete?"

"Uh, not really," I said.

"Well, like I said, I've had a little trouble learning to fly. I want ya to know that."

"Yeah, yeah, sure. C'mon let's get going," I said. "I got a bunch more students today."

Elwood shook his head and started to climb into the cockpit.

"Watch where you grab, Elwood!" I yelled.

It was too late. Elwood had placed his hand on a splattered bug so huge that its guts ran like day-glow fishing line alongside the airplane from just behind the cockpit to the tail wheel.

Elwood studied the bright colors on his hand for a few seconds, wiped them on his pants and climbed into the airplane.

At least he *tried* to climb in. Getting into the back seat of the Cub strained Elwood's coordination. It took him five minutes to settle into the seat, another five to fasten his lap belt.

It was a hint of things to come.

I remained outside the airplane, reached into the cockpit and gave the engine a few squirts of gas with the primer knob. Smiley's discount low-test poured from the leaky primer valve onto the floor of the airplane. All but the most imprudent pilots refrained from smoking in Moondog's Cubs.

I switched on the magnetos and flipped the propeller from behind in the manner of accomplished Piper Cub flight instructors. The old Continental engine coughed asthmatically a few times and went to work.

"How 'bout that!" I bragged as I climbed into the front seat, "she caught on the first flip!" I looked around to see if anyone else on the field had witnessed the miracle. Brookside instructors had been known to drop from exhaustion after an hour or so of hand-propping one of Moondog's dog-tired engines in the hot sun.

I lit a cigarette, taxied out and turned onto the cinder runway.

"You go ahead and take off, Elwood," I yelled over my shoulder.

"Please, Pete, you take off and then I'll try flying it in the air," Elwood said. He was trying to warn me.

I made the took off. The Cub struggled in the muggy air to clear the rusting hulk of a steam shovel abandoned at the end of the runway. Many such obstacles littered the airport, all of them as lethally positioned as anything ever concocted by the Mario Brothers. An immutable law of Moondog's held that all things would spend eternity on the exact spot they quit flying, running or breathing.

"Gotta watch out for that steam shovel, Elwood, it'd put a kink in your flying career for sure," I shouted. "Don't ever point an airplane at anything that can't run out of your way." More Pops Baker wisdom. Free of charge.

"Why don't you guys move it?" Elwood shouted back.

"Yeah, maybe we will someday," I replied.

It was another lie. The old steam shovel was certainly a lethal obstacle on takeoff but it was also the only barrier between the airport and the Polish neighborhood. Our neighbors' loathing of the airport had escalated with the increased flying generated by the guaranteed solo plan. Most of us preferred to take our chances with the steam shovel if we landed long rather than wind up in an unfriendly back yard, where we would have been treated like downed enemy fliers who had just strafed the parish church on Easter morning.

"Ya might also wanna avoid that drainage ditch alongside the runway, Elwood. It eats airplanes." I tipped the airplane and pointed at the ditch. Forty years earlier the ditch had been a sweetly flowing brook after which the airport was named. By 1962 it ran with a fetid cocktail of multi-colored, bubbling toxins on which floated a steady flotilla of garbage. The ditch was our Ganges, absorbing body and soul the remains of untold Aeronca Chiefs, Taylorcrafts, burned-out Lycomings, BT-13 landing gears, etc.

"And while I'm thinkin' 'bout it, try not to crash into Sam's Sheet & Scrap over on the right there." I pointed to the junkyard. "The Ripper'll get your ass if ya survive the crash."

"The Ripper?"

"Yeah, the junkyard dog. The Ripper's mean as hell, used to chase airplanes on landings. He'd follow them in and wouldn't let anyone out. His idea of fun, I guess."

"Does he still do that?"

"Not anymore! One day Pratt and Whitney got tired of the commotion. It disturbed their daytime sleep. They double-teamed The Ripper, 'bout tore his balls off. It was horrible. The Ripper ain't been back since. Just stay out of the junkyard and you'll be fine."

"Did you say Pratt and Whitney? Who are they?" Elwood asked.

"The airport cats. Christ, don't ever screw with them either. I've seen tigers I'd rather pet. Those cats hate everybody. Moondog only tolerates them because of the rats."

"Rats!?"

"Don't worry. We don't see too many during the day. But if you're ever around at night, stay the hell out of the hangar."

Thus was the new student apprised of the dangers, real and imagined, of operating an aircraft in and out of Brookside Airport.

At seven hundred feet the tired Cub threw in the towel and quit climbing. I aimed for the smoke stacks at U.S. Steel in the flats.

"When I give ya the signal, take a deep breath and hold it in, Elwood," I advised my student.

"Now what?"

"We're gonna get some free lift from the Bessemer Converters at the steel mills. You don't want to breathe the shit coming out of those stacks."

A few seconds before we were over the stacks, I gave Elwood the high sign. I gulped some fresh air, held my breath and entered a tight climbing turn. Hot air rising fiercely from the Bessies boosted the

Cub, winch-like, to two thousand feet. I turned away in the direction of the practice area and exhaled.

Elwood had not held his breath as instructed. He choked and coughed as if he had been gassed.

"I warned ya, Elwood," I said.

All an instructor can do is warn. The rest is up to the student. Elwood tapped me on the shoulder.

"Yeah?" I turned around.

A mostly voiceless Elwood motioned with a finger at a piece of wing fabric not quite attached to the framework. The loose, billowing fabric slapped gruffly against the wing ribs.

"Is that...choke...cough...serious?" Elwood asked.

"It'll keep your mind off the frayed control cables," I said. It was the answer Al gave me when *I* asked. "Okay, Elwood, let's quit screwin' 'round an' get to work. This is gonna be the quickest solo in history."

"You really...cough...think so?"

"Yep!" I said. "A few minutes to get you warmed up then back to the airport for some takeoffs and landings. An hour from now you'll be soloed. I'd bet my life on it."

It was an unfortunate, if foretelling, choice of words.

I pulled back power on the engine, which settled into a rhythmic wheezing. I suggested Elwood try some straight and level flight for a few minutes before we returned to the field to shoot takeoffs and landings. Then I'd solo Elwood, collect my five-dollar bonus and move on to my next student. Easy money.

I opened the cockpit door to allow cooling air inside. I lit another cigarette and leaned back to enjoy the ride. This would be a piece o' cake, aviation as the Wright boys surely intended.

"Okay, ya got it, Elwood," I hollered, holding up both hands to show that I had relinquished control of the airplane.

Without warning, the nose of the Cub thrust hideously upward. I didn't grab the stick. I wanted to see how Elwood would recover. The nose of the Cub started down. Good sign. Then it fell through the horizon. Bad sign. The Cub turned sharply right and entered a spiral. *Real* bad sign.

It was time for instructor intervention. I grabbed the stick. It wouldn't budge.

"Hey, c'mon, quit playin''round back there, Elwood," I yelled over my shoulder. "Let go o' the stick."

Elwood did not respond. I turned to look at my student. He strangled the stick in a death grip, pushing it full forward and holding it hard right. His other hand held the throttle wide open.

Reaching behind me, I attempted to peel Elwood's hand off the stick. His fingers had fossilized. Plant Number Five at Jones & Laughlin Steel loomed larger by the second as the spiraling Cub picked up speed. The control surfaces fluttered, announcing their intention to leave the airframe.

"Fer Chrissake, let go o' the stick, Elwood. You're gonna kill us!" I screamed in a voice a couple octaves higher than my normal register. I reached around again. This time I punched Elwood in the chest. The blow got his attention; he released the stick as if he suddenly realized he was holding a pit viper.

I leveled off the airplane at about one hundred feet while I probed my crotch for the cigarette that had popped out of my mouth. A group of steelworkers on break were yelling and giving us the finger.

"Oh yeah? Fuck you too!" I yelled back at the steelworkers. I returned their salute as well.

A flight instructor must never lose his patience. Without tolerance and understanding there can be no teaching. I took a minute to calm down while I prepared a short speech for my student.

"Heh, heh, now that's what we in the flying business call freezing at the controls, Elwood. Can happen to anyone. Now that we've learned about that, I don't guess we'll have to practice it anymore, huh?" I said.

I held my breath and circled over the Bessies again to regain lost altitude. As a precaution, I closed the cockpit door. The seatbelts were a bit threadbare and I feared being thrown from the airplane like Spikey the monkey, who at least had a parachute.

"Now let's try it again, Elwood. Just relax. I'm sure you'll do better."

Elwood did worse. My student proved incapable of anything except wild, inexplicable manipulation of the controls. If the airplane banked just slightly to the left, he countered with an abrupt and full deflection of aileron and rudder to the right. Other times his correction was in the same direction of the bank. I had no way of predicting his response. For Elwood there was no such thing as a neutral stick position. All he knew was full forward or full back, hard left or hard right.

He treated the throttle as if it were a pump, moving it from idle to wide open continually. The phlegmatic old Continental didn't like it but did its best to keep up with the erratic power changes.

Most students who have trouble learning to fly lack self-confidence. Not Elwood. He confidently tried his best to kill me. One exchange is forever etched in my mind:

"Push *forward* on the stick, Elwood, you're getting too damn slow!"

"No! I gotta pull *back* on the stick. We're too low!"

"We're going to be a lot lower if ya don't push the stick forward. Pleeease let me have the stick!"

No amount of flight instructor training could have prepared me to properly counter some of my student's more perverse gyrations. A series of parabolic maneuvers even resulted in moments of weightlessness. Cigarette butts, loose change, candy wrappers and a mummified rat, all undisturbed for decades on the floor of the Cub, floated around the cabin surreally. No one ever coaxed so much irregular behavior from a Piper Cub. My rear end bounced from one side of the cockpit to the other with a rumba-like motion.

After about 30 minutes of ineffable terror, it occurred to me that Moondog, a practical joker with a known taste for the macabre, had set me up. Elwood was probably an experienced pilot just trying to scare me.

"Real funny guy, that Moondog. "I'll bet that sumbitch put ya up to this, huh Elwood?" I laughed uneasily, having just recovered from back-to-back low-level spins. "Some joker, that Moondog. Heh, heh. Or was this Hangardoor's idea? That doggone Hangardoor! You guys sure had me fooled for a while."

"No, really Pete, I'm doin' the best I can," Elwood replied in a voice that told me he was hurt by the accusation. "I tried to warn you that I had trouble learning to fly before."

I turned around for another look at my student. Elwood was bright red with frustration. Sweat ran in rivers down his face, soaking his T-shirt. Tears swelled in his eyes. Here was someone who, for whatever reason, wanted to learn to fly. I felt sorry for him. I even quit disliking him so much for trying to kill me.

I had two choices: I could return to the airport and confess my failure to Moondog, who would be obliged, under terms of the guaranteed solo, to refund Elwood's money. Or I could flirt with death for the rest of the one-hour session.

I weighed my two options and decided to take my chances with Elwood. Besides, I am not a quitter. I became determined that Elwood would make some progress before we went back to the field.

Back to basics, I thought. We worked at simple straight and level flight for the rest of the hour. Nothing seemed to work. I even demonstrated how, if one let go of the controls altogether, the inherently stable Piper Cub would pretty much fly itself. When we landed, my new student had never managed to hold the wings level for more than a few seconds at a time. As I climbed out of the Cub my knees shook. If no one had been present, I would have kissed the ground. Perhaps a lifetime of flying wasn't going to be the pursuit of leisure I had imagined.

Elwood may not have learned much about flying from me but I learned a lot from him. One can read all one wants about potentially fatal airplane blunders but there's no substitute for witnessing them firsthand. Not that I recommend it.

In the next week I logged six more hours with Elwood. Not only was he still not showing any progress but, far worse, I wasn't getting paid for risking my ass flying with him. I decided to appeal to Moondog for relief.

Moondog and Al were supervising a painter working on a scaffold strung across the front of the hangar. The painter was putting the finishing touches on a mural depicting a shiny new yellow Piper Cub in a lazy turn above a storybook pastoral setting complete with brown and white cows. The Cub glittered against an azure blue sky dotted with puffy clouds.

Enormous black letters over the mural declared that Brookside Airport was home to "THE ACADEMY OF THE AIR." Beneath, in even larger letters, read, "R.P. 'MOONDOG' McCUTCHINSON, OWNER AND OPERATOR."

Moondog wouldn't have dreamed of spending a penny of his recent profits on the many items around the airport that needed repair, notably his Piper Cubs. But, like all men who feel they've made a contribution to the world, money was no object in his bid for immortality.

"Wuddaya think o' the name, Fusco? Pretty good name, huh? Gives the place some class, don'cha think?" Moondog said.

"The Academy of the Air? Yeah, that's what this place is. Sure, that's what I'd call it," I said with all the sarcasm I dared.

My boss sensed the disrespect and cast a baleful eye in my direction. I never became accustomed to looking at Moondog's face. I'm not certain if it was his wolf mouth, grisly bear eyes or the dark three-day growth of beard, which he had even on the rare days he shaved.

I swallowed hard and began my pitch. "Hey, Moondog, I don't know if ya noticed or not, but I bin flyin' with the same student all week. He's a little…slow and he's gonna be tough to solo. I'm thinkin' we oughta give him back his money, cut our losses before we spend much more time with him. Know what I mean?" I tried hard to sound matter-of-fact and in control.

There was no sign of empathy in Moondog's eyes. I had, in effect, just walked up to a vicious sleeping dog and kicked it square in the ass.

Moondog rubbed the tip of his chin with his thumb as he measured how much abuse to shower on his unfit, impertinent employee. Al snickered; he knew what was coming.

"Notice ya?" Moondog said, his voice rich with mockery. "Hear that, Al? This clown wants to know if I've noticed 'im flyin' 'round with the same student all week in my airplanes? Burnin' my gas. Wastin' my money. Fusco thinks we, get that Al? *we* oughta cut our losses and give the kid his money back. 'Magine that, Al, give the kid his money back? Ain't that some nervy shit?"

Al took a long drink from a bottle in a brown paper bag and inhaled ferociously on a straight Camel. He wiped his mouth on his sleeve and snorted smoke through his nose. His lifelong conviction that all pilots failed miserably when things got rough was once again confirmed.

I was very sorry I had brought it up.

"Yeah, ya bet your ass I bin noticin' ya," Moondog said, his voice shifting to dead serious. "And ya might as well forget about givin' anyone's money back and git that kid soloed or I'll start chargin' ya for the gas. Wuddaya think, Al, should we charge Fusco for the gas?"

Al snorted again in total agreement with his boss.

"Git back ta work, Fusco. Git that kid soloed!" Moondog said.

Moondog's absolute indifference to the welfare of others was astonishing, although I would learn over the years that it is a trait shared by all those who own the airplanes others fly. I walked away.

After a few more Elwood sessions, which had become daily exercises in the art of cheating death, I appealed to Hangardoor for help. He owed me a few favors and I thought maybe a change of instructors might help.

"Don't worry, I'll getcha off the hook," Hangardoor said magnanimously. "Ya know, sometimes it's all how ya handle a student. A really *good* instructor has gotta let a student know he believes in him, if ya know what I mean. I'll give him the stick as soon as we break ground. It's a little trick we *experienced* flight instructors use to show our new students we trust them. Pay attention. Ya might learn something."

I had planned on warning Hangardoor not to even consider letting Elwood touch the controls until they were at least three thousand feet but his condescension irritated me. I thanked him humbly and stepped back to observe an *experienced* flight instructor at work.

The exact moment at which Hangardoor showed Elwood that he believed in him was easy to determine. It was almost certainly when the Cub stopped climbing shortly after lift-off, turned right and entered a wide, wandering teardrop pattern over Sam's Sheet & Scrap. The Cub seemed drawn to the giant magnet dangling from the junkyard crane. Hangardoor and his student pirouetted several times around the crane at an altitude of about thirty feet. The crane operator jumped to the ground.

The Ripper added to the entertainment. Snarling and barking, the dog followed the Cub's progress around the junkyard, anxious to deal with the intruders should they fall into his squalid kingdom. I enjoyed every second of it, my pleasure heightened by the thought of Hangardoor fighting with Elwood for the stick.

The airplane made an unexpected steep turn and departed the junkyard. It headed straight for me. I almost didn't see it coming for the tears of laughter in my eyes. The Cub flew so near, so low, I could hear Hangardoor swearing at Elwood. To this day I don't like to dwell on how close I came to being the first instructor in history to be killed by his student *while standing on the ground!*

Hangardoor, I must allow, handled the situation very well. He executed a variety of dramatic recoveries, a gripping demonstration of flight instructor low-level survival technique. He finally wrenched control of the aircraft from Elwood and landed. He cut the engine as soon as he touched down and leaped from the Cub before it quit rolling.

It was perhaps the shortest flying lesson in history, about five minutes by most estimates. And Hangardoor was right, I learned something: No flight with a student at the controls is ever a certainty.

Everyone on the field, including Moondog, had witnessed the event.

"That bad, huh?" Moondog asked as Hangardoor walked by.

Hangardoor didn't bother to answer. He needed a drink, which he cadged from Al.

I felt vindicated. Moondog now had no choice but to refund Elwood's money. End of story. Not quite.

Moondog went to the office. I trailed behind, curious. Moondog picked up the phone and called Pops Baker, Brookside's foremost flight instructor before his retirement a year earlier.

Pops hung up on Moondog the first few calls. A persistent Moondog kept redialing.

"Pops, hear me out. I know you're retired now and I sure hate to bother ya, but I gotta little problem," Moondog said. He laid it on thick. "There's a student havin' a bit of trouble soloin'. These young instructors, they just don't have your touch. You were the best, Pops."

Moondog knew Pops owed him. He had let Pops instruct at Brookside after other airport operators in the area would no longer hire him because of failing eyesight and his unorthodox World War One teaching methods. Moondog also knew that Pops could not resist a challenge.

Pops agreed to take on "one last student."

"Pops Baker is on his way out to solo that kid," Moondog said to me after he put down the phone. "Pay attention. You're 'bout to see a *real* instructor in action."

The comment irked me. Somehow I found the courage to reply.

"Why don't *you* fly with Elwood if ya think he'd be so easy to solo?" I asked.

Moondog did not have a flight instructor's rating but he didn't let that stand in his way when there were too many students for us to handle. "I wouldn't think twice about soloing 'im. I might yet," he said.

At the time I thought Moondog was just talking tough, trying to impress me. As usual, I underestimated him. True outlaws don't make idle threats.

Pops Baker arrived about an hour later.

Pops had taught me to fly at another airport a couple of years before and it was great to see him again. He hadn't changed a bit. He still wore the same red suspenders and baggy trousers with pockets closer to his knees than waist. His eyeglasses, the thickest I have ever seen on a human, fueled speculation that he was, indeed, legally blind. His stubble of whiskers was permanently stained with an ever-present dark and odorous cheek-bulging chaw. Pops had a wild side to him and loved to spit tobacco out of low-flying airplanes into open convertibles. He rarely missed.

A man of calm, measured manner, Pops was the finest instructor I ever knew. He could teach a person to fly just by talking about it. He learned to fly in World War One and did little else but teach flying for almost 50 years. He never earned a good living at it. As a fitting end, he finished out his career at Brookside Airport working for Moondog. Considering his skill, Pops deserved better but, as he said many times, success in aviation has nothing to do with one's ability.

"It's all a matter of luck, a crap shoot," Pops told anyone who'd listen. "I know some guys who never could fly worth a damn who today is flyin' the big airliners makin' loads of dough while some of the best pilots I ever knew is flyin' junk airplanes in some jungle dodgin' poison darts."

Now here he was, over 70 years old, about to show us "young studs," as he called us, how to solo a student.

He and Elwood took off and were gone several hours.

"You think ol' Pops has got Elwood straightened out by now?" I asked Hangardoor.

"You know Pops. He could be standing in a cornfield right now watching that kid solo."

Quite possible. One of Pops' favorite tricks was to set the airplane down in a pasture. He would climb out and announce to his student that it was time to go it alone.

"Never give a student a chance to think about soloing," was Pops' philosophy.

He was a master at soothing the tense student. Once, when a student was having trouble relaxing at the controls, Pops crawled out of the airplane and sat down backward on the wing lift struts. He reached into the cockpit from outside and flew the airplane, even landed it that way. All just to show how easy it was to fly a Piper Cub.

Pops and Elwood returned, entered a short, snappy pattern and landed. Pops was flying the airplane, a bad sign. He believed that a good flight instructor could spend an entire career without touching the controls. Pops' color was bad. It looked like he might have swallowed his chew. He crawled out of the airplane and walked toward Moondog.

"How'd it go, Pops?" Moondog asked.

"Give the kid his money back," Pops said grimly without moving his lips. He started to leave. I caught up with him as he was getting on his bicycle. He could no longer see well enough to drive a car.

"You awright, Pops?" I asked.

"Yeah, I'll live," he said, wiping sweat from his glasses. He held the glasses at arm's length and aimed them at the sun. "Did I ever tell you that during both world wars I'd take cadets every other instructor on the field wanted to wash out? Worst damn basket cases you ever saw! A couple of months later those same cadets would be aces. They'd be winnin' air medals, fer Chrissake."

Pops had told me the story at least a hundred times but I kept silent as he continued his tormented epitaph to a long career as a flight instructor.

"Maybe I don't have the touch anymore," he said. "I've spent forty thousand hours flight instructing. Before today, I can't remember ever losing my temper, raising my voice or being scared in a cockpit. Hell of a way to go out, ain't it?"

Pops bicycled back into retirement, for good this time.

At least it would be fun watching Moondog beg Elwood to quit. Or, better yet, maybe we would have the unimaginable pleasure of seeing him refund Elwood's fifty bucks.

But pirates don't beg. And, as I was to soon learn, they never return your money.

Moondog waited for Pops to leave then walked over to the thoroughly demoralized Elwood, still sitting in the airplane, his head down in shame.

"Congratulations, kid, I've got great news for ya," Moondog said, his face breaking into a wide, devious grin that exposed several rows of teeth. "Mister Baker says you're ready to solo."

"He did?"

"Yeah, sure did, said you're a real ace," Moondog repeated. "You kin solo in the morning. Be here early. *Real* early."

Elwwod drove away. I was certain we'd never see him again.

"Hey, Al, is the yellow Cub with the one blue wing ready to fly?" Moondog yelled to his mechanic, who was in the hangar pounding the crap out of something with a pair of large pliers.

"No more than usual," Al yelled back.

"That'll do," Moondog said. "We'll need it in the morning."

I couldn't believe my ears. Of all the terminally ill Piper Cubs in the Brookside fleet, the worst by far was the one known as "the yellow Cub with the one blue wing." Al, in a moment of inspiration, had assembled the ship from Piper Cub parts he exhumed from the airport ditch and Sam's Sheet & Scrap, plus a few pieces he took off his disabled Buick. The engine had parts in it not deemed usable even by Moondog's low standards. Two of the pistons had once served as ashtrays in the office shack. The bent right landing gear leg had supported the airport mailbox since World War Two.

Al worked in the hangar for two or three days, cursing and hammering parts together like some mad scientist creating an aberrant life form. The airplane's component parts were all a different, unidentifiable hue of yellow. Except for the right wing panel, which was blue. The blue wing drooped a couple of degrees, giving the airplane a sad, whipped appearance. The ship possessed no paperwork, no official documentation that it really existed, which it didn't as far as I was concerned.

"So which one o' you guys wants the honor of test-flyin' her?" Al asked after pushing the finished product out of the hangar into the sunlight for all to admire.

We scattered. Al never admitted it but I know he was hurt that none of us offered to test-fly his baby. The forlorn, spurned Cub sat behind the hangar, an outcast among outcasts.

Until the Hungarian Air Force came along.

The Hungarian Air Force was our name for a half-dozen or so brave souls who had fled their native Hungary after the bloody revolt against Russian domination in 1956. They had all been pilots at one time in the *real* Hungarian Air Force but didn't speak English well enough to obtain United States flying licenses. They also had an air of casual daring about them that deterred other airport operators in the area from renting them airplanes.

Not Moondog. He recognized a kindred spirit in these courageous revolutionaries who had used rocks against the artillery and tanks of a repressive government. The yellow Cub with the one blue wing was theirs to use anytime they wanted for the price of the gas.

Joking in a strange tongue, the Hungarians would show up at the airport a couple times each week from their jobs as laborers at the steel mills. Two at a time, they'd take turns flying the yellow Cub with the one blue wing.

I once made the mistake of asking Amory, the unofficial commander of the exiled air force and the only one who spoke a little English, if the drooping blue wing panel made the Cub difficult to fly.

When Amory finally understood the question he smiled and replied, "Oh, no, iz make dem znappy roll en dem outzidey lupe eezy! Kom on, I tak yu up."

A couple of my students were standing nearby and heard the offer. They urged me on. No way, I thought. The pilots of the Hungarian Air Force had a dual reputation: They were known to be very good pilots but they were also certifiably nuts. I had sworn I would never get into an airplane, especially *that* airplane, with the Hungarians.

"Oh, no thanks, Amory," I said, "I gotta run." *Yeah, run like hell.*

"Bawk, bawk, bawk." My students turned the screws.

I couldn't look like a chicken in front of my students. I had to go. If my aviation career is remarkable for any one thing, it would be the unwise decisions that have characterized it almost from the first day.

"Kom on, yu like diz ver mooch," Amory pressed, pulling me along by the shirtsleeve toward the yellow Cub with the one blue wing. I resisted. I appealed for help from the mob like an innocent man being led to the gallows. All I got were more chicken sounds.

Amory pushed my unwilling body into the front seat. "Yu zitz up har yu zee reel gud how much da fun iz to fly wit peelot from da Hungaree!"

One of my students eagerly swung the prop. My only chance was that the motor wouldn't start. But of course it did. Amory shoved the throttle wide open. He taxied with the tail in the air past my waving students.

"Yu evar flies da upzidey down?" Amory asked, starting his takeoff roll from midfield.

"Not on purpose," I said. I reached up and did a magneto check. RPMs dropped precipitously. I pointed to the tachometer. Amory laughed, his instinctive response to everything.

"I teech yu how flies da upzidey down," Amory promised as we broke ground.

"This airplane barely flies right side up," I protested.

Amory just laughed.

Aerobatics tend to fall into three distinct categories: the simple loops and rolls almost every pilot has tried; the boring high-speed military public relations bullshit pomp; and airshow routines in graceless, overpowered bombs that test airplane more than pilot.

Unrelated to any of the above activities are aerobatics as interpreted by eastern Europeans, of which Amory was a master. The difference was not only Amory's skill, but his zero fear of death. I don't think it ever occurred to Amory he could be killed in an airplane, a feeling I've never shared. And, as exciting as Amory's flying may have been to watch from the ground, it could only be fully appreciated from inside the airplane while "zitting" in the front seat.

When I sensed Amory's deft touch on the controls, I relaxed. What the hell, I'd surely learn something flying with Amory. He was a natural-born pilot, a title many pilots think they deserve but damn few do.

Such were my thoughts even as, at one hundred feet, Amory rolled the yellow Cub with the one blue wing ninety degrees to the right and did a knife-edge climb. I looked straight down out the open cockpit door at Sam's Sheet & Scrap. The Ripper, standing on a spent and prostrate refrigerator, monitored our progress, licking his chops.

The knife-edge climb was merely Amory's opening act, a warm-up. He launched into a series of loops, rolls of every variety, a tail slide from four hundred feet and a maneuver that seemed to tumble us through the sky and, of course, "upzidey down" flight until the engine sputtered. *All of this in a Piper Cub with an airframe of suspicious provenance and, if I had to venture a guess, an engine with at least a million hours on it.*

I'll never understand how Amory cajoled so much out of that Cub. Then again, he only proved something I already knew: It's not the airplane, it's the pilot.

Amory talked me through a few stunts. I didn't understand his English too well but he was the kind of instructor who could speak to his student through the stick. Throughout, my only fear was that the yellow Cub with the one blue wing would come apart. Flying with Elwood, now *that* was scary!

"Hoo boy, iz gud fun, no? Now uz flies over da Lak Airy, mebbe find da bout to booz. Lotz gud fun!"

Bout to booz?

With the sun hanging low in the horizon, Amory crossed the Lake Erie shoreline and descended to about two hundred feet over the water. He scanned the horizon like a U-boat commander with a couple of spare torpedoes. "Look for dem bout. Bout wit da ore iz da bez to booz. Hoo boy!"

Bout wit da ore...? Bez to booz? Okay, so it was an ore boat we were after and we were going to buzz it. Big deal, I thought. Buzzing ore boats on Lake Erie was old hat, the first thing any pilot trained in a city on the shores of the Great Lakes learned. As fine a pilot as he was, it was highly unlikely that Amory could improve on my own technique for trimming the deck of an unsuspecting ore boat.

Amory soon got his chance when we spotted one lumbering west across the lake. "Hoo boy! Dar zay iz! Deze reel gud. Zun in hiz eye," he said devilishly.

He rolled the Cub hard to the left and lined up for the kill, approaching the boat head on. (Personally, I preferred to surprise the crew from the stern.) He stayed a little high, standard procedure for buzzing *any* boat since it lessens the chances of someone else on the water getting the airplane's tail number. The feds, with good reason, have little pity on those who buzz—ore boats or anything else.

Amory remained at two hundred feet until we were almost on top of the boat. Some buzz job, I thought. Way too high! Even as I underestimated him, Amory pushed the nose down abruptly into a steep power dive. He aimed for the bridge.

The yellow Cub with the one blue wing didn't have an airspeed indicator. It didn't need one. The vibrating airframe told me we were going too damn fast. Amory steepened the dive.

More speed, more vibration.

A few seconds later we were close enough to the bridge to see the faces of the crew but Amory didn't pull up. I started to shake almost as much as the speeding Cub. My rear end lifted off the seat but I couldn't let Amory know I was scared. Nor did he do it to scare me, I don't think. It was just the way they "booz da bout in de Hungaree."

The bridge crew spotted us. Their faces were full of horror and incredulity. In an instant the crew disappeared from view to the bridge floor. The unconditional surrender was what Amory wanted. He pulled up.

Into a loop.

I couldn't believe it was happening. Hanging from my seat belt at the top of the loop, my faith in Amory wavered.

"Hoo boy! Iz da gud fun no?" Amory yelled as he started down the backside of the loop. "Now da bez part. Yu wait, yu zee."

I didn't have long to wait.

Nearing the bottom of the loop, Amory aimed for the bridge again. I watched three crewmembers get to their feet and brush themselves off. At the sight of the re-approaching yellow and blue kamikaze, they disappeared to the floor a second time.

I've never seen anything funnier.

"Wut yu tink?" Amory asked, missing the boat by a few feet. "What zay one mar time we booz dem bout? We give tu dem reeel gud one mar time!"

"Naw,"I answered."I think we've scared those guys enough for one day."

"Okay," he said, performing a victory roll. "But yu like iz how we booz da bout, huh?"

"Like nothing I've ever seen, Amory," I admitted.

I spotted the Goodyear blimp over the lake about three miles away. I kind of hoped Amory didn't see it. But no such luck.

"Hoo boy!" he said. "Deez gud day. Never do I zee nutink lak deez, how you zay…bleemp? in my koontry. You kaplists, he got evertink."

Even the yellow Cub with the one blue wing could catch the Goodyear blimp. A few minutes later we were flying in formation with it. Amory attacked the blimp from the front, above and below. He got behind it and took advantage of the opportunity to practice for future revolutions.

"Rat a tat tat tat," Amory howled as he strafed the blimp's enormous exposed ass with countless rounds from imaginary machine guns. He swore an oath. "Deez how iz I shuz down dem Roosian komniz zumabitch bostards if I ev'r gitz chanz."

I thought it all great fun until I spotted the blimp's mooring lines trailing below and behind. I pointed them out to Amory.

"Hoo boy, deez bleemp mebbe he ketch uz lak dee feesh, huh?" Amory said. He pulled back the power, allowing the blimp to outrun the Cub. For a few anxious moments we flew among the mooring lines, which reached for us like counterattacking tentacles. Blimps are not nearly as defenseless as they might appear.

We landed as darkness fell over Brookside Airport, laughing like hell. I probably would not have ridden with Amory again but I'm glad I did it once.

I thought of my flight with Amory as Al, acting on Moondog's orders, dragged the yellow Cub with the one blue wing from behind the hangar and prepared it for flight. Which is to say he put a little air in the flat left tire and trimmed some wooden splinters from the prop tips with a pocketknife.

The Hungarians, I feared, would soon be an air force without an airplane again.

Not that any of us really expected Elwood to show up for his solo flight. Some of us *prayed* he wouldn't.

Even so, Elwood was waiting in his car when I arrived next morning.

"Ya really think ya wanna try to solo today, Elwood?" I asked, meeting my former student as he stepped out of his car. "Maybe we oughta shoot a few landings first."

"No, I don't think so. That won't help," Elwood said. His face was filled with dread and forced conviction. "I'm as ready now as I'll ever be. I gotta know if I can do this."

"I already know, Elwood," I said. "You can't!"

"Maybe," he said, "but I've gotta try to solo, no matter what."

For the record, I should confess to a lifelong regret for not asking Elwood what drove his potentially deadly obsession. Maybe it's better that I never knew.

At any rate, Elwood had, unfortunately, found the one airport operator in the world willing to give him the opportunity to try. Moondog, who had spent the night in the office shack, opened the door. He rubbed his eyes, stretched and scratched as if he had been hibernating. Girlfriend Betty snored in the background.

"You back?" Moondog asked Elwood.

"Yes sir," Elwood said. "I'm ready to solo."

"Well, all right. Ya jist better hope you ain't as fucked-up as everyone around here says ya are," Moondog said. He obviously had never read the *Flight Instructor's Handbook*, which is very specific when it comes to boosting a solo prospect's confidence.

One by one, the employees of Brookside Airport, and some of the students who knew what was planned, began arriving. If Elwood was serious about soloing, no one wanted to miss it. Hangardoor even skipped his morning nap.

Moondog personally helped Elwood into the back seat of the yellow Cub with the one blue wing. He spun the prop with a large hairy hand. The motor caught after several attempts. It dared not start.

Al sat up in the back seat of the Buick, awakened by the sound. He joined the audience.

Pratt and Whitney, who had never been known to show an interest in anything at Brookside Airport other than its rodent population, made a rare daytime appearance. The cats surely sensed something primal in the air, the timeless struggle for life itself, the scent of doomed men before battle. They crouched off to one side of the runway, staring fixedly at the action. Their nostrils flared in anticipation of blood and mayhem.

I also admit to a sinful fascination. The feeling was surely akin to that of my ancient pagan Roman ancestors as they sat in the Coliseum eating fried pepper sandwiches, drinking Chianti and handicapping the main event.

Elwood started taxiing to the runway. The Cub weaved like a drunk trying to pass a sobriety test. Random throttle movements gagged the old Continental, which spit up the water that came free with all Smiley's discount low-test.

Moondog looked around to see what witnesses might be present. "If this asshole kills himself just remember that he stole the airplane. Hear me?" he said out of the corner of his mouth as he waved to Elwood, still trying without much success to taxi the short distance to the runway.

To no one's great surprise, Elwood didn't make it. He snarled in a thick patch of milkweed. His solo flight had ended before it even began. I, for one, was relieved. Elwood started to exit the airplane.

Moondog had other plans.

"Just stay in the airplane, kid. You had your chance ta back out," Moondog said as he walked over to the weed-tangled Cub. His tone told Elwood that it would have been far more dangerous for him to get out of the airplane at that point than to continue. Moondog was not to be denied his entertainment.

Moondog lifted the Cub by the stabilizer. He dragged the airplane, some milkweed and Elwood to the center of the runway. He lined the Cub up on the runway and dropped the tail to the ground with a thud.

"Hang on a minute," W.W. Storm yelled, running over to the airplane. W.W. pulled a ballpoint pen from his pocket and drew a line on Elwood's pants, a few inches from his crotch. It was a Pops Baker trick.

Ya see this mark I just drew on your pants, Elwood?"

"Uh, yeah, I guess so."

"Well, when you go to land and get close to the ground, chop the power and pull the stick back to that line. Just try to stay lined up with the runway and hold the stick on that mark on your pants. It'll help, maybe. Okay?"

"Uh, yeah, sure, I guess," Elwood replied, studying the blue line on his pants like it was advanced calculus.

"If you're through playin' flight instructor, W.W., I got a student to solo," Moondog hissed as he reached inside the cockpit and pushed the throttle wide open. The engine yelped in pain; the yellow Cub with the one blue wing moved forward.

"The sign says 'Guaranteed Solo' and guaranteed solo is what ya gets," Moondog broadcast. "No one washes out of *my* Academy of the Air! Everyone graduates or dies!"

Moondog lit a giant, half-dollar cigar in honor of the moment as Elwood rolled down the runway, certainly more hopeful than assured.

As the Cub gained speed it jerked left and right. It bounced a few times as Elwood tried to yank it off the ground at too slow an airspeed.

A couple of hundred feet later the reviled Cub with the one blue wing became airborne. The easy part of Elwood's solo was over.

I was still congratulating myself for the excellent instruction I had given Elwood when the Cub leveled off at about twenty feet and headed for the derelict steam shovel at the end of the runway.

"Climb, Elwood! Goddamnit, climb!" I yelled, "pull back on the stick!"

Elwood couldn't hear me and I knew it. His solo flight might have ended right then except for a fortuitous crosswind that carried the airplane away from the steam shovel and over the junkyard. It cleared a stack of crushed automobiles by mere inches and continued drifting toward the steel mills in the flats. Hot air from the stacks shot the Cub almost straight up. The Cub's nose was cocked hard left, the right wing was down. Not pretty but Elwood was flying.

"Stay close! Don't lose sight of the airport, Elwood!" I yelled again. Our narrow, pot-holed cinder runway was the only place to land in the dense urban and industrial area. If Elwood could not find the airport again, he was doomed. I remember thinking that he was probably doomed anyway. Then, to my great relief, Elwood turned back toward the field.

"Hey, how 'bout that!" I said to the others. "He's comin' back to land!"

I spoke too soon. Elwood stopped the turn, descended and headed for a row of towering power lines away from the airport. I closed my eyes. I heard a collective gasp from the assembled crowd. When I opened my eyes, Elwood was on the other side of the power lines. He had flown under them.

"Now wuddaya think of that?" Moondog said. "This kid's awright!"

The Cub descended further and turned toward the flats east of the airport. It disappeared from view in the smoke from the mills. An edgy quiet fell over Brookside Airport. Long minutes passed. All eyes remained trained on the east horizon searching for Elwood.

"Anybody see 'im?"

"I don't see nuthin.'"

"Me neither."

"Not me."

"Hey, wait a second, I think I hear 'im," Al said. He leaned a booze-reddened ear into the wind to get a fix on the Cub. The sound of the engine grew louder but the airplane was nowhere in sight.

As the rest of us scanned east, I noticed that Pratt and Whitney were looking intently west. Had the cats tracked the Cub's every move like prey with their keen, carnivore eyes?

I turned around. All I saw was yellow and blue.

"Look out!" I shouted.

The Cub was no more than ten feet in the air and headed straight for our small gathering. It flew in a grotesque skid like a drunken avenging, suicidal angel. Elwood had circled the industrial flats at an extremely low altitude without hitting anything. Somehow the yellow Cub with the one blue wing had returned unerringly to its natal river. We all jumped to the ground.

Except Moondog.

"Real good navigatin', kid, now let's see ya land the son of a bitch," he roared as the airplane passed inches over his head. "And you guys didn't think the kid knew how ta fly. You assholes couldn't instruct your way out of a whorehouse."

Finding the field was one thing, landing on the field quite another. I crossed the fingers of both hands.

Elwood gained a little altitude and circled the airport a few times. The airplane made wild porpoise-like undulations I had never seen performed in *any* airplane.

Eventually he lined up with the runway, more or less, and began an approach. About 50 feet from the ground he lost his nerve, pushed up the throttle and made a string of near-stalls that passed for a go-around. The grimacing engine cooperated, but just barely. Elwood lined up several more times but lost his nerve at the last second and went around. It was difficult to watch.

Each time Elwood flew by he looked out the cockpit window at us, seeking help we couldn't give. His face was a picture of raw fear. I felt ashamed; I hoped no one would ever learn that I had anything to do with Elwood's death. It certainly wouldn't look good on my airline application.

My shame as an accomplice, however, battled with the esteem in which I held my former student. It's not everyday you get to see someone play against the odds with his life.

"How many times do ya 'spose he's gonna go 'round 'fore he lands? This is pretty annoying," Moondog wondered out loud.

"Yeah, I'm gettin' bored," Hangardoor said.

"He ain't goin' 'round too many more times," Al replied flatly. "There ain't much gas in that tank. Didn't think he'd need much to crash on takeoff."

Al hardly finished the sentence when the Cub's engine sputtered and quit cold.

Fortunately, Elwood was over the approach end of the runway. Unfortunately, he was about 100 feet in the air. With the engine dead we could plainly hear Elwood whimpering. All the ballpoint pen marks, Pops Baker wisdom and assorted flying tips in the world would be of little use to him now.

The airplane hung suspended and motionless for a long, silent moment before swooping to earth like a raptor after a mouse in the underbrush. The propeller windmilled idly in the dive. The yellow Cub with the one blue wing struck the runway so hard that it should have come apart. Miraculously, the rat-gnawed bungees not only held, but rebounded the ship high into the sky, as if earth itself was rejecting both machine and piteous human occupant.

Elwood had let go of the controls; he clawed with both hands at the side cockpit window, a captive on some nightmarish amusement park death ride. I looked away.

"That's good Elwood, don't touch nuthin'," I yelled over my shoulder. "Just hang on!"

The Cub seemed to fly on pure instinct, guided by forces both metaphysical and divine far beyond the understanding of anyone present that day. Again and again the ship fell to earth, caught its breath, and bounced back into the sky, each time a bit lower, a bit slower. Near the end of the runway the airplane tired of the sport and quit bouncing; it swerved to the right twenty feet from the steam shovel and rolled slowly, ignominiously, into the witches' brew at the bottom of the drainage ditch.

A factory whistle in the flats sounded a mournful quarter note. It signaled the first coffee break of the day and the end of Elwood's guaranteed solo flight.

All we could see of the Cub was the rudder, sticking out of the ditch, twitching.

"Good, that means he's alive," someone said.

"Not necessarily! A body'll keep movin' for a while after it's dead. Twitches just like that rudder," Moondog added, no doubt from experience.

W.W. and I got to the ditch first. Elwood was indeed alive. He remained in the airplane. His feet trembled uncontrollably on the rudder pedals.

"You awright, Elwood?" W.W. asked.

"I...think...so," Elwood managed through clattering teeth.

Elwood crawled out of the Cub and started to scale the side of the ditch on shaky legs. He soon lost his footing, fell and rolled to the bottom. He lay face down in a bath of putrid sludge, emitting gurgling noises I shall never forget.

It was hard not to smile.

Afraid Elwood might dissolve, W.W. and I went after him. We dragged the Creature from the Green Ditch out of the muck and brought him to the top. The crowd that had witnessed Elwood's solo flight greeted him with hollow cheers, not of congratulations but of relief.

Al studied the damage to the yellow Cub with the one blue wing. Its right wing, the blue one, was bowed. The prop was broken and the landing gear splayed. The hot engine, half-submerged, sizzled.

"Shit, gonna take me most of a day to get that airplane goin' 'gain," he said. Then Al had second thoughts. "The hell with that thing!" He flicked a cigarette into the ditch.

Pratt and Whitney saw that Elwood was alive and bloodless. They slinked away, disappointed by humans once again.

Moondog took a long, gratifying puff on his cigar. As far as he was concerned, the show Elwood put on was easily worth the price of an airplane, especially *that* airplane. He slapped Elwood hard on the back.

"Well kid, I knew ya had it in ya. Little tough on my airplane but what the hell, any landing ya walk away from is a good landing!" Moondog said, thus perpetuating one of the longest running and least contested lies in aviation. (A far more accurate definition of a good landing would be a landing after which the airplane remains usable.)

Elwood said nothing. He displayed all the classic signs of a near-death experience: pallid skin tone, sunken eyes, rubbery limbs and pulsating stomach, its contents moving ever upward. I stepped back.

In one sweeping movement Moondog produced a large switchblade. He held it high over his head and pressed the button. "Kertwaaack!" The knife snapped open; its razor-sharp blade caught the morning sun like a signal mirror.

At the sight of the knife, Elwood almost fainted. Moondog bit down hard on the cigar and spun the latest Academy of the Air graduate around by the shoulder. Elwood fell to his knees and slumped forward, meekly awaiting execution. Moondog clutched Elwood's shirttail. With two expert swipes he cut out a large piece of cloth. Elwood made the sign of the cross and collapsed to the ground.

I helped Elwood to his feet and asked him to say a few words. He wandered off without comment. I don't think he wanted to throw up in front of us.

In keeping with aviation custom, I marked Elwood's severed shirttail with his name, the date of his solo and the names of his many instructors. I tacked it to the office wall alongside the shirttails of other Academy of the Air alumni.

"Another satisfied customer!" Moondog proclaimed as Elwood drove away.

Some waiting students who had observed the solo demonstration left in a hurry, forfeiting dreams of flying along with their fifty bucks.

By that afternoon we put Elwood's improbable solo behind us and returned to our daily grind. Not for long, however. A couple of days later the bank closed in on Moondog. Our boss had never paid a cent on the airport note.

One step ahead of his creditors, Moondog and the corpulent Betty entered the B-25, the *Big Red Momma Bomma,* through the bomb bay. Betty's rear end became wedged. Moondog pushed from behind.

"They got thousand-pound bombs in this goddamned thing during the war. We oughta be able to get your fat ass in there," Moondog grunted as he struggled against Betty's weight.

He must have loved her very much.

With Betty finally inside the airplane, Moondog cranked up the *Big Red Momma Bomma* and took off. He treated the Polacks and us to one last ear-splitting, teeth-loosening buzz job, rocked the wings and disappeared on the southern horizon. I stopped short of saluting Moondog but in some perverse way I admired, even envied him. He lived life on his own terms. Few men can say the same.

I admired him a lot less when my last paycheck, for $34.26, bounced. Damn, I had big plans for that money.

Without its emperor, Brookside Airport collapsed in a matter of hours. As throughout history, the empire proved less able to survive the emperor's remedies than his vices.

Not wanting to believe that I no longer had a flying job and not knowing what else to do or where else to go, I went to Brookside Airport the day after the bank closed it. I just hung around.

Only Al remained; he was trying to get his old Buick up and running again with parts he had stolen from Sam's Sheet & Scrap in the middle of the night. His right hand was bandaged, compliments of The Ripper. Nothing personal, I'm sure, just a dog earning his keep at the junkyard.

Al had recycled a powder blue trunk lid from Sam's. I was holding it in position for him while he attached the bolts from inside when two men arrived. They identified themselves as repossession pilots and announced that the bank had sent them to pick up the B-25, Moondog's major asset, and anything else that would fly. They were mad as hell when I told them they were a couple days late on the bomber.

"Where'd this McCutchinson character go?" one of the repo pilots demanded.

"That way," I said, pointing south.

Al overheard the conversation. As usual, he was well into his cups. And plenty pissed. Al's last check had also bounced. He had even bigger plans for *his* money: Survival.

"Ya wanna know where that son of a bitch is?" Al asked from inside the trunk.

The repo pilot looked around, more than a little puzzled by the disembodied voice. He answered nonetheless. "Uh, yeah, we sure do. Where is he?"

"In Hell!" Al said, his voice echoing theatrically in the trunk. "That's where he is. In Hell! That's where the devil goes 'tween vacations on earth. Follow the bastard at your own risk! There's plenty more like him in Hell."

"Who the fuck am I talking to?" the repo pilot said. "Where are you?"

After a few more exchanges between repo pilot and the unseen Al, I grew bored and clued in the stumped repo pilot with a nod of my head toward the trunk. The repo pilot peeked into the trunk. When he saw Al, he looked at his partner and made a circular motion at his temple with his index finger.

The repo pilots accepted the fact that they were not going to recover the B-25. That left only the fleet of Cubs. They inspected each of them, keeping their distance like visitors to a leper colony. None of the Cubs was deemed airworthy; all received a summary death sentence.

"When was the last time anyone tried to fly these crates?" one of the repo pilots asked me.

"Uh, a few days ago," I admitted. "I gave a little dual in one of them."

"Well I'm sure as hell not flying any of them!" he said. "Nobody needs a flying job that bad."

That's because you already have a flying job, you asshole.

Using a grease pencil, the repo pilot wrote on the side of each Cub: "PULL ENGINES FOR SCRAP BURN AIRFRAME." Perhaps I should not have cared, but it broke my heart nonetheless.

Later that day, Al got his Buick running. He drove off to find another airport. Years later I heard that Al died in the back seat of the Buick, ranting with his last liquored breath about the ancient glories of the Pan Am flying boats and the incompetent, undeserving pilots that flew all airplanes.

Rest in peace, Al. I only hope in death you found the bliss that eluded you in aviation. You have plenty of company.

Sensing a good thing was over, an alarming number of hangar rats scurried in little groups over to Sam's Sheet & Scrap to explore the career possibilities. Pratt and Whitney followed their food supply. The cats, unsentimental to the end, never looked back at their airport home. In a more or less bloodless coup, they handily commandeered The Ripper's sleeping quarters, an upside-down Hudson Hornet under the only shade tree in the junkyard. Humiliated and homeless, The Ripper stood in the sun for hours, alternately licking his balls and barking crazily.

I knew how he felt.

A few surly characters in a dump truck came to the airport from Sam's Sheet & Scrap to pick at the bones. They cut the engines off the Cubs with a torch. They hauled away the engines and anything else that would melt to the junkyard.

Sam showed up personally in a bulldozer to finish the job. The smile on Sam's face gave me the feeling that he had been waiting for the chance.

I became a lone spectator to the end of Brookside Airport. It wasn't pretty.

Sam made quick work of the wooden hangar and office shack, which he formed into a funeral pyre. Then he combed the field. Nothing escaped Sam's trained arson's eye. He pushed load after load onto the pyre: the six engineless Cubs; the shirttails; the green velvet couch; Hangardoor's makeshift bed; the "GUARANTEED SOLO!" sign; numerous oil and gas-soaked airplane parts; explosive half-filled cans of nitrate dope and at least two or three tons of miscellaneous debris.

Still smiling, Sam doused the heap with gasoline. He was about to set it afire when he spotted the tail of the yellow Cub with the one blue wing sticking out of the drainage ditch. He drove his dozer to the ditch, lassoed the tail of the Cub with a rope and dragged the airplane across the field. After adding Elwood's baptismal Cub to the pile, Sam stepped back and threw in a match.

Wrathful flames engulfed the heaped remains of Brookside Airport. Dark smoke rose swiftly like an unstoppered genie free at last and in a hurry to get the hell out of town. Unable to follow the genie, I just stood and watched, contemplating my future in aviation as the fire blazed.

He is justly served;
It is a poison temper'd by himself.

Laertes to Hamlet

Prologue to Chapter Two

The Cleveland Plain Dealer obituary page gave only a few brief paragraphs to the quiet passing of Mafia chief Carmine Beneviaggio. Mob guys, even famous ones, who die in bed forfeit play on Page One.

The obit read,

"Carmine Beneviaggio, powerful don of Cleveland organized crime for five decades, died peacefully Tuesday afternoon in his swanky east side suburban home. He was 92.

"Beneviaggio, nicknamed 'Benny Smiles' because of a facial scar which made him appear to be perpetually smiling, was an innovator among mob bosses of his era. He espoused modern methods of operation. Beneviaggio was the first Mafia kingpin to use air travel extensively."

Air travel? Hah! Not that night he didn't!

Nagging fears and unanswered questions overrode the enormous relief I felt at the news of Benny Smiles' demise. Would that twisted grin of his still haunt my sleep now that he was dead? Could I retrain myself after almost forty years not to brace for instant, explosive death each time I started my car? Sure, Benny Smiles was gone but, more to the point, what about the other scary bastards with him that awful night? Were they also dead? Did it matter?

I'm Italian and I know how the system works. Mafia guys never close the books on unsettled scores. They harbor and cultivate revenge, pass it down generation to generation like a gold watch or trusty pistol. Let me think, who might be left to track me down after all these years? There was the limo driver. He looked like a gorilla, only uglier and bigger. As I remember, we didn't exactly hit it off.

The driver concerns me but he's not the one I fear most. No, not the limo driver.

If retribution for that dreadful night ever comes, it will have only one eye, a diamond-hard, pitiless eye. Sal the Peeper!

Sweet Jesus, anyone but Sal the Peeper!

2

An ancient galley slave enjoyed the ultimate job security of being chained for life to his bench. When the galley was sold, gambled away, seized in battle or repossessed, the slave stayed on in a kind of package deal. He suffered hourly floggings and endless shifts at the oar, but was at least guaranteed a bowl of gruel every day of his entire tenuous existence.

No such employment safety net exists for the professional pilot who suddenly finds himself with nothing to row. No one is as unemployed as an unemployed pilot!

Typically, re-entry into the pilot employment market begins with a few weeks of self-pity, anxiety and re-acquaintance with the scolding truth of one's expendability. Thus emotionally prepared for rebuff, the job hunt begins. It's never easy. The unemployed pilot is guaranteed only that he will hear on a daily basis that he is either too old or too young, that he has not enough flying time, too much flying time or the wrong kind of flying time. Without exception, the type-rating or license required for the available position will be the only one he doesn't possess.

Faced with such grim reality, some pilots become discouraged and quit the flying game despite the fact that an unspeakable alternative awaits them: working for a living.

There have been suicides.

Others—Hangardoor Herliwitz and myself come to mind—go into temporary retirement, vowing to return to flying when things improve. One of Hangardoor's sabbaticals lasted twenty-two years. Mine lasted a mere eight.

But that was much later. In the fall of 1962, I was determined to assimilate back into aviation as quickly as possible. After a pilot earns his first dollar flying airplanes, he's spoiled, ruined for any other type of occupation.

Undeterred by the Moondog fiasco, W.W. Storm and I began a systematic sweep of northern Ohio airports looking for work. The search fanned out from busy airports in Cleveland to less busy airports on the city fringe to distant, backwater country airports. We were buoyed by a popular and persistent 1960's rumor of an impending "pilot shortage," an unprecedented seller's market just around the corner in which every pilot in America could name his price.

Sadly, the projected pilot shortage was—and remains—a hoax, an elaborate deception that cruelly renews itself with each new generation. The supply of pilots always exceeds the jobs.

The good jobs, that is.

A caution: The pilot shortage hoax has become commercialized. Today it's big business. The hoax has spawned any number of "pilot hiring services." In exchange for exorbitant fees, these services offer such arresting advice for landing airline jobs as "wear a suit to the interview and don't pick your nose." Hopeful airline applicants, always looking for an edge, eagerly line up in the sheep barn for fleecing. Regrettably, airline pilots often operate the scams; they somehow manage to live with themselves. It's a safe bet that these pick-pockets never suffered much on the way up.

As if we required any more obstacles, W.W. and I discovered to our chagrin that every prospective employer knew of Moondog's notorious guaranteed solo plan. Bad news travels fast in aviation. Anyone who ever worked for Moondog was branded an outlaw by association. We deftly skirted the issue of our previous employer and even reacted with indignant outrage at the mention of his name. Knowing what to omit from a pilot employment application often separates the guy flying the airplane from the guy pumping the gas.

Aviation opportunity, it turned out, lurks in strange places. Our break came when W.W. and I stopped for a long lunch at a roadside tavern called Grandma's Bar and Grill and Groceries about forty miles west of Cleveland. Grandma's doubled as a gas station and doubled again as a fruit stand specializing, on that fall day, in pumpkins and apple cider.

We were sitting at the bar, eating hamburgers, drinking beer and talking big about flying. Someone at the end of the bar, his face half-hidden by empties, butted into the conversation. "Can you hot shots fly a twin-Beech?" he asked.

"We can fly anything," W.W. answered, his confidence augmented by the alcohol. Actually, neither of us had ever seen the inside of a twin-Beech—with the possible exception of a wrecked example in which I collapsed from exhaustion one night at Brookside Airport after a fourteen-hour day of flight instructing.

"Is that right? You can fly anything? You want a chance to prove it?"

The stranger, though he seemed unimpressed with W.W.'s bluster, unexpectedly offered us both a job.

"Me and my brother operate a bunch of twin-Beeches and some other equipment too. We could use you guys if you're really pilots and not just bullshitters. You want jobs or not?"

Flying job opportunities always arrive when an unemployed pilot least expects, usually after he's abandoned hope and wasted two weeks studying for a real estate license. Such unanticipated offers can catch a pilot off balance and cause him to lose his poise.

Pathetically eager, I could only shake my head in acceptance at the stranger as I choked down a mouthful of Grandma's gristle with a long swig of beer. "Hell, yes!" I gagged.

W.W., so cocky minutes before, managed little more than a grateful whimper.

W.W. and I had, by an unutterable stroke of luck, happened into the very gin mill favored on a twice-a-day basis by Nick Gorotny, half-owner of Gorotny Brothers Flying Service. Seems Nick and brother Ernie ran a charter outfit at an airport on the family farm west of Cleveland, not far from Grandma's Bar.

"I heard you guys talking about Moondog McCutchinson a few minutes ago," Nick said. "Ju work for that asshole?"

"Uh, kind of. Well, a little," I said. Shit, only nineteen years old and already my career ruined. Bad judgment, the most indictable flying gaffe of all, had marked me.

"Yeah, maybe we did," W.W. added, repentantly. "It was all we could find. But we never liked the prick!"

When had W.W. become so honest?

We both looked at Nick Gorotny, holding our breaths and fully expecting the ax to fall. Canned after not quite thirty seconds, a record even for me.

"Flown for worse," was all Nick said, holding up his beer to toast unnamed former miscreant employers.

W.W. and I breathed a sigh of relief. Dodging bullets is an important piloting talent.

Our lack of experience did not seem to be an issue. The only thing that mattered to the Gorotny brothers, Nick emphasized over more beers, was a pilot's willingness to work like a dog for very little pay. He reaffirmed his job offer, mostly because W.W. and I didn't argue with the terms of employment.

My flying career was taking on a disturbing pattern of servitude.

Nonetheless, Gorotny Brothers Flying Service was a definite step in the right direction, a chance to build flying time and maybe undo the damage to my reputation. The Moondog experience had surely been a fluke, an aviation anomaly that I could now put behind me. How could I have known that in less than a year I would leave the Gorotnys in disgrace and, far worse, on the run from the Mafia? A blemished resume would be the least of my worries.

Grandma was so impressed that W.W. and I had jobs with Gorotny Brothers Flying Service that she allowed us to run a tab. We changed from beer to boilermakers, bought a few rounds for the house and spent the rest of the day at the bar celebrating, right up to when Grandma threw us out, tab unpaid.

Next morning we drove through the Ohio countryside to report to work for the Gorotny brothers. Fair warning of coming events streaked by on a Burma Shave sign.

"WHEN YOU REACH/FOR THE SKY/MAKE SURE YOU DON'T/POKE YOUR EYE/*Burma Shave.*"

In those days I paid little heed to advice from anyone, certainly not bullshit Burma Shave platitudes. Unending rows of tall, plump corn along U.S. 20 spoke only of prosperity and abundance on that idyllic fall day. Consuming our usual breakfast of donuts, black coffee and cigarettes, W.W. and I drove on, as content as the grazing Holsteins we passed. Life was good.

Even my old DeSoto ran particularly smooth, missing on only two of its six scored cylinders. Like me, it must have felt the promise of renewed life and boundless opportunities.

"This is our big break, W.W.," I said. "I can feel it. We get a little time with these Gorotny characters and nothing can stop us! We'll be with the airlines before we know it!"

"Kinda countin' your chickens before they hatch, ain'tcha?" he said.

"You sound like a Burma Shave sign, W.W.," I said.

We drove past Gorotny Airport two or three times before we found it, at the end of an unmarked dirt road. It was unlike any other country airport W.W. or I had ever seen. Surrounded by lush fields of soybean and corn, also owned by the Gorotny brothers, one expected a grass runway and perhaps a few Aeronca Champs and Piper Cubs put to pasture. Instead, like a cleverly-camouflaged D-Day staging field, the airport had a lighted paved runway—well, kind of; both ends of the runway were paved but a stretch between them was grass—and harbored a random fleet of twin-Beeches, Douglas DC-3s and a couple of Stearman biplanes used for towing banners.

As if he didn't fly enough during the week, Nick Gorotny worked airshows on weekends in his North American P-51 "Mustang." Between airshows, the cowling of the P-51 remained continuously open in a perfect imitation of a hawk chick demanding attention.

The Gorotny brothers had, in effect, amassed their own air force from among the fatigued survivors of World War Two. They had purchased the aircraft one by one in the post-war surplus airplane market, a unique public feeding frenzy in which aircraft that cost the government millions of dollars were sold for less than the price of the aluminum.

More sophisticated pilots might have written off the airport as an aircraft wrecking yard or, at best, a flyable museum. But to a kid about to become part of it all, the ragged Gorotny fleet glittered like diamonds strewn about the Elysian Fields. That someone would actually pay me to fly these airplanes was overwhelming.

Not a lot of money, to be sure, since the Gorotnys were quick to exploit the "airplane dazzle disease," a debility endemic and incurable among young pilots. W.W. and I exhibited all the textbook symptoms: wide-eyed, drooling and slightly angular around the rib cage.

We met Ernie Gorotny, the serious brother. Blunt and unemotional, Ernie refused to learn anyone's name right away. He referred to all new hires simply as "the fuckin' new guy" for the first six months or so, maybe longer if you didn't distinguish yourself by getting on his shit list. (Ernie would learn my name in a record three weeks.) He offered W.W. and me a characteristically straightforward indoctrination to the world of charter flying.

"Main thing with this charter business is getting the job done, getting the airplane and the freight where and when you're being paid to take it. Nothing else counts!" Ernie began. "Nick told me you guys worked for that lunatic Moondog McCutchinson. That was kid stuff. Forget it. We're running a charter service here. That means somebody calls, we go. Anytime! Anyplace! Any asshole can fly an airplane, but not every asshole can get to where he's supposed to go on time. If you'd rather make excuses than fly, then go to work for the airlines. They're always canceling for some bullshit reason."

Going to work for the airlines was precisely what W.W. and I had in mind. And, to give Ernie his due, he called it exactly. I eventually went to work for an airline and we cancelled all the time for any number of bullshit reasons.

As Ernie continued his sermon on charter flying, I became bored and only pretended to listen. Feigned interest is a required job skill for pilots. Without it, a lifetime of ground schools would not be survivable, especially mind-numbing first-day company indoctrinations like Ernie's. All pilots have their own version of the "ground school gaze." I perfected mine in the first grade to make the nuns think I was paying attention while my thoughts raced to distant galaxies.

Much of this book was conceived in ground schools.

Reserving my enthusiasm for the flying, my thoughts and eyes wandered around the airport. I spotted an old Cadillac hearse, hushed and melancholy, abandoned near the hangar. The hearse rusted unceremoniously among tall thistles, country-sized spider webs and proprietary wasps.

"And another thing…" Ernie said.

"What's the hearse for, Ernie?" I asked, interrupting my new boss. "Free funerals part of the benefits here?" I thought it was funny.

W.W. gave me a dirty look for screwing with the man who stood between our future and us.

Although he didn't laugh, Ernie didn't seem to mind the question. He explained, with a trace of pride, that the derelict hearse was the first "airplane" in the Gorotny fleet. When they were getting started, he said, Nick and he had inconveniently won a contract to fly freight between Cleveland and Detroit before they bothered to buy any aircraft. While Ernie went to find an airplane, Nick purchased the hearse, which he equipped with a rotating beacon and surplus air raid shelter siren. Nick hand-lettered "MOTHER OF MERCY AMBULANCE SERVICE" on each side of the vehicle. He then pushed his talents with a libelous rendering of the Virgin, who clasped her overly-large hands in prayer and hope above a prone individual more suggestive of corpse than patient.

Each night for two months Nick loaded the Mother of Mercy with airfreight and ran wide open between Cleveland and Detroit, siren screaming and red beacon flashing.

"Did some of my best flying in that hearse," Nick later told me. "Some nights me and the Mother of Mercy made it to Detroit quicker than you could've in a twin-Beech. Can't tell you how many times the cops volunteered to escort me through the worst speed traps in Ohio and Michigan. Good goddamn thing they never looked inside."

There was a lot of Moondog in Nick Gorotny.

Ernie pointed to the hearse's successors, a line of Beech 18s, a work-horse unaffectionately known as the "twin-Beech" to the several generations of pilots who suffered—and are still suffering— in them.

"That's what you two'll be flying," Ernie said. "Nick'll give you a checkout this morning. Did Nick mention that you'll be flying along with some of the other guys for a week or so before we turn you loose? Until you're on your own we won't pay you, of course."

Of course.

"Oh, while I'm thinking 'bout it, all takeoffs will be made from this end of the airport," Ernie added.

"What about if the wind is blowing the wrong way?" W.W. asked.

It sure sounded like a legitimate question to me.

"What's that got to do with anything?" Ernie replied. His sarcasm and unconcern for safety brought back disturbing memories of our previous employer. "Costs money and time to taxi. Unless there's a hurricane blowing, don't let me catch you taxiing down to the other end."

We didn't get many hurricanes in northern Ohio. We did a lot of downwind takeoffs in heavily loaded airplanes. All part of the job.

Off in another corner of the airport were the burned remains of what had been a twin-Beech. I inquired about it.

"I'm glad you asked," said Ernie. "Last year I hired a couple young punks, kinda like you guys. I had just bought that twin-Beech and sent them to bring it home. After they landed, they decided to settle a bet."

"What kind of bet?" W.W. asked.

"Well, there was this switch on the panel labeled 'FLARES.' One bet the flares were still on the airplane, the other believed the military had long-ago removed them. So of course they flipped the switch to settle the argument."

"And...?" I asked.

"Do I really have to finish the story?" Ernie's face grimaced as he continued. "Four signal flares that had been minding their own fucking business in that aircraft since World War Two shot out the bottom of the fuselage. Instant twin-Beech bonfire! Any more questions?"

In every aircraft ever built there is at least one switch that, in league with a bit of misguided curiosity, can bite a pilot in the ass in more ways than can be imagined. A cockpit is no place for the impulsive.

With our indoctrination to charter flying complete, W.W. and I set off to inspect the twin-Beeches we'd be flying. We counted sixteen. The twin-Beeches were the backbone of the Gorotny fleet. Though not the stuff of legend, they were cheap, plentiful and reliable. More important, they could carry a considerable load in their square, stubby fuselages, which resemble a homemade travel trailer. When it comes to airplane design, utilitarian and ugly seem to go hand in hand.

From the time it was designed in the late 1930s, the twin-Beech could never decide what it was or what it wanted to do. During the war it served as a pilot, bombardier and gunnery trainer, freight and personnel transport, target tower, aerial mapper, sub spotter and leaflet dropper. After the war, it became the vehicle of choice for small-time charter operators.

The twin-Beech had any number of qualities to make pilots hate it. Not only was it a disagreeable handful in the air with one engine failed at gross weight, but it also enjoyed a well-deserved reputation for its take-your-eyes-off-me-and-I'll-make-you-pay-for-it ground handling. Pilot comforts were minimal; the twin-Beech was hot in the summer and cold in the winter. I've never heard anyone say anything really nice about the twin-Beech, unless "they sure built a lot of the goddamn things" qualifies as a compliment.

Like it or not, all new-hire pilots had to start on the twin-Beech. If a guy stayed around long enough and proved himself, he earned the opportunity to move into some of the Gorotnys' bigger junk for a bit more pay.

Later that morning, Nick gave W.W. and me our checkouts in the twin-Beech.

"Got much multi-engine time?" he asked me.

"Sure, I got time in a UC-78," I said.

Well, kind of. Until he wrecked it, Moondog owned an all-wood Cessna UC-78 "Bamboo Bomber," yet another unloved twin-engine, bastard-child relic of the last world war. My time in the "Bamboo Bomber" was limited to a few hours instruction from Hangardoor followed by a multi-engine rating ride with a federal examiner. The fed sat on the edge of his seat with his eyes closed for the entire flight. I think he agreed to give me the rating just so he could get back on the ground.

I had also logged a few hours in the "Bomber" with Hangardoor buzzing Lake Erie beaches and, of course, ore boats. Loud and imperturbable, the old wooden Cessna twin was ideal for such chores—but little else.

"It really doesn't matter what else you flew," Nick said, "'cause nothing prepares you for the twin-Beech except the twin-Beech."

I knew that much of the flying at Gorotny Brothers Flying Service was at night. I figured it was a good time to admit to Nick that I didn't have much time at night.

"What's the problem?" he said. "It's the same as flying during the day except you can't see anything."

Simple enough.

Nick first showed us how to start the Pratt and Whitney R985 radial engines without setting fire to the aircraft and the airport in the process. Before we took it up, Nick gave us a warning. "You have to fly this sumbitch all the time! It'd just as soon make a fool out of you on the ground as in the air."

"How 'bout single-engine performance," I asked in my deepest Clark Gable test-pilot voice. Performance on one engine is the true test of any twin-engine plane and the only topic worth discussing among professionals. I figured Nick would be impressed that I knew enough to bring it up.

Nick gave me a long look. He lowered his eyebrows, retracted his chin and moved his head back in amazement that I would ask such a witless question.

"I assume you mean if you lose an engine on takeoff when you're heavy as hell, which is just about every time you take off out of this field," Nick said.

"Uh, yeah, I guess," I said, unsure what Nick was trying to say.

"Well, I've flown twin-Beeches for years and they don't fly worth a shit on one engine when they're heavy," Nick said. "On takeoff, forget it! The only thing the second engine's good for is to fly you to the scene of the crash."

"Needed bigger engines, huh?" I asked.

"It didn't need bigger engines, it needed *another* engine," Nick said. "But they ran out of room. It might interest you guys to know that the military once jury-rigged the damn things with rockets strapped to the sides of the fuselage to help in the event of an engine failure on takeoff."

"Sounds pretty cool. How'd that work?" W.W. asked.

"Not good! All the rockets did was burn a path to the scene of the crash. The fire made it a little easier to find the wreckage at night and drag the bodies out, I suppose. Any more questions about engine-out performance?"

W.W. and I shook our heads. Some aviation subjects take weeks to explain. Useless esoterica such as runway analysis graphs, mean aerodynamic chord and the tropopause—whatever the hell that is—can remain a mystery throughout a pilot's career. The truly important subjects, namely those dealing with breaking one's ass, can be covered quickly.

"You gonna pull an engine on us today, Nick?" W.W. asked.

"Probably not. We need all the airplanes we got. Can't afford to lose one."

Made perfect sense to me.

We spent the rest of the morning practicing takeoffs and landings until Nick felt that W.W. and I handled the twin-Beech well enough not to kill ourselves or, more to the point, not to wreck one. The rest was up to us—and the airplane. With all due respect to training departments everywhere, instructors don't teach pilots how to fly airplanes, at least not airplanes such as the twin-Beech. The airplane teaches a pilot how it wants to be flown, how it *must* be flown. The trick is to survive the training process.

The twin-Beech proved an adept, if resentful, educator.

After a couple pro bono trips with some of the more experienced pilots on the field, I was on my own. Within a week the twin-Beech covered the first item on the syllabus. Exactly as Nick had predicted, it made a fool out of me. Such was my callowness that it didn't take the entire airplane to accomplish the feat, merely a landing light.

The landing light story: By the early 1960s there were no two twin-Beeches alike in the world. The military or civilian owners had modified all of them for any number of purposes. The landing light on one of the Gorotny mutants was installed on the front of the nose compartment, which was hinged and swung up and back to allow access to a small additional freight area. I made a short trip in the ship one night from Gorotny International, as we called our home base, to Defiance, Ohio. Good weather. Short trip. Easy money. Before I left, I stuffed one last small piece of freight in the hinged nose compartment and hurriedly—and carelessly—secured the latches.

While I don't remember ever making a real good landing in the twin-Beech, that night in Defiance I thumped down a bit harder than usual. The improperly latched nose compartment, landing light and all, came undone and swung open and back on the second bounce. The zillion-candlepower light shined directly into my eyes from about a foot away. I was instantly blinded. Unable to see where I was going, I ran the airplane off the narrow runway into the dirt.

I managed to shut down the engines, but not before the props had stirred up a ton or so of dust. In my reduced-vision state, the reflection of the dust in the bright landing light created the illusion of smoke. I thought the airplane was on fire. I swung open the small escape hatch over the pilot's seat and stumbled out of the cockpit onto the ground. Hopping around, I shook imaginary flames away from my body and yelled "Fire! The airplane's on fire! I'm on fire! Help!"

A couple of truck drivers, waiting to pick up the freight, observed the entire operation. They walked out to the airplane.

"What in hell you talkin' 'bout fella? There ain't no fire," one of the truck drivers said. "You bin smokin' some o' that merrywanna, ain'tcha? C'mon, quit messin' around and move this thing to the ramp. We gotta get the freight unloaded."

I climbed back into the aircraft, restarted the engines and somehow taxied the airplane to the ramp without the benefit of sight. While the truck drivers unloaded the freight and made tasteless jokes at my expense, I struggled blinkingly to regain my vision. The airplane was needed back at Gorotny International and mere blindness would not have been an acceptable excuse for Ernie. After about thirty minutes, with a bit of my vision restored, I flew home.

Somehow W.W. had already heard the story. He began calling me "Searchbeam" before I was out of the airplane.

Nothing on earth is so fragile as a pilot's reputation. Other professionals protect and cover each other. A doctor can maim or kill any number of patients and his colleagues will remain quiet, even take the stand and swear to his competence. Same for lawyers, who won't usually rat on one another unless there's a few bucks to be made.

Pilots do not extend the same courtesy. Screw up just once in your flying career and, unless you depart this world in the effort, the mishap will follow you and be told with increasing fervor and embellishment for the rest of your life. Aviation has been called a brotherhood. It's not. It's more like a neighborhood bar.

Fifteen years and a few flying jobs later, I was trying to get some sleep one night in a recliner held together with duct tape in a drafty room provided for freight pilots at Chicago's O'Hare Airport. Two pilots a couple recliners down from me were swapping twin-Beech stories. One of them related the one about the landing light. He was talking about me!

"...and they called the guy 'Spotlight' from then on! Must have been a goofy bastard."

"Whatever happened to him?" the other pilot asked.

"I heard Spotlight got killed later in another twin-Beech."

My scholarly, reverential devotion to the historical accuracy of flying stories is well known. Though dead tired, I felt obligated to set straight the raconteur. I unglued myself from the duct tape stuck to my pants and walked over to the two pilots.

"Scuse me," I said.

"Yeah?"

"It was 'Searchbeam,' not 'Spotlight.'"

"Huh?"

"The guy you're talkin' about, they called him 'Searchbeam,' not 'Spotlight,' after the miscue with the landing light."

"How do you know?"

"Because I was there when he returned to the field. You should have seen him groping his way out of the airplane. We laughed for days."

"What was his name? You remember?" one of the pilots asked.

"Let me think," I said. "Oh yeah, I remember. His name was W.W. Storm. He's still around. He was not killed in a twin-Beech crash like you said. Not that he didn't try. But you're correct about one thing."

"What's that?"

"He was a goofy bastard."

W.W. rubbed the landing light thing in pretty good for a couple of weeks until the incident with the monkey. As an aside, the occurrence of monkeys in the first two chapters of this book has far more to do with the quality of flying jobs I was able to find at that stage in my checkered career than it does with an overactive imagination.

The monkey story: A few of us were hanging around the office one slow morning listening as Nick relived his war exploits. Nick, in a P-47, was hard on the tail of some hapless Nazi prick. He was just about to squeeze off a few rounds when W.W., in a hysterical voice, unexpectedly called in on the airport radio.

W.W. had left a couple hours earlier for Cleveland Hopkins to pick up a load of rhesus monkeys to fly to Buffalo, where the animals would face an exotic, painful future at some medical lab. We hauled monkeys all the time. Except for the smell and the racket, it was just another charter.

For some reason W.W., presumably with his load of monkeys on board, was headed back to the field.

"Ya read Three Nine Delta?" W.W. asked in a voice higher-pitched than normal.

"Yeah, W.W., this is Pete, what's up? Goin' the wrong way, ain'tcha? Buffalo's east o' here." I have an informal approach to radio communications.

"Fuck you! Just meet the airplane, bring the shotgun and a first aid kit, a big one," W.W. said. His plaintive call would become legend at Gorotny International.

"A big gun or a big first aid kit?" I asked.

"I'm gonna kick your ass when I get on the ground! Can't talk any more, got my hands fu…" The transmission ended abruptly without further explanation.

I grabbed the rusty double-barreled shotgun and picked-through first-aid kit we kept in the office and ran outside just in time to see W.W. make a very slow pass over the airport. An object fell from the airplane into an adjacent pasture.

W.W. landed. Blood, pieces of raw flesh and bits of fur covered the top of the left cowling and wing. There was also blood on the propeller. Shaking and cursing, W.W. climbed out of the twin-Beech. Blood flowed from his right hand like a burst fountain pen. Brother Ernie was present, understanding as ever.

"Please tell me this mess on my airplane was your lunch and not a monkey," Ernie said as he surveyed the grisly evidence. "Because if this was a monkey I will get charged for it and I will in turn have to charge you. You won't believe what a monkey costs, buddy."

"It *is* a monkey, Ernie. Well, it *was* a monkey," W.W. said, averting his eyes from the gore. While he studied the damage to his red-soaked hand, W.W. explained that during climb-out from Cleveland

Hopkins one of the monkeys escaped from its cage and entered the cockpit, frantic and mad as hell.

Knowing he couldn't fly, much less land, with such a distraction, W.W. said he hit the cockpit trespasser with a flashlight. This caused the monkey to take cover under the instrument panel, where it began to pull and chew on the wiring and play with the rudder pedals. At that point, W.W. said he decided to divert to Gorotny International.

"Why didn't you just land back at Hopkins?" one of the other pilots present asked.

"I didn't wanna get the FAA involved," W.W. said.

Cleveland Hopkins was crawling with feds who seemed to have nothing better to do than screw with people trying to make a living flying.

"Good thinking!" Ernie said. "You did one thing right. Please continue."

"Well, I reached under the panel about the time I got back here and grabbed the monkey," W.W. said. "The little fucker sunk his teeth into my hand. He wouldn't let go so I held him out the window, thinking the slipstream would pull him off my hand. What else could I do, Ernie?"

"How'd the blood and fur get all over my airplane?" Ernie said.

"After a while the monkey let go of my hand. Somehow he grabbed onto the wing," W.W. explained. "I thought, with any luck, I might get the airplane *and* the monkey on the ground. I even slowed down to make it easier for the little guy to stay on the wing."

"I don't have all day to listen to this. What happened to that monkey?" Ernie said. Like all bosses, Ernie didn't like long stories.

"The monkey crawled up to the cowling and then…" W.W. paused, as if recalling something horrible.

"And then what, goddamnit?" Ernie said.

"Well, it, it kinda stuck its head into the prop. It was awful, worse thing I ever saw in my life!"

Ernie was the only one not amused. "Wait'll you find out what a monkey costs," he said. "A monkey costs more than a pilot."

The dozen or so relatives of the recently departed primate howled wildly in the background, no doubt demanding equal time to tell their version of the story.

In keeping with the liberal sick-leave policy of charter operators everywhere, W.W. doused his hand with half a bottle of war-surplus iodine and wrapped it in yellowed bandages. He hosed down the airplane to destroy the evidence while Ambrose, the Gorotny brothers' sole mechanic, spliced the chomped radio and instrument wiring. W.W. climbed back into the twin-Beech and flew to Buffalo, short one passenger and the use of one hand.

My landing light mishap was mostly forgotten as W.W.'s monkey story was told and retold. Each pilot who heard it added his own touches. My version held that *all* the monkeys got loose. While W.W. battled for his life in the close combat of the cockpit, one of the monkeys landed the twin-Beech. Landed, in fact, more smoothly than W.W. ever could except in his dreams.

There's no such thing as a factual flying story; damn few remain unaltered for very long.

Weeks turned into months at Gorotny International. Flying charter in twin-Beeches, while spawning a disproportionate number of entertaining stories compared to the rest of aviation, proved to be more hard work than fun. Each trip opened another window into the realities of flying for a living.

The Gorotnys ate and slept aviation and expected nothing less from their pilots. As brother Ernie often reminded us, he didn't hire pilots, he bought them. If he so much as suspected one of his pilots of screwing off, he'd find a chore for him on the family farm. Which pretty much explains how I learned to drive a tractor and run a cornpicker. Later in life I would fly brand new jets, have a lot of time off and make big money. To fully appreciate such a great job requires a sense of perspective. Some pilots have it; most don't. I pity them.

A day off at Gorotny Brothers Flying Service was rare, so rare I can't remember having one. Not that I minded. The idea that someone was paying me an almost livable wage to fly airplanes remained a dream come true, good fortune beyond my wildest expectations at the time. Only years later, after I went to work for the airlines, did someone explain to me that the idea of the flying game was to get paid the most for flying the fewest hours, none at all if possible.

It's somehow sad and a little suspect how many pilots working for the airlines never go near an airplane. And never want to. These pilots inexplicably prefer office politics, paperwork and endless committee meetings to flying. They gladly forfeit their line positions for long-term or even lifetime chief pilot, training department, pilot union or other extraneous office positions. It changes them; they don't think it does, but it does. Some return to line flying but with rare exceptions they're never the same. Flying is the most elemental of pleasures and nothing robs the soul of the capacity for simple joy as a whiff or two of rarified air.

Other than extra money, a choice parking spot, government-issue dark tie and the optional self-satisfied smile, I'm not sure what the office guys get out of it. It all seems kind of Faustian to a dumb kid from Cleveland's West 65th Street who wanted only a chance to fly airplanes. Then again, I was born without a single management chromosome—a deficiency for which I give daily thanks—so perhaps I just don't understand.

When winter hit northern Ohio, the twin-Beech learning curve turned vertical. Winter flying can be brutal in any airplane, even more so in a twin-Beech. Tricky crosswinds and icy runways proved a treacherous combination in an airplane not known as forgiving even on a dry surface. Ice build-up on props and flying surfaces took away performance from an airplane that had none to spare.

The twin-Beech cockpit heater, essentially a container full of raw gasoline, had a cruel tendency to overheat and trip the thermal relief circuit breaker. In any other airplane, the pilot could simply reset the breaker. But on the twin-Beech the breaker had to be reset from the outside, not an appealing alternative when airborne. Twin-Beech pilots in the northern climes wore clothing that would have been excessive on an Everest climb.

The brothers Gorotny ground deicing procedure was a special treat. The pilot first drew a few gallons of Ernie's precious ethylene glycol—he inventoried the supply every day to make sure we didn't use too much—from a fifty-five gallon drum in the hangar. After thinning the glycol with icy water in a five-gallon can, the mixture was warmed on an oil-fired space heater. The pilot, using a frozen mop, swabbed the ice-encrusted aircraft with the deicing brew. Even on a good night you soaked your shoes and slipped off the airplane at least once. On the twin-Beeches in the Gorotny fleet with suspect prop alcohol dispensers, we rubbed the props with a gooey anti-icing mixture. The stuff was the chemical equivalent of bear grease and much better suited at preventing chapped hands than prop ice.

A bit of warm food to eat at destination on a wintry night, it sometimes seemed, could spell the difference between life and death. Thermos bottles were bulky, fragile and required too much advance planning, not a strong suit of mine. A better method was to simply jam a couple cans of Campbell's soup between the cylinders and cowling before starting the engines. On arrival, *voila*, warm soup. It wasn't in any flight manual, but it worked. Admittedly, both cans didn't always make it to the destination.

A favorite winter story at Gorotny International involved a corpse W.W. was transporting out of state for burial, everyone's least favorite duty. Pressure changes at altitude in the unpressurized twin-Beech could cause the body to moan or even sit up en route.

The body W.W. was transporting to its place of eternal rest that night not only sat upright, but also froze in that position in the unheated cabin. After W.W. landed, he almost had a heart attack when he saw his passenger sitting upright, a la Lazarus.

After convincing himself that no blessed intercession had occurred in the twin-Beech, W.W. attempted to return the body to prone. Outside, an impatient undertaker was waiting in his hearse, laying on the horn. The cabin door did not open right away so the undertaker entered the airplane. He found W.W. cursing at the body as he tried to straighten it.

When W.W. returned later that day, he related with unrestrained glee how the miffed undertaker drove away with his customer sitting next to him in the front seat, the heater on full defrost.

On another night, I arrived at the airport, late as usual. Since trips were assigned on a "first come, first serve" basis, I lost out on a choice freight run to northern Canada to another pilot named Bruce Black. I drew a body run to Kentucky instead. As mentioned, everyone hated flying stiffs. (It wasn't until I began flying airline passengers full time that I came to realize dead ones were infinitely preferable to live ones.) I envied Bruce and the money he was going to make on the long Canada trip, since we were paid by the hour.

My envy was short-lived.

Bruce got his first clue that he was not flying an ordinary charter when the two guys who delivered the "freight" would not allow him to handle it. No problem. Bruce stood off to the side of the airplane and lit a cigarette.

His second clue came when one of the loaders rushed over and pulled the cigarette out of his mouth. As the loader stomped the butt he sternly warned Bruce not to combine any type of flame with his freight.

"Ya mean I gotta fly all night and can't smoke?" Bruce whined. "I'll never make it!"

"Ya might not make it anyhow," the loader joked. His partner shook his head and laughed in agreement.

The comment aroused my attention. I walked over to the airplane to investigate.

The "freight" consisted of about a mile of primer cord, a hundred or so "shaped charges," each capable of putting the twin-Beech into moon orbit, and eight or ten dozen boxes containing 50-pound donuts of C-4 explosive, each capable of putting the twin-Beech *and* the moon into orbit around Pluto. I backed away.

"What is this shit, anyway?" Bruce inquired.

"Plastique!" one of the loaders said as he carefully positioned the last box of C-4.

"Plastic? You mean I'm flying plastic all the way to Canada?" Bruce said. "How come I can't smoke around plastic?"

"Not plastic, you idiot, *plastique!*" the loader said. "You know, like for cutting mountains in half or turning rivers around. Like in BOOM! BOOM! Got it?"

"Yeah...I think so," Bruce said.

While Bruce Black contemplated the possibilities of a premature, if spectacular, end to his flying career, I said a silent prayer for the guy who went to all the trouble of dying just so I could fly him to Kentucky.

"Okay, you're all set, pal," the plastique loader said to Bruce. "Good luck. This is the second time we've tried to ship the stuff this week."

Ernie came out of the office with the airport's rusty double-barreled shotgun, a handful of shells and a moth-eaten blanket. He handed them to Bruce.

"What this for?" Bruce asked.

"You're gonna be flyin' over bear country up there in Canada. If you have to make a forced landing, these things'll come in handy," Ernie said. "Only one barrel works on the gun so make your first shot count."

"Which barrel?"

"I'm not sure," Ernie said. "You'll find out when you go to use it."

"What's the blanket for, Ernie?" Bruce asked.

"You can make a tent out of it or send smoke signals or something if you go down." Ernie said.

"What am I supposed to eat?" Bruce said.

"I don't know," Ernie answered, tiring of the conversation. "Maybe the bear. Cook it good. Bear meat's full of all kinds of nasty shit."

One could never accuse Ernie Gorotny of not looking after his pilots.

Bruce took the impromptu survival gear from Ernie and climbed daintily over the chancy cargo to the cockpit. Seated in the cockpit with the shotgun still in his hand, Bruce reminded me of Gabby Hayes on a stagecoach. He opened the window. He started to speak but didn't. The look on his face was telling. Bruce wanted badly to quit on the spot and tell Ernie to stick the twin-Beech, plastique, iffy shotgun and blanket up his ass.

But he went.

As pilots have always gone.

As pilots will always go.

The northern Ohio winter weather forced us to design our own instrument approaches at airports that did not have one, notably Gorotny International. We all had our own idea on the subject. When the ceiling and visibility at the airport were low, I flew a predetermined radial off the Cleveland VOR station and descended to about five hundred feet. I timed myself so that I would know—more or less—when to turn toward the airport. This was made much easier at night thanks to the orange neon top hat of the Top Hat Lounge near the airport.

A hard left turn of about forty degrees overhead the top hat glowing through the fog lined up the airplane with the runway. Nothing to it—provided that someone had remembered to turn on the runway lights. It was also helpful to know, well in advance, that the strings of lights along the road leading to an all-weather, all-night drive-in movie located near the airport looked a lot like a runway in the dark. This might be a good time to apologize, however belatedly, for any *coitus interruptus* I may have caused drive-in movie patrons one foul night while rummaging around in the fog at fifty feet for Gorotny International.

When the weather was *really* bad at the field, Ernie assigned one of his idle pilots the job of sitting in the airport pick-up truck parked with its nose in the air on a wooden ramp at the end of the runway. While Ernie coordinated with the inbound flight on the airport radio frequency, the pilot in the truck rapidly sequenced the headlights from high to low beam, a kind of poor man's approach light system.

Inevitably, I drew the perilous pick-up truck/approach lights duty one night. As I flashed the hell out of the headlights, I watched W.W. break out of the fog, make a playful dip at the truck, pass overhead a few feet and land behind me. I would much rather have been in the twin-Beech.

The Gorotnys, between rare, unpredictable and short-lived peaks of prosperity, operated on a frayed shoestring during that particular winter. Every time a pilot left Gorotny International, he risked running into someone to whom the Gorotnys owed money. Gorotny Brothers Flying Service thus avoided certain airports, where its airplanes—and pilots— were persona non grata. A list hanging in the office divided airports into two categories: "safe" and "avoid."

I was assigned a charter to Minneapolis one frigid night. After checking to see that Minneapolis was still on the "safe" list, I departed. My instructions were to wait on the freight at a certain fixed-based operator. After landing, I parked the airplane and retrieved two cans of Campbell's turkey noodle soup from the cowling. Juggling the hot cans from hand to hand, I walked into the office, bought a soda and sat down to have dinner. After dinner, I sat on a couch to wait on the freight. Waiting on freight or passengers to arrive is a major part of every charter pilot's existence, far more dreaded than engine failures.

I lit a Lucky and took out my pocket edition of Shakespeare. Even though I had blown off high school and flunked out of college in a record six weeks, I read a lot in those days. It was an attempt to fill in the educational gaps created by my inability and unwillingness to pay attention in any formal setting. Shakespeare held a special attraction, mostly because I identified so much with the suffering of his star-crossed characters. I was deep into King Richard's kidnapping when the freight truck arrived.

I pretended to be busy with pilot matters so that I could get out of helping load the airplane. I ordered fuel and took as long as I could to file a flight plan back to Cleveland. After the airplane was loaded, I went out to the ramp to fly it home.

Not only had the airplane not been fueled, but some moron had parked a fuel truck in front of it. A second moron had parked a fuel truck behind the airplane. Both trucks were locked and abandoned. I suspected the worst and began searching for clues. I found one, a note attached to the airplane's windshield wiper. It read, "You owe $800.45 for fuel. Pay up and we'll move the trucks."

Sensing it might be a long night, I quickly assessed my resources: half a pack of Luckies, two rock-hard Tootsie Rolls, some stale saltines, most of the second can of noodle soup and a grand total of one dollar and seven cents. I called Ernie, collect. He refused the charges the first two calls and only accepted them when he heard my voice rising abusively through the operator.

"You shouldn't swear on the phone, Fusco," Ernie said. "You could go to jail for that."

I could go to jail for a lot longer if I did what I'm thinking right now, Ernie.

"Ernie, there a note on the airplane that says you owe money for gas. I checked the 'safe' list before I left tonight. Minneapolis was on it."

"Damn, I meant to put it on the 'avoid' list," he said. There was a long pause. "How much we owe them bastards?"

"Eight hundred dollars," I said. "Eight hundred dollars and forty-five cents to be exact."

Another pause. "You think you can move one of the fuel trucks and get the airplane out of there?"

"How am I supposed to do that? Break into the truck and hot wire it?"

"It's been done before. Ya know how?"

"You trying to get my ass kicked for me, Ernie?" I yelled into the phone.

A couple guys working in the office eavesdropped on the conversation. One of them locked the cash register while the other kept on eye on me, as if he had just heard on the radio that an armed man fitting my description had escaped from death row.

"Actually, I won't need that airplane 'til things pick up around here." Ernie was thinking aloud over the phone.

"How do I get home, Ernie?"

"You got any cash on you?"

"About a buck. Make that seventy-five cents. I'm gonna buy a candy bar."

"I just ain't got the money to pay that gas bill right now," Ernie said without apology. "Do the best you can." He hung up. The son of a bitch hung up!

Until then I didn't realize how well Shakespeare captured the universal condition of men. At that moment, I knew exactly how King Richard must have felt when, held hostage by some nasty Germans, he appealed without success to his evil brother John to ante up the ransom. Evil John, who would soon became evil *King* John due to Richard's misfortune, told his brother about the same thing Ernie told me: "I just ain't got the money to pay that ransom right now, Richard. Do the best you can. And oh, by the way, go fuck yourself."

The truck drivers who had delivered the freight were my first hurdle. They were waiting for me when I walked out of the office and demanded to know when I'd be leaving for Cleveland. The freight they had loaded into the twin-Beech was high priority, they said. Heads would roll if it didn't get to where it was going.

Faced with such unhappy customers, who happened to be big, mean-looking unhappy customers, I naturally avoided the truth. The twin-Beech was a complicated airplane, I explained, and it would be another half-hour before the magnetos were cool enough to engage and the encapsulated reverse-polarity batteries powering the Shippler navigation devices were fully charged.

This early practice in bullshitting an uninformed public would later prove invaluable in my airline career. Sometimes, however, it pays to know whom you are bullshitting. An annoyed passenger once asked me the reason for the lengthy mechanical delay we were experiencing with our Boeing 737. I could have told him the truth, that mechanics were looking for nothing more prosaic than a hydraulic leak. But what fun would that have been?

Unusually inspired, I told the passenger that the aircraft flight control specialists were changing out a defective inverse flap-warping device in the right wing spoiler of the Boeing. Such a device, I patiently explained to him, was necessary for mach lateral flight in the jet stream. When I finished, the passenger handed me his card, which identified him as a "senior systems engineer" for the Boeing Aircraft Corporation.

Caught red-handed, what could I do but laugh? He didn't. With the possible exception of the men who designed the Curtiss C-46 "Commando"—exhaustively covered in the next chapter—most aircraft engineers don't seem to possess a sense of humor. It's probably better that way.

As casually as possible, I climbed into the twin-Beech and gathered the stale saltines and a handful of relightable cigarette butts from the coffee can ashtray. I walked away, past the truck drivers. Slowly, the way one does from a growling dog.

"Where ya goin' buddy?" one of the drivers growled.

"Uh, I gotta go to the other side of the field to get the special form to file the required, uh, interstate barograph flight plan. Be right back, guys," I said, waving at them.

I walked in the freezing night air toward the bright lights of the main cargo area, about a half-mile away. In the cargo area I hoped to catch a ride home on someone's jump seat.

A caution: Begging cockpit jump seats is an acquired piloting skill. It's not as easy as it may appear. Some pilots, especially senior captains for major airlines, allow the job to swell their heads so much that it doesn't allow much room for anyone else in the cockpit. They react to a request for their sacred cockpit jump seat as if someone were asking to borrow their new Porsche to enter in a demolition derby. I've seen a few big-time airline jerks actually sneer at pilots of lesser status who had the nerve to ask for their jump seat.

Freighter pilots, however, invariably take pity on stranded brothers. Wandering around the ramp, I asked every freight jockey I saw if he was headed anywhere toward Cleveland. One poor kid flying cancelled checks to Cleveland in a single-engine Cessna explained that he'd like to help but the cancelled checks filled the entire cabin, sometimes dangerously overloading the airplane and throwing off the center of gravity. I felt a little guilty. I wrote a lot of three-dollar checks in those days.

I spotted a candy vending machine. Everything was sold out except for a row of Zero Bars, my least favorite candy bar. The machine swindled me out of several quarters before it delivered. I choked down the Zero Bar, gave the candy machine a retributory kick and resumed my hunt for a ride home.

About an hour later I came across a crew flying a weary DC-6 for a freight outfit with the peculiar name of "Zantop Air Transport." The captain welcomed me aboard, no questions asked. He and the other crewmembers even shared their smokes while I entertained them with the story of my predicament. They all had similar stories. The crew flew me to Detroit where I waited six hours for another Zantop flight to Cleveland Hopkins. I didn't get home until late the next night, cold-soaked, near-starved and mad as hell. At Ernie? At aviation? At myself? I wasn't sure.

Ernie paid the fuel bill a month later. He sent W.W. and me to Minneapolis to retrieve the airplane. The fuel trucks were gone but some spiteful prick had let the air out of the tires. While W.W. went to look for compressed air, I borrowed a can of red paint and a brush and painted "Eventual Air Lines" on the side of the twin-Beech. Ernie knew I was the vandal but couldn't prove it. He made he remove the paint anyhow.

To this day when someone tells me they are thinking of becoming a professional pilot and ask what to expect, I relate the broke-hungry-stranded-cold-as-hell-pissed-off-in Minneapolis story. I don't tell it to amuse nor to trouble them. I tell the story only to warn them. It's important for a wannabe pilot to know that while Ernie Gorotny may be long gone, his species is far from extinct.

I'd soon have a much better story to tell. Read on.

*   *   *   *

As spring begrudgingly arrived in northern Ohio, I came as close to liking the twin-Beech as a pilot could hope, which is to say that I didn't hate it as much as I did at first. Despite its reputation, the airplane never really let me down. It pulled me through thunderstorms, ice, engine troubles and a few sticky situations of my own making that I am too embarrassed to chronicle even in *this* book. I thought I had seen it all but I hadn't seen anything yet. The twin-Beech was about to fail me in a grand manner that would make everything else that would ever happen to me again in an airplane seem like once around the patch in an Ercoupe.

The drama began on an unseasonably warm, rainy day during what had been a very wet spring, even for Cleveland. There was no flying that day. That didn't mean, however, that there wasn't any work. We had loosely-defined job descriptions at Gorotny Brothers Flying Service; Ernie had a couple of the pilots cleaning out the cow barn. I hid from him in the hangar, where I pretended to help Ambrose, the Gorotnys' mechanic.

Sandy-haired and baby-faced, Ambrose was single-handedly responsible for keeping the entire Gorotny fleet airworthy, a daunting task considering the brothers owned more airplanes than some Central American air forces. Ambrose was slow-paced but deliberate, a master of the fine art of calculated negligence, the system by which, to one degree or another, *all* aircraft in the world are maintained. He knew down to the last turn of a wrench or tap of a hammer the bare minimum amount of time and effort it took to keep the variety of aircraft in his care flying. Lack of spare parts was his major problem. Much of Ambrose's days were spent in the ongoing juggling act of cannibalizing one airplane for the sake of another. Aircraft were sometimes asked to sacrifice vital organs so that another could live one more day.

We were working on Oh Four Romeo, queen of the Gorotny twin-Beech fleet. The aircraft had been the personal transport of some Strategic Air Command honcho during its military career. Oh Four Romeo was the only twin-Beech on the field still in the passenger-carrying configuration. Its aluminum skin was still a little shiny and mostly oil free, brand new by the standards of Gorotny Brothers Flying Service. The slightly ratty interior was appointed in blue leather with six passenger seats and a stocked bar, which Ernie inventoried even more devoutly than he did his precious barrel of deicing glycol.

The Gorotnys used Oh Four Romeo for the rare passenger charter. Normally, only Nick or Ernie flew the charters because the passengers, so relieved after a flight in the drafty, noisy twin-Beech, usually tipped out of all proportion to services rendered—particularly when they got drunk, which they usually did, on the free booze.

Ambrose, with damn little help from me, had just changed a troublesome carburetor on Oh Four Romeo's right engine. We towed the airplane out of the hangar into the rain to run it up. "Okay, hop inside and give that sucker a try," Ambrose said, wiping his hands with an oily rag.

I did as ordered and cranked the right engine. It gave the characteristic Pratt and Whitney gurgle, expelled some smoke, and began to run smoothly. Not for long, however. The engine began to miss and back-fire. The carburetor we—make that Ambrose—spent two hours installing was no good.

"Damnit!" Ambrose said, throwing the rag to the ground. He walked around to the side of the hangar and kicked through a forest of weeds in the rain, as if looking for something. I would have rather returned to the dry hangar, but my curiosity got the better of me. I joined him in the search.

"What're we lookin' for, Ambrose"

"Aw, last week I got pissed at another carburetor that was giving me fits and threw the goddamn thing out the hangar window. It's out here somewhere. I'm gonna try it on Oh Four Romeo if I can find it."

"Uh, if it didn't work last week why ya gonna mess with it again?" I asked.

While we searched the weeds among dozens of other similarly rejected parts for the heretofore junk carb, Ambrose took the opportunity to educate me about one of aviation's stranger enigmas.

"Pete, ya see that piece o' shit DeSoto you drive?" Ambrose asked. I readied myself. Mechanics have trouble with plain English. They speak a language all their own; most of what they say is not easily translatable by pilots. So far I had no problem following him, however.

"Sure I see it," I replied. How could I miss it? My black four-door 1948 DeSoto, acquired under favorable terms from a brother-in-law, was more artifact than automobile. Both rear quarter panels were rusted so badly that only a brownish-red outline of metal remained to suggest that it once had rear fenders. Springs of unequal tension caused the car to list hard to starboard, so that it seemed to be in a high speed turn even when parked. Not that high speed was anywhere in its repertoire. The DeSoto was equipped with an odd, early attempt at an automatic transmission known as "Fluid Drive." One simply put one's foot on the accelerator and a couple of miles later the car could be moving at up to 40 miles an hour, depending on wind direction and velocity. The car was tired and unreliable, a candidate for the crusher even on the days it started. I hated it and it hated me.

"Well, here's how it works," Ambrose continued. "If that piece o' shit DeSoto of yours dies, it stays dead 'til ya fix it. Period! End of discussion! But not airplanes, they're different."

"They are?"

"Sure. All ya gotta do is leave 'em alone for a bit. Just go do something else, smoke a cigarette or something, and airplanes'll fix themselves. I can't explain why, but I know it's true. I've seen it too many times. The more complicated the airplane or the part, the truer it is. Airplanes fix themselves!"

I didn't buy Ambrose's explanation but time would prove him right. Over the years I would shake my head in wonderment as I observed Ambrose's unlikely theory in action. Sometimes just walking away from a Convair 640, Lockheed Electra or Boeing 727 or 737 and getting a cup of coffee would be enough. A circuit breaker that wouldn't stay closed would close, a pump that wouldn't pump would pump again, a dead radio would suddenly broadcast crystal clear. Even the flight and engine computers on the "next generation" aircraft accede to this unaccountable rule. It's especially true if one goes through the trouble of locating a mechanic. When he arrives, he often finds nothing wrong. The pilot, of course, looks like a fool.

"That's it?" I said.

"Yep, that's it. Airplanes fix themselves! Cars don't. Boats don't. Lawnmowers don't. But airplanes do. Ah, here it is!" Ambrose announced. He picked up the carburetor gingerly, a biblical shepherd coming across a lost lamb.

We pushed Oh Four Romeo back into the hangar. Ambrose went to work removing the bad carb. I took advantage of a brief let-up in the rain to walk out to the mailbox on the road for the day's mail, keeping a sharp eye out for Ernie. In the mail was a letter from the Cleveland FAA office addressed to a *Chester* Gorotny.

"Hey, Ambrose, who's this Chester Gorotny?" I asked when I returned to the hangar. "He's got a letter."

"Just put it with that stack of letters there on the shelf under the Champion Spark Plug box. Careful how you handle that box," Ambrose said.

I mindfully lifted the spark plug box and inserted the letter on a large stack of Chester's unclaimed mail. A hand-written note taped to the box proclaimed, "Chester, a hell of a brother and a hell of a pilot. Rest in peace."

Armed with a large wrench, Ambrose was engaged in battle removing the recalcitrant carburetor. When he had it off the engine he threw it out the open window into the weeds, where it would presumably repair itself.

"So, who's this Chester?" I asked again.

"Who?" Ambrose said, annoyed. "Lester? Lester who?" Most mechanics are as deaf as pilots. It's the engine noise and the large hammers they use.

"*Chester!* Not Lester. Chester Gorotny." I repeated. I was determined to learn more about the third brother, apparently deceased, who collected his mail under a spark plug box from the great beyond.

"Oh, all right," Ambrose said. He put down the wrench and lit a cigarette. "Chester was the third Gorotny brother, the real crazy one. Best airshow pilot who ever lived."

"Get killed in an airshow?"

"No, Chester didn't get killed in an airshow. He was too good a pilot to get killed in an airshow. Got his ass killed towing banners. That answer your question?"

"How do you get killed towing a banner?" I asked. Towing banners was one of our jobs. Nothing could be easier or, at least I thought, safer.

Take off, toss out a line with a hook on the end of it and make a low pass to grab the banner line strung between two poles. Then fly over a designated area and circle for an hour or two. The hardest part was staying awake. The only real danger was to people on the ground. Once, a banner advertising Pilsner of Cleveland beer came loose and fell into Cleveland Municipal Stadium during an Indians game. It settled in the box seats along the third base line, unquestionably the most exciting thing the long-suffering Cleveland fans saw that dismal season.

As I waited to hear how I might expect to get killed towing a banner, I patted my empty pockets in the manner smokers have of showing another smoker they are out of cigarettes. Ambrose offered me a Pall Mall.

"Most people who smoke buy their own cigarettes," he said. "Did anyone ever tell you that?"

"Sure, all the time," I said. "Now, back to this Chester guy."

"Well, there's all kinds of ways to get killed in airplanes," Ambrose said, drawing on his cigarette. "Back then things were real bad here. We couldn't afford a real banner-towing hook so we used a modified small boat anchor."

"A boat anchor?"

"Right, a boat anchor! It worked so good that we kept using it for years till that day when Chester missed the banner line and the anchor hit the ground and dug in. It started to furrow just like he was towing a plow behind him."

"Then what?"

"Figure it out! Before Chester could disconnect the towline, the anchor pulled him right outta the sky like he was on the end of a kite string. He crashed out on the road, right on top of a police car. Chester died in the crash."

"How 'bout the cops?"

"They were all right...after a couple months."

"Damn, never heard such a thing," I said. "So what's the deal with the spark plug box?"

"Those are Chester's ashes," Ambrose said with a sigh. "But not all of them, mind you. Chester mentioned once that when he died he wanted his ashes thrown out of an airplane. Nick and Ernie took the ashes up in a twin-Beech and tried to throw them out. Matter of fact, it was this very same airplane, Oh Four Romeo. The ashes kept blowin' back in, so Ernie and Nick felt that Chester must have changed his mind. They saved what ashes they could, put them in that spark plug box and there lies Chester. Some of his ashes are probably still in the airplane, so he gets to fly now and then. End of story. Back to work."

Ambrose ground his cigarette out on the hangar floor.

"How come he still gets letters?" I persisted.

"Mostly, they're from his ex ol' lady's lawyer in California and the FAA. The ex wants money and the feds are still trying to pull his ticket." Ambrose laughed hollowly as he selected a wrench from a toolbox the size of a small building.

"Wouldn't it be easier if somebody just told them that Chester was dead?"

"Ah, screw 'em," Ambrose said, becoming reflective. "This way it's like still having ol' Chester around."

I didn't think Chester would mind so I opened the latest letter from the feds. It proved to be a bureaucratese eulogy to an aviation career.

> Dear Mr. Gorotny,
>
> This letter is to inform you of the ongoing investigation into the incident of Aug 10, 1959. Several witnesses, including two law enforcement officers injured as a result of your alleged negligence, have entered depositions with this office. The officers maintain the aircraft you were flying, a Stearman biplane, N84296, appeared to be attached to a rope which was in turn inexplicably attached to the ground, causing your aircraft to be pulled out of the sky.
>
> As you know, this office is in possession of the banner-towing apparatus used on that day. An extensive three-year examination of the device by a number of experts from both the National Transportation Safety Board and the Federal Aviation Administration has determined that the device in question is quite possibly marine in origin rather than the aviation type approved by the Administrator for the aerial towing of banners, pursuant to Federal Air Regulation 91.10 and 43.21.

Considering your continued and unexplained lack of cooperation in these proceedings, it is the decision of the Administrator that your airman's privileges shall be denied until further notice and/or a further decision at hearing, the time of which shall be determined upon your receipt and reply to this letter.

Poor Chester, hounded past the grave by his ex-wife's lawyer and some FAA clowns. Even the gestapo used to let a guy alone once he was on ice.

I went back to work handing tools to Ambrose. A few hours later he managed to get the salvaged carburetor mounted on Oh Four Romeo. We again towed the airplane out into the rain and cranked up the engine. The carb rescued from the parts limbo performed flawlessly. The engine purred like a kitten.

"Works like a charm," Ambrose said happily. "What I tell ya? Airplanes fix themselves! Last week that carb didn't work. Now it does. Okay, let's get this thing gassed up. Ernie told me he's workin' on gettin' a charter tonight for some big mucketymucks."

"Who are they?"

"Don't know," Ambrose said. "Ernie wasn't too sure, just said they were big shots. It's all we got for tonight. Sure been slow around here."

"Well, they won't be needin' me," I said, looking at my watch. "I got here late today, might as well go home a little early to make up for it. See ya, Ambrose."

As I got into my car, the weather that had threatened all day moved in with a vengeance. The skies mutated from purple to green to black. The rain changed to silver sheets of water, which untamed winds pushed horizontally across the ground. Lightning shot from the clouds at random targets on the airport and in the surrounding cornfields. Thunder rocked the pavement under the old DeSoto.

Thus was the stage set, the sound effects turned on and the house lights darkened for a two-act tragicomedy in which I had a starring, if unwilling, role.

I inched my way home through the rain with little help from the sliver of sun-baked rubber on the DeSoto's windshield wipers.

I was pleased that there was no flying that night—except for the passenger charter that Ambrose had mentioned and Ernie or Nick would probably fly it. There wasn't a chance Ernie would let me fly his big deal twin-Beech Oh Four Romeo on a passenger charter in this weather, especially with important people on board.

After stopping for a hamburger and a couple beers at Grandma's Bar and Grill and Groceries, I drove home to my little rented room and drifted off into a deep, dreamless sleep to the rain against my window.

Destiny, patient as ever, awaited my return to the airport.

Act One:

"Riiing...Riiing...Riiing..."

The phone awakened me. I looked at the clock. It was 2 a.m. I figured it was probably Bunny, one of my girlfriends, who might be feeling a bit lonely.

"Yeah...hello, who's this? Bunny? Bunny, is that you? Hi, sweetheart. I miss ya, baby. I was gonna call ya. No kidding. C'mon over," I answered drowsily. My sleepish pulse rose at the prospect. I was never too tired to entertain Bunny.

"No, this ain't Bunny! Who the fuck is Bunny? Wake up, goddamnit! This is Ernie. I got a passenger charter for ya, something real big."

"Ernie...? Oooh, no," I moaned. My dream date with Bunny evaporated in a clap of thunder.

"Yeah, Ernie! You remember me, your boss. Get your ass out to the airport."

"Right now?"

"No, next Wednesday afternoon! Yeah, right now! I got a passenger charter for ya. The people are on their way out to the airport. They wanna go to Newark and you're takin' 'em."

"Newark? You looked outside, Ernie?" I mewled.

About that time, as if to help me make my case, lightning lit up the room and sizzled the phone connection. A prolonged million-decibel burst of thunder disrupted our conversation.

"This is one hell of a storm, Ernie." Still mewling.

"Hey, no problem for a pro like you," Ernie said. "I was gonna fly this trip myself but something else came up. Just take these guys to

Newark and wait on 'em. They said they're only gonna be there about twelve hours. You can sleep in the airplane. These guys, they sound like big shots. Take care of 'em and maybe you'll get a nice tip."

"I don't wanna nice tip, Ernie. I wanna go back to sleep."

"Be at the airport in a half hour! And stay outta my booze! I know what's on the airplane. Goodby." Click.

I wasn't anxious to get out of bed and fly in the foul weather but since Ernie was the kahuna and I only a lowly subject, I got dressed and drove back to Gorotny International. Everything in aviation is governed by seniority of one sort or another.

On the way to the airport, dense rain and strong gusts of winds slammed against the front of the DeSoto like a warning from some unidentified advocate. Go back, go back, the elements seemed to say. I pressed on, ignoring the portents the way pilots do in the pursuit of duty or glory or, in my case, a paycheck. I hoped the big shots Ernie mentioned would change their minds. Who'd want to fly in weather like the stuff trying to break through my windshield?

My heart sank when I saw a black limousine waiting near the office. Damn, they showed. The lights were out on the limo. Two guys wearing dark overcoats and wide-brimmed hats stood guard as patiently as gargoyles near the limo in the pouring rain without umbrellas, getting soaked. *They were standing in the rain!* I parked, grabbed a month-old newspaper discarded on the floor of the DeSoto and covered my head with it. I ran over to the limo, toe-dancing like a circus poodle around the larger mud puddles.

"Hey, you guys been waitin' long? Got here as soon as I could. Some freakin' storm, huh?" I hollered over the rain and thunder. A good charter pilot must establish rapport with his passengers. The two men looked at me but didn't say anything.

A flash of lightning allowed me a momentary glimpse at their faces. The closer of the two scowled at me, as if trying to decide if I was there to steal something. I swallowed hard, then even harder when I got a good look at the character on the far side of the limo. He sized me up with a sullen, coal-black left eye. A drooping eyelid hung like funeral bunting over his right eye.

I smiled wanly at the two men. They bared their teeth in return. I sensed this was not a pleasure trip.

"Who you?" demanded the one with the solo eye, which seemed all the more piercing from having to do double duty.

"My name's Pete, I'm your pilot," I shouted over the storm as politely as possible.

"Where da...machine?" the other guy asked.

"The machine?" I said, amused. "What kind of machine? What're you talking about?"

"You a...joker or sumptin' like dat?" he said, taking a step in my direction.

His one-eyed partner solved the riddle and stopped the advance before intent changed to deed. "He mean the airplane. Where it at?"

"Oh, the airplane? Sure. It's parked near the hangar, all ready to go," I replied. I pointed in the direction of Oh Four Romeo. "Why don't you move the car over there. Let's get out of this rain."

My savior directed his good eye into the limo and motioned with his head toward the airplane parked outside the hangar. The limo glided to within a few feet of Oh Four Romeo. The two guard dogs and I followed in the pouring rain, which dissolved the newspaper I held over my head. I picked up my pace, extracting wet globs of newsprint from my hair as I ran.

When we had all assembled near the airplane the driver's door popped opened. The driver, a tall, broad-shouldered guy with a gloomy face, jumped out with an umbrella and opened the rear door. A small, impeccably dressed man about 60 years old, presumably the boss, sat in the back seat. A gorgeous woman, long-legged, blond and magnificently busty, sat next to him. The blond was so unlike the west side Cleveland babes I ran around with that she could have easily passed for a different life form.

It pleased me that the boss didn't have the same grim expression as the others. To the contrary, the little guy seemed happy, so happy he was smiling. He acknowledged my presence with a nod and a smile.

I'd be smiling too buddy, you lucky bastard!

The babe, like all truly beautiful women, acknowledged no one's existence but her own—and the guy picking up the tab. She and the little happy guy slowly emerged from the limousine while the driver held the umbrella over their heads. Not one raindrop ever touched boss or blond.

The same could not be said for me. Drenched, I opened the cabin door to assist the boss and his stunning companion into the airplane with the aid of my prized seven-dollar five-cell chromed flashlight that I had recently purchased. The boss stopped short of the cabin door to survey the twin-Beech.

"How old dissa machine?" he asked.

What is this "machine" stuff with these characters?

I looked to the one-eyed guy but he didn't seem inclined to correct his apparent employer's choice of words as quickly as he had corrected his rain partner's. I assumed the boss, too, meant the airplane.

I was a smart ass in those days and I wanted very much to say something like, "dissa machine so old we dona even keepa tracka no more," or "you would no driva to Newark in a machine dissa old, thata for sure." But I didn't. There was an indefinable quality of power and finality about the little guy that warned against wisecracks. Instead, I summoned all my charm and diplomacy.

"Sir, it's not the age of an aircraft that matters, it's the condition and the loving maintenance it receives," I said in my best used car salesman's voice. The image of Ambrose kicking through the weeds for the discarded carburetor flashed in my mind.

The boss pursed his lips and accepted my explanation with another nod, though I sensed reservations. He and the blond proceeded warily into Oh Four Romeo, guided by the beam of my prized new flashlight. I followed, inches behind the babe, drooling. I left the boss to fend for himself while I helped the blond with her seatbelt. Leaning over the most beautiful woman in the world to show her how the belt worked, I was engulfed in an intoxicating cloud of perfume that probably cost more than I earned in two months. My knees went weak; I almost collapsed on top of her. I took as much time as I dared to strap her in, swallowed another whiff of perfume for the road and wobbled away from heaven on rubbery legs.

The driver went to the trunk of the limo for the baggage. I hopped out of the airplane and followed him to offer my assistance, anticipating the first of several nice tips Ernie had mentioned.

"Need some help? That stuff looks pretty heavy," I said, reaching around him to grab one of the bags. It weighed a ton; something inside clanked. As I struggled to lift it, the driver snatched my wrist and applied slightly more pressure than required to turn carbon into diamonds. I dropped the bag. The wrist hurt for a month.

"Just tryin' to help," I said. "You didn't have to break my wrist."

The driver looked up from his unloading chores. He seemed unable to believe that I was still there. "You wanna help, go 'way, go flya you machine," he said.

I retreated to the machine. At that point in the drama I figured my passengers were musicians and perhaps a bit touchy about their instruments. Maybe the babe was the vocalist. She could sing to me anytime. I play a little piano. We could talk shop. They were probably going to Newark for a concert. I'd ask her for some free tickets upon our arrival, maybe an autograph.

After my five passengers were seated, I made my way to the cockpit. My waterlogged sneakers squished embarrassingly. I heard the boss say something that sounded like Italian to the limo driver. I was halfway into the cockpit when the driver tapped me on the shoulder with an inhumanly large knuckle. The shoulder hurt for a month.

"Whatsa you name?" the limo driver asked.

"Pete."

"You last name?" Inquisitorially.

"...Fusco," I answered, reluctantly. Pilots treasure their anonymity.

"Foosco? Italiano, no?" he said.

"Yes, yes sir," I answered. "Full-blooded. First generation!"

He relayed this information to his boss, who appeared reassured by the news. As if dying in the rain in a blazing twin-Beech crash with a coombah pilot at the controls would make it any more fun. I was negotiating the foot-high main wing spar to access the cockpit when the driver grabbed me by my sneaker. He had another question.

"Mister Beneviaggio wanna know if you have lotsa, how you say?…experience flya dissa machine?" the driver asked.

Mister Beneviaggio? Did he say "Beneviaggio!?"

Just hearing the name caused me to bark my knee hard on the spar and crack my head on the cabin's low ceiling. Not *thee* Mister Beneviaggio, I hoped, not Carmine Beneviaggio, the Cleveland Mafia chief?

I looked over my shoulder and casually stole a peek at the boss in the dim, flashlight-lit cabin. He had not been smiling after all, at least not intentionally. I spotted the famous scar, which curved upward from the corner of his mouth to the top of his cheek. The scar wasn't one of those phony half-inch wide Hollywood jobs but a thin line all the more chilling for its irony and understatement. It made him only *appear* to be smiling.

Shit, could this be the character they called "Benny Smiles," the guy who sent men on one-way midnight swims in the oily Cuyahoga River with a single word from that laughing mouth? Until that moment, I always assumed Benny Smiles existed only in the *Cleveland Plain Dealer*.

And if he was Benny Smiles, then even the most casual reader of the Cleveland papers knew that the one-eyed character must be Salvatore "Sal the Peeper" Mercurio. Sal the Peeper was a captain in Benny Smiles' family and his most trusted button man. Benny and Sal had been in the news a lot lately, something about a hostile takeover of assets belonging to an Irish gang. Sal the Peeper's specialty, according to the *Plain Dealer*, was shooting people and cutting them up, not necessarily in that order.

All the puzzle pieces suddenly snapped together: the limo; the three goons and their happy boss; the dynamite girlfriend and her hundred-dollars-a-drop perfume; flying to Newark in the middle of the night in a twin-Beech from a country airport instead of on United Air Lines' morning flight from Cleveland Hopkins; the clanking inside the heavy suitcases; the smell of wet mohair and garlic in the cabin; why that rotten bastard Ernie didn't want to fly the charter himself.

"Hey, kid, you no heara me? Mister Beneviaggio aska you a question. You good *pilota* or no?" the driver asked again. He sounded confused and irritated by my unexplained, stunned silence.

"Oh, sure," I replied, trying to remain calm in a den of wolves. "We're highly trained. They wouldn't let me fly this machine, uh, I mean airplane, in this kind of weather if I didn't have lots of experience."

Benny Smiles and his associates seemed content with my answer, which was a wholesale lie. It was not the time to explain to the Cleveland don that charter flying is essentially an entry-level position, a place to build flying time to land a better job. That, if I had lotsa, how you say?... experience, I wouldn't be here at oh-dark-fucking-thirty flying a war-surplus twin-Beech. Nor did he have any particular need to know that inexperienced charter pilots lose more customers while honing their skills than beginning heart surgeons. I wasn't about to tell him, for instance, that I had never taken off in the kind of storm that raged without letup over the field. I also saw no need to share that to date the only passengers I had ever flown were caged monkeys and a couple of stiffs, none of whom had much choice in the matter.

Not that I had anything to fear. Professional pilots never give a second thought to who's riding in the back. The rule of thumb is as old as aviation itself: Get one's own fat ass to the destination and everyone in the back of the airplane will land with you. All I was going to do was fly them to Newark. Sure, there was a thunderstorm to fly through but the airplane was full of gas and I'd probably fly clear of the weather in fifty miles or so. These stony guys would be eating out of my hand after a few minutes' worth of the kind of carnival ride in store for them. Buckle up boys. You might want to hold on to your fedoras.

With the grilling over, I entered the cockpit and strapped into my seat. I chortled with satisfaction at the knowledge that these real-life mafioso might be a bit afraid of flying all the way to the east coast through lousy weather in a small airplane with a young *pilota* at the wheel. I stopped short of rubbing it in, however.

It was their time to be scared. Mine was coming.

"Oh, I almost forget," the driver said. His large upper torso burst through the little curtain that separated me from the passengers. He handed me an envelope stuffed with fifty-dollar bills.

"What's this?" I asked.

"Money, lotsa money. *Molto soldi! Cabeesh, paisano?*" He gave me a playful rap on the arm. The arm hurt for a month.

"Oh, yeah sure, but you don't have to pay me cash. Mister Gorotny will mail you a bill. You can send him a check."

The driver leaned into my face. His beady eyes narrowed insistently. "Mister Beneviaggio no likea check. He no canna trust you with the money, *Capitan* Foosco?" He sniggered at his little "*capitan*" joke, an honorific he bestowed on me with the type of contempt he no doubt reserved for people he was about to plant in fresh cement.

"Oh, sure, sure you can trust me. I think I'm bonded," I said, having no idea what "bonded" meant. I stuck the money in my shirt pocket and checked it every ten seconds.

Aided by my prized flashlight, I located the battery master switch, which was in a different place in every twin-Beech on the field. (The joke was that the brothers Gorotny had a standardized fleet until they bought their second airplane.) The limo driver remained half in the cockpit, looking around. He seemed impressed with all the switches.

"She pretty, how you say...complicate, huh *Capitan* Foosco?"

"Yeah, she sure is," I said, trying to act nonchalant.

What he didn't know and what I wasn't going to tell him was that half of the switches were no longer connected to anything; some of the others were probably rusted shut. While he watched, I cranked up the left engine to get a generator on line. The engine turned over a couple of times, barked softly once or twice and started. I ran up the rpms a bit and turned on the cabin lights. The storm worsened. Strong winds shook the airplane.

The driver seemed content with my performance and returned to the cabin. I pulled the cockpit curtain closed, breathed a sigh of relief, lit a cigarette and went to work starting the right engine.

That is, I *tried* to start the right engine. I primed it and held the starter switch. The Pratt and Whitney turned over, coughed a few times and backfired loudly but failed to start.

I tried again. All I got were more backfires, each progressively louder. A backfire from a radial engine sounds a lot like a shotgun blast and can be disconcerting to anyone riding in the cabin. I stuck my head through the curtain to comfort my passengers and assure them nothing was wrong.

"Just a backfi..." The word froze in my throat.

All three of Benny's boys held large pistols, each pointed in a different direction, ready for a counteroffensive. Sal the Peeper had an automatic leveled at me. The muzzle of the .45 caliber didn't bother me nearly as much as the muzzle of Sal's .50 caliber good eye. Any lingering doubts I might have had that the little smiling guy was *thee* Don Carmine "Benny Smiles" Beneviaggio quickly faded.

"Honest, guys, it's just the engine backfiring," I said. I appealed to the boss with an imploring look, one coombah to another.

Benny Smiles surveyed the situation. He made a godly motion with his hand and the three men reholstered their weaponry. The blond, who had found the stocked bar, tossed down a drink without ever looking up from a magazine she was reading. Nor, I'm sure, would she have paid much notice if Sal the Peeper had emptied his pistol into me. The babe sat facing me. Her knees were spread. Not much, but enough. I had an unobstructed view up her tight skirt but I couldn't chance a peek. Prudent men didn't trespass on Benny Smiles' turf.

"You stop foolin' 'round up there," Sal the Peeper said reprovingly. "You hear me? *Cabeesh?*" His sinister lone eye sized me up and passed judgment. He administered the *mal occhio*, the evil, condemning eye so dreaded by Italians. I grew up hearing about the *mal occhio* from my father. Supposedly, the intended victim got headaches if the curse took. But that was Old Country stuff, mere stupid superstition. I humored my dad even though I was far too sophisticated to believe in such foolishness.

I nodded in total cooperation to Sal the Peeper and retracted my head, turtle-like, into the cockpit. The headaches started almost immediately.

The thunderstorm had stalled directly over the field. Directly, it seemed, over Oh Four Romeo. A bolt of lightning struck the ground not more than fifty feet from the aircraft. A violent series of gusts pushed at the tail, rocking the airplane like a rowboat. Rain hammered the aluminum skin with an elusive rhythm of thirty-second notes. The left engine, which I advanced to nearly full throttle to keep the battery charged, whirred noisily above it all.

During my next attempt to start the right engine, I primed the hell out of it. This caused another backfire but it still didn't start. I looked through the curtain to apologize again for the backfire. Maybe Benny Smiles would intervene again, maybe not.

Sal the Peeper leaned forward in his seat, glowering, his brow furrowed. The funeral bunting fluttered angrily over his bad eye. His right hand went inside his coat, grasping something. I got the message. Sal the Peeper didn't want to hear it. Nor did he appear to be the type of fellow accustomed to issuing two warnings. I smiled pliantly and closed the curtain.

Pete Fusco

"Okay, you stop foolin''round up here in dissa machine. You heara me, Foosco?" I mimicked Sal the Peeper mutedly to myself as I got back to work. Again I cranked the right engine, urging it on with the same invectives normally reserved for my piece o' shit DeSoto.

"C'mon, you dirty bastard son of a bitch!" I said. It usually helped. As I held the starter, I looked across the cockpit out the right window. The Hamiltan Standard propeller resembled a lazy windmill turning in the rain. The engine didn't start but it didn't backfire either. I was thankful for that at least.

An aircraft engine starter can get awfully hot when overused so I gave it a rest. I lit another cigarette and sat back in the seat to take a short break before trying again to start the disinclined engine. The storm worsened further, shaking the airplane in a kind of preview of what we could expect once we got in the air.

I tried the right engine again. It turned over but didn't start.

I peeked in the back. Benny Smiles, his limo driver and Sal the Peeper had lit up big five-dollar heaters. They were playing cutthroat pinochle in a cloud of blue smoke. The fourth guy, apparently a junior mob man, busily poured drinks for everyone. He couldn't seem to make them quickly enough for the blond, already tanked and doing her best to deplete Ernie's liquor. She drank as fast as the apprentice could pour while she read her magazine. She wore the expression of practiced boredom common to all gorgeous women.

Watching the party, I rehearsed how I might tell *thee* Benny Smiles that he would have to wait until morning, when Ambrose showed up for work to fix the problem with the engine. Then Benny and his gang could depart in broad daylight so that the whole world would know he was going to Newark. I'd have to tell him that *Capitan* Foosco, his hotshot *Italiano* pilot, had let him down. Maybe I could explain that the uncooperative engine was a blessing in disguise since it was not an ideal night for flying anyway. Sure, that would help. Would he understand about the questionable carburetor Ambrose had reclaimed from the weeds?

No, I decided not to tell him about the carb. That was pilot stuff that a passenger would never understand. Besides, men like Benny Smiles were only interested in results, not excuses. His business was wealth, power and death, not carburetors.

I tossed my half-smoked cigarette out the cockpit window, gathered my nerve and turned to break the bad news to my passengers. I rehearsed two or three times how I would tell them that we were not going anywhere. I reached for the curtain. A large fist clutching a pinochle hand dense with hearts pulled it open from the cabin side. It was my old friend the limo driver. We were face to face, his cigar so close to my nose that I could feel the heat. Up close, he was even uglier and scarier. Much uglier. Much scarier. It was my opportunity to explain about the engine that would not start.

"Oh, yeah, hi. Sir, about this right engine…"

I never had a chance to finish the sentence. He didn't give me a *chance* to finish the sentence.

"*Capitan* Foosco," he said, chortling at his little *capitan* gag again, "Mister Beneviaggio wanna know where we are."

"Where we are?" I blurted it out. Holy shit, these guys didn't know we were still on the ground! The pounding, incessant rain, the noise and vibration from the left engine running at almost full power for the last ten minutes and the wind whipping the airplane like a tree branch made them think we had taken off and were in the air. They thought we were flying!

With anybody else as passengers, the situation would have been funny. Briefly, I thought of all the mileage I'd get out of the story at the airport if the brunt of the joke were on anyone else in the world except the Cleveland don. A U.S. senator perhaps. The Pope. Anyone but this guy.

"Hey, *Capitan* Foosco, you hear me okay? Mister Beneviaggio wanna know over where we are." The driver's voice had an edge. "Whatsamatta wi' you, you hard o' hear? Mebbe you needa one o' dosa ting you putta in you ear, huh?" To make his point, he stuck a sausage-sized finger two inches into my ear. The ear hurt for a month.

I couldn't speak, my mind too busy trying to cast a perspective on what was happening. At that point—before I escalated the situation past all sanity—it was nothing more than a simple misunderstanding with a simple solution. Just finish what I started to say, just tell the ugly bastard that we were still on the ground and couldn't get the second engine started. I'd apologize for the inconvenience, return the envelope stuffed with the lotsa money and part friends. They'd understand. We were all Italian, after all.

But I didn't do it. For whatever reason, *I did not do it!* And, if someday I could get an explanation for what possessed me to do just one of the many stupid things I have done in my life, it would be to understand what caused me to tell *thee* Mister Beneviaggio's driver that we were high over the east side of Cleveland on our way to Newark. Making good time, in fact. My best guess is that fear of failure—I knew these guys wouldn't react well to failure—and something now popularly known as "denial" played a large part.

"*Grazie, Capitan* Foosco," the driver said with ever more scoffing emphasis on the "capitan." He turned to report the good news to his boss. "We over da east side, Mister Beneviaggio. Mebbe ovah you house, huh?"

The boss chuckled, a cue that caused everyone in the airplane to chuckle. Except me.

In near panic I went back to cranking the right engine. With a little luck, I'd get the engine started and get the piece o' shit twin-Beech off the ground and save the night yet. The end of the runway was only about ten yards away. My passengers need never know. I could be airborne in a matter of minutes—if I could just get the right engine started. The propeller spun around promisingly for several minutes; the engine gurgled and seemed about to light off a few times. No backfires. My heart gladdened.

Then the prop rotation began to slow like a sluggish giant winged insect that had spent the whole day mating and wanted only to rest and die. After about ten more seconds, the prop stopped turning altogether. I pushed on the starter switch so hard I thought I might break it off. But the prop would no longer move. The starter was overheated. I'd have to wait a few more minutes until it cooled to try again.

The rain against the airplane changed tempo. It took on a grieving, arrhythmic jungle beat. The cockpit grew unbearably hot and sticky. I slid open the side window for some fresh air and smoked a cigarette that seared my dry throat. I thought of all the people I wanted to murder. Number one was Ernie Gorotny for giving me the trip. I'd finish off Ernie quickly, not let him suffer too much. But not

Ambrose. I'd slowly strangle him and put to rest once and for all his bogus theory of aircraft self-resurrection. While I squeezed his neck, I would repeat his words to him. "All ya gotta do is leave 'em alone for a bit. Just go do something else, smoke a cigarette or something, and airplanes'll fix themselves."

Fix this, Ambrose.

The jury would understand.

Long minutes passed. The driver whisked aside the curtain and stuck his head in the cockpit again. Flying for the airlines, federal law protected me from such unsolicited visits. An airline passenger could get three to seven in the joint for just knocking on a cockpit door. Not that night. Nor did it escape my attention that the thin curtain that separated me from some very dangerous men was decidedly unbulletproof.

"Hey, *Capitan* Foosco," he said, "Mister Beneviaggio wanna know where we now."

There was no turning back. I was committed, the die had been cast. I threw myself into the absurd scenario. I grabbed the yoke as if I were flying the airplane and gave a studied look at an oil-stained, wrinkled military chart left on the floor of the airplane from World War Two.

"Lemme see here," I said, tracing my finger over the chart, which covered an area just south of the Yukon Territory. Philipsburg was the first city that came to mind. "Yeah, here we are, over Philipsburg. Yeah, that's right, Philipsburg, Pee Aay. Makin' darn good time. Have you guys in Newark pretty soon."

We would have had to be flying faster than sound to be over Philipsburg at that point but he bought it. He left to once again report our excellent progress to his boss. I peeked into the cabin. Benny Smiles shrugged knowingly at the news as if to say, "Wudda you tink? Thata my coombah flya dissa machine." I wondered how many men had ever pimped Benny Smiles and survived. I tried not to think about it too much.

The driver returned to the cockpit yet again, this time with a question of his own. "How 'bout dissa storm? She bad, huh? *Madonne!*"

What the hell, what did I have to lose? I told him that the weather radar showed we'd be in the stuff for a while, but that it was no big deal.

I pretended to dodge around some cells. Not only did Oh Four Romeo have no weather radar, I had never even *seen* a weather radar set. Once more the goon bought it. He returned to the pinochle game, perhaps with a little more respect for *Capitan* Foosco's remarkable flying skills.

The reality of the situation I had created settled over me like a cloud of doom. My stomach churned and I began to feel ill. I swung open the cockpit escape hatch above my head for more fresh air. The rain and the swirling cool air from the left prop blast soothed me. I looked up into the open hatch like a man trapped at the bottom of a very deep well.

I tried the right engine again. I desperately wanted to get the damn thing started, not only to avoid having to tell the boys that we were still on the ground but also for revenge. The boys in the back had run me through a wringer. I longed to get even. I wanted to get airborne, find the biggest storm cell in the area and centerpunch it. That'd keep the son of a bitch limo driver in his seat. The right motor did not understand my need and failed to turn over.

It occurred to me for the first time that I could simply climb out of the cockpit through the escape hatch above my head and run for my life. The gang wouldn't even know I was missing until the next time Benny Smiles ordered his driver to check up on me.

I talked myself out of it. Abandoning an airplane with passengers aboard is contrary to the unwritten code of pilots of all vessels. Unthinkable! In a moment of weakness, Conrad's Lord Jim deserted the foundering Patna full of sleeping, Mecca-bound pilgrims. The half-swamped Patna beached itself a week later, leaving Lord Jim to plumb the depths of shame for the rest of his life. Captain Smith of Titanic fame; now there was a role model! Smith stayed with the leaky Titanic to the cold, bitter end and *Capitan* Foosco would stay with Oh Four Romeo. Cowardly breakout was not an option.

Not just yet.

Once more I attempted to start the right engine. It refused to even turn over. My guts, cramped into a square knot, tightened another turn. My mind blanked. I began to lose my nerve, afraid to keep up my scam and afraid not to.

Heavy rain poured into the cockpit through the open hatch. I hardly noticed. I was too busy rehearsing stories for my passengers.

I could tell them that it was all a big joke; that I was just screwing around with them. No, they'd never buy it. A sense of humor was a definite liability in their chosen profession. They made the jokes. Not me. Scratch that. I'd come clean and beg forgiveness, tell Benny Smiles I panicked and appeal to his compassion. Forget it. Forgiveness and compassion did not exist in his world. A *Plain Dealer* story I read a couple months before alleged that Benny Smiles once had a guy shot for taking his parking spot. Sal the Peeper was the chief suspect but the district attorney had so far found no one willing to testify.

It's not like Benny's boys would have any trouble with me. The math was easy: one smart-assed, unarmed charter pilot against three trigger-happy racket guys. *Capitan* Foosco would be just a little middle-of-the-night pistol practice for them. The best I could hope for was that they'd give it to me fast and clean, no torture. I resigned myself and tensed in the cockpit seat the way men do in the electric chair while anticipating the juice. Like a rat thrown into the cage as a snack for the sleeping rattlesnake, I knew it would be only a matter of time before the scent of my fear betrayed me.

I lit another cigarette before I realized that I already had one burning in my hand. A long arcing ash fell from the cigarette to my lap. I remembered Ambrose telling me how some of Chester Gorotny's ashes were still in the airplane. A dead copilot was just exactly what I didn't need at that moment but it somehow fit.

The open escape hatch above my head jiggled invitingly in the wind. Lord Jim beckoned. "Go ahead pal," he seemed to say. "Haul ass! Cowardice is very underrated. Given enough time to stew about it, there would be no heroes."

Captain Smith held me back. "Stay with the ship! You hit the bloody iceberg, now live with it. Stay, it's the sacred duty of command. Go down with the ship, die like a man."

I weighed the two choices: Lord Jim lived to sail another day. Captain Smith didn't make quite as good a case, considering that he was still awaiting rescue at the bottom of the Atlantic.

I tried the right engine again but there was not a hint of movement out of the prop. The overheated starter was useless, all hope gone. In a few minutes the driver would be back for an update. I knew I couldn't continue the charade. I'd crack the next time he poked his gruesome mug through that curtain into the cockpit.

Lord Jim whispered into my ear. "Bail out or die in this miserable airplane like the *gavone*—Italian lowlife—you are. The sooner you get away from Benny Smiles and his band of killers, the better."

Smith was at my other ear. "Stay!"

"Haul ass!"

"Stay!"

"Haul ass!"

Panic nudged my reins; cowardice never had an easier sell, twenty seconds tops. Chester Gorotny's ashes may not have wanted out of that airplane, but I sure as hell did!

Act Two:

I hastily devised my craven plan. I transferred the left engine, still screaming at almost full throttle, to the smallest gas tank. The engine would run out of gas and quit in about twenty minutes, more than enough time for me to get in my DeSoto, allot the required five minutes to start the piece o' shit, and travel a few miles down the road. I'd at least get out of pistol range.

With a deep breath, *Capitan Gavone* donned a dress and frilly bonnet, raised the pitch of his voice, pushed aside the women and children and made for the life boats. Screw Captain Smith and *Titanic!* The bastard got what he deserved. Hello Lord Jim, where do I sign for my life of shame?

Head first, I snaked out of the escape hatch onto the wet, slippery aluminum surface of the left wing. My butt was only inches from the spinning propeller, which swung like a vindictive scimitar. I thought about W.W.'s luckless monkey as I oozed on my belly down the wing.

I passed by the small cabin windows and looked directly into Benny Smiles' face. He was studying his pinochle hand. His trademark scar smiled at me, taunted me. Sal the Peeper struggled to keep his good eye focused on his cards. Benny and Sal both had an ace of hearts on the little table between them. The driver held a ten of spades in his hand, moving it back and forth in front of his face as if he were afraid to trump. Did one trump Benny Smiles or Sal the Peeper with impunity? I couldn't spare the time to learn and really didn't want to know. I did, however, take time for a quick glance up the babe's skirt. Why not? I was probably already dead. At the wing trailing edge the prop blast made me lose my grip on the slick surface. I did a modified half gainer off the wing into a muddy puddle. No points for style.

Hurting all over but feeling tremendous relief, I got up and ran on unsteady legs for my DeSoto. In the car I rooted through my pants pockets for the keys while I reached into my shirt pocket for a cigarette. I felt a fat envelope. Sleeping Jesus! Benny Smiles' ill-gotten money! I had *his* money in my pocket. The jury was still out on whether one could desert the mob in an airplane with the engine running after telling them they were in the air and live to tell about it, but there was plenty of precedent for what happened to guys who stole money from these people. It wasn't done. Their justice was entirely too far-reaching and complete. Like the Mounties, they always got their man. Unlike the Mounties, they always got a swift conviction.

The thought of going back to the airplane to place the cash in the cockpit was not very appealing, but my options were extremely limited. I could go back and risk getting caught or leave with the money and cower in my rented room until Sal the Peeper found me and took aim with his good eye while the limo driver dug a shallow grave for *Capitan* Foosco outside, next to the garbage cans.

I had no choice. A return trip to Oh Four Romeo was imperative—foolhardy but imperative.

Approaching cautiously, I clawed my way uphill on the wing against the prop blast. The wing had become a water slide in the heavy rain and I fought for every inch. I stopped for a look into the cabin window. The driver still held his trump card indecisively. "Go ahead, trump the little laughing fucker," I said, not too loudly. "It couldn't be any worse than what I'm doing! At least you have a gun to shoot back with."

Benny's scar again smiled at me, as if it had a life of its own and shared this private, very risky stunt with me. Could the scar communicate with its landlord? I had enough to worry about without adding that possibility. I broke away from the window and scaled another couple feet up the wet wing to the cockpit. A few feet from the cockpit I tossed the envelope with a hook shot into the open hatch. Nothing but cockpit!

I had no guarantee they'd find the money in the cockpit but at least I tried to return it. Wet, but all there. What else could I do? Knock on the cabin door like the UPS man and hand it to them?

Again I fought spinning prop, wind, rain, slippery aluminum and panic as I made my way back down the wing. Again I took a forbidden look at the babe. Again I fell off the trailing edge into the mud. I was getting good at it.

I scrambled for my car, turning once to look back at the airplane. A flash of lightning illuminated Oh Four Romeo and its pilotless passengers. It also lit up the derelict Mother of Mercy ambulance/ hearse. The crudely painted Virgin on the side had changed her expression from one of hope to one of despair, as if even she could not intercede in my behalf with Benny Smiles. "Sorry *Capitan* Foosco," the Virgin seemed to say, "these guys are too connected. They're out of my league. Good luck, my son."

A long, steady volley of deafening thunder followed. Was it the storm or the wrath of Benny Smiles? Did he just find out his coombah pilot had split? Once again, I hoped his boys would at least find the money. Benny might go easier on me. Although from what I knew about the Mafia, double-crossers were hated even more than thieves. Try as I might, I could not put the situation into any encouraging perspective.

I reached my car a second or two later, took a precious couple minutes to decompress, then jammed the key in the ignition like a knife. Normally I sweet-talked the engine for a minute or two but the occasion called for immediate, maximum abuse.

"Start, you miserable cocksucker!" I bellowed at the DeSoto.

"Rrrr…rrrr…rrrr…varooom."

By some small miracle—perhaps as much as the Virgin could muster under the circumstances—the motor caught on the first try. Nor did it quit the first four or five times I tried to engage it as it usually did. I drove back to my rented room wide open, the speedometer flickering near a record 45 miles an hour. The sloppy gears in the Fluid Drive transmission made noises more distressing than normal; they ground out an unholy refrain that sounded a lot like "SalthePeeperSalthePeeperSalthePeeper." Every car behind me looked like a long, black speeding retaliatory limosine.

I considered leaving the country, or at least the state, but if Benny Smiles wanted me he'd find me no matter where I went. With eleven dollars in my pocket and a car that had been driven the equivalent of ten times around the earth, I wouldn't get very far.

When I reached my rented room, I fell into the hard bed without bothering to take off my wet clothes. For an hour or so a nameless, irrepressible dread prevented sleep. I kept wondering how many of the Mafia's rigid codes—all punishable by varying degrees of death—I had violated? I finally forced myself into a troubled sleep. Twice I awoke sweating from a nightmare in which Sal the Peeper had stuffed my bullet-ridden body into the rusty trunk of my DeSoto. Not a shiny Caddy or a Lincoln, but my rusty DeSoto! His boss stood behind him directing the operation.

Smiling, of course.

All I ever wanted was a flying job, a lousy flying job. Was that asking too much of life? How could this have happened? In typical pilot fashion, I blamed everyone but myself.

I awakened with a start to the rising sun outside my window. The storm had passed, retreated back to its cage. Maybe there had never been a storm. Nor an Oh Four Romeo, nor a Benny Smiles, nor a Sal the Peeper. I tried to convince myself that it had all been a nightmare. My soggy clothes forced illusion to surrender unconditionally to reality.

My first impulse was not to return to the airport and test Ernie's version of justice, which I knew would be at least as severe as Benny Smiles', although perhaps without an execution. But there was always the chance that Ernie would listen to my explanation and understand. I drove to the airport with sleep-flattened hair to face the music Ernie had surely been rehearsing.

At the airport twin-Beech Oh Four Romeo, the scene of such high drama only hours before, sat guiltlessly in the exact spot I had abandoned it and my passengers. The escape hatch over the cockpit was still open. A disquieting wind swept across the field under a warmthless sun, much like the day-after descriptions of Verdon written by the few soldiers who had survived the carnage.

The Virgin's expression was hard to read.

As I expected, Ernie was waiting on me, as was Ambrose. Their expressions were a much easier read: the bearing of a team of prosecutors with all the goods necessary for conviction. I predicted a brief trial, with about as much right of appeal as the victims of Vlad the Impaler.

"You bin to Newark and back already?" Ernie the Impaler asked.

"No, I never got there. Hell, I never left the ground, Ernie," I said, talking fast and boldly, acting as if *I* were the wronged party. "I couldn't get the right engine started. Must have been that carb me and Ambrose changed out yesterday. Should have left the damn thing in the weeds. I did my best, Ernie. Really! But I couldn't get that goddamn right motor started. I gave those guys their money back and left. They were some scary bastards, let me tell ya! Sal the Peeper was with them!"

"Sal the who?"

"Peeper! Sal the Peeper. Jesus, don't you read the papers, Ernie?" I said, looking around, certain a sniper rifle was trained on my ass.

"No!" Ernie said. "I'm sorry to report that I've never heard of such a person."

It wasn't looking good for me. The best I could hope for was that Ernie did not know the whole story. As much as I feared uttering a hurried confession before receiving last rites from Sal the Peeper, I feared even more that Ernie and the boys at Gorotny International knew the truth. The Benny Smiles caper was the aviation screw-up equivalent of DiMaggio's 56-game hitting streak. It would likely stand forever and overshadow all other records for charter pilot idiocy. Life wouldn't be worth living. I might as well be dead.

Then again, maybe I was making too big a deal out of it. Perhaps when Benny Smiles and his entourage saw I was no longer in the cockpit, they picked up the sopping money, carefully opened the cabin door, saw they were still on the ground, got into their limo and drove away. They might have been too embarrassed to tell anyone. Maybe they had a sense of humor after all; maybe they laughed their asses off all the way home. What a great story it would be to tell the other mob guys when they finally got to Newark and, someday, to their grandchildren. We Italians readily laugh at ourselves.

I tried hard to imagine my passengers of the night before laughing at themselves. It wouldn't come.

"Kindly explain this note I found in the airplane," Ernie said. He handed me Exhibit A, a piece of paper scribbled with the scratchy handwriting and desperate spelling and grammar of a guy expelled for life from the third grade for loan sharking and extortion. Most likely the limo driver, I thought.

The note read, *"cappattan foosco yu tink yu funie no. why not yu tak us nuwurk. we not go newerk wee luse lotz money. yu maka we luuk badd. mistur benevagiio no like dat. who yu work for, mebbe peepel what not ower frennd. we fine out see yu gin."*

The blood drained from my face. I almost fainted.

"This must be from the passengers," I said, trying to hide my anguish. I dropped the note, my death decree, to the ground. "Like I told you, Ernie, I had a little trouble with the right engine. Couldn't get it started and we didn't fly. I returned the money and went home. Simple at that!"

"Bullshit! That was a thousand dollar charter you flushed down the toilet," Ernie said. His face turned purple. "By the way, just who *do* you work for?"

"I work for you, Ernie," I answered.

"Don't count on it," he said, hinting at the verdict.

Ernie pointed to Exhibit B, a pile of empty liquor bottles. "The bar on the airplane's empty," he said denouncingly. "Every single drop of liquor. You think that shit's free?"

"The blond, Ernie," I whined. "Oh boy, could she put it away!"

"Blond? What blond? Her name wasn't Bunny by any chance, was it?

"Bunny? Bunny who?" I asked, my voice rising in despair.

"Weren't you expecting a call from some bimbo named 'Bunny' last night when I called?" Ernie launched into final cross-examination.

"Oh, no, it wasn't Bunny," I said. "Bunny's a redhead, only drinks beer, just takes two or three to get *her* going. No, it was the blond babe. She was one of the passengers. God, so beautiful, like from another planet, Venus or somewhere like that."

The last answer from the accused would have convinced a jury of my closest relatives that I had emptied the bar, with or without help from Bunny. It certainly convinced Ernie.

My case was hopeless. Who was I going to call in my defense? Ambrose? Not a chance. The limo driver? Oh sure, he'd square it with

Ernie—right after he drove over me with the limo. The blond? She didn't even know she was in an airplane. Don Carmine Beneviaggio? He was far more accustomed to handing out indictments than acquittals.

"Goddamnit! Did you get laid in my airplane, Fusco?" Ernie railed.

Like any good prosecutor, Ernie had saved his cheapest shots for last. He moved in for the kill.

"Maybe you sent the passengers home because you didn't want to fly in a little rainy weather then you got drunk and got it on with Bunny. That how it went? Something very peculiar happened here last night and I'm gonna find out."

Not from me, Ernie, not in a million fucking years.

"I'm gonna try that right engine myself," Ambrose said. "It ran fine yesterday." Ambrose's own reputation as a mechanic, after all, was at stake. He climbed into the airplane. His head appeared in the cockpit a few seconds later.

"Shit, the cockpit's soaked," Ambrose yelled. "What were you doin' in here?"

"He was drinkin my booze and gettin' laid!" Ernie answered for me. "You better hope that motor doesn't start, Fusco."

The motor! Of course! Why didn't I think of it? The right engine, the root of my problems, was also my defense. They'd see! It wouldn't even turn over. As much as I used that starter, it had probably welded itself together. And, if by some miracle the engine *did* turn over, that junk carb would make it kick and backfire all day without starting. The carb, the very source of my undoing, would exonerate me. I watched Ambrose go through the starting procedure. They'd see!

Lots of luck getting that engine started, Ambrose.

"Errr, errr, errr, errr," the right engine not only cranked over but it started. Immediately. Uncomplainingly. No backfiring. No kicking. No coughing. To this day I don't think I have ever heard an engine, any engine, run so silky-smooth.

So accusingly smooth!

Ambrose's words, somewhat modified, pounded in my ears: "Airplanes fix themselves. Leave 'em alone for a while. Go get a cup o' coffee, go pull something real cute on some mob guys, get on Benny

Smiles' shit list. When you come back everything'll be working again. You'll be making new acquaintances among the fish at the bottom of Lake Erie, but the airplane will be good as new."

"Sounds like it's running great to me," Ernie said, his voice well past scorn.

The prosecution rested its case.

Numbed, I listened to the right engine on Oh Four Romeo ridicule me with all nine sweetly humming cylinders. There was nothing left to say. I had tried my best but failed. As Ernie told me that first day, getting through is what counts in the charter flying business. There's no room for bullshit excuses. You get there or you don't. Any asshole can fly an airplane, he had said. If you'd rather screw off than fly, then go to work for the airlines.

The airlines never seemed so far away.

Ambrose shut down the engine and looked out the cockpit window at me. "Young kids!" he said. "You can't trust young kids with these things. Too damn complex for 'em."

"Your last check oughta just about cover the booze you and Bunny sucked down," Ernie said with unambiguous finality. He walked away.

My trial was over. The punishment was that I was free to go. But go where? I stood there for a long time, more removed from flying than I had ever been, banished not from paradise but from a place somewhat lower. The worst part was admitting to myself that it wasn't Ambrose or Ernie or Benny Smiles or a disinterred carburetor that put me in this position. It was my own brashness and stupidity. I hadn't weighed the consequences before I made my decision. Looking back, I suppose I should consider myself lucky to have learned such a critical lesson of powered flight while still safely—more or less—on the ground.

On the way home I stopped at Grandma's Bar and Grill and Groceries to ease the pain. With my last few dollars and a little extended bar credit, I drank beer, smoked cigarettes and grieved like the Ancient Mariner to the other patrons well into the morning. Grandma, who at first seemed sympathetic, threw me out just before last call. I skipped on the bar tab.

That afternoon I awoke with a hangover and out of work. Again. I chalked up the Benny Smiles debacle to experience. In those early days it seemed that I was always chalking up some unpleasant experience to experience.

Then I did what any disgraced pilot and marked man in my position would have done. I moved on.

...and they worshipped the beast, saying who is like unto the beast? Who is able to make war with him?

Revelation

Prologue to Chapter Three

The Curtiss C-46 "Commando" chained to the ramp called to mind a circus elephant tethered for stomping its handlers. As I approached, I speculated that the chains were nothing more than a subtle reminder to some renegade non-sked freight operator that he was a tad behind on his payments, perhaps a year or so.

Closer examination revealed a more serious problem. The mighty C-46, indestructible veteran of wars and humbler of able men, had been visited by its only natural enemy: the FAA.

The fed left his mark, an official red tag attached to a padlock on the cargo door. I read the tag,

"This aircraft, Curtiss C-46 N611Z, has been found by a Federal Aviation Administration maintenance inspector to have 14 (fourteen) airworthiness discrepancies. By order of the Administrator, this aircraft is declared nonairworthy and is hereby grounded. It has been restrained by physical means. To tamper with this aircraft, its physical restraints, or this tag is a violation of federal law."

Tamper? Tamper with a C-46? Tampering is something one does with a lawnmower or jury, not a C-46. No one I ever knew "tampered" with a C-46 and got away with it. And what was that about 14 airworthiness discrepancies found by the crack fed? Only 14? Hell, 14 discrepancies wouldn't have been enough to cause even the most prudent of the old penny-a-mile gang at Universal Air Transport to look up from his morning pint.

I caught a reflection of myself in the vast greenhouse of glass that surrounds the pinched, pointy nose of the C-46, reminiscent of the end of a plump banana. Many years had passed since I sat on the other side of that cockpit window, a cheeky kid learning painful lessons about flying and myself from this reproachful beast. The C-46 was my first big airplane. I went on to fly larger airplanes but I never flew anything bigger. Truth is, there is nothing bigger than a Curtiss C-46.

Scornfully, I rattled the heavy chains that bound my old teacher to the ramp. Only the FAA would be naive enough to believe mere chains could restrain a C-46. It was no accident that the C-46 came by the nickname of "Dumbo."

I took no little comfort in the hard-gained knowledge that if ol' Dumbo really wanted to be free it had the heart and the strong back to do it—and take those ridiculous chains, eight or ten tons of that concrete ramp and a few dozen silly-ass feds along for the ride of their lives.

At night, of course.

By the summer of 1965 I had been employed, more or less steadily, as a pilot of small single and twin-engine airplanes for about three years. My earnings came to less than $10,000. Total! In the great lottery that is aviation I had yet to hit even one number in six. It was time to move up to the bigger airplanes and the bigger bucks. I was as ready as I'd ever be.

I targeted Universal Air Transport, a non-scheduled freight airline that operated a fleet of about forty Curtiss C-46 "Commando" aircraft out of Detroit's Metro Airport. Universal used the C-46s to haul tons of chartered freight each night for the automotive companies, whose laughable inability to keep their plants supplied with parts guaranteed the airline a steady business of last-minute, desperation charters.

Unlike the major airlines, which required that a pilot applicant survive a death march through a personnel department full of scary, non-pilot types, the chief pilot still did all the interviewing and hiring of pilots at Universal Air Transport. I had enough flying time, especially after I stretched the truth a bit, to gain an interview with Captain Weir, Universal's chief pilot.

I stood outside his office for a few minutes, summoning my nerve and charm. I conducted a last-minute survey of my appearance: haircut not more than a week old; snappy green plaid sports coat with sky blue trousers, both of which I had hung outside a steamy shower that morning to get the major wrinkles out; borrowed paisley tie; matched argyle socks and shined brown shoes. Nothing boosts an applicant's confidence like being well dressed. I had even shaved. I was ready for an astronaut interview.

Captain Weir came across as a nice guy at a time when chief pilots were expected to be tyrants. Flight schools, charter services, corporate aviation departments and airlines simply found the pilot everyone hated and promoted him—or her—to the chief pilot's office. Nice guys need not apply. (Today, the trend is toward sensitive types.)

As I sat across from Captain Weir at his desk, I faced the most difficult judgment call a pilot applicant will ever encounter, trying to guess what the guy doing the hiring wants to hear that day. Or, more important, what the guy doing the hiring *doesn't* want to hear that day. Captain Weir, to my relief, did not play games. After less than a minute of forced pleasantries, he told me what I could expect flying for Universal Air Transport.

"You'll make a decent buck, but this is some pretty rough flying here, mostly middle-of-the-night trips," Captain Weir said. He conversed in short, splintered sentences because of a curious habit of vigorously rubbing his hand over his face while he spoke. The second he opened his mouth, his hand moved to his forehead and started a journey south that ended under his chin. After a few seconds spent kneading the chin, the hand crawled back up his face. During its pole-to-pole jaunt the hand traversed his mouth in synchronization with his words, much like the World War One fighter planes that fired bullets through the propeller.

"And that C-46 ain't for everybody," he continued. "It's a big, mean airplane. Some guys can't cut it. You better know what you're getting into. Got time in anything big?" he asked, scanning my application disinterestedly.

He paused for my answer; his hand took a short break. Years of the unusual activity had turned Captain Weir's face into a kind of living putty. There seemed to be no cartilage left in his nose, a pliable, bulbous mass that took new form with each pass of the hand.

Naturally, I acted as if rubbing one's face while speaking was normal behavior. I briefly toyed with the idea of doing it myself but dismissed the idea. Even I have limits on what I will do for a flying job.

"I've been flying mostly twin-Beeches," I answered, not expecting him to be impressed. He wasn't.

"Oh yeah, twin-Beeches, sure," he yawned. "Hey, I see here you worked for the Gorotny boys over there in Ohio. Nick Gorotny's an old buddy of mine. We flew in the service together, showed those krauts a couple o' things, let me tell ya. Me and Nick once double-teamed some son of a bitch in an ME-109. Blew his Nazi ass right out o' the sky!"

"Oh, you know Nick Gorotny?" I said.

"Yeah, real well," Captain Weir said. "I just talked to him a month or so back."

He spent the next twenty minutes reliving World War Two, as Nick Gorotny had done many times. I pretended to feed on every word. Captain Weir drew a little swastika on an eraser and handed it to me.

"Tell ya what, you be the ME-109," he said. "Hold that eraser up about right here."

Captain Weir positioned my hand carefully. (Chief pilots are very detail-oriented.) He found two pencils, which became he and Nick in their P-47s. He stood up and maneuvered the pencils over and around the eraser while he made P-47 and machine gun sounds. Suppressing an urge to laugh, I tried to elude the double-team, though not very hard. Captain Weir made me drop the eraser when the fatal shots had been delivered. As I remember, I made noises like that of a shot-up airplane spinning in. I don't have *that* many limits on what I'll do for a flying job.

Captain Weir's right hand, still clutching a pencil, returned to its facial journey. The pencil threw off his hand-mouth timing. Key words became muffled. Listening to him required all my concentration. I leaned closer. Thinking.

I had not known Captain Weir and Nick Gorotny were air corps pals. This was something I might be able to use. God knows, I had little else going for me. Normally, the trick in pilot interviews is to follow the lead. Volunteer nothing. But I changed tactics and decided to play up the Nick Gorotny angle, *anything* to divert Captain Weir's attention from the employment gaps on my application and conspicuous lack of flying time and past employer references. If I could get him talking about his old buddy Nick, maybe he wouldn't ask me under what circumstances I had left the Gorotnys. I had somehow omitted my dishonorable departure from the application.

Actually, conditions were so bad and pilot turnover so brisk at Gorotny Brothers Flying Service that, except for my several much-celebrated performances, no one there would have even remembered me. Except maybe brother Ernie—bastards have long memories.

I took a chance and threw the Nick card on the table.

"Good ol' Nick," I said. "Hell of a pilot, must have been some great fighter jock. Boy, you guys sure had it rough over there, huh? I might be talkin' German right now if it wasn't for you guys, heh, heh. Nick gave me my checkout in the twin-Beech. Yeah, good guy that Nick."

"Yeah, good ol' Nick," Captain Weir said. "Say, I've heard his brother Ernie's a pain in the ass, a real prick. Is that right?"

I could easily have done an hour on Ernie Gorotny without saying anything nice about him but I feared Captain Weir might be testing me. Perhaps Ernie, too, was an "old buddy." I played it safe.

"Ernie a prick? No way!" I said, acting offended on Ernie's behalf. "Ernie's a super guy, never asks his pilots to do anything he wouldn't do. A real fair boss, too, always gives his pilots the benefit of the doubt."

I hated myself for days.

Captain Weir changed the subject. "You got any problem staying awake at night?" he asked.

I knew where he was going with the question since, as he had already warned, Universal was a hard-core night-freight operation. I was ready for him.

"None at all," I answered, playing the insomnia card I had up my sleeve. "I'm a real night owl, hardly ever sleep. Don't need any."

Truth is, the best bed in the finest hotel has never made me as drowsy as a cockpit seat. It's known as "dozing for dollars" in the flying business.

My shameless renunciation of sleep did the trick. Captain Weir hired me, though it might have had more to do with the fact that Universal Air Transport was short of pilots. Then again, there was an outside chance that I may have wowed him. I could not have cared less. What counted was that I was the newest pilot on the Universal seniority list. All I wanted at that point was to get the hell out of that office.

Captain Weir seemed to have the same idea. He stretched mightily. I sensed he had tired of the interview. Chief pilots deal with a million piddling details each day, a working condition that over time severely limits their attention spans. Lucid conversations lasting more than thirty seconds with a chief pilot are rare; with an *assistant* chief pilot, fifteen seconds would be a world record.

It's a result of the terrible burden of chief pilots. They spend their days babysitting pilots who have somehow crossed the line, including but not necessarily limited to incompetents of every ilk, malcontents, boozers, quarrelsome captains who pick fights with copilots, quarrelsome copilots who pick fights with captains, quarrelsome captains and copilots who pick fights with *everyone* and pilots too stupid to realize that racial, sexual and religious harassment laws pertain even to them. Unsurprisingly, it's always the same untidy group.

Chief pilots must also deal with the pilot crazies, who have always found refuge from sanity in airline cockpits. The nuts come in every variety, from mere amusing eccentrics to dangerous raving lunatics. Some of these characters' antics wouldn't be tolerated for a minute if they sold aluminum siding yet are considered acceptable in the left seat of a Boeing 777.

Worst of all chief pilot duties is the requirement to memorize and catalogue every detail of The Big Picture, a jigsaw puzzle of seemingly unrelated technical and economic abstractions far too complicated and horrifying for the average line pilot to contemplate, much less understand. Chief pilots rely on their working knowledge of The Big Picture to explain inequities of the industry to line pilots. Personally, if anyone ever allowed me a glance at The Big Picture, I wouldn't look. I'd much prefer a sneak peek at Hell.

I should point out that modern-day airline chief pilots bear damn little resemblance to their earlier counterparts. Their importance has evolved steadily downward so that today they are concerned almost entirely with policing pilot groups for proper haircuts and shined shoes. Oh yeah, and making sure the line pilots wear their fucking hats.

At any rate, my business with Captain Weir was over. I thanked him and got up from the chair to leave.

"Say, by any chance are you the kid Nick Gorotny called 'Flashlight' or 'Headlight' or something like that?" Captain Weir asked. He grinned for the first time, an inscrutable chief pilot grin. "Nick told me a lot of funny stuff about that asshole."

It was "Searchbeam," damnit! If you're gonna spread the story, at least get it right!

I tried to read Captain Weir's face. Did he know I was Searchbeam? Was this another test? A chief pilot trap? Why the shit-eating grin? Would my past make any difference since he had already hired me? Best not to tell him, I thought. After all, it was his "old buddy" Nick Gorotny himself who told me never admit to anything in the flying business unless you're certain someone has clear 8 by 10 glossies of the event. "Tell your lie and take it to the grave," was Nick's motto. Mine, too.

"I think I heard about that clown. Something about a landing light, wasn't it? The guy thought he was on fire," I said, scrunching my face like I was trying to recall the story. "Must have been a real idiot. But that all happened before I worked for the Gorotnys. Never knew the guy."

"Guess not," he said, tapping his fingers on the desk. Again I started to leave. I got as far as the door.

"I don't suppose you know anything about the kid who told the mob guys they were flying when they were still on the ground then got scared and jumped ship, do you?" Captain Weir asked. "I've heard some flying stories in my day, but that one takes the cake."

You got that right, fella.

"Wow! He pulled a stunt like that on the mob? That sure took nerve," I said, feigning surprise. "No, I never heard about him. Glad it wasn't me. A guy could get himself killed like that."

Until that moment, I wasn't certain if the Gorotny brothers knew what really happened that awful night with Benny Smiles and the gang. Somehow they must have learned the truth. How many other people knew? Did every wannabe racket guy in the country know? What a great way to win instant adoption into Benny Smiles' lucrative family business—bring him the head of the wise-ass coombah pilot that made a fool of him. Was spreading the story that spiteful bastard Ernie's idea of revenge?

Even though it had been a while, I vowed to redouble my security measures. Which meant that I'd have to remember to roll up the windows on my ancient DeSoto. The door locks didn't work.

After that, I *really* couldn't get away from Captain Weir's office fast enough. My business with him was finished. The only legitimate reasons to hang around the chief pilot's office are to finagle time off or get your ass chewed. I hadn't given him a reason—yet—to chew my ass and even I didn't have the nerve to ask for time off my first day on the job. I thanked him again and left before he had a chance to recall any more stories.

Besides, only fools and butt-kissers with dreams of their own empire hang around the chief pilot's office for the hell of it. It can't be repeated too many times: A successful flying career is one in which the chief pilot never learns your name.

Once outside, I breathed more easily. I walked out to the Universal Air Transport ramp for a close look at a Curtiss C-46, my new mount. There were a few four-engine DC-6s and DC-7s scattered about, but they were way too senior for me to fly. As a new guy, I would start on the Curtiss C-46 "Commando," which made up the majority of the fleet. I counted about twenty on the ramp. Some of these same ships had unflinchingly hauled imponderable loads over the Himalayas and flown vast stretches of the Pacific in World War Two, ducked into blockaded Berlin after the war, served in Korea and, later, became the spurious tools of the CIA in southeast Asia. Drug smugglers think highly of the C-46's capabilities to this day.

The Universal fleet of battered, fading war heroes and fugitives from justice rested in Detroit's smoggy morning sunlight. This was not exactly the major airline I dreamed of, but it was a step in the right direction. Universal Air Transport was a shot at the big iron, an opportunity to break the chains of slavery and impoverishment that come as standard equipment with all small airplane flying jobs.

I approached one of the C-46s head-on and marveled at the sheer bulk that had earned the airplane the title of "Aluminum Overcast" when it first flew in the late 1930s. The C-46 was one of the largest twin-engine airplanes ever built. It spans over a hundred feet and weighs about fifty thousand pounds fully loaded.

If the C-46 was one of the largest twins ever built, it was also one of the most ungainly, a triumph of substance over style. A cruel, comic book caricature of an airplane, the fuselage design seemed inspired by an over-inflated football. Actually, two footballs, attached one on top of the other like Siamese twins joined at the stomach. A curving seam that hinted of a grin ran alongside the fuselage where the upper and lower sections joined. The seams met at the crimped, pointy nose, giving the C-46 an eternally puckered expression. As a final touch, an apparent prankster in the Curtiss design department placed an oval air vent in the tip of the nose; the vent resembled nothing so much as a glowering eye. Viewed from the front, the impression was of a mythical winged Cyclopean beast that had been goosed.

From my perspective on the ground, the C-46 didn't look like it would be difficult to fly, but I reserved judgment. As with most airplanes designed before World War Two, the C-46 was built to do a specific job and pilots were simply expected to fly it, no matter how inharmonious the alliance. Pilot comfort and ease of operation were not primary considerations. (A persistent rumor, never substantiated, held that the C-46 designer's wife had run off with a pilot.)

Make no mistake, the C-46 was *not* an antique even in 1965. Rather, it compared more to an aging samurai—weary, a bit slow and odd-looking, but still capable of kicking ass and always worthy of respect. Endearing terms such as "gentle" and "ladylike" that pilots use to describe, say, the Douglas DC-3, a pre-war contemporary of the C-46 but no equal in *any* category, didn't fit.

Incidentally, no one who flew the C-46 ever called it a "Commando." "Commando" was a bullshit wartime public relations label, the product of military propagandists. From the beginning, pilots called the C-46 "Dumbo," mostly because it lumbered, made noises like and, depending on what you were hauling, smelled like an elephant. Dumbo's tail wheel configuration made it even *look* like an elephant, a large truculent bull in rut cooling its fat ass in the river.

Along with the normal dents and wear that betray an aircraft's age like growth rings in an oak, the C-46 I examined that day had a string of neat aluminum patches on the right side of the fuselage near the tail. The patches, Purple Hearts of a sort, indicated that at some point in its long diverse career the aircraft may have annoyed someone in possession of an antiaircraft gun.

My tour of the aircraft took me to the left main landing gear. I kicked the giant tire, a pilot gesture of affection akin to slapping the ass of an old girlfriend. My foot rebounded off the tire at an oblique angle at twice the speed of the kick, striking the ground and scuffing my shoe. For a second or two I got the odd feeling that the airplane had kicked me back in an act of premeditated malice.

I put the ridiculous notion behind me and worked my way to the dented left engine cowling. I looked up at the storied Pratt and Whitney R2800, one of the twin hearts of the beast. I hugged the bottom blade of the huge propeller and reveled at modern man's ability to create wondrous, if not always eye-pleasing, machines.

A voice interrupted my silent soliloquy to the C-46.

"Hey buddy, better watch out when you're standing underneath those babies," chuckled a passing Universal Air Transport pilot. The straggler, his shirt hanging out the back of his pants, was just getting in from a hard night of flying. Another pilot walking with him shook his head.

"Must be a new guy," the other pilot said.

"Huh?"

"Look at your shoulder, ace."

I turned my head. Even as I rhapsodized about the unique charm of my new friend Dumbo, angry dark engine oil dripped from the cowling on my best, and only, sports coat. I stepped back from the airplane. As I blotted the oil with my best, and only, handkerchief, I began to see the C-46 in the new light of adversary rather than ally. I would soon learn that the C-46, like all mythical beasts, did not make friends and gave no quarter to its victims—in the air or on the ground. Ol' Dumbo belonged to a select group of man's more predatory inventions. Like bumper jacks, pressure cookers, radial-arm saws and Vincent Black Shadow motorcycles, the C-46 was known to hunt humans for pure sport.

My enthusiasm hardly diminished, I walked around to the side of the airplane and climbed aboard via a ladder hanging from the opened cargo door. Ineradicable smells of aviation past and present, human and inorganic, confirmed and suspected, overwhelmed my senses. Burned gasoline, overheated hydraulic fluid, mildewed leather, moldy rubber and rotting plywood floors shared the stage with stale cigarette smoke and the sweat of the several thousand pilots who had practiced their trade here.

I climbed out of the airplane and walked backward to take in the full expansiveness of the C-46. There was a scent, no, a *fragrance*, of promise in the air that not even the pollutants spewing from Detroit's nearby auto plants could mask. I was overcome with delight— prudently tempered with apprehension—at the idea of flying such an airplane. My pulse raced.

Universal Air Transport's graveyard lay just behind the ramp. I spotted a burned-out fuselage; the charred stringers cast a spectral outline of a C-46. Crashed airplanes, with all their mortal implications— dust to dust, that bullshit sort of thing—are irresistible to pilots. I asked around and learned that the C-46 went straight into the ground in clear weather a mile out on final at Detroit Metro Airport. The captain, it was determined, had suffered a massive heart attack and slumped forward on the yoke. The copilot, a kid my age, died in the crash. I added the reality to my list of ways one can buy it in an airplane.

At a local bar, I met some other pilots whom Captain Weir had also hired that day. Their backgrounds were not much different from mine. The aviation world, I learned, was full of Moondog McCutchinsons and Ernie Gorotnys. I wasn't certain if it made me feel better or worse. We swapped stories and lies and celebrated hard all weekend.

Ground school started on Monday morning. The class of about thirty pilots was comprised mostly of low-time guys like myself in the fledgling stage of our careers, plus about a half-dozen veterans making the rounds flying for every C-46 operator on earth. Talk about stories! Talk about lies! Everyone in the class with a C-46 type-rating started as captain. The rest of us would be copilots.

Some of the old C-46 hands only flew in the north during the spring and summer. In the spring they flew salmon by the untold ton out of Alaska. As summer approached they worked their way to Michigan, where they'd haul auto parts for outfits such as Universal. At the first hint of a cold breeze in October, they returned, like buzzards, to their home base in Miami International Airport's notorious "Corrosion Corner." They were known as "Miami Feather Merchants," though I don't recall why. Many of the Feather Merchants were famously out of shape and overweight; their faces showed the strain of years of night flying and the heavy drinking it inspires. I mentally practiced the impossibility of pulling their dead, slumped bulk off the yoke a mile on final.

Federal regulations required all of us to get a week of C-46 ground school, to be taught by a guy named Ike. White-haired, small and bird-like, Ike came across as a little grouchy until you had known him eight or ten years. He was, to our great surprise, still an active line pilot, even though he looked to be much older than the maximum age of 60. Eternally elusive about his year of birth, Ike's age was, and always will be, the best-kept secret in aviation. Historians are far more likely to learn the fate of Amelia Earhart.

Without introducing himself or acknowledging our presence, Ike began to draw a fuel system on the blackboard using six or seven different colored chalks. Right off the top of his head! I was impressed. After about an hour, Ike was still working on his masterpiece that, for all its artistic merit, bore scant resemblance to the C-46 fuel system shown in the manual issued to me. The C-46, for instance, had only two engines. The fuel system Ike was drawing had *four* engines.

"Say, pardon me, sir, but I have a question," said one of the aspiring copilots, who had also spotted the discrepancy. The C-46 veterans in the class couldn't have cared less what Ike was drawing. Most of them slept off hangovers.

"Goddamnit! Lemme finish what I'm doin'," Ike snapped. The inquiring pupil withdrew the objection.

As Ike created great art in chalk, one of the Miami Feather Merchants passed out dirty magazines from a well-traveled leather flight bag. Some of us learned quickly from the veterans and napped. For years I thought that no sleeping aid, prescription or otherwise, could induce sleep like ground school. But I was wrong. Toward the end of my career, the airlines began replacing ground school instructors with "computer-based-training."

In a scene right out of Kafka, pilots are chained by headsets to unsmiling, unblinking computer screens in a darkened room for ten hours at a time to learn aircraft systems. The computer, designed by geeks who think it's easier to send an e-mail than pick up a phone, doesn't much care if the student falls asleep. To the contrary, it *encourages* sleep. After the nap, the screen is still on the same damn page, waiting with the patience of a Russian chess champion or, more accurately, a medieval torturer waiting for his subject to revive. At best, the training computers are ineffective; at worst, they're demeaning. Like all computers, they rebuff the supple human minds that created them.

I never dreamed that I'd someday miss ground school instructors and their endless blackboard diagrams, loaded questions and tired repertoire of corny jokes.

Computers also provide flight guidance in all the new airliners and corporate jets. While they can only bore you in ground school, they can kill you in the air. The airborne computers are wonderful tools—until they become a distraction, at which point it'd be less dangerous to have a poker game and naked babes in the cockpit. Computers have been known to lure pilots to their deaths as surely as the siren Lorelei once seduced unwary sailors to shipwreck on the reefs.

Nor is distraction the only danger. A number of airline accidents have been blamed directly on computers. In most cases faulty information, whether from pilot input or from the computer, was at fault. Alas, man has always been slow to adjust to new technology. One hundred thousand years after the discovery of fire, he still burns his fingers. And always will.

Only the cybergeeks masquerading as pilots truly love the airborne computers.

About an hour later Ike, slapping chalk off his hands, addressed the class. "Remember," he began, "there is no such thing as a stupid question. There is, however, such a thing as a stupid answer. Okay, now let's cover the DC-6 fuel system."

Ike had spent most of the morning drawing the wrong fuel system! Stretching from my nap, I scanned the room, wondering who had the balls to tell him. Even though I've never learned when to keep my mouth shut, it wouldn't be me. Not that day. This Ike guy was too touchy. He spotted my C-46 manual. I tried to cover it with my hands.

"You got the wrong manual, sonny. That's for a C-46," Ike said. "This is a DC-6 class."

"I don't think so, sir," I said. "Of course I could be wrong." It's always wise to leave oneself an exit in debates with ground school instructors.

When Ike realized that everyone in the room had the same manual, he hit the roof. "Goddamnit! Why didn't someone tell me before I went through all this trouble drawing the wrong fuel system. Shit! Let's go to lunch."

Ike continued on similarly for four days, interspersing some of his favorite movies—some related to flying, some not—to break up the long afternoons. The movie I remember, mostly because Ike made such a big deal out of it, involved a crash test performed by the FAA using a Douglas DC-7. The feds topped off the old Douglas with thirty thousand pounds of 145-octane gasoline and flew it via radio control through two telephone poles. The flaming results would not have surprised anyone except the FAA.

"Take another good look, gentlemen, at your government in action," Ike said, running the film a second time. "That was a perfectly good DC-7 that the feds destroyed with your tax dollars. Some poor bastard could be earnin' a living in that DC-7, puttin' beans on the table with it. Hell, why didn't those asshole federales ask me? I'd o' told 'em what was gonna happen if they flew a 'seven full of gasoline 'tween two telephone poles."

We all laughed but Ike was serious.

Many years later, in another airline ground school, I watched the sequel to that film. The feds, perhaps convinced that the blackened remains of the DC-7 were a fluke, repeated the test. In the sequel they sacrificed a perfectly good Boeing 707, seventy thousand pounds of kerosene and two more telephone poles. The outcome was similarly unsurprising. I thought of Ike, gone but not forgotten.

Over the years the movies have given way to an endless stream of videos. The videos, many produced by self-ordained experts, have elevated the ground school ritual, never exactly riveting, to tortuous levels.

The video that earns mention in this book is a paralyzing treatment of weather radar by a retired airline pilot we all nicknamed "Starchie." Starchie's two-hour arcane discussion of thunderstorm avoidance has become a standing joke among a captive audience of airline pilots. For Starchie, the weather radar set was a life's work, worthy of unceasing, tireless analysis. Five minutes into the video I began to doubt that Starchie had ever flown in weather. Five minutes later, just before I lost consciousness, I began to doubt that he had ever been in an airplane.

I happened to know that Starchie's credentials were legitimate, however, and that bothered me even more. He was obviously one of those pilots who wrongly believe that flying airplanes is rocket science, which is to say he *made* it rocket science. The less complicated the task or system, the harder guys like Starchie work to make it difficult.

It ain't that hard, Starchie. All thunderstorms are pretty much alike. Just turn on the radar and fly away from the red spots. Frankly, I'd rather be burned at the stake than have to sleep through that video again.

On Friday morning Captain Weir poked his head into the classroom and informed Ike that the airline was in immediate need of our services. I awoke from my nap. Ike passed out a written exam, which had me worried until he began giving out the answers. I got a 78.

Ground school, to everyone's enormous relief, was over.

"We'll start flight training this afternoon," Ike said. He read names from a list. "Fusco, Irwin, Cinotto and Knudsen report to me at three this afternoon. I'll be your flight instructor. Try to stay out of the bars 'til then."

That afternoon the other three pilots and I left Terry's Lounge, a Universal pilot hangout, and reported back to Ike, who had the unenviable job of training the four of us to fly a C-46. We followed Ike like ducklings out onto the flight line and into Dumbo. I made the mistake of trying to help the aging Ike up the cargo door ladder. He brushed my hand away.

"Sonny, the day you have to help me get on a goddamn airplane you have my permission to shoot me," Ike said. He scooted up the ladder with astounding agility for a man who looked at least seventy.

Ike did not live to see the "age 60" rule rescinded. It's a shame, because he had been a poster child for the movement. Ike could have flown any airplane safely into his eighties. He almost did! On the other hand, however, I've known pilots who should have quit the day they turned forty.

As we followed Ike to the cockpit, we laughed, joked and talked big about our flying exploits. Ike turned around short of the cockpit door; he eyed us until we quieted down. "Okay, gentlemen, please give me your undivided attention."

We were about to be briefed. My eyes glazed. I've never been good at taking directions. I hate briefings.

"Gentlemen, I know you're all great lovers," Ike began. "If you guys told me that you got laid last night I'd believe you. I have no reason not to."

We looked at each other, wondering where Ike was going with the dialogue, unlike any airplane briefing I ever heard.

"Furthermore," he continued, "if you told me you all won fifty bucks in a poker game last night, I'd believe you. Why the hell not?"

More looking at each other. More wondering.

"Yep, I'd believe anything you guys told me," Ike said. "Anything, that is, except how good you fly. Please quit talking about how good you fly 'cause you're about to get a chance to show me. In an airplane that knows the difference! The moment of truth, gentlemen, is at hand."

Ike's students became very quiet.

With the ground rules established, I was somehow elected to be the first to get a chance to show Ike, my three fellow students and Ol' Dumbo how good I could fly.

Nervous and unsure, I buckled into the right seat and wriggled uncomfortably in unfamiliar surroundings, a mortal astray in the cave of a mythical beast. The cockpit sat unusually high because of Dumbo's tail wheel configuration. Large side windows extending down past my waist magnified the effect of height above the ground, which seemed far below, about a mile or two. No large airplane ever favored its pilots with such an uncluttered panorama of the passing landscape as did the C-46. Today's younger pilots, who bury their heads in computers connected to autopilots, may be surprised to learn that it was once considered sound practice to look out the window now and then.

The C-46 cockpit was vast and cold, not snug and cozy like those of the twin-Beech and other small airplanes I had been flying. The throttles stuck up about a foot with coffin-shaped knobs on the end. Nothing about the C-46 cockpit said relax and enjoy. Everything said "Ready thyself for humiliation, *sonny.*"

My three classmates sat behind me on a jump seat the size of a sofa. None of them said much; their turn was coming and they knew it.

This C-46 had a strangely different smell than the one I inspected that first day on the ramp. It smelled of rancid cooking grease with more than a hint of fried onions that overrode all the normal freighter aircraft smells.

"Somebody bring their lunch with them?" asked Jack Irwin, a guy we called "Crash" because of his poor luck with the babes. "Smells like a diner in here."

"It *was* a diner once," Ike said. "After the war, some idiot in Florida took the wings off this thing and poured the belly full of cement. Turned it into a restaurant. Imagine that? Sounds like something the feds might do, don't it? We needed more airplanes a couple years ago and bought it from the restaurant owner. Got most of the cement out but not the onion odor. C'mon, let's quit screwin' around and get this over with."

Ike gave us a quick review of the cockpit layout, including the hemp escape rope.

"Normally this rope is long enough except when I'm teaching new guys," Ike said. "Then it's about ten thousand feet too short." Instructor humor. Requisite forced laughter filled the cockpit.

I read the checklist, after which Ike got an okay from the ground crew to start engines. I looked out the right window and counted the passing propeller blades as Ike held the starter. When the appropriate number of blades had passed, Ike threw fuel and ignition to the engine. A grand, satisfying cloud of blue-gray smoke issued forth from the exhaust stacks and from everywhere else inside and around the cowling. The beast was awake.

After we started both engines, Ike told me to taxi the C-46. I pushed the throttles up a little and moved ahead slowly. The twin R2800s mumbled under their breath. I touched the brakes to keep the airplane going straight.

"Stay offa the brakes," Ike instructed. "Learn to taxi this thing with the tail wheel. Use a little differential power if you have to, but stay offa the brakes. Any jerk can taxi with the brakes."

The expander-tube brakes ratted on me with loud, elephantine squeals each time I touched them. Eventually, I made it out to the runway and got the airplane lined up. Ike reminded me to lock the tail wheel.

"Everyone screws up at least once in a career and takes off with the tail wheel unlocked in a C-46. But it's so goddamn hair-raising I guarantee it'll only happen once and that ain't gonna be today," Ike said. He reached down and locked the tail wheel.

"Okay," Ike said, "you all get one free takeoff. I ain't gonna pull an engine on you this time. Just get her rolling and take off. Nothing to it. Let's see how you do, sonny."

Sounded simple enough. Sure the C-46 was big, but an airplane's an airplane. How much different than a twin-Beech could this thing be? Confidently, I glanced behind me at my classmates huddled together on the jump seat, silent and expectant. Their lives were in my hands. I pushed the throttles up to takeoff power. The props screamed on each side of us, a conversation-halting, panic-instilling shriek of a mistreated animal that had broken loose of its cage and looked to settle old scores.

All this time the beast had still been asleep and I didn't even know it! It was wide awake now. After a couple hundred yards, it was in full battle stride. I pushed on the yoke a bit and Ol' Dumbo lifted its tail. I held on for dear life, pumping the frying pan sized rudder pedals to keep the beast straight.

Since spoken communication on takeoff was out of the question, Ike held up one finger for V1, the decision speed, after which we were committed to flight. I was pleased with myself for so easily taming the C-46. I may have even smirked as I prepared to rotate the ex-diner into the air.

Without warning and despite his pledge not to fail an engine, Ike reached up and pulled the power all the way back on the left engine. He shot the beast in the left leg at full gallop to duplicate the loss of an engine at lift-off, the most critical stage of flight. Dumbo lurched hard to the left; I applied full right rudder and held up the left wing. It felt like I was holding up a Caddy by the bumper. No airplane would ever feel so big again as that C-46 felt at that moment. Everything else I had ever flown suddenly seemed like a kiddy-car. An all-out physical and mental war followed. Cold sweat rolled off my forehead, burning my eyes.

In those days pilots were required to memorize a lengthy list of emergency items that had to be called out after an engine failure.

I did my best, flying the airplane and spouting commands, only forgetting about half of them. I also neglected to call for Ike to retract the gear.

Ike leaned into my ear and yelled, "Since you slept through ground school, sonny, you might have missed the fact that the landing gear on this monster retracts. Wanna see if it works?"

"Oh yeah, gear up!" I said. Laughter came from the jump seat behind me. Pilots can be cruel.

With the gear up, climbing out on one engine became notably less of a challenge.

After we gained some altitude, Ike restored power on the left engine. He pulled back the props and it became a little quieter in the cockpit, which is to say I could almost hear myself think. Had Ike forgotten his promise that we would all get "one free takeoff" with both engines running?

In a voice just below a scream, Ike explained the double cross. "I was just trying to teach you something, sonny. In this business there is no such thing as a free takeoff, especially in a C-46. Even though it may never happen to you in your whole career, you have to be ready every takeoff to lose an engine. This thing'll fly on one engine, even when it's heavy, but you got to do your part, you got to do everything just right. If you hesitate to react you'll be out of control. You'll die like a goddamn doctor in a Bonanza."

As his students digested the advice, Ike continued. "And don't worry too much about all that memory item crap. If you lose an engine on takeoff when fully loaded, you're not going to have enough spit in your mouth to say *anything* for a good five minutes. Just fly the airplane. Do what you have to do and stay alive. And don't just react. Think it out first! Remember, God creates the emergency, men create the crash. There is no such thing as an accident!"

It would make a good bumper sticker.

Ike's deep mistrust and grudging respect for all things mechanical, combined with his understanding of human nature in life and death situations, was his gift to us that day. Incidentally, it took the feds and the airline industry thirty years to catch up with Ike but lengthy emergency item memorization is no longer required or recommended. Even panicked, one can always read from a checklist.

Out over Lake Erie we tried a few stalls, actually "approach to stalls," in which the recovery is begun at the first hint of a stall. The beast objected to the exercise. Near the stall speed, the airplane shuddered and bucked, the signal to pour in the power, lower the nose to the horizon and hang on. After an hour or so of stall recoveries, steep turns and slow flight practice, I began to get a feel for the steadfastness and honesty of design built into the C-46. I also started to understand the love-hate feelings pilots have for it.

Ike told us he once spun a C-46 "just because I was in the mood to do it." Our eyes widened. Spins were for little airplanes, not something the size of a liberty ship. Fortunately, Ike wasn't in the mood that day for spins.

We did some more air work and returned to the airport. This is what I had been waiting for, my first landing in Dumbo. The airplane bounced so high that Detroit Metro tower thought we were on a missed approach.

"Give me a little warning if you're gonna bounce that high again," Ike said with a wide grin, "so I have time to get my oxygen mask on." More instructor humor. More forced laughter.

After a few tries, Ike almost taught me how to land the C-46. I must confess that for the year or so I flew Dumbo, I never really got past the point where I didn't feel like just a passenger on landing. But that's not to say I didn't enjoy flying the beast. Under ideal conditions the C-46 could be compared to a big, fat, fifty thousand pound Piper Cub. Under conditions less than ideal, it couldn't be compared to anything.

A few days later it was time for our check rides.

"Everybody takes it once around the patch," Ike announced. "You can scare me but if you don't kill me you're a Universal pilot."

After we all scared Ike but managed not to kill him, he released us to the line. Training was over; learning was about to begin.

Universal Air Transport was a true nonsked airline; there was no scheduled flying. Pilots lived by their phones, waiting for a call, which usually came in the middle of the night. For reasons never made entirely clear to me, airfreight is a nocturnal activity; like a tarantula, it moves best after dark.

Universal's main customers were the Detroit automotive companies. Auto plants tend to live on the edge when it comes to spare parts. Rather than shut down an assembly line in, say, Indianapolis, the auto companies would charter a Universal C-46, fill it with bumpers, transmissions or anything else needed to keep the line rolling, and the day would be saved. At least in theory.

My first trip was a 2 a.m. departure for Cleveland, on to Kansas City and back to Detroit. I was paired with a captain named Jimmy.

Short and round, Jimmy had a funny way of walking, a kind of robotic shuffle requiring a minimum of energy in which his feet never actually cleared the floor. The seat of his uniform pants shined like the Hope Diamond. His food-streaked tie, if boiled for an hour, could have provided a hearty meal and hot coffee for a family of four. His leather flight kit, patched with duct tape, rusting rivets and countless sutures, had lost the will to remain upright. It slumped hard to port, resembling nothing so much as the rotting carcass of a beached invertebrate.

Though Jimmy was only in his thirties, his hair had already begun to turn white. A disproportionate number of night-freight pilots seem to have white hair, possibly for the same reason that ocean creatures which live at dark depths lack coloration.

Jimmy let me fly the first leg to Cleveland, where we would pick up a load of auto parts for Kansas City. The weather was clear between Detroit and Cleveland so we flew across Lake Erie without an instrument flight plan. It was an ideal night, Jimmy assured me, for flying low across the lake.

"Ever done that 'fore, pardner?" Jimmy asked in a pronounced Southern accent different from any I ever heard before or since.

"Oh sure, lots of times," I said. I had never flown low over the lake at night, however, and never in anything the size of the C-46. Nor was I certain what Jimmy meant by "low." The word means different things to different pilots.

Another Cleveland-bound C-46 crew that took off just before us seemed to have the same idea. We spotted them flying low over the water a few miles ahead. The shadow of the aircraft trailed ghostlike on the moonlit lake.

"Take 'er down reeeal low over the water and keep the speed up," Jimmy said. He moved the throttles forward. "We's gonna sneak up on that sumbitch and go under 'im."

Under 'im?

Breaking the rules in an airplane is never smart but almost always fun. Flying low in a large airplane is a mostly forbidden pleasure and thus very satisfying. I jumped at the chance to take Dumbo down

Naturally, I assumed Jimmy was only joking about going *under* the other aircraft. Probably just some bullshit captain bravado, I thought. Fly *past* or *over* the aircraft close enough to scare hell out of the crew, perhaps, but not *under* it.

I leveled off at about 100 feet, roughly the same altitude as the lead aircraft. Its blazing exhaust stacks guided us like signal flares. The moonlight illuminated our greenhouse cockpit. The unusual view of the lake was thrilling.

It would get more thrilling.

"I said take it down *low*. C'mon now, take it down *low*, goddamnit!" Jimmy urged. "I'm gettin' a nose bleed up here. C'mon, we's gainin' on 'im. Push 'er down."

Reluctantly I eased the nose down lower, then lower. We were about fifty feet off the water. I was certain we were throwing spray off the props. The unusual perspective of the lake became somewhat less enjoyable. I remembered a bit of advice I once received from one of the airport bums at old Brookside Airport named Perry Meier. Even the best pilot in the world, he had warned, can only hope to *tie* the low altitude record.

"Hold what ya gots now, don't goes any lower. They's ore boats out here." Jimmy said.

I thought of how much Amory of Hungarian Air Force fame would have appreciated the opportunity to let loose on an ore boat at night in a C-46.

"This'll do it," Jimmy said, pushing the throttles wide open. The twin Pratts grunted their approval of the caper. I glanced at the exhaust stacks; they glowed an angry blue, the color of unleashed power.

The aircraft ahead, about 50 feet above us, was silhouetted in the moonlight. We were going much faster than our prey, which appeared to have stopped. I held the altitude steady and, not totally believing what was happening, flew under the other airplane. A minute later we were well ahead of it.

"Good job, man," Jimmy cackled. "Sumbitch never knew we was a'comin'. That'll teach 'im to fly so goddamn high. Now go 'head and

pull up and rocks the wings. Ya gots ta rub it in a little. Bet them guys
pissed their pants!"

Them guys!

"Is this something you guys do all the time?" I asked in a weak
voice as I rocked the wings half-heartedly.

"Not all the time," he said.

"Good," I said.

"'Cause if you did it *all* the time, " Jimmy said, "It'd be lots
harder to sneak up on 'em. It's 'bout havin' fun, pardner, 'bout stayin'
interested when ya gots to fly all night. When ya bin flyin' nights fer a
long time, ya looks fer ways to entertain yourself. It's kinda like being
a vampire. I never met me a vampire, but ya kin bet yer ass they does
what they does mostly ta stay entertained at night."

Still working on the connection between freighter pilots and
vampires, I spotted Cleveland Hopkins. Steady lightning to the west
foretold the weather waiting for us on the Cleveland-Kansas City
leg. More entertainment. Not that there promised to be any shortage
of entertainment landing at Cleveland, which was using the south
runway even though the wind was blowing out of the west at over
twenty-five knots.

I flew in and out of Cleveland Hopkins Airport for many years.
Any similarity between the direction of the wind and the runway in
use has always been strictly coincidental.

Twenty-five knots would have been a hefty crosswind in any airplane
but particularly in a C-46. I landed with full right aileron and hard left
rudder. The touchdown was reasonably smooth and in most aircraft
the difficult part of the landing would have been over. Not in the beast.
When the tail wheel hit, the wind caught the billboard-sized vertical fin
like a schooner sail and tried to push the nose around to the right toward
the boonies. The C-46 didn't object. I did. Still holding full aileron and
rudder, I advanced the right engine to keep the airplane straight.

"Okay, youse doin' good, man, but don't let up yet," Jimmy urged.
"Youse gonna have to fly this thing all the way to the ramp tonight
so don't let up. Ya might even have to tweak the brake a little to keep
'er straight. Don't even *thinks* 'bout lettin' up."

Making the mistake of thinking the battle was over, I pulled
the right engine back and relaxed the controls the merest amount.

The beast sensed a weakness and pounced. It lurched to the right. I corrected but it was too late. The right main gear was in the grass, the left main still on the runway. Runway lights passed under the nose. The beast, and its devious ally the wind, had prevailed.

"Aw, ya let up, man. Told ya not ta let up," Jimmy said. He didn't sound the least concerned. Amused, if anything. My mishap seemed to fit his definition of "entertainment."

I fought to keep the runway lights beneath us till we slowed. I might add that this all happened some years before the advent of centerline runway lighting. I humbly take credit for inventing the concept that night.

After we had stopped, I taxied back onto the runway. The right main gear neatly clipped off a runway light. The C-46, genetically closer to a bulldozer than to an airplane, paid no notice.

"I think we hit that runway light," I said. "Wudda we do now?"

"*We* didn't hit anything. *Youse* hit the runway light," Jimmy said. "Let's see ifin the tower seen anything 'fore we decides what we's gonna do. One of the main 'vantages of flyin' 'round at night is usually there ain't no witnesses. Or least nobody what gives a shit."

The night shift at Cleveland Tower did indeed miss the runway light mishap. Or was too tired to fill out the necessary paperwork. Or maybe they just didn't give a shit. Some air traffic controllers in those days were a lot like freight pilots.

We kept quiet and taxied to the ramp.

"Sorry if I scared you, Jimmy," I said, sheepishly.

"Hell, take lots more'n that to scare me," he said. "Besides I don't cares if a copilot scares me, jist as long as he don't bore me."

I don't think I bored him.

"Should we tell somebody 'bout the light?" I said.

"Since youse still kinda green mebbe I might better clues you in on a few things," Jimmy said. "When ya screws up in an airplane ya gots four choices."

"Four?"

"Yep. Ya kin tells the truth, which nobody ever does 'less they's crazy. Or ya kin tells the *right* lie. Or ya kin tells the *wrong* lie."

"What's the fourth?" I asked.

"What we's gonna do. Ya doesn't say shit ta nobody. Ya gettin' any o' this, pardner?"

While the ground crew loaded the airplane for the flight to Kansas City, I checked the weather and performed the ton of paperwork required before each flight. I discovered that Jimmy had added a little extra fuel. On the smaller airplanes I flew, I always put on a little "grandma" fuel but I figured this was the Big Time and foolishly assumed that the numbers had to add up. The extra weight of the fuel Jimmy had added in error would cause us to be about 900 pounds over maximum takeoff weight. Good damn thing Jimmy had a copilot as sharp as Pete Fusco to point it out to him.

"Hey, Jimmy," I shouted across a room full of Universal pilots smoking cigarettes and cigars and drinking strong coffee out of paper cups. "Ya got too much gas on this thing. We're gonna be too heavy for takeoff."

The room became uncomfortably silent. The other pilots looked at me, as if I had just given up my grandmother to the cops. Jimmy started in my direction.

"Man, ya really are new, ain't ya?"

"Like I told you, this is my first trip." I said.

"Never would've guessed." Jimmy put his arm around my shoulder and blew cigarette smoke disdainfully on the paperwork I was trying to show him. He lowered his voice and looked around as if the feds might be monitoring. "It's a long ways ta Kansas City from here and they's some nasty weather out there. That's why we gots the extra fuel. Get it?"

"Yeah, but we'll be overweight, won't we?"

"Lemme lets ya in on a lil' secret 'bout aeroplanes," Jimmy said, looking around again. "They'll fly when they's a little heavy, but they won't do shit without gasoline. They's gonna be times in your career when ya'd rather have fuel than pussy. Remember that, pardner. Extra fuel's better'n brains. Hell man, extra fuel's right up there with prayer."

With the fuel issue settled, Jimmy happened to notice all the weather I had written down.

"What's all that?"

"The weather, every city between here and Kansas City. I got us all the terminal forecasts and sequences, winds aloft, you name it."

"Youse sure peakin' out early, pardner. That there's a lot o' work fer nuthin," he said.

"How so?"

"Look, we's got plenty o' gas and we's gonna go anyhow. Who cares what the weather is? I'd rather be 'sprised. The weather's never as bad as they says—'cept sometimes."

It all made perfect sense to me. I filed a flight plan to Kansas City and followed Jimmy to the airplane. I've only pretended to check the weather ever since.

We took off and turned to the west. Jimmy was flying. He climbed to eight thousand feet. Lightning, nature's beacon to warn pilots of rocky shoals ahead, flashed like artillery fire on the horizon. A solid line of severe thunderstorms ran north and south as far as the eye could see and at least four times higher than the C-46 could climb if it had rocket power.

Jimmy's chief concern was lunch. He ate a couple sandwiches, from which he took large indiscriminate bites in the manner of a reef shark. He drank coffee out of a dented thermos that might have seen action in the trenches of the Somme. He casually studied the weather ahead. After he washed down two or three donuts with a last swig of coffee, he fished an old army poncho and a giant roll of duct tape from his flight bag.

"Don't 'spose ya knew 'nough to bring a poncho or tape, huh?" Jimmy asked, busily taping the numerous window seams around his seat.

"No, sure didn't" I said. "Nobody said anything about it."

"They's lots o' things in this flyin' business ya gots ta figure out fer yourself. Wanna borrow some tape? It's gonna git mighty goddamn wet in here."

"No thanks," I said, not wanting to believe it could possibly get wet enough *inside* the C-46 to require a poncho or taped window seams. My DeSoto, yes, but not the big-iron C-46.

After Jimmy completed his waterproofing procedure, he let go of the controls, reclined his seat and laid back.

"Ya looks too wide awake fer your own damn good. Go 'head an' takes it fer 'while. I'm gonna git me a lil' nap," Jimmy said. "We's gots a long night 'head o' us. Lotsa nymphocumuli ahead."

"Nymphocumuli? Don't think I ever heard of that," I said, mentally reviewing my extremely limited knowledge of cloud types. All clouds look pretty much the same to me.

"Yeah, nymphocumuli—fuckin' thunderstorms!" my mentor said as he closed his eyes.

I asked Jimmy to stay awake long enough and fly the airplane while I performed the preparatory pilot rituals necessary to flying any large airplane. I began by accidentally dropping my ball point pen on the cockpit floor. I dove after it, squeezing my body between the seat and the center pedestal.

"Mise well kiss that pen goodby," Jimmy said. "Never saw nobody find nuthin' dropped on a cockpit floor, fer sure not in Dumbo."

For five minutes I rubbed my hand over the sticky accretion of human and man-made deposits covering the floor. After slicing my thumb on the razor-sharp seat rail, I gave up the search. The pen joined a thirty-year collection of other pens, Zippo lighters, buttons, loose change and eyeglasses lost forever on the cockpit floors of every large aircraft in the world. Jimmy was right. When an object is dropped on a cockpit floor, it stays dropped.

Jimmy handed me the chewed stub of a pencil and I returned to the task of readying myself to take over the airplane. In smaller airplanes I just jumped in and went; but this was the Big Time.

I adjusted the rudder pedals and my seat five or six times to pinpoint the ideal position. (Landing and sleeping positions are the most important.) I arranged my charts in the geographic order I would need them. Next I tweaked the instrument panel lighting, adjusted my reading light and rooted through my flight bag for my prized seven-dollar five-cell chromed flashlight and E6B computer, a cardboard handout from Aeroshell held together with a plastic rivet. I fiddled with my headset and fine-tuned the radio squelch knob, etc, etc.

Jimmy watched my routine with annoyed wonderment until he could no longer contain himself.

"Ya gettin' ready fer brain surg'ry over there or what? Youse workin' 'tirely too hard, pardner. We's gonna be in Kansas City afore ya gits thru screwin'round. Now if youse was tapin' your windows or sumpin' 'portant, that'd be dif'rent. If ya wants ta do brain surg'ry, go fly for United. They's the brain surgeons, they makes a big deal outta ever goddamn thing."

"You really think I'm working too hard at this?" I asked. His comment surprised me. I had never been accused of working too hard at *anything*.

"Ya sure as hell is," Jimmy said. "Looky here, the secret ta flyin' is ya gots ta *let* it happen, not *make* it happen. The less ya does, the better ya flies and the easier 'tis. Youse never gonna make the long haul if ya works that hard at it. Hell, the best pilots I knows is the laziest people. They saves themseles fer 'mergencies, not plannin'. No one kin pay 'tention all the time in this business and be any good at it. If ya ever flies with some asshole who pays 'tention all the time, watch 'im close. He's gonna kill ya. Is *any* o' this sinkin' in?"

When I signaled Jimmy that I was at last ready to take over the yoke, he lay back in his seat. "Now don't go fallin' 'sleep on me," he said. "Nuthin' makes me madder'n wakin' up and findin' my co-pilot asleep." Jimmy closed his eyes and sighed in resignation to his role as teacher of the uneducable.

While I'd been known to nod off at the yoke, there was almost no chance of it happening that night. The "nymphocumuli" loomed ahead, a big-league, dues-paid-up Midwestern summer squall line. Wrathful mountain-sized clouds hurled jagged fluorescent bolts of lightning at each other and at the ground. They seemed impatient for our arrival.

Airborne weather radar had been around for a number of years by the middle 1960s, but was far from standard equipment on the Universal C-46 fleet. The C-46 didn't need it, wiser men than I had determined. My plan was to dodge the worst of the weather as we encountered it. The rules had been established centuries before in the days of sail: Aim for the dark spots at night and the light spots during the day.

There were not a lot of dark spots. In lieu of dark spots, the lightning itself sometimes offers a nanosecond glimpse of an opening in the clouds, a canyon of opportunity and safe passage. I saw plenty of lightning but no openings.

I asked Cleveland Center if anyone had gone through the weather recently.

"No, you'll be the first to try tonight, Universal," the controller said. "Let me know what kind of a ride you get. Deviate as much as you need."

I turned up the cockpit lights so that the lightning would not blind me. I stole the trick from Ernie Gann's *Fate is the Hunter.*

"Hey, turn those lights out!" Jimmy said, as unimpressed with Gann's timeless wisdom as he was with the weather ahead."They keeps me awake."

I dimmed the lights again. The air remained smooth even though the boiling wall of weather was only about a mile away.

Captain Jimmy, trained at great cost by Universal Air Transport and entrusted with the safety of the C-46 and everything in it, fell sound asleep. His snoring was audible above the engines. I was pleased with his show of confidence, though I'm sure Jimmy trusted more in Dumbo's survival skills than mine. The C-46 was built for this. No, that's not quite correct. The C-46 *lived* for this.

I hunkered down in my seat, loosened the grip on the yoke so that I would ride with the storm instead of fight it and waited. I knew what a *small* airplane felt like in a thunderstorm—something akin to a butterfly on three large cups of Starbucks—but I wasn't certain how the beast would handle the weather.

A tightness gripped my stomach, the same primordial, encoded fear that made primitive man cower piteously in his cave during thunderstorms. But I was modern man and far too smart for that. So smart, in fact, that I was about to fly directly into the storm. Dread's probing fingers crawled my spine but I was prepared, if not entirely eager.

The angry clouds, bloated with rain, swallowed us alive and began to chew. I did my part, banking left and right chasing elusive dark spots. It went pretty well for a few minutes as I skirted the whitest and worst cells in a kind of sloppy aerial hopscotch.

Then I ran out of dark spots.

With little other choice, I held on and drove straight ahead into the core of the storm, into a world of fire, wind and water. Hail smashed against the cockpit windows with the power of cannon shot. The same expansive cockpit windows that made flying the C-46 on nice days such a treat only added to the terror of flying into weather.

Lightning illuminated the cockpit. It cast a cerulean blue glow on the sleeping Jimmy sprawled flat in his seat like Doctor Frankenstein's cursed monster on recharge.

Several times the storm rolled us almost on our side before I could right the airplane. Dumbo, while not as stable in violent weather as some airplanes, compensated with impertinence. Its Cyclopean eye glowered unblinkingly, defiantly into the storm. The beast took the blows in stride, always back on its feet breathing steadily, taking on all comers like Popeye post-spinach. As the battle raged, I'm certain I heard Dumbo whisper to the elements, "Is that all you fuckin' got, rookie?"

As if in answer, the skies delivered a sizzling, mile-long sidearm lightning bolt that smacked Dumbo square on the nose with an accompanying cherry-bomb discharge. The theory that lightning is the power source of life takes on added relevance when one is struck by it in an airplane. Assailed by billions of unbridled volts, it's easy to visualize such an ungovernable force jump-starting a lifeless planet without letup for eons until by chance or design—take your pick—it caused a puddle of swampy goop to throb. I had the discomfiting feeling that the lightning, having seen how badly the life experiment thing had worked out, was trying to reverse the process, beginning with Jimmy and me.

Heavily charged air bathed the airplane in St. Elmo's fire. Otherworldly blue flames rolled around the props and licked at the windshield with long skinny spider legs anxious to wrap us for later use. Early Italian sailors thought these same static charges on lines and sails a guiding torch from Saint Elmo, a second-century martyr who earned his arguable connection with the sea by having his intestines spun out on a ship's windlass. It was win-win for old St. Elmo and the Church in those days before ship-to-shore radio. If the sailors weathered the storm, they returned to sing the saint's praises and make willing donations to the parish. If they didn't survive the storm, who was ever going to learn that Elmo had forsaken them?

My right foot and leg felt damp. As Jimmy had predicted, the lower windows at my side were leaking freely. The intrusive water defied gravity and moved up, down and sideways inside the cockpit. It channeled along the window frames and ran contemptuously down my leg and into my new twenty-nine dollar flying boots. The weather, not content to torment me from outside, was coming *into* the cockpit.

Jimmy snored on. I envied him and wondered if I would ever reach a point where I could sleep in weather like this. The more brutal the pounding, the better Jimmy slept. Dry and cozy, he snored in synchronization with the props and nature's tantrum. As for Dumbo, built like a Depression-era bridge and tempered by war, the storm was a mere passing diversion during another long ride into the night.

An Eastern Air Lines flight checked on the Cleveland Center frequency. The Eastern airplane was behind us and not yet into the weather.

"Center, is anybody gettin' through this line ahead?" the Eastern pilot asked in an edgy voice.

"I have a Universal C-46 going through now. I'll ask him how the ride is," the controller replied. "Universal, how's the ride where you're at?"

I picked up the mike and was about to give a blow-by-blow of the severe weather. There were no holes in it and I was going to warn the Eastern flight to stay away, get the hell out of there. He was probably flying a Martin 404, a peacetime airliner not nearly as stout as a C-46. I'd be a hero. Eastern, which had never bothered to reply to my resumes, would have no choice but to hire me—after a congratulatory dinner in my honor.

Jimmy stirred. He had been listening to the radio while sound asleep, an acquired skill and the mark of a real professional. He waved me off, indicating he would talk on the radio. No doubt he wanted to tell Eastern personally about the nasty weather and give them the benefit of his expert assessment. He stretched and grabbed the mike.

"No problem attal where we's at, jist a nice, smooth ride," Jimmy said, barely able to hold the mike to his mouth in the turbulence.

The Eastern pilot heard Jimmy's reply and followed us into the squall line. He started whining soon after.

"Center, be advised there's moderate to severe turbulence and very heavy rain in this stuff," he said. "We're almost unable to control the aircraft. We're turning around and getting out of here. We'd like clearance back to Cleveland. Who'd you say was getting through?"

"Universal, a C-46," replied the controller.

"Oh!" he said. "For sure we're turning around."

"How come you didn't tell Eastern what kind of weather we're into?" I asked Jimmy.

"They really didn't tell me how green ya was," Jimmy shouted over the water pummeling the windshield. "Pardner, no matter what, never tell nobody what's goin' on inside the cockpit. What happens in the cockpit stays in the cockpit 'til ya dies, or at least 'til ya retires. That radio'll hang yer ass every time. The less ya says, the better."

Captain Jimmy was right and the feds knew it. Hence the arrival of cockpit voice recorders a few years later. The gadgets hang above a pilot's head in the cockpit like a fly on the wall, as damning as a written confession, as revelatory as a suicide note. Sometimes, they *are* the suicide note.

"Besides, I hates Eastern," Jimmy added as an afterthought.

"Why's that?"

"They wouldn't hire me."

"How come?"

"Not real sure, 'cept the guy who was interviewing me didn't know shit 'bout flyin' and I kinda pointed it out to 'im, I guess."

"That'd do it."

"Reckon so. Now, if the 'mergency's over I'm gonna try ta gits back ta sleep."

Thus blanketed in protective secrecy but still getting bounced around pretty good, I had no choice but to wait until we broke out on the other side of the storm—wherever that might be. Turning around like Eastern Air Lines was not an option. Universal Air Transport and other non-scheduled airlines of the day paid their pilots by the mile, computed from departure to destination. Had we gone back to Cleveland and waited out the weather we would not have been paid for the effort. Even going to an alternate airport if the weather at the destination was below landing minimums did not count. I worked for many different types of compensation in my flying career. The pennies-a-mile arrangement was by far the most compelling. When a Universal Air Transport airplane didn't get through, no one got through. Period!

A couple of miles later, after one last furious thrashing, the storm spit us out the other side into a clear, peaceful night sky. The beast droned on under the stars. I scored the round a draw.

With some difficulty, I managed to wake Jimmy when I had Kansas City in sight. It was his leg and his landing.

"Ya makes the landing, pardner, ya needs the practice. This time stay off the runway lights. One runway light and one fart in the cockpit per night is the legal limit," Jimmy said. "Hey, youse pants look wet."

"Yeah, maybe a little," I said, squishing in my seat.

The landing at Kansas City was uneventful. The taxi to the gate wasn't. Kansas City Ground Control advised us in a jittery voice that the number two engine was torching flames. One adventure seemed to follow another in a Curtiss C-46.

"This guy prob'ly don't know what he's talkin' 'bout, but ya better goes back and have youself a look-see," Jimmy said.

I made my way to a window on the right side of the fuselage, from where I could see the engine stacks more clearly. I saw the flames. Not just little flames but belching, snarly yellow and orange Halloween flames that shot back all the way to the tail of the aircraft every time Jimmy so much as touched the throttle on the right engine.

I deduced, based on my limited knowledge of physics, that raw 100-octane gasoline was somehow being fed directly onto the hot engine exhaust stacks. I worked my way to the cockpit with the news.

"It's bad, Jimmy," I reported. "Every time you touch the throttles, that right motor turns into a dragon."

"We'll have maintenance take a look at it," he said.

Jimmy wrote up the torching engine in the logbook and gave it to a mechanic with the unsettling nickname of "Hammer."

"Maybe a hole in a fuel line or something, huh?" I offered.

"Oh, is that right? Who's the mechanic here, anyhow?" Hammer shot back. Even those few mechanics that don't hate all pilots hate pilots who make suggestions.

Not at all pleased that we had interrupted them from their dominoes game, Hammer and another surly mechanic started the engines and taxied the C-46 to a spot where they could run it up. A hand-written sign on Hammer's giant toolbox did little to reassure me. It proclaimed a universal dictum among airplane mechanics, then as now: "IF IT AIN'T BROKE DON'T FIX IT. IF IT IS BROKE TRY TO CONVINCE THE PILOT THAT HE DON'T NEED IT."

Jimmy and I watched the right engine torch all the way to the run-up area. The airplane looked like a traveling bonfire. If anything, the torching had gotten worse; flames shot well *past* the tail. After a few minutes in the run-up area, Hammer taxied back to the ramp. He shut down the engines and walked over to where we were standing. He scribbled a barely legible entry in the logbook and handed it to Jimmy.

"Ground checks okay," he said, looking Jimmy hard in the eye. It was mechanic's lingo meaning he wasn't going to do anything about it. "Looks normal to me," he said.

Hammer was playing the old mechanics stall game, begun by Wilbur Wright the first time Orville complained about a loose flying wire on the Flyer. Hammer was willing to try anything rather than actually fix the problem. If he could convince Jimmy to fly the ship to Detroit, then the Detroit mechanics would have to repair it. He was betting—with our lives—that it would get there.

Unlike today, copilots in 1965 were expected to agree with the captain's decision. If the captain went, the copilot went, as simple as that. The thought of flying a blowtorch back to Detroit terrified me. I already had several demonstrations that night of just how hard it was to scare Jimmy.

Hammer waited on Jimmy's counter while I held my breath.

"Tis normal, huh?" Jimmy asked.

"Yep. Norrrmal," Hammer said, smirking and standing his ground.

"Alrighty," Jimmy said. He scratched his head a second or two. "Here's what we's gonna do. Me and my pardner here is gonna grab us a couple bunks and git us a little shuteye. Last time I looked there was two motors on that bitch. If the torchin's 'norrrmal' like you say, then the other engine oughts ta do it too. When ya gits the other engine to do the same 'norrrmal' kinda thing, wake us up and we'll fly 'er back to Detroit."

It was a masterful comeback, for which no mechanic appeal existed. Hammer was beaten and he knew it.

Complaining to each other about wise-ass pilots, Hammer and the other mechanic gathered their tools to fix the troublesome engine. I scored one for Jimmy—and me—in the great survival game that is flying. A career involves many such exchanges with numerous non-flying types from mechanics to controllers to simulator instructors to chief pilots to the FAA to the NTSB to all levels of management, all of whom are more than willing to tell a working pilot what to do and how to fly the airplane while they sit on the ground. They never seem to figure it out: PILOTS ARE THE ONLY PLAYERS IN THE GAME OF FLYING. EVERYONE ELSE IS JUST A FUCKING WATER BOY. Non-pilots bet their Christmas bonus or next promotion on their decisions; pilots play the game with somewhat higher stakes.

Covered head to toe with grease, Hammer woke us about six hours later with the news that the engine was repaired. He reluctantly showed us the "norrrmal" fuel intake manifold with the "norrrmal" eight-inch crack in it that he had removed from the engine.

Strangely enough, he had no hard feelings. He lost that round, but only because Jimmy was a cagey veteran. Tonight it might be a new captain still learning the ropes that Hammer could talk into limping back to Detroit in an ailing airplane.

Refreshed by the nap, we took off for Detroit about nine a.m. It was a treat to fly during the day even though the sun was in our eyes. To the south we could see some scattered puffs of clouds, benign remnants of the storm that littered the sky like beer cups on an Irish soccer field after a riot. I was flying.

"You used one of these autopilots before?" Jimmy asked. He began playing with the autopilot on the C-46, which was robustly safety-wired to the disengaged position to prevent its use.

"Never," I said. "Shit, I've never even seen one before. But these don't work anymore, do they?"

"Some don't, some do," Jimmy said.

I suspected that Jimmy was about to share yet another facet of his vast aviation knowledge.

Curtiss had installed a crude, early version of an autopilot when they built the C-46 during World War Two. To save money and the hassle of maintaining the autopilots, most freight outfits, including Universal Air Transport, had decommissioned them. The airlines either removed the autopilots entirely or, as in the case of the ship we were flying, safety-wired the switches closed and pasted a placard on the device that warned, "AUTOPILOT INOPERATIVE. DO

NOT ATTEMPT TO ENGAGE. ENGAGING AUTOPILOT COULD RESULT IN LOSS OF AIRCRAFT CONTROL." There was nothing tricky about the wording. I was convinced.

Not Jimmy.

"Yeah, some of these things works, but, naw, ya wouldn't know that," Jimmy said. He reached into his shirt pocket for the little red book all pilots carry. The books are for keeping flight times but pilots write all kinds of additional pertinent information in them: girl friends' phone numbers, gambling debts, etc.

"I keeps a record of which ones of these things works and which ones doesn't."

"That's nice," I said.

"Now lemme see here. Yep, this here aeroplane has a good 'un. We gits to jist ride along on this leg. We's gonna let ol' Jack fly us home, pardner." "Jack" was a reference to the Jack & Heinz Company, wartime lowest-bid makers of the device.

"That's some pretty strong safety wire on that thing, Jimmy," I said. "Ya suppose there's a message there?"

"That's why I carries some pretty strong wire cutters with me," Jimmy said. He began excavating through his flight bag for the cutters to free "ol' Jack." He unearthed a variety of items I never saw any other pilot carry in a flight kit. But no wire cutters.

I was both relieved and disappointed. An autopilot, even one designed in the Stone Age, was a luxury, like weather radar, that I didn't allow myself to think about. I had never flown anything equipped with an autopilot. For all I knew, autopilots were science fiction, a World's Fair exhibit, something to look forward to in the next millennium—or my next life. Hand-flying airplanes for hours on end can be pure drudgery. Engaging the wired-off, placarded autopilot was very tempting, if for no other reason than just to see one work.

However, I knew that once an aircraft component was decommissioned, it was forgotten. Universal Air Transport made only a pretense of maintaining many aircraft components essential for airworthiness. It certainly didn't maintain anything decommissioned.

Then again, the worlds of maintenance and flight departments do not fly in formation. Rather, they orbit each other, sharing many of the same forces but governed by different rules, written and unwritten. Pilots and mechanics, for instance, each have their own definition of "airworthy." There was a good chance the autopilot might work fine but, just to set the record straight, I wouldn't have cut that safety wire for a million dollars.

"I don't mind hand-flying," I said, hoping I could dissuade Jimmy from disturbing the autopilot from its grave. "I actually kind of enjoy it."

"That's cause ya's new an' don't know no better," Jimmy said, still searching through his flight kit.

To my dismay he found a pair of rusty wire cutters, which he held up triumphantly.

"After ya bin flyin' fer a couple more years yu'll do anything to keep from hand-flyin'. Now jist hang on and keep 'er straight and level while I cuts the wire and engages this lil' gem. You're in fer a treat, pardner, a real treat."

He was right about that.

Jimmy cut the safety wire. He twisted mightily to break free a crude, saucer-sized knob more appropriate to a submarine or cement truck than an airplane. A sharp, grinding noise accompanied by metallic chattering followed. As I held the yoke and my breath, I could feel powerful forces inside the beast taking control away from me.

"Okay, jist let 'er go and sit back," Jimmy said, very pleased with himself.

I was reluctant to give up the yoke to invisible hands.

"Ya gots ta catch up with technology, pardner," Jimmy urged. "C'mon, let 'er go."

I released the yoke. The airplane flew straight ahead. Jimmy winked at me, as if we were putting one over on the airplane, getting a free ride, cheating the beast out of the fun of making us work.

Sure enough, the beast stayed on course and on altitude. We were indeed flying on autopilot. I slid my seat back in cheerful disbelief and lit a cigarette. I knew the reprieve that an oar stroke must have felt when the sail was raised or the guy with the whip had to visit the head.

"Now this is flyin' the way it was meant ta be, the way God planned it, all relaxin' and no work," Jimmy crowed. He launched into a tiresome scientific treatise about the workings of autopilots.

Jimmy assured me that, in the event I lived long enough to become as good a pilot as he, someday I would also be able to discern such aircraft fine points. I was in the middle of a vigorous yawn when the airplane began drifting to the right. I started to reach for the yoke.

"Jist stand by, pardner. Have a lil' faith in ol' Jack," Jimmy said. "He'll figure it out and git us back on course."

When it became obvious that "ol' Jack" had no interest in whether or not we were on course, Jimmy twisted the autopilot knob out some more. There were more grinding noises but the adjustment worked; the airplane flew straight ahead once more.

"Needed some fine tunin' is all," he said. "Hope youse payin' 'tention to what I'm doin'. Ya could learn sumpin' here, pardner."

As Jimmy continued the lecture, the right wing dropped. The airplane turned about twenty degrees. The little faith I had in 'ol Jack vanished. I grabbed the yoke. It wouldn't move.

"Level the wings," Jimmy said.

"I can't!"

Jimmy tried his yoke, twisting hard to the left to level the wings and recover from the turn. Like mine, his yoke wouldn't budge.

"Sometimes this happens," Jimmy said, his voice not yet discernibly tense.

"Sometimes this happens?"

"Sure, no problem." Jimmy went to war with the yoke. He got it to move a small amount but the beast ignored the control input. The ship began a series of short, staccato dives each followed by a neck-snapping pull-up. The airplane pitched up one last time then nosed down hard. Bank angle increased. We were out of control. I readied myself for death, imagining what the last few minutes of life might be like with Dumbo in a grave-yard spiral. With any luck, the feds would find Jimmy's fingerprints on the autopilot knob and clear me. The world would know that I had tried to play by the rules at least once.

Jimmy attempted to rewind the autopilot knob to its original position. The knob didn't seem to screw in quite as easily as it had screwed out. Every turn of the knob brought more unsolicited inputs to the control surfaces. We lost several thousand feet while we made two descending steep turns over the corn fields and pastures of Missouri.

"Let's both git on this sumbitch," Jimmy said.

Jimmy and I grabbed our yokes and braced our feet on the instrument panel for better leverage. We became locked in a death struggle with the beast, the old story of men attempting to tame their own technology run amuck. As we yanked on the frozen yoke, the airplane dropped another thousand feet and carved another full turn in its descent toward the ground. Bank angle exceeded sixty degrees.

"Pull harder!" Jimmy yelled in a reedy voice.

I was somehow pleased that something could get his attention.

"If we pull any harder, we're gonna snap something," I said.

"I was beginnin' ta wonder if youse was ever gonna figure that out, pardner" Jimmy said. "Pull harder!"

I pulled harder.

"Twiiing! Twaaang! Raaang!

The autopilot's snapped tendons banged around against aluminum far away inside the airplane. The autopilot disengaged. We were back in control.

After Jimmy told the "right lie" to center, we climbed back to altitude. Jimmy took out his little red book, licked the tip of his pencil and made a notation. I assumed this particular airplane was now off the list of those with working autopilots.

"Not sure whether or not I'd try thisun 'gain," he said.

Not sure?

Hand flying had never seemed so fulfilling. We got back about two in the afternoon. I drove to the small apartment I had rented and collapsed on my bed, knowing that when the sun went down the Universal schedulers would have another trip for me. I fell asleep with a better understanding of the connection between vampires and freight pilots. There must be some advantages to flying night freight, but in twenty years of it I never came up with any. Unless one considers flying unshaved and stripped to one's skivvies on hot nights an advantage.

A month or so later I was again teamed with Captain Jimmy on a 2 a.m. departure to St. Louis. The weather was great, clear as a bell, and I looked forward to it.

Jimmy was a bit impetuous—he once landed at Detroit Metro on an ice-covered runway instead of diverting because, he explained to the chief pilot, that's where his car was parked—but he was always fun. He loved to rib copilots but always treated them as equals, not as underlings subject to his whims. He did not require homage, as do some captains. He knew something that many professional pilots never figure out in a forty-year career: Keep the crew happy; a happy cockpit is a safe cockpit. If your crew's not happy, captain, you're not a professional.

This seemingly self-evident concept is difficult, if not impossible, to teach. The airlines and corporate flight departments recognized the importance of cockpit harmony about 1980. To their credit, they've spent millions of dollars on "Crew Resource Management" classes trying to reach the jerks. They'd have a better chance of training the Wolfman to stay home and watch television on moonlit nights. Nor is the Wolfman analogy far from the mark. Many otherwise congenial pilots only begin to grow hair on their palms and sprout fangs when they settle into the captain's seat. The cockpit is their full moon, the stimulus that transforms them into assholes.

These clowns might be amusing except for the fact that their arrogance and aggressiveness occasionally results in broken bodies and twisted aluminum. A frightening number of airline accidents have been traced to the captain's refusal and inability to weigh any opinion but his own. Consequently, the feds and airline check airmen are constantly on the alert for pilots who don't adhere to the CRM principles of common respect and open communication. But the jerks, again like the Wolfman, are crafty and hard to trap. They can change their demeanor to fit the occasion. With a fed or check airman in the cockpit, many would win an Academy Award for their charade of cockpit unanimity.

Given the choice, I'd much prefer to take my chances with a supernatural carnivore in a dark forest than fly again with some of the captains I dealt with in my career. Or even a few of the copilots, for that matter. The jerks don't just make flying dangerous; they also make it work. They take the fun out of it. Somewhere in the hottest depths of Hell there's a private room reserved for the jerks. There they'll be free to whine on the radio, micro manage and nitpick each other's techniques, tyrannize and write-up everyone, make endless moronic announcements over the PA and deny the Devil the jump seat for eternity. When they become bored, they can holler down to the next hotter level and discuss the weather with pilots who insisted on sharing their political and religious beliefs in the cockpit.

A wise old captain I once flew with early on summed it up best: "Treat everyone on the crew with respect, as if someday they might have to pull you from a burning wreckage. Don't ever give anyone a reason to think twice about it.

I can't say that I ever flew with anyone that I would have left burning in the wreckage but there's definitely been a few I would have thought twice about.

The good guys, of course, will enjoy a far different hereafter than the assholes. They'll all own little red biplanes stored in air-conditioned hangars at celestial airports with two-mile-long grass runways. Gasoline, cold beer, table dances, cigarettes and fatty foods will be provided at no cost.

Captain Jimmy, a natural-born storyteller who contributed more to this book than he'll ever know, kept me entertained with outrageous flying yarns all the way to St. Louis. It was a hot summer night and he took off his uniform shirt. His T-shirt sported a C-46 with the nose painted to resemble a howling dog's mouth. A caption over the dog/airplane read, *"Cargous Caninus."* Jimmy was a true freight dog if I ever knew one. And I've known a bunch.

We were having a lot of fun, probably more than the law allowed. Things were going *too* well. That's why I wasn't surprised when the tail wheel would not extend on the approach to St. Louis Lambert Field.

Jimmy broke off the approach and called for me to raise the landing gear. I asked the tower if we could circle near the airport while we addressed the problem. Anywhere we'd like, the tower voice said. Jimmy climbed to four thousand feet and flew wide, freestyle circles east of the field. We tried again to lower the gear. Same thing: two greens on the main, a red on the tail wheel. Jimmy reached over and retracted the gear.

"Tail wheel's hung up on the uplock. Guess ya gits ta play with the shepherd's hook, pardner," Jimmy said. "I hates ta send ya back there but ya really ain't a C-46 driver till ya's done the shepherd's hook. Since I've done it before, I'll wait here."

Ike had mentioned the so-called "shepherd's hook" during our abbreviated, drowsy ground school. I recalled that the hook was used to somehow manually lift the hundred-pound tail wheel off of the uplock. All I knew for certain was that it was stowed above the tail wheel bay on the wall of "J" compartment, the furthest aft compartment.

Equipped with my prized seven-dollar five-cell chromed flashlight but without a clue of what I was going to do when I got there, I headed for the back of the airplane. At best, aviation is an inexact science; much of it is necessarily learned on the job. With any luck, there'd be some printed instructions.

Seven tons of automotive parts, stacked to within a foot of the ceiling, stood between "J" compartment and me. Several heavy boxes had fallen off the top of the freight bins and obstructed the narrow aisle alongside the freight. With the aisle blocked, I was going to have to climb *over* the freight. I returned to the cockpit to inform Jimmy that it might take a while to get to the back of the airplane.

"I'll be a few minutes getting back there," I said. "I'm going to have to climb over the bins. The aisle's blocked."

"Might wanna take off yer shirt and pants," Jimmy suggested.

I should have known better but instead chose to ignore Jimmy's advice. Fully clothed, I began a Sisyphean crawl over the bins full of automotive parts. Not quite past the second bin, a Chevy truck differential, obsolescing even as the paint dried, reached up and ripped the left sleeve and epaulet off my uniform shirt.

"Shit!" I yelled. The shirt was one of two official pilot-type shirts I had to my name.

Jimmy heard me and laughed. "Didn't think yud'd git *that* far," he said. Copilots hate when captains are right, though not nearly as much as captains hate when copilots are right.

Ten feet of slow progress later, I dropped my prized flashlight into a bin full of front-end assemblies. While retrieving it, a giant cotter key honed to a razor's edge cost me the other shirtsleeve. I'm not sure what ripped the crotch out of my trousers.

The playful Jimmy couldn't resist pulling a few G's along the way. The G-forces pinned me to the freight and slowed my progress. I expected as much and would certainly have done the same to him if the roles were reversed.

After a few more obstacles, I made it to the rear of the airplane and "J" compartment. The compartment, about the size of a hot tub, was recessed into the floor of the airplane. We called it the "orchestra pit." The shepherd's hook hung exactly where Ike said it would be, right over the tail wheel bay.

Ike, however, never mentioned anything about a rat.

Yet there it was, directly below the shepherd's hook. The rodent's demon-red eyes glowed in my flashlight beam. I attempted to scare it away with loud curses and even blitzed it with ignition switches I found in a freight bin. It didn't budge. There was no way in hell I was climbing off that last freight bin with the rat on the floor. I hate rats. No, let me be honest. I *fear* rats.

I tried a few more scare tactics, even made some goofy cat noises. The rat just stared at me, not the least intimidated by my antics. As Jim cut lazy circles in the night sky over St. Louis, I started another low crawl back to the cockpit, drawing heavily on my infantry training. I knew Jimmy would have some ideas about how to take care of the rat. He seemed to know everything else about the freight-flying business.

"Rat? Ju say 'rat?' He have a ticket? No rats flies free on Universal Air Transport."

"I'm not kiddin', Jimmy. A rat, a big one!" I held my hands about two feet apart.

"We got's ta get that tail wheel down, pardner," he said, unimpressed by the size estimate of Superrodent.

"How would you handle the rat, Jimmy?"

"Personally, I'd jist stomp the lil' bastard, or mebbe give 'im a dirty look. That'd be 'nough right there for it to commit su'cide. But you bein' a yankee an' a city kid an' all, ya might wants to grab that CO_2 bottle over there and take care of 'im."

"We don't have a fire, Jimmy, we have a rat!"

"Man, this airline's jist gots to start teachin' you new guys the 'portant things in ground school," Jimmy said. He turned around in his seat and flipped on the overhead cockpit light. He studied the condition of my clothes—what was left of them.

"The rat do that? He *is* a big 'un."

It wasn't that funny. The shirts were four bucks each; the trousers set me back nine, on sale at Sears.

"So what do I do with the C02 bottle?"

"Ya needs a chem'stry lesson too? Just spray the shit out o' that rat. The C02'll freeze it, make that little bastard harder than Chinese 'rithmetic. C02's better'n a shotgun, works on wasps too. I ever tell you 'bout the time..."

"Sounds like a good plan to me," I said, interrupting yet another Jimmy story. Armed with the lethal C02 bottle, I started to leave the cockpit. I couldn't wait to get at the rat.

"Hang on a minute, pardner," Jimmy said. He had further instructions. "Now when that rat thaws a bit, it'll come right back ta life. And don't asks me how, it jist will! So, when ya gits it froze reeeal good, use the bottom o' the bottle ta mash it."

"Gotcha!"

"One more thing," Jimmy added.

"Yeah?"

"Don't quits poundin' too soon. Rats die hard."

"Gotcha!" I started to leave. Jimmy stopped me again.

"What!?"

"By the way," he said, "I could use a set o' shocks for my pick-up, a '52 Chevy. See what ya kin do for me on the way back."

Universal Air Transport pilots felt free to maintain their automobiles with parts they hauled. General Motors never seemed to miss them, though it might explain why some cars arrive at dealerships lacking components.

My progress over the top of the freight bins was lizard-like and a lot faster on the next trip since the condition of my clothes was no longer an issue. In a few minutes I was again face to face with the rat. It hadn't moved. To my credit, I gave it one last chance to scurry up out of the orchestra pit and hide under the freight bins. I tossed two dozen more ignition switches at it. But the rat nimbly sidestepped my pitches and held its ground. It stared into the flashlight beam, sizing me up with little verminous eyes, flicking its hairless pink tail defiantly.

"You had your chance. Say your prayers," I said, arming the fire extinguisher. From atop the freight bin, I reached out as close to my adversary as possible and let loose with a white, noisy cloud of C02. I emptied the entire bottle. "Take that, you little bastard," I said through clenched teeth. It felt good. *Damn* good.

A ghostly-white tail, no longer flicking, pushed up through the spray on the compartment floor like a too-late flag of surrender. I shivered at the thought then went into action again. I jumped off the freight bin and, before the rat had a chance to even think about thawing out, I finished the job. I smashed it with the bottom of the empty CO2 bottle for a long time. When the rodent was thin enough to slide under a bank vault door, I hit it once more for good measure, discarded the bottle and grabbed the shepherd's hook.

I lifted the cover off the tail wheel bay. The lights of St. Louis twinkled far below. The twin Pratt and Whitney 2800s rumbled outside like distant, racing locomotives. I studied the tail wheel apparatus for a few minutes with my flashlight, trying to decide where to lift it. After I figured it out, I held the flashlight in the crook of my neck to keep it directed on the operation and, using both hands, lifted the tail wheel off the uplock with the shepherd's hook. I wiggled the hook free of the tail wheel, which fell and locked into the down position with a gladdening clunk that rocked the back of the airplane.

Another job well done by Pete Fusco, first officer and *rattus gargantuous* exterminator extraordinaire.

Out of the corner of my eye I saw the rat move. It *moved*. I swear it did! I recoiled. My prized flashlight fell away from my neck and headed for the open tail wheel bay. I grabbed for the flashlight. I caught it.

And dropped the shepherd's hook out the bottom of the airplane.

"Shit!"

I watched the hook for a long minute as it fell away from the airplane in a wobbling spiral. It disappeared in the night lights of St. Louis.

Without knowing exactly why I did it, I picked up Superrodent by the tail—maybe it hadn't moved after all—and dropped it out of the airplane. It just felt like the thing to do.

One more time I fought my way back to the cockpit, gashing my right flying boot on a radiator. I reported to Captain Jimmy.

"I killed the rat."

"Good. And I see we gots a green light on the tail wheel. *Real* good!"

"Uh, Jimmy, I got something to tell ya."

"What?"

"I dropped the shepherd's hook out of the airplane. It was an accident." I was afraid he'd be pissed.

After a long moment of silence, Jimmy turned to me. His face lit up. "Dropped the ol' shepherd's hook right outta the airplane," he said to himself. He started laughing. "Imagine that? Imagine a shepherd's hook, a goddamn *shepherd's* hook, fallin' straight from Heaven! Hey, what if it landed right in front o' some drunk leavin' a bar? What wouldn't ya gives ta see the look on that guy's face? Hell, man, that'ud make *me* quit drinkin'. How 'bouts the rat? Didja throw the rat out too?"

"Yes, as a matter of fact I did," I said, surprised he had asked. "But I'm not sure why."

"Who cares *why* ya done it? Main thing is ya *done* it. They's hope fer ya, pardner. Ya gots potential."

The entertainment prospects of a shepherd's hook and freeze-dried, flattened rat falling from the night sky amused Jimmy out of all proportion. Between bouts of unmanageable hysterical laughter, he asked if I'd land the aircraft at St. Louis. Everything is funnier at four in the morning.

As a footnote, I have related the shepherd's hook story with some reluctance. Liability claims, I'm told, have no statute of limitations. A belated legal reprisal is not entirely out of the question. I've assuaged my guilt over the years by believing that the hook and the dead rat really did fall near or, better yet, on *top* of, a drunken wife-beater or other scoundrel who took it as a sign and reformed. The guy might have even seen it as a calling and turned to preaching. Perhaps somewhere in St. Louis there's a church called "The First Church of Jesus Christ Bombardier." I'm the patron saint.

A footnote: Aviation has its ironies. About fifteen years later, Jimmy needed a job and hired on to a night-freight outfit at which I was flying captain on a Convair 640. Jimmy found himself flying copilot for *me!*

"What say, pardner?" he said on the night we were to fly together, then restated the best piece of advice he had ever given me and which had, alas, come to pass: "Always treats the copilot right, 'cause someday the sumbitch could be the captain."

I treated him with the respect due any former teacher. To my great delight, Jimmy ribbed me all night from the right seat. When he wasn't sleeping.

*   *   *   *

The Christmas holidays approached. Production at the auto plants slowed and Universal Air Transport's business slowed along with them. Actual furlough notices soon followed rumors of pilot furloughs for those of us hanging by a thread at the bottom of the seniority list. Ominous aviation rumors always come true and are usually worse than expected, while good rumors materialize only infrequently and seldom live up to their advance billing.

I got a call on Christmas Eve morning informing me that I was to fly one last trip later that day, after which I could expect to be furloughed until spring.

The trip would be with Bill "Firecan" Haddock, a kind of pilot time capsule from an earlier age in aviation. Firecan, who had learned to fly in the 1930s, fiercely objected to any new aviation technology, especially the advent of jets. Jet-powered aircraft, he maintained, were inherently dangerous. They flew too high, landed too fast and were an insult to time-honored and revered devices such as the reciprocating engine and propeller. Firecan felt that jets were no closer to true airplanes than the turbine-powered bomb that held the speed record at Bonneville was to the 1950 Mercury he drove.

"Jets! What a lotta bullshit! Who'd want to fly on an airplane powered by blowtorches connected by a garden hose to a wing full of lamp oil?" went a favorite Firecanism. "Those jets are nuthin' more than firecans. You won't catch me on no firecan!"

Naturally, he became known as "Firecan." The merest indiscretion or stray comment could earn a pilot a nickname at Universal Air Transport. Al Roberts, a frugal character who had repaired a hole in his uniform trousers with a rubber tire patch, lived out his days as, naturally, "Tirepatch." Once a nickname was bestowed, there was no appeal.

Women pilots, according to the gospel of Firecan, presented an even greater threat to aviation than the jet engine. He told anyone who would listen that women were better suited for making peach preserves than flying airplanes. A lot of pilots back then felt the same way. Some still do. If the business of aviation carries any shame, it's the institutionalized exclusion of women—and minorities—that marked the first 75 years or so. I'm as guilty as anyone. How could we men have been so stupid? Welcome aboard ladies. You sure look cute in those hats.

Despite his reactionary convictions, Firecan was really one of the most pleasant people I've ever known. His querulous front was part of his charm and also a defense mechanism, a shield against unwanted encroachments of the modern world.

Firecan and I were to fly spare airplane and ground handling equipment parts from Detroit to Universal Air Transport outstations in Cleveland and Boston then return to Detroit. We also had on board about 300 frozen turkeys, the company's Christmas present to outstation employees. We were heavy.

The turkey bit appealed to my Christmas spirit. I stopped on the way to the airport and purchased two Santa Claus hats, one for Firecan and one for myself. As I expected, the flinty Firecan didn't think much of the idea. He studied the Santa hat as if he had never seen one before.

"What in God's name am I 'sposed to do with this damn thing?" he asked, puffing on a cheap cigar, which he was never without. He rubbed a stubble of beard on his chin quizzically before answering his own question. "Shit in it?"

"It's Christmas Eve, Firecan," I appealed.

"So what?" he said. "You're pretty happy for a guy 'bout to be laid off, ain't ya? You oughta be standin' in some bread line 'stead of pretending you're Santa Claus out wastin' your money on stupid-lookin' hats."

"Aw, c'mon, Firecan, everybody oughta be happy on Christmas Eve," I said. "Hell, I've worked for nine solid months. That's the longest I've ever worked at one time. I got a few dollars saved up and I'm ready for a break." In those early days I never considered flying to be a full-time, year-round occupation. I actually looked forward to layoffs, seasonal or otherwise. I once even volunteered to be fired, but that's another story.

After much persuasion, Firecan and I walked out to the loaded C-46, wearing the Santa Claus hats and carrying our leather flight bags. Firecan was chomping his cigar and griping. I whistled a Christmas tune and made plans for squandering the money I had saved.

We left Detroit for Cleveland about four in the afternoon. The weather was clear and unseasonably warm when we departed. Halfway across Lake Erie at 7,000 feet the temperature fell a few degrees. We flew into snow and light icing conditions on the edge of a snowstorm brewing over the lake, all part of the "lake effect" that makes living on the shores of the Great Lakes so quaint.

The icing was not a great concern since Dumbo could handle a lot of ice. At the time I had no idea just how much.

"Got a little ice on the leading edge of the wing, Firecan," I said, looking out my window. "Wanna use the boots?" As a young copilot I was always overeager, a condition that corrected itself with time.

"Nah," Firecan said, looking out his window at the left wing. "Let 'er build up a little more before you use the boots. That much won't even faze this big windwagon. It eats ice."

Unlike modern jet aircraft that run heated air from the engines to the wing at the flick of a switch, the C-46 was equipped with deicing boots. They required patience and finesse. A little experience didn't hurt either. The trick was to wait until the wing accumulated just the right amount of ice before hitting the switch, which inflated the rubber boots in a sequence along the leading edge of the wing and tail, expanding the boots and breaking off the ice. Too soon and it would do little good, too late and you could have too much ice on the wings to break off. The worst possible situation was to have the deicing boots inflated under the accumulating ice, expanding without any effect inside an icy shell. But that could only happen during severe icing conditions and we were a long way from that.

I had never experienced severe icing. Fact is, I thought it one of those fanciful weather phenomena dreamed up my meteorologists to fill weather books that no one ever read. And even if severe icing did exist, it was the kind of thing that only happened to other pilots.

Cleveland was overcast when we landed. A north wind was hard at work pulling moisture from Lake Erie and magically, secretly transforming it to snow inside the clouds.

Firecan kept an eye on the weather but I paid no notice. I was having too much fun throwing frozen turkeys out the cargo door to the waiting ground crew. Firecan wore the Santa hat but refused to "ho ho ho" along with me. I didn't mention it but with the hat raked off to the side of his head and the cigar in his mouth, Firecan resembled the Grinch far more than Santa Claus.

We had only been on the ground a few minutes when December's early darkness fell on the airport like someone had pulled down a shade. Even as I "ho ho hoed," the air took on a bittersweet dampness. The temperature dropped. The ceiling lowered, as if the skies could no longer support the weight of the snow within. It began to snow heavily, a Christmas Eve present for kids in Cleveland.

"What a revoltin' development," Firecan said, looking at the falling snow. Just about everything was a "revoltin' development" to Firecan Haddock.

"Just a little snow for Christmas Eve, Firecan," I said. "I love it!" I began whistling *I'm Dreaming of a White Christmas.*

"Yeah, maybe if you was home sittin' in front of a fireplace with a couple tomatoes on your lap and a hot toddy, but you seem to forget we gotta fly all night in this stuff," he said. "Let's hurry up and get the hell out of here before these assholes close the airport and we get stuck in Cleveland 'til spring. Shit, we still gotta go to Boston and back to Detroit before we're done. Let's get this windwagon in the air."

Firecan and I helped the ground crew finish unloading the aircraft. We still had a considerable amount of freight, including some very heavy fork-lift parts, bound for Boston. And more frozen turkeys.

I closed the cargo door while Firecan cranked up the engines. The altimeter had fallen considerably in the short time we were on the ground. Wet snow, the kind that packs with one hand into the hardness of a hockey puck, covered the airport. We had the aircraft de-iced, taxied out and took off. Firecan was flying. He turned east, climbed to nine thousand feet and headed for Boston.

And directly into the teeth of the worst winter storm in twenty years. Postage stamp-sized snowflakes pelted the windshield. From inside the cockpit, the impression was that of a biblical swarm of white locust unleashed by some pissed-off Old Testament prophet.

Using my prized seven-dollar, five-cell chromed flashlight, I watched ice accumulate on the nuts that secured the windshield wipers. No matter the airplane, the wiper nuts are always the first parts to pick up ice. With a little experience, a pilot can judge how much ice is on the airframe just by looking at the nuts. They were lightly coated with bristly rime ice, the so-called "fuzzy nuts" stage. No big deal.

"The nuts are a little fuzzy, Firecan," I said. "I'll check the wings." I inspected the wing leading edges. A neat white line of ice ran along the boots.

"Much out there?" Firecan asked.

"A little."

"Keep an eye on it," he said. "No sleepin' for you on this leg." He knew me pretty well.

We flew about seventy-five more miles into the precipitation. The clouds thickened; the white locusts flew in tighter formation against the windshield. I checked the wiper nuts again. They had progressed past fuzzy. Enough ice had accumulated on the wings to warrant use of the boots. I inflated the boots and the ice broke away.

"The boots work," I said.

"Good, we're gonna need 'em," Firecan said, reaching up to give the props a shot of alcohol. Ice flicked off the props onto the side of the fuselage with the sound of distant tin drums. Watchful but unalarmed, we continued, certain that we could deal with the weather. The beast, after all, was at home in any habitat; it had avoided extinction for many years by sneering, no, *spitting*, in the face of conditions far worse than this.

After another thirty miles or so, the precipitation grew so thick that my flashlight could not penetrate well enough to illuminate the wing. I needed the "Grimes Light," a hand-held, zillion-watt light gun that hung on the bulkhead behind the copilot. The Grimes Light was also handy for spotting deer on airports and cars with lovers parked along airport fences.

As I turned around to reach for the Grimes light, I knocked my book of William Blake poems to the floor. The book opened to *The Fly*, one of my favorites. Blake hinted at coming events.

"*...I dance and drink and sing
Till some blind hand shall brush my wing.*"

It was not the time to ponder Blake's genius. I grabbed the Grimes Light and aimed it at the wing. An inch of ice jacketed the entire leading edge. Walnut-sized ice balls had swallowed the wiper nuts. The fight was on.

I was busy as hell, taking turns running the boots and cycling alcohol to the props. Ice broke off the leading edge, avalanched across the wing and disappeared behind us into the dark sky. Ice thrown from the props pounded the sides of the fuselage, the sound of not-so-distant tin drums. I changed the prop pitch now and then so that the hubs would not ice up. My old pal St. Elmo joined in, unleashing his blue flames of static electricity against the windshield. Had he come to lead us to safety with his torch? I sure hoped so.

Indicated airspeed began to decrease. Firecan bumped up the throttles in response. He hunkered down in his seat. I didn't like the look in his eyes, that of the inborn human dread of the elements at their spiteful worst. We were a testimony to the cruel duality of nature. How beautiful the falling snow must have looked from the ground, the perfect Christmas Eve diorama. Inside the cockpit it felt less and less like Christmas. William Blake would have loved the irony.

"Tell center we want to descend," Firecan said.

Center cleared us down to seven thousand feet. Instead of increasing, the temperature dropped a degree or two. We were in a temperature inversion. Ice accumulated at a faster rate.

I flicked the glass on the temp gauge with my index finger, the conditioned if irrational response of pilots who don't want to believe what they read on an instrument. The needle didn't move. It seldom does.

We descended to five thousand. The temperature rose again; the ice worsened.

"See if center knows the tops," Firecan said.

I asked center about the tops. The controller told us that another pilot recently reported the tops of the clouds in the area at eleven thousand feet. Firecan decided to try to climb out of the icing. I obtained clearance for eleven thousand feet.

Like a weary mountain climber with a burdensome backpack near the summit, Firecan added power and started uphill. We needed six or seven thousand feet and we would be in the clear on top of the clouds, where at least some of the ice would flake off the airplane like cheap paint.

During the climb the ice formed almost faster than the boots could get rid of it. The props drank our limited supply of alcohol with the eager thirst of a wino. Ice flew off the prop blades in a cannonade against the fuselage. From the cockpit it sounded like stowaway lunatics in the back of the ship were banging on garbage can lids with hammers.

Dumbo seemed up to the challenge. The props chewed through the heavy freezing precipitation. At ten thousand feet we caught glimpses of the moon and stars through the ragged cloud tops. Encouraged, we kept flying east, further into the ice. Airspeed continued to bleed as the ice metastasized on the wing behind the boots and on other parts of the ship that could not be deiced.

Firecan, who understood large radial engines better than any man I ever knew and always respected their limitations, grabbed the throttles and pushed them forward. Manifold pressure edged into the red band.

"Check your manifold pressure, Firecan," I said.

"Fuck the manifold pressure!" Firecan said. "They made a million Pratt and Whitneys. They only made one Firecan."

And one Pete!

I laughed uneasily and lit a cigarette. I had watched other captains exceed engine limitations, some on a regular basis, but never Firecan. He was undoubtedly the most prudent pilot I had ever flown with. When Firecan overboosted those engines I became worried.

But even with the extra power, we were too heavy with accumulated ice to reach the clear sky above the clouds. We wasted another five or ten minutes trying. The moon and stars peeked through the overcast, teasing us. Or perhaps they were luring us, drawing us into a trap as cunningly as a pack of wild dogs. Truth is, we lured ourselves. It was Christmas Eve and we wanted to deliver our spare parts and turkeys to Boston and get back to Detroit by morning. Christmas played far too great a part in our decision to press on. Some permutations fit in the flying equation better than others. Don't ever let Christmas kill you.

Hanging in the tops, we enjoyed one last peek at the moon and stars. Firecan pushed the throttles almost to the stops to reach them.

It didn't help; the beast was too loaded with ice to climb another foot. We sank into the overcast, back into the icing, back into uncertainty.

While we had been trying to climb on top, the precipitation in the clouds below had changed from wet snow to large sleety pellets that stuck to the airframe with renewed stubbornness.

"What a revoltin' development!" Firecan said. "We shoulda turned around the minute we got into this shit, but that ain't gonna help much now. We gotta get this thing on the ground. We oughta be abeam Buffalo. It's probably the closest airport. Maybe we can duck in there. Tell center we're gonna descend and turn toward Buffalo."

The aircraft we had that night was equipped with Wilcox radios, unsophisticated high-output devices built at a time when transmitting *through* mountains was the norm. They were known as "Hogcallers." Nonetheless, a half dozen calls to center went unanswered. Ice on the radio antennas had silenced us. Ice on the navigation antennas prevented us from even determining our position. I kept trying to raise someone, all the time wondering just how soon the steadily decreasing airspeed would equal the stall speed, which increased with each pound of ice. When the two speeds met, the C-46 and its crew of two would fall out of the sky like a giant snow cone.

"Can't get anyone on the radio," I said.

"We're on our own, goddamnit," Firecan said. "Let's hope there ain't anybody below us. Not that anyone else'd be stupid enough to fly into this."

Firecan started a shallow turn to the left and rolled out in the general direction of Buffalo. He descended to five thousand feet. The temperature dropped again.

"How much ice is on your carb air intake?" he asked.

I shined the Grimes Light on the carburetor air intake. The intake, normally the size of the proverbial breadbox, was choked with ice. I couldn't have jammed both fists in it at once. If the intakes closed much more, the air-starved engines would quit. Ice can kill you in a variety of ways. I told Firecan what I saw.

"Shit!" was all he said. The word covers most adverse airplane situations. "Shit!" is often the last word spoken on the cockpit voice recorder. The word shares, according to a casual survey I've conducted of cockpit voice recorder transcripts of crashes, about equal billing with last desperate appeals to the Creator for mercy.

"Still better than gettin' shot at, isn't it Firecan?" I said. I knew Firecan had seen action as a pilot in World War Two. I meant it as a joke to lighten things up a bit but Firecan seemed to be thinking seriously about the comment. He looked at me.

"I've been shot at and I've been in ice. I'd take gettin' shot at over ice any day," he said.

I regretted mentioning it.

Firecan descended further to about four thousand feet. The clouds thinned a bit as we flew north. Ice stopped accumulating as rapidly but the ice on the airplane seemed as intent on remaining as a drunken party guest. The boots fought a losing battle, inflating gamely but ineffectually under the heavy layer of ice. No, not exactly *ice* anymore, more like white army ants on the march against a large animal in distress.

Prop alcohol was spent; the blades were caked with ice. The prop domes grew irregular, vestigial stumps of ice that turned crazily. The airplane began to vibrate as if Dumbo, disgusted with its inept operators, was attempting to shake loose its frozen riders on its own.

"We shouldn't have wasted that time trying to climb out of this. Jesus, but this happened quick! Never saw ice like this in my life." Firecan said. His voice was a mixture of self-recrimination and apology for my imminent death.

"We were only in it a little while, Firecan," I said. "Who could have figured it would build this fast?"

"I sure didn't! Try getting Buffalo VOR. We can't be that far away." Firecan said.

I tuned in Buffalo VOR but heard only static. Little red flags on the VOR head told me I was wasting my time.

Firecan descended to a little less than four thousand feet. The Allegheny Mountains were somewhere below and he dared not drop any lower. Sweat poured from his forehead. He went into an intense survival mode, playing out precious airspeed a half-knot at a time to hold altitude.

The props howled a pained, tuneless soprano. I've forgotten most of the details of that night, but not the sound of those screeching props. Nor will I ever shake the nagging existential angst that comes with once having been eyeball-to-eyeball with the ugly face of Death. It never goes away.

Pilots live with a suppressed awareness, just below their consciousness, that a million unpleasant things lie in wait. It comes with the job. I could accept the fact that we had flown into severe icing and might lose our lives. What I had trouble accepting was the suddenness of it all, just how *quickly* things went to hell that night. In a matter of minutes, the always uneasy truce with the elements had escalated into a hopelessly one-sided contest.

And if I learned one thing that night, it's that the great aviation writer Ernie Gann was wrong, dead wrong, about fate being the hunter. Bullshit! Fate is *not* the hunter. Bad judgment is the hunter; presumption is the hunter; ineptitude is the hunter; stupidity is the hunter. Pilots who die in airplanes often stalk themselves all the way to their own graves.

Firecan and I had done just that. We had, in effect, dialed Death on the phone. The worst part was waiting for someone to answer.

Luckily for Firecan and me, ever-dispassionate Death seems to make up the words to the song as it goes along. Retribution shares the melody line with exoneration. Airborne fortunes can change rapidly; that night they changed in our favor. Not a lot, but enough.

The heart of the storm had moved—uncharacteristically—south of Lake Erie. Precipitation thinned steadily as we flew north toward Buffalo. The temperature warmed a bit. Some ice broke away from the antennas and we got our Wilcox Hogcallers and navigation radios back. I tried the Buffalo VOR again. A faint Morse code identification leached through my headset. The red flags disappeared from view. Needles snapped to attention. Buffalo was a little to the left. The C-46 carried no Distance Measuring Equipment. We guessed Buffalo Airport to be about seventy-five miles away.

"I got Buffalo VOR," I said.

"First good news since we left Cleveland," Firecan said. He tracked toward Buffalo. "We're probably still gonna die but at least we'll know where we were."

We were encouraged but, even with almost full power, we couldn't hold altitude. The beast descended inexorably, its foot stuck in the tarpits. Gravity tugged at us. Nature may abhor a vacuum but it absolutely detests anything too heavy and too slow to fly.

"I bin savin' a little power," Firecan said. He pushed the throttles to the stops. The engines shrieked dissatisfaction; they warned of impending failure.

"I think we're gonna void the warranty, Firecan," I joked.

"I wouldn't have it any other goddamn way," he said.

The airplane quit descending quite as fast.

"I guess we'll give them turkeys away to poor folks in Buffalo!" Firecan wisecracked loudly out of the corner of his mouth. Not that he fooled me. He had bitten his unlit cigar in half. All my cigarettes were gone; I relit smashed butts that I had already relit once. At one point, I lit the tip of my finger with my Zippo.

A voice cackled on Buffalo Approach Control frequency. The controller was talking to another pilot, something about the airport being closed. The pilot inquired about weather at other airports, the weather in general and even the white Christmas they were having. The conversation seemed like it would last forever. We couldn't wait that long. Since the other pilot wouldn't shut up, I transmitted *over* him—no problem for a Wilcox Hogcaller. I keyed the mike button and more watts of power than that of many commercial radio stations put me on the air on top of the other guy. I told Buffalo Approach in the calmest voice I could manage that we were iced-up and headed for his airport.

The controller informed us that the airport was closed because of deep snow on the runway. Stand by, he said, and he'd find out about other airports in the area.

"Stand by my ass! Ask him if it's still snowin'," Firecan said.

"Is it still snowing at the field?" I asked.

"No, the snow's stopped. We have overcast skies at four hundred feet. It's clear below. There's eight to ten inches of heavy snow on the runways. Plowing crews are working on runway five now. I repeat, the airport's closed!"

"Tell 'im that it's real good the airport's closed," Firecan said, "'cause we wouldn't want to have to wait for anyone else before we can land. Tell 'im we're covered with ice and we're landing at Buffalo! Tell 'im he can kiss my ass if he don't like it."

I relayed the message to approach control, editing it for broadcast.

"Just tell us what you guys need," the controller said. "I'll start by getting the snow plows off the runway. There's not many targets tonight. I should be able to pick you up on radar."

"Now that's one government employee I don't mind payin' for," Firecan said. "Tell 'im to turn on the approach lights and any other lights they've got down there. Tell 'im we're either gonna land on runway five or the highway outside the airport!"

I left out the part about the highway.

"Universal, are you declaring an emergency?" the controller asked.

"What about it, Firecan?" I said. It sounded like a good idea to me.

"Hell no! That ain't gonna help."

I still smile when I think about it. In the years since, I've seen pilots declare emergencies for the smallest mechanical annoyance. But Firecan, waiting for Death to pick up the phone, wouldn't even consider it. Declaring an emergency was something only the new crop of pilots did, not crusty old pros. For one thing, it would have required paperwork, a by-product of the modern age that Firecan loathed almost as much as jet engines and female pilots. As it turned out, we filled out a lot of paperwork anyway.

"We'll do what we're gonna do and worry about it later," he said. "You can declare all the emergencies you want when we get this thing on the ground."

Somehow it made perfect sense to me at the time.

A long minute or two later the approach controller picked us up on radar. He said we were fifty miles out. We were at two thousand feet and still descending despite Firecan's best efforts.

"Tell 'im I'm gonna go direct to the compass locator for runway five and intercept the localizer there," Firecan said. "That'll save a minute or two."

I relayed the request to the controller.

"Good luck, guys," he said.

The old Curtiss bucked to announce a stall several times, but trudged on, seemingly as intent on living as Firecan and I. What had been a complicated equation was now a matter of very basic mathematics. We were at a given altitude at a given distance and the airport was at a given point. From here on, our survival was strictly a matter of pass or fail. No retakes. No grading on the curve. Definitely no points added for neatness. Unlike my elementary and high school days, there'd be no making it up in the summer.

Ice covered most of the windshield; only a few clear patches allowed us to see outside. I glanced at the wing through one of the gaps in the windshield behind my right shoulder. My mouth fell open. Everything I could see was blanketed white. The boots had long since lost the battle. They were entombed uselessly beneath a couple inches of ice. Ice on top of the wing had formed into drifts, an Arctic snowscape in miniature. I quit looking out the window.

"How bad's that wing?" Firecan asked. I think he already knew the answer but was just trying to keep me in the loop. At any rate, he was far too busy to look for himself.

"Pretty bad!" I said. "At least an inch thick. From what I can see, the ice runs several feet back from the leading edge. The boots are buried but I'll give 'em another try." I reached up to cycle the boots.

Firecan grabbed my hand. "Don't use those boots!" he said. "The last thing we need right now is for the ice to break away from that leading edge."

"Why's that?" I asked. I thought Firecan had lost his mind.

"If it breaks off at the leading edge, the ice on the wing behind it will make a spoiler," he said. "Then for sure we're dead."

I went from praying that the ice on the wings would break off to praying that it wouldn't. A pilot's prayers must be quite specific.

"You'll intercept the localizer at the locator in about two miles," the controller advised. "The plows are getting off the runway now. I've called the crash trucks for you, even though you guys don't seem to want to declare an emergency."

"Yep, that's definitely one government employee I don't mind payin' for," Firecan said. Using the ADF needle and the controller's advance notice, Firecan captured the localizer with no wasted motion to eat up airspeed or altitude.

We were five miles from the runway. Our altitude was a mere six hundred feet. We continued to sink. The engines had been at maximum power for what seemed like days. I kept waiting for them to disintegrate. Even Pratt and Whitneys have limits.

About three miles out and lower than I care to recall or report, we broke free of the clouds. I saw the ground through a small clear spot about the size of a coffee can on the ice-covered forward windshield. If we made the runway, Firecan would have to land the airplane looking out the same hole. No way, I thought.

"I can see the ground, Firecan," I said.

Firecan nodded but didn't say anything. He was far too busy trying to keep a glacier flying on the localizer. We'd only get one shot at the airport; go-around was not an option. If we strayed much from the localizer we were doomed. I remember thinking we were probably doomed anyway. My dad's insurance business never sounded better.

The controller asked our altitude, which was about one hundred feet.

"Tell that guy to quit bothering us," Firecan said.

I repeated the message word for word. The controller understood. The radio fell silent. There really wasn't much left for anyone to say.

Airspeed was well below published stall speed. The airplane continued to descend but, more important, it continued to fly. Well, not exactly *flying* at that point, but a more than acceptable imitation.

Through the small unobstructed spot in the forward windshield I saw a brightly lighted Christmas tree lot pass under us. All the tree shoppers looked up. They pointed at the howling, wobbling, football-shaped ice sculpture passing over their heads. Ah, the show business that is aviation.

I spotted the approach lights, the most beautiful Christmas lights I will ever see in my life. The runway and runway lights were not visible due to the deep snow but I saw the lights on the snow plows sitting off to both sides of what I assumed was the runway. The plowing crews had a front row seat for the arrival of the unplanned visitor from Planet Ice. I privately speculated that we'd crash about a half mile short of the airport, right on top of a highway full of last-minute Christmas shoppers.

"I can see the approach lights, Firecan," I said.

Firecan acknowledged by pursing his lips and setting his jaw a bit tighter. A mile out the beast shuddered, again advertising a stall. Firecan cashed in about fifty feet of altitude for a knot or two of airspeed. Dumbo agreed to the trade and kept going. By virtue of its beastly will and little else, it *kept going.*

"Runway's dead ahead, Firecan." I said, peering out the little opening in the windshield. "Ya think we're gonna make it?"

"Ask me that about a minute from now," he said out of the corner of his mouth. He bit through another unlit cigar. "Shit, these cigars cost seven cents apiece."

Firecan joked because he knew that the slightest bit of panic in his voice would contaminate the cockpit instantly. I laughed as much as the situation permitted.

The landing lights illuminated a chain-link airport fence, the only thing between us, the runway and the morning newspapers. Christmas is a slow news day. Our failure, our imprudence, our *epitaph*, would surely make page one above the fold, the headline in the *Buffalo Evening News* a roaring sixty-point Bodoni: "CARGO CREW KILLED IN CRASH ON HIGHWAY, UNEXPLAINED FROZEN TURKEYS LITTER SITE."

"You gonna use the gear, Firecan?" I asked.

"I bin thinkin' 'bout it," he said. "What the hell, we're here now. Go ahead and drop the wheels. I'll trade places with you at the windshield." While he continued to fly the airplane, Firecan leaned toward the center of the cockpit and trained his eye on the one small iceless patch of windshield. What he was about to try was the equivalent of docking a submarine using only the periscope.

I lowered the landing gear. The increased drag caused the ship to sink a few more feet. Firecan had decided not to use the flaps. They were probably too ice-bound to come down anyway. Even if they came down, there was the chance one side might hang up. We had enough problems already.

"Think we got a shot at clearing that fence, Firecan?" I asked.

"Either that or take the goddamn thing with us to the coffee shop," he said. His tone implied more faith in the C-46 than in the fence. He unbuckled his seat belt and leaned further forward to get a better view out of the ice hole.

"We're not gonna clear the fence," Firecan muttered, mostly to himself, "but we'll make the airport...and we're still right-side up. Two out of three ain't bad."

Firecan instinctively jammed the throttles, which were already at the stops. It was maddening not being able to see outside. I kept telling myself that we were in a C-46. Like rats, they die hard, or so I'd heard. We'd be okay unless the cockpit hit the fence first. If the landing gear behind us hit it, too bad for the fence. The approach lights were a mere formality. I waited.

"Here comes the fence," Firecan yelled. "Hang on!"

I'm not enough of a writer to describe the sound in the cockpit of a Curtiss C-46 main landing gear ripping out a length of chain-link fence by the roots. Those who have listened helplessly, eyes watered and fists clenched, to their skull giving up a wisdom tooth to a pair of dentist's pliers have a place to start. To belabor the point, it's a good thing no one ever tried to land a C-46 on an aircraft carrier. If the arresting cables didn't snap, Dumbo would have dragged the ship to the center of Kansas.

The fence trailing off the gear became a garden rake that harvested the approach lights. Airplane, fence and dismembered lights touched down at the runway end in a kind of slow motion writhe with the engines wide open.

Firecan slapped the throttles closed. The beast rolled a few hundred feet in the deep snow and stopped. Nothing pretty about it but we were alive, a stunning endorsement of Curtiss' unloved ugly duckling, Pratt and Whitney's warrior engines, Firecan's magnificent flying skills and our sheer dumb luck. A *lot* of sheer dumb luck.

Crash trucks fought their way through the snow to reach the airplane. The plowing crews hollered at us from the ground. They asked if we were okay and, in the same voice, demanded we move the aircraft, fence, approach lights and all, off the runway. The plowing crews acted like they were pissed at us. *Pissed at us!*

I suppose they had their job to do too.

The crews looked far away to me; their voices came from another dimension. I lacked the energy to do anything but stare at them like a penguin out the little ice hole. I think I gave them the finger. It's what I would have done in those days.

For all kinds of reasons, moving the airplane was out of the question. "I think this Curtiss windwagon's done enough for one day," Firecan said. "What do you think?"

I agreed, nodding my head in deference and homage to the beast.

Firecan shut down the engines. The terminally-strained Pratts coughed out a long sour note followed by a guttural death rattle. An odor of burned oil and scorched metal reached the cockpit. The engines had given their all.

Dumbo dominated the white landscape like a monument to itself, a metaphor of survival and human folly.

It began to snow again. Large flakes fell gently on the stilled beast, unconquered, unconquerable.

I forced open the frozen side window, reached outside and rubbed my fingers over the craggy armor plating of ice on the airplane. Velvety snow landed on my hand and melted, rebaptizing me. Oddly, I felt no great relief. I was just tired, completely exhausted. I could have fallen asleep on the spot. I thought about my mother, how I'd have to call and tell her I wouldn't be home for Christmas. I'd leave out why; she worried too much as it was. I knew I'd spend that Christmas in Buffalo in a bar. I *wanted* to spend that Christmas in a bar. I *needed* to spend that Christmas in a bar. I *did* spend that Christmas in a bar. What's more, I bought a drink for every son of a bitch who wandered in.

Without saying a word, Firecan pulled a couple of cigars out of his flight bag and handed one to me. We lit up and puffed extravagantly, filling the cockpit with an evil-smelling indigo fog.

I'm not usually at a loss for words but I couldn't think of anything to say. As the reality of the unpleasant death we had escaped by inches settled over me, I had the urge to bawl like a baby, let it all out. But pilots don't cry. Somewhere in the measureless reaches of the Federal Air Regulations it's forbidden.

It remained for Firecan to capture the spirit of the moment.

"Pretty good cigars, huh?" he said, slumping back in his seat. He blew an elliptical smoke ring, which he reconfigured pensively into a figure eight with the tip of the cigar. The wobbly digit drifted like a ghostly apparition toward my open window. "Yep, *damn* good cigars!"

I turned to Firecan to acknowledge how wonderful a seven-cent cigar could taste under such ideal circumstances. I let out a choked laugh of glorious life and felt the top of my head. We were still wearing our Santa hats.

"Merry Christmas Firecan, you old fart," I said, pointing to his hat.

Captain Firecan looked at me and felt his head. Then he smiled, a big, untroubled smile, a Christmas Eve smile.

"Never deny a man the right to deceive himself"

Dave Beall, airline pilot and cynic

Prologue to Chapter Four

Someday aviation historians will realize that all the prop-driven airliners of the 1940s and 1950s are gone, as extinct as dinosaurs but without the fossilized remains. They'll wring their hands and ask what became of them? How could so many historically significant aircraft have simply vanished? It'll be in all the flying magazines. There'll be a website: www.greatgoneplanes.com.

If the historians should happen to ask me, all I'll be able to tell them is when and where these aircraft were last seen alive. It was in the late 1960s. They were crammed like convicts on death row into a nondescript patch of flaking asphalt and oil-soaked coral shell ramps in the northwest quadrant of Miami International Airport.

Outsiders and wiseasses called the area "Corrosion Corner." Pilots who worked there preferred, simply, "the Corner." The Corner in those days was something of a final roll call for all the great, near great and not-so-great propeller-driven aircraft discarded by the airlines of the world. Few of these aircraft escaped a stop in the Corner on their way to oblivion. Like a well-run whorehouse, the Corner had something for everybody: a sampling of Lockheeds, from the stately, long-legged Constellations to virile Lodestars; hulking Boeing 307s and their bulbous and awkward sons, the Stratocruisers; anything with propellers ever built by Douglas, up to and including the DC-7, grande dame of all the propliners; irrefutable Curtiss C-46s; exotic, bewildering immigrants such as the Vickers Vanguard and Bristol Britannia; even a few early jets, most notably the lovely but star-crossed deHaviland Comet, which had a tendency in its airline days to implode in flight. Obsolescence ruled the Corner.

As if just being in the Corner wasn't enough humiliation for these aircraft, their replacements were plainly visible to them on the south side of the same Miami airport.

Here the major airlines added to their fleet of new jets almost daily. The jets arrived with such rapidity that one suspected they were being hatched from pods in a greenhouse. Shiny and loud, they broadcast the unswerving progress and dull future of commercial aviation. As much as I longed to fly for the airlines, the south side looked kind of boring.

Pilots who flew from the Corner shared much in common with the airplanes they flew. Both operated on the edge of mainstream aviation, faced an uncertain future and took their chances a day at a time. There was nothing boring about the Corner.

Corner pilots drank, swapped stories and looked for flying jobs in any number of bars located nearby. Of these, Bryson's Bar across the street from the Corner remains the most celebrated. Steven Spielberg is said to have patterned the patrons of the alien freighter pilot saloon in Star Wars after the Bryson's regulars. But Spielberg didn't have a clue. Even the most menacing and repulsive of his intergalactic cutthroats would have run screaming from the Bryson's crowd—especially if they had encountered Three-fingered Hank, to name just one.

4

Looking back from a distance of forty-some years, the wonder is not that I got to Miami International Airport's notorious "Corrosion Corner" in 1967 but that I didn't get there *sooner*. I was an ideal candidate. A stop in the Corner was *de rigueur* for downward-hurtling flying careers such as mine. No matter what I tried, I just couldn't get out of aviation's slow lane. A job with the major airlines seemed more unattainable than ever, despite the fact that they were hiring steadily. I had managed to get a few interviews but they hadn't gone well. Little wonder. I had no college, a few pesky violations and no time in anything even remotely modern. I also struggled against, as First Sergeant Hunt had reminded me daily during my involuntary army stint, a "piss-poor attitude, private."

The Corner chapter of my life began with a phone call from my old friend W.W. Storm during the winter of 1967.

W.W., who had dropped out of sight around the Cleveland area that fall, called collect from Miami. My normal response to collect phone calls in those days was to feign a bad connection. I'd bellow into the phone awhile then hang up. But since it was my parents' phone I accepted the charges. Besides, I had lost touch with W.W. and was curious as to his whereabouts.

"Where the hell you bin, W.W.?

"Miami," he said.

"Wuddaya doin' down there? "You're not in jail are ya? I can't help you with bail money."

"No, I'm not in jail! I'm working," W.W. said. "I'm flying out of the Corner.

"As in 'Corrosion Corner?'" I asked.

"Yeah, as in 'Corrosion Corner,'" he said. "And you ought to get your ass down here, too."

"W.W., I've never heard one good about Corrosion Corner. A lot of the guys at Universal Air Transport worked down there in the winter. You shoulda seen 'em."

"*Seen* 'em? I'm *workin'* with 'em!"

"Yeah, well Corrosion Corner sounds like a better place to *end* a flying career than start one," I said. "No way I'm comin' down there."

I already knew all about Corrosion Corner. Or thought I did. Nothing about the place sounded promising: junk aircraft; lawless operators and smugglers; unpaid vacations in squalid Third World jails; long trips into the night in junk aircraft over vast stretches of shark-invested ocean to places with unpronounceable names; little pay in return for hard work, etc. In other words, a lot like the flying jobs I was able to find in the north but on a grander and more punishing scale.

"Oh, like you've got so much going for you in Ohio flying twin-Beeches," W.W. said. "No, wait, don't tell me, let me guess. You're still waiting for Universal to call you back."

"There's a chance," I said, convincing neither W.W. nor myself. My furlough from Universal Air Transport, which was supposed to last only a few months, was in its third year. Like the spurned movie diva Norma Desmond, my heart raced each time the phone rang, certain that Universal needed my services once again. Waiting to be called back from furlough generates even more pilot anxiety than merely being unemployed.

"You can have a different flying job every day if you want down here," W.W. said. "All kinds of good stuff to fly."

"Like what?" I asked.

"Like a DC-6, for instance," W.W. said. "Flew one the other day down to Aruba and back."

"You mean somebody trained you in a DC-6 just for one trip?"

"Not exactly. You don't have to be trained in the airplane just to ride along as copilot. They don't have many rules down here."

"Neither did Moondog or the Gorotny brothers," I reminded him. "You makin' any money?"

"The DC-6 job paid a hundred bucks. In one day!" he said, rubbing it in. W.W. knew as well as I that it took a week to earn a hundred dollars flying a twin-Beech in Ohio. I was temporarily speechless.

"And some jobs pay even better," W.W. said. "Weather's good, too. I know you're freezin' your ass off in Cleveland."

No argument on that point.

"What're the babes like down there?" I asked. Some things can't be left to chance.

"Same as the ugly ones you run around with in Cleveland, only tanner. There's lots of Cuban babes, too. Ain't nuthin' like 'em in Cleveland, or in the world for that matter. More arriving every day. Come on down to Miami. You won't regret it."

Whether or not I would ultimately regret the decision to go to Miami that long-ago winter is an issue I'm still dealing with. At the time, however, the promise of abundant flying jobs and some decent money was tempting indeed. Except for a little flight instructing and some occasional charter work, there wasn't much reason for me staying in the north. To make matters worse, some of the local operators wouldn't hire me anymore. A few wouldn't even allow me on their airport.

As an added lure, that winter had been particularly ferocious, even for Cleveland. Sunny Florida in the winter seemed an ideal place to search for my future in aviation. Or at least hide awhile and soak up a few rays until it found *me*.

In the end, however, it was W.W.'s portrait of the Cuban babes that clinched it.

"Give me three or four days," I said. "...or maybe even a little longer."

"You must still be driving that piece o' shit DeSoto, huh?"

"No, even worse," I said.

"I won't ask."

"Good."

"By the way, when you get here, try not to say 'Corrosion Corner.'" W.W. cautioned. "And *never* 'Cockroach Corner!' The guys don't like that. We just call it the 'Corner.'"

"I'll try to keep that in mind," I said. Somehow I had never envisioned the pilots who flew out of Corrosion Corner as sensitive types.

"When you get here, come to Bryson's Bar. It's off 36th Street, right across from the Corner. I'll probably be there. If I'm not, someone'll know where I am. See ya."

In 1967, I had been employed in the pilot bush leagues for about five years. While still mostly optimistic about my future, I no longer approached new situations with the soaring hopes that had characterized my early days. Sinking finances, yes; soaring hopes, no. Just where in the hell was all this easy money in flying that everyone kept telling me about? Time had taught me to temper my aviation expectations, much like the lab rat that gets an electric shock on the nose three out of every four pokes at the food button. I had reached the point where I could forecast conditions of any new flying job—invariably grim.

Yet, as I packed my plaid Bermuda shorts and snazzy Hawaiian shirt adorned with hot pink Hibiscus, I had no feeling for what lie ahead in Miami and Corrosion Corner. If I had, I might have elected to remain in Cleveland that winter, forage from my parents' refrigerator and freeze my ass.

In preparation for the Florida sunshine, I purchased a pair of mirrored sunglasses that made me look like a cop and began a grueling, week-long southern odyssey in a rheumatic, petulant, chronically-over-heated 1953 Jaguar sedan that I picked up cheaply when my despised DeSoto would no longer respond to resuscitation. The day I had watched, with unchecked glee, my old DeSoto being shredded I thought I could never learn to hate a car as much again.

Until I bought a used Jaguar.

While it didn't look too bad, the Jag routinely boiled over even in the sub-freezing Cleveland winter temperatures; taking it to Florida bordered on lunacy. The car's first protest came just south of the Cleveland city limits in the form of an electrical fire that filled the interior with acrid smoke. I drove for two hundred miles holding my head out the window, steering with my knees while I cupped my hands over my ears to prevent frostbite. The fire burned itself out but the headlights, turn signals, horn and radio never worked again.

A couple days later, the Jag snarled mutinously through the Smoky Mountains, planning retribution with every mile. By the time I arrived in Miami it had declared unrestricted war on me. The car vented steam from every bodily opening, including the glove compartment. I left the Jag stewing in its juices at the Traveler's Motel, economical residence of choice for Corner pilots. I asked directions and walked the eight or ten blocks to Bryson's Bar to find W.W.

I hesitated at the entrance to Bryson's and looked through the window. Some of the patrons sat in small groups, obviously planning big things over drink. Others sat alone and brooded, as if bemoaning lost opportunities in aviation or love. Still others were raucous, spending money freely on a wide variety of painted ladies. Bryson's looked like my kind of joint. I checked my wallet and entered.

W.W. spotted me. He was hanging out with some other pilots at one of the tables that lined the walls. It was only 10 a.m. but they all looked as if they'd been at the booze for a while. As in all bars, time had a way of standing still in Bryson's.

"Hey, Searchbeam, where the fuck ya bin? I could have *walked* from Cleveland quicker," W.W. blared across the room. "C'mon over."

W.W. introduced me to the others at the table with, "This is Searchbeam, the asshole I was tellin' ya 'bout that jumped ship on the Mafia guys. Did that take some brass gonads or what? Just left 'em sittin' there, the engine running and everything! What was that badass's name? Benny Miles or something?"

"*Smiles!*" I said, looking over my shoulder. "Benny *Smiles*, goddamnit!"

"How 'bout the other guy, the one who's gonna find you someday and cut your dick off? Hal the Sleeper or some dago mob goombah bullshit like that, wasn't it?" W.W. laughed so hard at the recollection of my horrific night in the employ of the Cleveland don that he choked on his beer and turned momentarily blue. I made no effort to help him.

"*Peeper!* Not Sleeper. *Peeper, Sal* the Peeper," I said. "You wouldn't think it was so damn funny if you'd been there. I wish you'd shut up about it."

"Like you'd shut up about it if it happened to me."

W.W. had a point. I would have towed his forwarding address on a banner over Cleveland.

The others at the table snickered. They had no doubt heard the story many times before. I feared W.W. had taken out an ad heralding my Miami arrival in the *Florida Underworld Gazette.* Way too many racket guys lived in Miami for my comfort. I had planned on relating W.W.'s monkey-out-the-window story, honed and embellished to perfection over the years, but it seemed woefully anticlimactic. The Benny Smiles story is hard to top.

"So, how long ya plan on stayin'?" W.W. asked.

"Just till I find something better," I said.

The answer caused another round of snickers at the table.

"Yeah, right. Like the rest of us," W.W. said. "Some guys been here thirty years waiting for something better to come along. They die here, get buried in the Corner."

More snickers.

Let them snicker, I thought. I had a plan. Well, at least I was going to work on a plan. Meanwhile, I'd hang around the Corner, check out the Cuban babes, make a few bucks and build flying time in more advanced (by Corner standards) aircraft than what I had been flying. Then I'd reapply to those airlines that hadn't already turned me down, my attitude well in check, and sweet-talk the personnel department assholes.

And next time I wouldn't be so damn honest on the psychological tests. Although did it really make a difference that I look at the contents of the bowl afterwards? Didn't everyone? Did I really want to fly with someone who didn't?

I'd also learn not to throw away little flat sticks when they came in the mail. That's exactly what American Airlines sent me when I applied. I thought it some kind of a mistake until I read the accompanying instructions. They wanted a stool sample. American Airlines pilots, widely regarded in the industry as the "Sky Nazis," appear to outsiders to have a decidedly anal approach to flying airplanes. It must all start with that little flat stick.

There was also the challenge of getting past the pilots who did the final screening of applicants for the major airlines. I can't prove it but my experience suggests that the airlines cull the worst nutcases and limp dicks from their seniority lists and assign them the task of interviewing perspective pilots. I'll never forget one ex-navy pilot type at Delta Air Lines looking down his nose at my application and scorning my Lockheed Lodestar, twin-Beech, DC-3 and C-46 time.

"Were you ever in the military?" he asked.

"Yeah, army."

"And just what did you fly in the...army?"

"A deuce and a half," I said.

"A what?"

"A deuce and a half," I repeated. "That's a truck."

"Oh," he sniffed, then giggled. "So you're a...*civilian* pilot?"

"Yeah, that's right."

It was the classic aviation confrontation: military-trained pilot against civilian-trained pilot. Even though ex-military and civilian pilots exist side by side in the world of professional aviation and work surprisingly well together, each group harbors suspicions. Civilian pilots secretly believe that their military counterparts are better suited to dropping bombs and strafing bridges while the military-trained pilots believe that civilian pilots are better suited to selling shoes. The simple truth is that a bad pilot is a bad pilot, no matter how he or she becomes one. The military produces as many ham-fisted bunglers as any civilian flight school.

The Delta interviewer ushered me into a second office. He asked that I sit in a rocking chair. How fun, I thought. I love rocking chairs. Another pilot entered the room, along with a fat guy who introduced himself as a psychiatrist. The shrink had darting, calculating eyes full of malice and the cackling laugh of a James Bond antagonist. I got the feeling he was packing a gun.

I'd rock and get dirty looks; I'd not rock and get different kinds of dirty looks. I knew the fun part was over when the three began asking questions. Their grilling would have shamed a tribunal of 16th Century papal inquisitors. They were searching for signs of heresy. No problem. Heresy has always been a specialty of mine.

"If you were a copilot with Delta Air Lines, under what circumstances would you take an airplane away from the captain?" the shrink began.

It had never occurred to me to take an airplane away from *anyone*. Among the guys I flew with, it just wasn't done—unless of course someone was trying to kill you. Elwood of my Piper Cub days came to mind.

"If he was trying to kill my ass," I said, apparently without enough hesitation to suit my inquisitors.

"Oooh?" the shrink said. He smiled like he knew he had me. "And do you think that just because someone was trying to, as you so eloquently put it, 'kill your ass,' that alone would be enough justification to take an airplane away from a captain at Delta Air Lines?"

"That's enough justification to take an airplane away from God Almighty," I answered. Again, too quickly.

"Please don't take the Lord's name in vain. We at Delta Air Lines take our religion very seriously," said one of the pilots, "and, besides, let us not forget that God Almighty is *not* a Delta Air Lines captain."

"I guess He's not arrogant enough, huh?" I said.

I knew I was done and wanted out of there. I feared for my life. One of the pilots directed me out of the office with a limp-wristed, backward motion of his hand. I left quickly, before they had a chance to find the thumbscrews.

Somehow I'd learn to pick my quarrels with aviation more carefully in the future.

What the hell, there were plenty of other airlines out there. I'd keep trying. Oh, how I envied the pilots flying for the airlines, several of which had crew bases in Miami. The pilots of Eastern Air Lines, Braniff International, National Air Lines and Pan American World Airways seemed to have it all: big bucks and lots of babes. The mere thought! Like the brand new, sassy jets they flew, the future belonged to them and they knew it. Noses held high, those cocksure big-time airline pilots in their toy-soldier uniforms—I hate uniforms but I'd make the sacrifice—and big, expensive watches didn't walk through airport terminals. They strutted.

The Corner pilots I met so far didn't strut much.

As an aside, if someone had told me in 1967 that in twenty-five years Eastern, Braniff, National and Pan Am would all be swept into the wastebin of aviation history, as forgotten as the Toledo & Great Lakes Railroad, I would have laughed in their face. I would have downright howled had they predicted that the Corner would be going strong in the new millennium flying jets that once belonged to these same defunct airlines. Yet that's how it turned out.

The lesson? Place or take no bets on a pilot's future. The God of Aviation Yet-to-Come is a capricious sort with a sense of humor every bit as cruel as that of the sulky deities that reside in smoking volcanoes.

The God of Airline Deregulation, created and ordained by politicians in the 1980s, proved even crueler—and completely humorless. Its victims are legion. Among the first was the myth known as the "Brotherhood of Airline Pilots." Deregulation turned airline against airline, pilot group against pilot group, brother against brother.

The above divinities, in league with the devious bastards—all of them masters of the "legal swindle"—who run the airlines and manipulate aviation finances and oil prices, virtually guarantee that flying airplanes for a living will always be a roller coaster ride.

But worth it.

After W.W. told the Benny Smiles story again to the few pilots in the world who hadn't heard it, I became acquainted with some Bryson's regulars. Corner pilots, I concluded after an evening of drink and discussion, fell into two general categories: those like myself only in the Corner temporarily (I hoped) and those who had found a home in the Corner. Those who had found a home in the Corner also seemed to have found a home at Bryson's. The pilots who hung out there possessed a "fly anything, anywhere, just don't bore me" approach to the game.

Flying was their business but it was also their life, unsteady, difficult and sometimes perverse, but their life nonetheless. A pilot needed wits, skill, adaptability and a certain amount of daring to survive in the Corner. A sense of humor didn't hurt, either. These same attributes, notably the sense of humor, were missing in many of the big-time airline guys I knew. Big bucks, lifetime security and an unflagging sense of self-importance seem to negate the need to smile.

To accommodate the odd working hours of Corner pilots, Bryson's was open twenty-four hours a day. There was even an adjacent package store where one could grab something for the road. Conveniently located across the street from the Corner, Bryson's was to Corner pilots what the Ravenite Social Club was to John Gotti and the gang, a place to unwind and drink for eight or ten hours at a time, look for ways to earn a quick buck and, of course, a place to entertain women. Which included some local working girls in a wide range of ages and prices. While I feel reasonably qualified to describe the characters and flying conditions of the Corner, I will defer to persons better trained than myself in the social sciences to analyze and chart the parallels between Corner pilots and whores.

In the interests of fairness and historical accuracy, I should mention that Carole's Pool Bar at the Traveler's Motel down the street from Bryson's also earned a reputation in its day as a Miami pilot hangout. The pool bar, however, catered mostly to the pilots from the major airlines. It closed at an unreasonable three a.m. and thus was not considered suitable for the needs of Corner pilots. All that remains today of Carole's Pool Bar is a small sign. Bryson's is still going strong, 24 hours a day. Mention my name but please don't tell them where I am.

My Corner briefing lasted well into the early morning hours. I returned to my room at the Traveler's and collapsed.

I awoke at the crack of noon and left the motel to check out the Corner possibilities for myself. For several hours I roamed amidst a dizzying array of aging airline workhorses that had made it to the Corner by many different routes, some more circuitous than others. I've always been fascinated by old airplanes and the Corner proved to be a gold mine. My first impression was that I had entered a flying museum. However, after watching a salvage crew cut up a gearless, engineless Douglas DC-4 for scrap, I changed my mind.

The Corner was anything *but* a museum. Museum denotes permanence and a high degree of guardianship. There was no evidence of either. The only commodity that seemed in shorter supply than ramp space in the Corner was compassion for unproductive airplanes. When an airplane could no longer work, it was discarded like a Dixie Cup or middle reliever with shoulder problems. At best, the Corner was a last defiant outpost, a place for an airliner to fly a few more years before being junked. Or, even worse, sentenced to a life at hard labor in Central or South America, where it would be maintained by methods frowned upon even in the Corner.

It pained me to think how well my battered, overcooked Jag and I fit into the scene.

Curiosity drew me to a hulking Russian-built turboprop something-or-other marked with quirky, indecipherable lettering. The ship, ugly even by the high Russian standards of airplane ugliness, was a hammered-together flying garbage can built without love or caring. It advertised, to anyone astute enough to notice, the foreordained end of the Soviet Union decades before the event. How it flew at all was a mystery, how it got all the way to Miami without losing a wing was beyond human comprehension. The ship had been converted to a freighter but looked like it had once carried passengers. I pitied the poor suckers who had once flown on Air Gulag.

A guy was painting over the strange lettering on the side of the airplane with cheap paint out of a disobliging spray gun that acted as if it, too, were Soviet in origin. I asked him what kind of an airplane it was.

"Dunno," he said, "can't pronounce it. It's Russian. That's all I know. A Shitski, or Crapski, or something like that."

"Gonna try to get it flying?" I asked. I assumed from the appearance that the aircraft was not in working order.

"We *bin* flying it," he said, a bit testily. "Getting ready right now to go to Caracas."

Good luck.

"You looking for a job? My copilot quit on me this morning."

Imagine that.

"You could tell your kids someday that you flew a Shitski."

Yeah, if I live that long.

"No thanks," I said, "I've already flown enough Shitskis to last a lifetime." It was not like me to turn down a flying job but I couldn't get away from that particular operation fast enough. However, I was encouraged that work seemed easy enough to come by in the corner. I resumed my search.

The afternoon Florida air was sticky and oppressive; just breathing was a chore. I had about decided to relocate my job search back to the air-conditioning and cold beer at Bryson's when I spotted a guy with a cast on his right arm loading a DC-3.

Tall and thin with a pencil-thin mustache and black slicked-back hair, he looked like the pilots I worshipped in the old movies when I was a kid. I had acquired a few hours in Gooneybirds and decided to inquire about a job. The hundred bucks I borrowed from a Cleveland girlfriend wasn't going to last long and I wasn't sure if they extended credit to pilots at the Traveler's Motel. (They didn't.)

"Uh, how ya doin?" I asked.

"Who wants to know?" he said, without looking up from his one-armed loading chores.

"Uh…me," I said. "Need some help flying the 'three?'"

"I need some help *loadin'* the son of a bitch," he said, struggling to lift another box inside the airplane. The cast on his arm didn't help much. "Then maybe we'll talk about flying it."

As we loaded boxes into the 'three, sweating like hogs in the swampy climate, the guy finally identified himself, though only as "Art." He seemed friendly enough, if a bit secretive. He told me that sometimes he just flew the DC-3 by himself, not the smartest, most legal or easiest thing to do—especially with only one good arm—but Art seemed far more concerned about privacy than he was about the safety of flight. I figured Art for a loner and maybe a little shady.No problem.

Art's cargo consisted of dozens of large boxes of toilet paper, laundry detergent and a ton or two of Coca Cola. Stories of smuggling in the Corner abounded; but considering the prosaic nature of the cargo we were loading Art was obviously not involved in that sort of thing. Yet, all the while we loaded the DC-3 he acted suspicious and asked me a lot of questions. What I didn't know at the time was that no one ever smuggles anything *out* of the United States.

"I'm leaving in about an hour," Art said. "I'm gonna make a stop first in Kingston to drop this stuff off for a hotel then I'm flyin' down to Quito in Ecuador. It's a long damn flight and I could use some help. Got any over-water time?"

"A little," I said, not really certain if buzzing ore boats on the Great Lakes qualified as "over-water time."

"I'll pay you two hundred dollars plus a bonus depending on how things work out. You ain't a cop or anything like that, are ya?"

"No," I answered. "I hate cops."

I didn't really hate cops but I figured it couldn't hurt to act a little tough in the Corner. I also didn't have a clue as to what Art meant by "bonus," but acted like I did. To tell the truth, while I had a vague notion of Kingston's location, I had never even heard of Quito, Ecuador. Faking it plays a bigger part in one's flying career than most non-pilots would want to believe.

"Ecuador's a long way," I said, pretending to know. It sounded like a safe speculation.

"Couple thousand miles, plus what we gotta add to go 'round Cuba since the dirty commie bastards won't let you fly over it," Art said. "Got any 'three time?"

"Some," I said.

"You're gonna have a lot more by the time we get back. You'll have to fly the whole way down and most of the way back. I've made this trip twice in the last week and I'm beat to death. Gotta get me some sleep."

"I can handle it," I said. At the time I thought Art was only kidding about me flying most of the trip.

Art's DC-3 was one of the rarer Wright-powered versions. It was in reasonably good shape for an aircraft over thirty years old, especially one flying out of the Corner. Angry, freehand lettering on the left side of the cockpit identified it as the *Azore Whore*.

"Quite a name for an airplane, Art," I said.

"Oh, yeah, named her after my fourth ol' lady...or maybe my fifth, can't remember," he said. The comment said everything I needed to know. I wasn't married but I knew all the stories. I changed the subject.

"Got the Wrights on her," I remarked knowingly. "You like them better than the Pratts?"

"Wrights! Pratts! Who gives a shit? Wright parts are cheaper," he said. "I'd fly her with Volkswagen motors if they'd do the trick."

Practicality was king in the Corner.

After we had the *Azore Whore* loaded, I did a quick walk-around inspection and noticed fluid leaking from the left prop hub.

"There's evidence of a leak on the left prop," I reported back to Art.

Art walked around to the prop. "Well, so there is," he said. He wiped away the incriminating fluid with the palm of his hand.

"Okay, evidence of leak removed. Let's get the hell out o' here!"

Maintenance delays were not much of a problem in the Corner.

We took off about two in the afternoon, nothing but clear blue sky to the south. I was flying. Art told me to take up a heading to the northwest and not climb too high.

The northwest? I had assumed Kingston, Jamaica and Quito, Ecuador were south. I did what I was told and turned to the northwest. We flew over a Miami suburb.

"See that street to the right, the one that has the little bend in it?" Art asked.

"Yeah, I think I do. What about it?"

"Slow down and fly over that street."

"How come?"

"That's where I live! Slow 'er down, I'm lookin' for something."

"What's that?" I said, pulling the power back. "Maybe I can help you find it."

"Okay, see that pink house under the light pole, the one with the heart-shaped swimming pool?"

"Yeah." *How could I miss it, Art?*

"I think my new wife's playin' around on me," Art said. "I'm told her boyfriend drives a maroon Harley. See anything down there that looks like a maroon hog?"

"No, sure don't, Art," I said.

"I don't either. Great! Turn 'er around. Let's go to Yamaica, mon."

I banked the *Azore Whore* sharply to the right. For no particular reason, I looked down just in time to see a maroon Harley ease furtively, eagerly, around a bend in the street and pull into Art's driveway. Art couldn't see it out of his window. I didn't mention my discovery. What purpose would it have served?

"I feel better," Art said.

"Yeah, must be a good feeling to know your wife doesn't play around on you when you're gone," I said.

Hope that biker puts the toilet seat down when he leaves, Art.

I passed over the Florida Straits and took up a southeasterly heading to avoid Cuba since in those days one could get shot down flying over Cuban airspace. The Bahaman Islands to the east charted our course like dropped breadcrumbs. Compared to the cheerless gray landscape and dirty accumulated snow of the Midwest in winter, the setting was straight out of a storybook.

The *Azore Whore* turned out to be a pretty sweet-flying old bird. Like a lot of the planes in the Corner, it smelled faintly of pigs and flowers. To this day there remains a steady business in the transportation of breeding pigs from the United States to countries in Central and South America. I don't understand why, unless American pigs might know something foreign pigs don't. The pigs usually survive the trip pretty well. The airplanes never fully recover.

Flowers come the other way, from south of the border into the United States. They're no bargain either. The cloying fragrance of a ton or two of carnations makes a pilot feel like he's lying in state, definitely not recommended for anyone with touchy sinuses. The *combination* of lingering hog and flower scents is well beyond anyone's power of description.

Cuba came into view to the right. Art glared at the island. Corner pilots hated Cuba, not because of politics but because Fidel Castro prohibited aircraft of United States registration from flying over it. For Art, it was a matter of simple economics.

"There's gotta be a million other islands in the world," Art sighed. "Why did those dirty commie bastards have to pick Cuba? Flying around that island has cost me a bundle. What I wouldn't give for a load of bombs to drop on those commie pricks."

Personally I had never given the politics of Cuba—or anyplace else—much thought. Ideological opposition is for serious thinkers who don't have to worry about making a living. However, I had once read that Castro gave speeches routinely lasting seven hours. Attendance mandatory! That more than anything caused me to flip Fidel the bird on the way by.

Art and I talked for another half hour, mostly me asking questions for which I got no answers. In the middle of a sentence, he slouched in his seat and fell sound asleep, leaving me to ponder what he would have done if I hadn't come along. Art seemed capable of a kind of self-induced coma. I studied his chest to see if it was moving. Now and then he confirmed he was still alive by inadvertently pushing on a rudder pedal or bumping the throttles with his arm cast. Some pilots claim they can't sleep in airplanes, but those pilots never flew out of the Corner.

It occurred to me that I should have asked for more pay, considering that I was going to do all the flying. A negotiator I'm not. However, there was still the "bonus" Art had mentioned, whatever that might be.

I flew through what the sailors call the Windward Passage between Cuba and Haiti and headed for destination Kingston, Jamaica. A pilot's thoughts tend to align with the type and age of the airplane he's flying. The thirty-year-old DC-3, which was fighting a war when I was born, took me back to a simpler time in aviation when every flight was an adventure. And then further back, to the age of sail and exploration. I imagined the exhilaration and relief my pillaging seafaring Italian ancestors must have felt when welcomed to a new world by these same comforting waters. No gold, but plenty of sunny beaches and babes.

I put my feet on the bottom of the instrument panel and tuned in some frenzied Latin music on the low-frequency radio. I thumped my fingers on the yoke as I tried to keep time to perplexing Cuban tempos. There wasn't a happier pilot in the world. On that day I could have flown to the ends of the earth, even as I wondered wistfully whether I would ever get to fly an airplane that wasn't built before I was born—or one that didn't smell of pigs and petunias.

We landed at Kingston. Workers from an island hotel met the airplane and unloaded the supplies. Art ordered the fueler to top off the *Azore Whore* to its 800-gallon capacity while we got something to eat. In the airfreight business, when you get a chance to eat, you eat, hungry or not. I downed two hamburgers and resupplied myself with a giant cup of hot coffee and a couple packs of Luckies. I was ready for anything.

After pulling Art into the airplane by his arm cast, we departed for Quito, Ecuador. Quito, I deduced from looking at a chart, was 1300 miles straight south of Jamaica. It lies on the Equator like a road marker. Most of the flight would be over open water, about seven or eight hours flying. It would be a stretch for a DC-3, a bigger stretch for a tired pilot in a DC-3.

"Just hold your heading, no matter what kind of weather we run into," Art said. "Otherwise God only knows where we'll wind up. We might be breakfast for the headhunters."

Art chuckled at his mention of "headhunters," a sick private joke of some sort. I returned a knowing, tough-guy Corner laugh.

"It's gonna be dark when we get there," I said, looking over the worrisome approach to Quito, inconsiderately located high in the mountains. "Is that a good idea with all those mountains?"

"Trust me, you're better off landing at places like Quito at night when you *can't* see the mountains," Art laughed. "If you saw the mountains you're gonna have to fly around, you'd never land there. Just stay on the published approach and you'll be fine. The *Whore's* been in there many times. She knows the way. Besides, I'm gonna conduct a little business down there. Dark's the only time to conduct business. I like dark."

As was his style, Art offered no further details. I assumed the business he was going to conduct had something to do with my bonus. Art fell asleep, as quickly as if he had a switch implanted somewhere on his body.

I plodded on into the night, hour after hour, whistling tunes to keep awake and trying to ignore the lulling cradlesong of the twin Cyclones. With the possible exception of ground school or a chief pilot meeting, nothing puts a pilot to sleep quicker than sitting between two large radial engines. I tried to ignore the fact that we were over the open waters of the Caribbean in an antique airplane, a detail far less lulling than the Wrights' cradlesong. There were a lot of things below waiting to eat us if anything went wrong.

The chart showed Panama ahead and to our right. The mere thought of the effort involved in digging a ditch across a continent made me yawn. I wanted to go to sleep like Art but fought it. Sleeping in airplanes is something best done in shifts. I found more Latin music on the radio, hoping it would disrupt my body's insistent circadian sleep pattern.

Many hours later, I picked out a row of brooding lights that I assumed were cities on the coast of Columbia. I tuned in a navigational aid in Cartagena.

Art stirred. His reddened eyes cracked open. He looked out the window. "It's pretty clear tonight," he said groggily. "Just fly the volcanoes along the coast. They'll take ya to Quito." It was his sole contribution to the entire flight.

"So that's what those are," I said to myself. The "city lights" I saw were active volcanoes. So this was the "rim of fire," a line of testosterous flaring volcanoes along the Pacific coast of South America. Mister Weisnoski had talked about this very thing in tenth-grade geography class. He would have been proud of me for finally figuring it out, might even have boosted my final grade to a D.

Flying out of the Corner, I concluded, was one big field trip.

I followed the volcanoes until I picked up the powerful Quito compass locator. The weather was clear at the airport, which sits in a valley nine thousand feet above sea level surrounded by even higher mountain peaks. Quito is one of those airports that scoffs at everything a pilot is taught to beware. It challenges a pilot, *defies* him to enter. I contacted Quito Approach Control. A muddled voice in broken English gave us clearance to descend into the unknown. As I descended, the mountain peaks, silhouetted by moonlight, rose above me. Looking up at mountains is instinctively discomfiting to a pilot. I chanced a guess that more than a few aircraft had made unplanned landings into those mountains, sullen stone guardians with standing orders to punish the incautious. To this day, arriving or departing Quito remains one of the more sporting propositions in aviation. The engine-out takeoff "escape routes" worm through a lethal funhouse maze of narrow valleys and plateaus.

Art had contracted with a Miami importer to pick up a load of woolen sweaters and native kitsch. The kitsch included volcano-shaped ceramic ashtrays, cutesy Noah's Arks filled with animals—inexplicably, only one of each species—and a dozen or so different types of crudely-carved and painted wooden statues of Jesus with a resemblance to Che Guevara.

Art left me in charge of a group of loaders while he walked over to a dark corner of the ramp.

I watched him rendezvous with a short, wild-eyed forest dweller lurking in the shadows. The man was dressed only in a loincloth and feathered armband. Moonlight reflected off his dark, oiled body. He radiated a fierceness out of all proportion to his diminutive stature. I didn't think such people existed except in my father's collection of National Geographics. In the National Geographics, however, such colorful types were armed only with blowguns, not an automatic rifle like this character.

Rifle, blowgun, it didn't matter; he didn't look like the kind of guy I'd pick a fight with in a bar.

The native held two sacks, which he opened one at a time while Art inspected the contents with a flashlight. Art and the native were soon involved in what looked like heated negotiations over the sacks.

Neither seemed to speak the language of the other but both seemed to understand perfectly that unless a satisfactory amount of money changed hands, Art was not going to get the sacks that he coveted. Whatever Art's haggling skills might have been, it was obvious even at a distance that he was no match for the noble savage.

Eventually a deal was struck. The native studied Art's arm cast for a moment, smiled at the notion and disappeared into the shadows from which he came.

Art hurried back to the airplane, grinning like he had just purchased a Rolls for half the sticker price. He stopped for a few minutes to talk to a little girl about twelve years old. He gave her some money, patted her on the head and returned to the airplane.

"That was nice of you to give that beggar girl some money," I said.

"Beggar girl? What beggar girl? That's my Quito wife," he said. "I just don't have time for her tonight. How long did you say ya bin in the Corner?"

"Not long enough, I guess." *Or maybe too long.*

Again I helped Art climb into the *Azore Whore* with his two sacks. He unfastened a panel on the rear bulkhead spuriously marked "DEADLY HIGH VOLTAGE! DO NOT OPEN! DEATH COULD RESULT!" After carefully depositing the sacks in the opening, he refastened the panel and stacked some bundles of sweaters in front of the bulkhead.

"What's in the sacks, Art?" I asked, knowing he wouldn't tell me.

"Your bonus," he said, without further explanation.

Dawn broke about the time the loading was finished. I got my first clear look at the high, make that *real* high, *real* steep terrain to the east and west of the airport. If the Spanish invaders who had settled Quito knew that someday it would require an airport, they might have picked a more suitable location. Then again, they might have considered it a great joke on future generations.

Art and I each found a comfortable spot on the woolen sweaters and slept a few hours. I highly recommend fifteen hours of hand-flying a DC-3 as a cure for insomnia.

Refreshed from the long nap, Art even helped fly home. He sang a few country songs.

"You got a pretty good voice, Art," I said. "Ever sing professionally?"

"Sure as hell did. I once sang at the Grand Ole Opry, believe it or not."

"I believe it," I said. "What happened? How come you didn't stay with it?"

"Some woman fucked it up for me," Art said.

I wanted to pursue the issue but I settled for the condensed explanation. Besides, every pilot I had ever known blamed his reverses on a woman. I would have much rather heard her side of the story.

I asked again about the sacks. Art just grinned. In keeping with his cryptic manner, he seemed to want to make it a surprise or something.

"It ain't drugs, is it, Art?" I asked. Getting busted in Miami would not be fun. One of the guys at Bryson's told stories of third world dungeons with better accommodations than Miami's jails. (Several Central American countries allowed conjugal visits and even offered room service and a wine list.) I already had enough rough spots on my application to explain to the airline interviewers. Time in the joint would be a hard sell, possibly beyond my sweet-talking abilities.

"No, no way. No drugs! I wouldn't mess with that shit," Art said. "Besides, I don't know who to sell it to."

After stopping in Jamaica again for fuel we arrived in Miami about four in the morning. A front had settled over south Florida while we were gone; it had rained all day. Misting clouds hung low over the airport.

A fat, sleepy, supercilious U.S. Customs officer stepped inside the aircraft and inspected the woolen blankets and native kitsch. He spotted the bogus "DEADLY HIGH VOLTAGE" sign on the rear bulkhead and made a move like he was going to investigate. I was about to be busted for smuggling without the slightest idea of what I had smuggled, an accessory to a crime I didn't even know I had committed. I started thinking up an all-purpose story.

The customs guy thought better of the idea. Either the sign bluffed him or it was just too much extra work for a government employee. He sighed and begrudgingly admitted us back into our own country.

Art waited until the fat customs officer was out of sight and cursed him harshly. He went to the bulkhead to retrieve the two sacks he had purchased from the Ecuadorian forest dweller. I followed, directing the lighthouse-like beam of my prized flashlight on the operation. Art unfastened the "DEADLY HIGH VOLTAGE" panel and reached inside. He grabbed one of the sacks, looked inside and handed it to me.

"Take a couple out of there," Art said. "It looks to be a good batch." He jammed his left arm back into the bulkhead opening up to the shoulder and groped around blindly for the other sack.

Good batch? Of what?

I opened the sack and reached inside, curious but wary. I grasped an object about the size of a tennis ball with some of the same fuzzy qualities, as well as several oddly familiar indentations.

Maybe it's some kind of tropical fruit. Great! I'm hungry.

Uncertain of what I held in my hand, I pulled out the object and shined the full intensity of my five-cell on it. I discerned a facial pattern: eyes, nose, mouth and ears. Coconuts have little faces on them but it was not a coconut. No, not a coconut nor any other kind of tropical fruit that I had ever seen.

Perhaps it was a monkey head, a discovery revolting enough, considering my past experience with monkeys in aviation, to make me want to drop it back into the bag. But as I turned the object around in my hand I determined it was not a monkey head. No, it was definitely no monkey. The details of the face were too fine, the expression too intent, too pensive, too...*human.* I was holding someone's head, someone's very small head. Someone's *shrunken* head.

"AAAH!" I yelled, flipping the offending head over my shoulder and out of the opened cargo door onto the ramp. The little noggin rolled a few feet and came to rest, face down, in a puddle.

"Hey, what's going on out there?" Art snapped. "Be careful with those goddamn things. They're worth a lot of money!"

Art was having trouble reaching the second sack and was a bit aggravated.

"A lot of money? Who would want these things?" I asked, shuddering and gasping for breath in the thick, wet early morning air.

"Are you crazy? Lots of people want 'em, museums and collectors."
Art's patience was gone.

"Goddamn freaks!"

"Yeah, some of them too. There's a lot of strange bastards in this
world, in case you ain't noticed."

I'm beginning to, Art.

"How come you have to smuggle them in, Art? They illegal?" I
imagined myself trying to gloss over my felonious involvement with
shrunken heads at the next airline interview.

"Not really illegal exactly, but the customs guys will confiscate
the heads if they find 'em. I guess the crybaby liberals in this country
don't like shrunken heads. There's an embargo on 'em or some such
silly shit. They don't understand that it's just business. Say, you're not
some kind o' fuckin' liberal, are ya?"

"I don't...think...so," I said. *But I'm starting to wonder, Art.*

"I'll have those heads sold by this afternoon. Get five or six
hundred each. So be careful with 'em," Art repeated.

Be careful with 'em? Some poor slob got his head lopped off
and shrunk down to the size of a spud and Art worried that I might
hurt it?

My curiosity, however, was piqued. I jumped out of the airplane
and picked up the head I had thrown onto the ramp. I wiped it off
on my pants, took a deep breath and again shined my flashlight on
the tiny face. I forced myself to look at it.

Despite my initial horror, I found nothing at all frightening about
the shrunken head. Quite the contrary. The face possessed a salving
aspect, far less menacing than, say, G.I Joe or a statue of a martyred
saint. I was drawn to the eyes, or, more accurately, eyelids, stitched
closed with exacting sutures a plastic surgeon might envy. Though
lacking eyes, the face stared at me. The unseen eyes radiated serenity,
a peace very deep and cosmic. The mouth, also sewn closed, gave
hint, almost a whisper, of bliss unattainable in this life. The face
spoke not of death but of rebirth. It seemed to say, "Look into this
face, pal, and fear not. Good things await."

The head studied me rather than the other way around. What
magic was this? How could this man, no doubt a pitiless, brutal
warrior who had lived and died so violently, speak to me through eyes

forever blind and lips forever silent of a reconciliation and happiness in death so intense as to be almost palpable? No one ever came close to persuading me of the existence of an afterlife. Not the priests; sure as hell not the nuns.

But wait, hadn't grumbly old Father Downey told us in the fifth grade that soldiers who die in war go automatically to Heaven? I wondered if this former combatant qualified since, as I recalled, certain restrictions applied. The soldier had to be a Catholic in the service of the United States military fighting a country that didn't believe in *our* God. Getting iced by a communist was most desirable. If the soldier were Irish, like Father Downey, the trip through the pearly gates was expedited.

Most of the fifth graders bought it, but Father Downey's spiel sounded like a lot of bullshit to me at the time. Suddenly I wasn't so certain. As I contemplated the evidence, Art found the other sack.

"Hey, quit screwin' around out there and grab this other sack! You can keep the head you tossed out the door and take a couple more. Don't take any with tattoos or red hair."

"How come?" I asked.

"They bring the most money. Shit, you don't know much. How long you bin around the Corner?"

"Too long," I muttered.

"How's that," Art asked.

"Say, Art, is it just me, or do you also see something in these faces?" I asked, holding the head—custodian of so many wonderful secrets—close, looking for a crack in the door for a peek at the unknown.

"Yeah, I see something." Art said.

"What? What do you see, Art?" I asked expectantly, pleased that even a philistine like Art could not deny the message in the faces.

"I see about five or six one-hundred dollar bills in every one of those mugs." Art was living proof, if anyone still needs proof, that it doesn't take a great deal of cash to block the view to Paradise.

Admittedly, the money I could have gotten for the heads was tempting. But my early education at the hands of the priests and nuns of the Church of Martyrs placed far too much emphasis on superstition and guilt. It was bad enough I had lent a hand, however unintentionally, to such morbid commerce. For all I knew, these men might have been killed and their bodies mutilated just to fill Art's standing order.

I declined the heads. I knew that if I had taken just one to sell or keep as a souvenir to haul out only on great occasions after much drink, I would spend the rest of my life dodging its ethereal stare in my dreams—not to mention any tribal curses that may have accompanied this indigenous product of Ecuador.

"I really don't want any, Art," I said, surrendering my tiny, enigmatic new friend.

Art shook his head like he didn't understand. He gave me an extra hundred dollars instead.

The sun started to rise. In the dim first morning light I watched Art one-handedly sort the shrunken heads on the floor of the airplane like a greedy kid arranging and evaluating his baseball card collection.

"See ya later, Art," I said.

"Oh, yeah, see ya. Say, come back tomorrow about two in the afternoon if you're interested in more work," Art said without looking up from the heads.

"More heads, Art?" I asked. Weakly.

"No, *langostas*," he said, vague as ever.

I nodded my head, pretending to know what he was talking about. I didn't plan on working for Art again, but I didn't tell him what I thought about his shrunken heads. In aviation, it's not wise to burn bridges, even though I had gotten pretty good at it.

The long airplane ride into the night and enlisting stares of the butchered heads and likely associated hexes had been too much. I badly needed to put a little distance between the Corner and me. I drove away from the airport in the direction of the Florida swamps. The Jaguar, of course, overheated, a normal occurrence on any trip of more than six miles in any temperature above minus 20F. Only those enormous double-articulated locomotives once used for hauling coal over the Allegheny Mountains generated more steam than that goddamn Jaguar.

For once, the car's timing was perfect. I pulled off the road and climbed out. I slumped down beside the car and beseeched the sun's rays to purge me of my wicked deed. I fell asleep in the grass, not the brightest thing to do in southern Florida.

A scouting party of fire ants, gram for gram the most savage and unmerciful life form on earth, awakened me an hour later. I drove back to the Traveler's and slept for many hours. When I got up, I headed straight for Bryson's, intent on drinking away the experience with the shrunken heads.

W.W. was there. He and some guy I hadn't seen before were hunched over a table along the wall. They were engaged in what looked like serious conversation. At Bryson's, the horseshoe bar was for recreational drinking. Business and the entertainment of babes were conducted at the tables.

"Hey, Searchbeam, I was just gonna call ya," W.W. said. "Shake hands with Hank."

I shook Hank's hand. At first I thought he was giving me some kind of Knight's of Columbus or Shriner handshake or something. His hand wasn't one hundred per cent; it didn't feel right. When he took his hand away I noticed Hank was missing his index finger. It hardly took my attention away from the wig he sported, an unwashed, knotted jet-black affair that looked like it may have once been a football helmet involved in numerous big games. The right sideburn of the wig covered his ear. I fought an urge to straighten it.

"Where ya bin?" W.W. asked.

"Equador. I hand-flew a DC-3 twenty-eight hours. Or maybe it was twenty-eight hundred hours. I'm not sure." Mention of the trip made me sleepy again.

"What the hell were you doin' down there?"

"You wouldn't believe me if I told you."

"Bring back any heads?" Hank casually interrupted in a deep, boozy, knowing voice.

"No, no heads," I lied. "No goddamn heads!"

"Heads? What kinda heads?" W.W. asked.

Corner pilots were always interested in new initiatives.

"Wuddaya guys talkin' 'bout?" W.W. pressed. "What kinda heads? Is this something I need to know about?"

"Trust me, ya don't need to know. Please shut up about the heads, W.W.," I begged. "Keep studying babes instead. Someday you might get laid."

"Never mind the heads, they're nuthin' compared to what I can offer you," Hank said. "Have a seat. Me and your buddy is talkin' big things."

A hefty barmaid thundered over to our table, breaking up the conversation.

"Hey Hank, there's a guy from the Corner on the phone," she said. "He's lookin' fer a flight engineer on a Connie. You interested?"

"Not a bit," said Hank. "No more o' that penny-ante stuff for me. I got my own airline now. Tell that guy to stick that Connie up his ass."

My ears perked up. "You hirin' pilots, Hank?" I asked, greatly relieved that the subject had changed from shrunken heads.

"If you're just lookin' for a flyin' job I can't help ya much. If you're lookin' for a chance of a lifetime then we oughta talk."

Hank thus cast the line delicately into the water like a champion fly fisherman. I left the safety of the submerged log and swam over. W.W. was already there. Our eyes greedily surveyed the bait.

Hank explained how he had flown out of the Corner working for other people his entire life. He didn't recommend it. There were better things. In a few days he would take delivery of a relatively low-time, almost like-new Douglas DC-7, a long-distance "C" model. He said he had purchased it from Pan Am, which was replacing its piston fleet with jets. As he spoke he accented his words with the missing index finger, a striking demonstration of the brain's refusal to accept the loss of a body part.

"There's plenty of life left in that old Douglas," Hank said. He scratched his right ear underneath the wig with the missing finger. "Eventually gonna get another one just like it. You guys got a chance to git in on the bottom floor."

Hank gave us a chance to savor the seductive wiggle of the bait. W.W. and I swam around the meal in ever tighter circles. Hank waved the waitress over to the table for another round of beers. On my tab, of course.

The Douglas DC-7, while undeniably a great airplane in its day, was in 1967 a sailing ship in the age of nuclear power. True, a few of the airlines were still operating piston-powered equipment but the battle was lost. Aviation had sold out. The direction was inexorably toward the unromantic, screeching but efficient jets.

However, a DC-7 certainly seemed like an upward move for W.W. and me. Hank knew what his two fish were thinking. The time was perfect for the Three Great Lies of Pilot Hiring, which, except for periodic technical updating, remain unchanged and in widespread use even today. One or more of the Three Great Lies are part of all pilot hiring. No defense exists for them when told under the right circumstances, especially by a master such as Hank.

"Ya know, we ain't gonna be operating that old DC-7 forever," Hank said as he began chain-smoking my cigarettes. "It won't be long and we'll be gettin' some jets. Probably some new Boeing 727s, sumpin' like that."

It was Great Lie Number One, which in the late 1960s was intended to assure the potential new-hire pilot that the piston junk would soon be replaced by jets. Hank executed Great Lie Number One perfectly, with just the right amount of downplay.

W.W. and I started to bump the bait with our noses. We positioned to strike.

Now that he had our attention, Hank transitioned effortlessly into Great Lie Number Two, the promise of rapid upgrade and big money.

"Now, since you guys don't have a type-rating in the DC-7, I'll have to start you both as copilots and won't be able to pay ya much," Hank said. "Course it won't be for long. Soon as ya get a little time in the 'seven I'll check you out as captains. We'll be talkin' 'bout thirty grand a year."

At the mention of captain and thirty grand, a confoundingly unimaginable amount of money to earn in a single year, W.W. and I finished our beers in one long, delirious gulp. Great Lie Number Two is emphasized the most and never underplayed since it is meant to set the hook. Which it did.

After a pause so precisely timed that I shiver in admiration for Hank's skills even after these many years, he effortlessly launched into Great Lie Number Three. This is the promise of a transformation from freight to scheduled passenger-carrying operation in the near future. He played us like a violin.

"We're gonna have to start out flying nonsked airfreight at night just to get things going," Hank continued, swigging his beer and wiping his mouth on his sleeve. "But what I'm really planning is a first-class, day-time, scheduled passenger airline operation. With terrific-lookin' hot stewardesses. You guys like girls and blow jobs and stuff like that, don'tcha? Hell, I'll even let you guys hire the girls. You kin interview 'em. Know what I mean?" He laughed wickedly.

The oral sex addendum was Hank's personal touch to the traditional freight-to-passenger Great Lie Number Three. Icing on the cake. The irresistible draw.

Hank needn't have bothered. W.W. and I looked at each other; we were unable to believe what we had happened upon. In Bryson's, no less. But I didn't get to be a pilot by being stupid. I had some probing questions.

"Uh, what's the catch, Hank?" I asked, salivating.

"Well, I wouldn't exactly call it a catch, but I'm gonna need some investment money if you're interested in getting into this airline right from the beginning, on the ground floor so to speak," Hank said, downing the rest of his beer and looking into my empty pack of Luckies with undisguised agitation. He ordered more beer and smokes. On W.W.'s tab this time.

"I'm just gonna go 'head and put this on your tab again," he said, no doubt confident that the Three Great Lies of Pilot Hiring had been successful. "We'll call it a down payment on the future."

"How much is this airline investment gonna cost us," I asked. I had about four hundred dollars and was starting to wish I had taken a couple of the shrunken heads. When the stakes are high enough, one readily abandons scruples and scoffs at potential curses.

"Everybody so far has come up with one thousand dollars," Hank said. "But where else are ya gonna buy into an airline for a grand?"

W.W. and I looked at each other again. I saw the same despair in his eyes that he must have seen in mine. A thousand bucks was a fortune. I knew guys who had retired on less.

"You guys have about a month to raise the money," Hank said. "All the shares will probably be sold by then."

"You got a phone number, Hank?" I said, astute businessman that I am.

"I'm in and out of this place a lot. Look for me here."

Over the ensuing years I've learned to be suspicious of people offering business propositions in bars and reluctant to give their phone numbers. Telemarketers come to mind.

After Hank left, supposedly to begin negotiations on a second DC-7 with Pan Am in New York, a Corner pilot named Tommy Spotts happened by our table. Guardedly, so as not to give away too much of the deal, W.W. and I told him about our good fortune.

"This guy wasn't missing a finger by any chance, was he?" Spotts asked. He held up three fingers of his right hand in perfect imitation of Hank's impairment. "Maybe even wears a wig that looks like a floor mat out of a Cuban taxicab?"

"Yeah, could be the same guy," I said.

"Sounds like Three-fingered Hank," Spotts said. "That old crook wouldn't be tryin' to sell you guys shares in an airline would he?"

"Yeah...maybe something like that," W.W. said.

"He's been at that game for years," Spotts said. "But he's never managed to come up with an airplane. Just make sure you see an airplane sitting on the ramp before you give him any money."

It sounded like good advice. W.W. and I resolved not to give Three-fingered Hank a cent until we could see and touch the DC-7.

We sat in Bryson's till early in the morning, discussing our airline dreams—and where we might find the cash to finance them. I remembered Art telling me to show up at 2 p.m. that day if I wanted to fly. I hadn't planned on working for Art again but my sudden urgent need for money made me reconsider.

That afternoon I reported to the *Azore Whore* as instructed. Art introduced me to another pilot named Jack Morgan, with whom I would fly that day. To where and for what purpose Art didn't explain. I had learned not to ask such questions, since Art probably wouldn't have told me anyhow. I knew only that it had something to do with *langostas*, whatever they were.

I recognized Morgan from Bryson's. He was a regular, a hard-drinking, hard-smoking, babe-chasing character. My kind of pilot.

"Say, Morgan, I didn't get a chance to stop at K-Mart yesterday for supplies," Art said. "You don't mind takin' care of that for me do you?"

K-Mart? What am I getting into this time?

"No problem," Morgan said.

Corner pilots were certainly multifaceted, I thought.

Art pulled three one hundred dollar bills from his wallet and handed them to Morgan. "Just get the usual stuff. This time, try to find some beads. Last trip, they said they wanted beads, made a big thing about it."

Beads? Were we going to buy Manhattan?

Morgan explained the mission on the way to K-Mart. "We're gonna buy a lot of K-Mart crap and bring it down to Cat Island in the Bahamas. Then we go meet some other guys who'll have a load of *langostas* for us. We'll trade them the K-Mart crap and some money for the *langostas*. Simple as that. Art might even give you a cut of the take, depending on how many *langostas* we bring back."

"I got a question, Morgan."

"Yeah?"

"What the hell are *langostas*?"

"Lobsters, man, warm water spiny lobsters. They don't have no claws," Morgan said.

"Lobsters? Aren't we going through a lot of trouble just for some lobsters? What's the big deal?"

Morgan shot me a rebuking glance. I sensed he was about to add to my knowledge of the peculiar brand of aviation as practiced in the Corner.

"Lobsters are a little uh, ya might say 'out of season' right now. Can't get 'em through the normal channels. Art contracts people with nothing much else to do but catch 'em for us."

"You mean *poach* them?"

"Uh, yeah, something like that. We get 'em from the natives and fly 'em back to Miami and Art sells 'em to restaurants at a nice profit. Everybody's happy except the *langostas*." He laughed.

"Isn't poaching illegal?" I asked.

"It's only illegal if you get caught," Morgan said. "Nothing's illegal if you don't get caught!"

Oh well, if I could explain fifty-dollar guaranteed solos, murdered monkeys, pissed-off mob guys, encounters with airport chain-link fences and shrunken heads to the airlines, I sure as hell could justify a few barrels of out-of-season lobsters. Everyone likes lobster. I sure did—at the time.

In K-Mart, Morgan and I first threw every package of beads we could find into a shopping cart then started walking the aisles. We drew on Morgan's vast bartering experience with native people of the Bahamas to determine what might please them. He spotted a bin full of K-Mart crap with a sign that proclaimed everything in the bin cost a dollar.

"Bingo!" he said, fishing through the bin full of limp spatulas, sunglasses with missing lenses, soft metal drill bits, dull filleting knives, artificial baits with no track record, sewing kits with all red thread and every other imaginable useless item on the face of the earth.

"Wow, we struck it rich!" Morgan said. "Those clowns down there'll go nuts over this stuff." He set off to find the store manager.

"Hey pal, how much for the whole dollar bin?" Morgan asked the manager after he found him.

"The sign says the items are a dollar each."

"No, I want the whole bin. Take two hundred dollars? Nobody's ever gonna buy any of that junk, anyhow."

Morgan obviously had been through this before. After more dealing, the manager settled on two hundred and twenty-five dollars. Art would have been proud of his protege, maybe even allow him to negotiate for shrunken heads someday.

We loaded four shopping carts with the contents of the dollar bin. On the way to the checkout counter, Morgan spotted a rack of beef jerky.

"Another bingo!" he cheered. "Those island characters love beef jerky." He emptied the rack.

We paid for the jerky and K-Mart crap and pushed the carts out to Morgan's car. The haul filled the trunk and the back seat.

"You live around here, Morgan?" I asked, making idle chatter as we drove.

"You might say that. I live in my car." Up until that moment, I didn't think things could get much worse for me in aviation.

"We better stop and eat," Morgan said. "It's gonna be a long night. I know a great Mexican joint. Ya like Mexican food?"

"Sure, love it."

We stopped at a place called the *Taco Mucho*. Morgan was right, it was a great joint. The green chile shrimp enchiladas were outstanding.

They were so good that I ordered a second helping, along with a second side of pineapple *pico de gallo*. We used Art's money to pay the bill and the dollar tip. I was ready for the long night Morgan promised. I didn't know then but it would be one of the longest nights of my life, right up there with the Benny Smiles adventure.

The *Great Langosta Caper* was on.

The flight down to Cat Island in the Bahama chain took just under three hours, most of which was filled with Morgan's lengthy accounts of his sexual conquests, heroic bar fights, surefire dog track and *jai alai* strategies and enough flying stories to fill another book. By contrast, my own stories were not worth the mention. I just listened. Today I wish I had taken notes.

We arrived at Cat Island about dusk. Morgan brought the *Azore Whore* down low, banked hard over the water, scattered a couple dozen pelicans and lined up with what looked like the beach.

"Gonna land on the beach?" I asked. It had been done before. A DC-3 can land just about anywhere.

"No, there's a strip just to the left of the beach," he said. "See it?"

I didn't see the strip. What I *did* see were several wrecked, half-submerged aircraft in the water, all of which suggested that we were about to land on a runway with a higher than average degree of sportiness.

The runway was a short, narrow, unlit crushed coral and sea shell affair carved out of the jungle growth on the edge of the water. Morgan landed and turned the *Azore Whore* around at the end of the runway. The tail of a twin-Beech stuck up out of the surf to my right; it moved with the waves like a piece of aluminum seaweed. Good place for it. That was one twin-Beech some poor guy wouldn't ever have to fly again.

Morgan scanned in the direction of a dirt road. A set of headlights flashed erratically at us.

"Great, Raoul's right on time. That's rare. Usually he gets too drunk and forgets to come. Then we gotta go in town and look for the son of a bitch."

"Who's Raoul?"

"Our Cat Island contact."

"He's got the *langostas*, huh?" I asked, happy that the operation was going so smoothly. Hell, I'd be back at Bryson's by 1 a.m. The place would just be warming up. I had this thing going with a Cuban babe named Lulu.

"Oh, fuck no, Raoul doesn't have the *langostas*. The *langostas* are on Rum Cay about fifty miles southeast of here," Morgan said.

I got an uneasy feeling. "Uh, how do we get there?"

"By water," Morgan said, matter of factly.

"Wouldn't it be easier to just fly the *Whore* over?"

"Rum Cay doesn't have an airstrip. We have to take the boat from here."

At the mention of a boat, I began to feel ill. I can't even look at a *picture* of a boat without grabbing onto something. I also happen to be afraid of the water, even water *not* famous for its shark population.

"A boat? You mean I gotta get in a goddamn boat?" I whined. "I hate boats. Nobody said anything about a boat."

"I guess you could stay here," Morgan said. "But we're not supposed to land here. We don't have landing rights or some such bullshit. If the local cops come out, you'll probably spend the night in jail."

"Jail!?"

"Well, not really a jail, more like a loony bin. The cops park a jeep in front of the door to keep you inside. Just don't sleep, keep moving around till I come for you. The rats aren't too much of a problem but watch for the scorpions, especially the big red ones. And just about any of the spiders you see could kill you. Don't talk to anyone in there. You wouldn't believe the characters in that place."

"I can imagine," I said.

Morgan looked at me. He shook his head. "No, you *can't* imagine! This ain't Cleveland, Ohio."

I figured I'd take my chances with the boat. I prayed it was a big one. It wasn't. Or a new one. Wrong again. Maybe the sea would be calm. Strike three.

"Whose gonna drive the boat?" I asked.

"Raoul, the same guy driving the truck."

"Didn't you say he drinks a lot?"

"Not to worry. No law against drinking and running a boat," Morgan explained. "Boats run on booze."

"Are we gonna be in the Bermuda Triangle?" I asked. I wasn't sure where it was.

"Oh, hell yes," Morgan said, "but that'll be the least of your worries. By the way, if Raoul's been drinking don't piss him off. He's a touchy bastard. When he's drunk *and* pissed, he turns wild."

An essential member of Art's *langosta*-bootlegging team, Captain Raoul was a taciturn, swarthy, shirtless local with a tattoo of a sinking ship on his back. His appearance instilled a great many things. Confidence was not one of them. To my chagrin, Raoul *had* been drinking, steadily for the last thirty or forty years by my best estimate.

We loaded the K-Mart wampum into the back of Raoul's rattling truck and drove a short distance to where his boat, the *Toot Toot Tootsie*, was docked. I didn't expect a cruise ship but I didn't expect the *African Queen* either. No, that libels the *African Queen,* which at least had a roof and didn't list. And Bogie only had to put up with warm beer, leeches and Hepburn's grief. We had fifty miles of Atlantic Ocean to cross. At night! With a crazy at the helm!

We climbed aboard the *Toot Toot Tootsie.* I began to get woozy. And, despite Morgan's warnings, I soon managed to piss-off Raoul. My crime? I'm not certain if it was my refusal to give Raoul my snazzy Hawaiian shirt with the pink hibiscus that I was wearing or my innocent inquiry as to the location of the life vests, an extravagance Raoul apparently felt unnecessary. He responded to the question as if it were an attack on his skills as a sailor which, of course, it was.

"You friend pretty funny guy, hah mon?" Raoul said to Morgan. "Maybe he like go reeel fast, do some tricks, hah?"

Raoul opened a beer bottle with his back teeth as he pushed the throttle wide open. The bow of the *Toot Toot Tootsie* lifted straight up out of the water.

"Now ya did it, ya got him mad," Morgan said to me out of the corner of his mouth. "Better hang on."

"Hang on? To what?"

Raoul had guessed that I was afraid of boats. It pleased him no end and spurred his playful side. Unfortunately, what the *Toot Toot Tootsie* lacked in aesthetics and safety features it made up for in speed. Raoul cut a half-dozen terrifying donuts among the Cat Island reefs; he looked back at me and guffawed drunkenly.

In the open water Raoul aimed for the swells, which proved as impenetrable as concrete bridge abutments. Bahamian waters are only calm in cruise ship advertisements. Each swell stopped the speeding *Toot Toot Tootsie* dead and hoisted her about ten feet into the air, after which the boat returned stern-first to the sea, landing with hull-crushing force.

The moonless night added to the horror. I knew what it felt like to ride a rapid locked inside a 55-gallon drum.

I was too frightened at that point to be seasick, but as Raoul tired of the game and took up a more or less steady course for Rum Cay, my stomach rose to the occasion. Morgan sensed that I wasn't doing too well, probably because I was sprawled on the bottom of the boat, whimpering.

"You all right?" he asked.

I was too sick to respond, nor even nod my head. I lay face down in a layer of burnt oil, diesel fumes, seaweed and seawater that leaked into the boat. My stomach communicated with my brain; they discussed the second order of green chile shrimp enchiladas and side of pineapple *pico de gallo* in great detail.

"Hey mon, tell you friend no puke in mah boat," the sadistic Raoul said to Morgan.

It was too late. Nor was it ordinary puke; from what I recall, it was more like the spilled insides of a gutted barracuda.

A lifetime later, the boat slowed and we wormed our way up a narrow, black, pestilential cove that cut into Rum Cay. I hung over the back of the boat and watched the slowed motor gurgle bubbles to the surface in imitation of my stomach. Low-hanging jungle growth brushed my head. I imagined every hungry poisonous creature on earth crawling or slithering down my snazzy Hawaiian shirt. The *Toot Toot Tootsie* pulled up to a makeshift dock and came to a blessed stop.

With much effort, I managed to sit upright. On the dock were dozens of stacked barrels.

"What's in the barrels, Morgan?" I asked in a strained voice that was mostly breath.

"The *langostas*," he said. "Lots of *langostas*. This'll be a good haul. You can take a few with you when we get back to Miami. They'll cook 'em for you at the Traveler's. They're delicious with plenty of butter and lemon, just a little oregano. Fried plantains on the side."

That time I managed to clear the boat. Mostly.

The locals were delighted with the K-Mart crap, most of all the beef jerky. They chewed it loudly with great zeal as they loaded the barrels of *langostas* aboard the *Toot Toot Tootsie*. All the while they cracked cheap jokes at the expense of the fledgling buccaneer in the snazzy Hawaiian shirt hanging halfway out of the boat.

At the dock, no less.

Raoul had no choice but to take it easy on the five-hour trip back to Cat Island because our heavy cargo threatened to swamp the *Toot Toot Tootsie*. The slow progress over the swells added to my agony, as did the sound and aroma of doomed *langostas* sloshing around in the barrels.

As if that wasn't bad enough, Captain Raoul ate a couple *langostas* raw and smacked his lips at me above the drone of the engine. He threw the remains into the sea.

"That for the sharks, mon," he whooped.

Sharks? So what! Bring 'em on! I welcomed the promise of a speedy end by a frenzied school of hammerheads, the more the merrier. I no longer cared about anything. Prone in my berth on the floor of the boat I drifted into delirium.

Ever the wannabe writer, I plotted out *The Revenge of the Langostas*. In the end, the *Tootsie* goes down like the *Pequod*. The *langosta* barrels break open and the creatures devour the evil Captain Raoul, bit by bit. It'd be awful, take hours. All hands are lost except for me. I am spared by Providence to fulfill some noble mission undisclosed to me at the time. I survive clinging to a floating barrel. The *langostas* stay with me, nourish me with their lives until my rescue. Humbled and inspired by Nature's selflessness, I become a better person, maybe even a vegetarian, or something goofy like that.

No amount of fantasy, of course, could distract me from the seasickness. I free fell into an abyss of self-pity. Would my suffering in aviation never end? Which of the Fates had I failed to placate? I implored the rankled Fate to identify herself and spell out the terms of appeasement. What would it take? Perhaps I could sacrifice a chicken or fatted calf when I recovered or, more immediately, a boatload of *langostas* and Raoul's freshly ripped-out, still-throbbing heart.

My only consolation was that things couldn't possibly get any worse for me in aviation. Surely, I had depleted the Fates' gamut of pilot indignities.

Not quite.

When we arrived at Cat Island, I wasn't much help reloading the illicit cargo from the boat unto Raoul's truck. Nor did my condition allow me to ride in the cab; I traveled in the bed of the truck with my tasty, smelly friends the *langostas*.

At the airplane, I used my last strength to crawl into the cockpit of the *Azore Whore* while Morgan and Raoul transferred the cargo.

Morgan made the take off. At his urging, I opened my cockpit window and flew with my head out in the slipstream all the way to Miami. Morgan tried to be a gentleman about the whole thing, which is to say he didn't laugh too much.

After we landed, Morgan conveniently neglected to stop at U.S Customs since we couldn't hide the *langostas* as easily as Art had hidden the shrunken heads. Art met the airplane; he and Morgan unloaded the barrels. Too weak to even climb down the ladder, I simply rolled out of the cargo door onto the ground. My sole contribution to the *langosta* importing operation, besides providing entertainment for everyone, was to hose down the right side of the airplane.

As a fitting end to the *Great Langosta Caper,* Morgan and Art, still handicapped by the arm cast, dropped one of the barrels. It burst open; *langostas* large and small took off across the ramp. Boy, could they move! I watched Morgan and Art run down a few dozen but I was too sick to truly appreciate the humor. A good number escaped. For several weeks their shells, picked clean by gulls and cockroaches, littered the Corner and reminded me of my ordeal.

Art handed me my money, a hundred dollars. If I hadn't needed the money so badly to launch my airline career, I would have burned it. I turned down the two squirming plump *langostas* Art held in front of my face and raced for an unseen place to pay yet more tribute to the sea. I didn't eat a lobster again for twenty-two years.

Then things began looking up.

*   *   *   *

A few days later I met a doe-eyed lass, whose name I don't remember even though we meant a lot to each other for a couple weeks. For reasons as baffling today as they were then, the doe-eyed lass thought I was cute and even, at times, amusing. I moved out of the dingy Traveler's Motel and into her Coral Gables apartment. I play piano and the doe-eyed lass even had an antique Steinway grand willed to her by a grandmother, who, more important, had left her no little cash. She also owned a brand new car, which was fortunate because she refused to set foot in the Jaguar. I finally had a base of operation, complete with flush babe, piano and a new car that didn't overheat.

They also serve who stand and wait.

In addition, the airline deal with Three-fingered Hank grew more promising by the day. W.W. Storm and I ran into Hank at Bryson's and learned that he actually had a DC-7 we could see and touch.

"Yep, I got 'er, prettiest thing you ever saw," Hank exulted. "Pan Am towed it over to the Corner this very morning. You guys got your money? I can't wait forever."

"Not exactly," I said. "But we're gettin'close."

The gods had done this to me before, allowed me within reach of a goal then yanked the rug out from under me. Divine torture is by far the worst.

"Well, ya got a week or two," Hank said. "I can't fly 'er right now anyway. She needs a little maintenance."

That the ship needed maintenance came as no surprise. It certainly aroused no suspicion since the DC-7 was the type of aircraft that required maintenance within a few minutes of leaving the assembly line. Hank said the ship was being repainted as we spoke and invited the two of us to come by and see it.

The following day W.W. and I drove to the Corner. As advertised, there was Hank *and* a Douglas DC-7, a long-range "C" model. Maybe once, I thought, the cynics who handicap the game of aviation were wrong. My patience had finally paid off. Screw the Fates!

Hank, a mechanic as well as a pilot, was in the process of removing the cowling from the number four engine. He was perched atop his maintenance vehicle, a converted bakery delivery van with "Macaluso's Freshest—From My Kitchen To Your Stomach" still painted on the side. I poked my head into the van. It smelled of cheese blintzes and hydraulic fluid.

"Ain't she a beauty?" Hank said, waving at us with three fingers and a thumb. "Need to swap out a couple cylinders on this number four engine, maybe work on the radios a little but otherwise she's in great shape."

I had never seen a man so proud, so happy or so anticipatory. Unless it was W.W. or myself.

The DC-7 was undeniably a beauty. Granted, the airplane was twenty years out of step with the rest of the industry, but to W.W. and I even an old DC-7 represented the unobtainable: Prestige. Big money. Day flying. Passengers. Stewardesses!

The aluminum skin, still shining from the last buffing it got at Pan Am, fairly sparkled in the broiling Florida afternoon sun. This truly was the "Douglas Racer," the last in a long line of Douglas piston-engine airliners and by far the sleekest and fastest. I thought of Firecan Haddock and how much he would have loved it.

Hank removed the cowling from the number four engine and handed the pieces down to W.W. and me. I was awed by the sight of the R3350 engine, the redoubtable Wright "sprinkling can," so called because of its inclination to ooze oil. A pilot need only worry when an R3350 *wasn't* dripping oil, according to Hank. The motor, which traced its oily roots back to Kill Devil Hill, stuck out of the wing obscenely in all its naked, massive beauty.

"Hey, Hank, you got a name for this airline?" I asked. "We're gonna need a name, aren't we?"

"Who ya think you're dealin' with? 'Course I got a name."

"Uh, what is it?" I asked.

"You guys go check out the left side of the airplane and ya can read it for yourself," Hank beamed. "Had it painted on yesterday."

Beaming also, W.W. and I walked around to the left side of the ship, curious as to the name of the airline of which we would soon be part owners and captains. I stopped short when I saw it.

Hank did indeed have a name for our airline. There it was, in yellow, gold and the pulsating purple of a fast food joint, the name of the airline that I would help start, the airline where I planned to spend a career, be a big shot, hire and fire, the airline into which I was about to sink my money, hopes and dreams.

"TRANS CELESTIAL AIR TRANSPORT."

Trans Celestial Air Transport? I had the feeling of shattered expectations that had become so familiar to me in my flying career, probably the same feeling loyal Ford buyers must have experienced when they learned that the company's hot new offering for 1957 was to be known as the "Edsel." I felt embarrassed for the DC-7.

"Wuddaya think, W.W.?" I asked.

"I dunno. I kind o' like it," he said.

"You would."

"Oh yeah? So wudda you think about it?"

"Remember the day when that asshole Moondog hired that guy to paint 'The Academy of the Air' on the front of the hangar?" I said. "Remember how we all felt? Kinda stupid?"

"Yeah...."

"Well, I feel the same way now."

It got worse; there was also a logo. W.W. and I stepped back to appreciate it fully, the way one does to study a fourteen-foot Caravaggio canvas. It was no Caravaggio. A swollen black circle covered the vertical fin and rudder. A constellation of silver stars repeated, in a semi-circle against the black background, "TRANS CELESTIAL AIR TRANSPORT." Under the letters were two objects that resembled winged rockets, precursors of the cruise missile. The two rockets were on a collision course.

"Hey, Hank, you sure 'bout that name?" I asked when I returned to the number four engine. Hank had his head buried between the engine and the firewall.

"Hell yes, I'm sure about that name," Hank said, his voice echoing off the firewall.

"Where'd ya come up with it?"

"I did a survey," he said.

"Oh, yeah? Who'd ya ask about it? The guys at Bryson's?"

"Yeah, matter o' fact I did. They all think it's a great name. Some pretty sharp guys hang out there, case ya hadn't noticed."

I hadn't.

"How 'bout that logo? Where'd ya come up with that?" I said.

"I saw something like it on TV once, kind o' borrowed the idea," he said.

"What were ya watchin' at the time, Captain Video?" I cracked.

Hank didn't respond.

I thought it odd that Hank had not painted the name and logo on the *right* side of the ship. "PAN AMERICAN WORLD AIRWAYS" was clearly discernible under a thin coat of cheap silver paint, as if the name were trying to burst through the cover. I speculated that the airplane objected to her new, lesser role in aviation—not to mention her new name—and was trying to assert her identity and the esteem she once enjoyed as a pampered star of the Pan Am fleet.

"How 'bout the right side of the airplane, Hank? Ain'tcha gonna paint the name on it, too?" I asked.

The hot sun, a recalcitrant cylinder nut and my pressing questions seemed to be eroding Hank's patience but he nonetheless took time to educate me.

"People never look at the right side of an airplane, only the left side, the side they get into. Costs money to paint both sides. If you're gonna be an airline owner, you oughta start thinkin' 'bout such things."

I was reasonably certain that the major airlines painted the company name on *both* sides of their airplanes, but I didn't push the issue. Hank had a large wrench in his hand and I stood within easy range. At least Hank had the airplane and everything was right on schedule. Perhaps when I became a shareholder, I could negotiate with the board of directors for a new name, on *both* sides of the airplane.

"You guys got a bunch of questions. But how 'bout the money?" Hank asked, surfacing from under the motor mount. He sucked the back of a hand that he had smashed between the wrench and the cylinder.

"Not yet," W.W. and I said in unison.

"Let's see...today's the nineteenth. I'll give you guys till the end of the month to raise your share. Ya can find me at Bryson's."

That much I already knew.

As W.W. and I walked away, I noticed lettering under the left cockpit window. Hank had named her *Princess*. I approved of the name, a giant step up from the *Azore Whore*. No doubt about it, I was making progress in aviation.

"I'll be back, *Princess*," I said.

"Did you just talk to that airplane?" W.W. asked.

"I guess I did," I admitted. I've always talked to airplanes. I thought all pilots did.

"Might want to spend a little more time in Bryson's and a little less time in the sun," W.W. said.

I relayed my desperate financial position to the doe-eyed lass that evening. She had an idea. Her father was chairman of a large corporation that had recently purchased a new Learjet. At her request, he made a few calls and learned the chief pilot was looking for a copilot. The airplane was based in posh West Palm, about an hour's drive away. Her father set up an appointment for me with the chief pilot, who, I was cautioned, would have the final say.

A corporate job? Of course! Why hadn't I thought of it? I could fly for her father's company and still own shares in Trans Celestial Air Transport, where I could retreat to if the corporate job didn't work out. If I had a steady flying job with a company the banks had heard of, I might even be able to borrow money for the shares in Trans Celestial. Hell, if I had some Learjet time, the big time airlines couldn't possibly turn me down. Aviation, which until then had been a contracting universe for me, began to expand.

I'd no doubt have to schmooze the corporate chief pilot clown a bit, but I could do that with the best.

I had to work fast. First, I'd need a suit for the interview. I didn't know much about corporate flying, but the corporate pilots I had seen all wore suits. I hated suits almost as much as I hated the toy-soldier uniforms the airline guys wore, but I'd do it.

Since I was saving my money to buy into Trans Celestial Air Transport I shopped, against the protests of the doe-eyed lass, at a discount clothing store called Weinrab's. Weinrab's seductive ad read, "Suits to suit you, prices to please you!" That day Weinrab's offered a suit special for $29.95. With two pair of pants!

The doe-eyed lass, familiar with my taste in clothes, accompanied me as an advisor. She urged me to buy a better suit but a suit's a suit, I figured. I went for the special, located on a rack in a darkened room in the rear of the store. My first choice was a rose-colored beauty that would have been dynamite with the maroon shirt and mustard tie I selected.

The doe-eyed lass shook her head and dug in her hooves. At one point, she screeched and became wild-eyed. (Women betray their true nature at the least likely times.) I knew there was no way I was getting out of the store with anything that suited my tastes. I stood helplessly by as the doe-eyed lass picked out a dark blue suit. She assured me that corporate pilots wore dark blue suits. I whined but it didn't help.

Mr. Weinrab altered the dark blue suit personally while the doe-eyed lass picked out a white shirt and subdued tie. Later that day she shined my scuffed shoes and took the new shirt out to be laundered and heavily starched.

I got a haircut and, the night before the interview with the corporate chief pilot, I worked hard at erasing the scoffing grin that I began to perfect in the second grade as a defense against total indoctrination by the good nuns of the Church of Martyrs. I was ready for the world of corporate aviation. Nothing could stop me now.

I awoke early the next morning, showered, shaved and splashed on a few handfuls of *Old Spice*. I dressed in my new duds. The starched shirt acted like a back brace and made me walk funny—like a corporate pilot. I looked in the mirror and hardly recognized the awkward image reflected back at me. I kissed the doe-eyed lass goodby and drove off for my appointment with the jet age. I was so pumped up that I briefly considered asking the doe-eyed lass to marry me. Her father was certain to like me as much as she. Hadn't he set up the interview for me? I'd be fixed for life with a robber baron for a father-in-law.

The Jag made the trip to West Palm Airport with just one water stop. Despite the uncharacteristic peace offering, the first thing I planned to do with my big corporate pilot paycheck was shop for a new car. I'd shoot the Jaguar. Better yet, I'd *drown* it. I'd drive right into the surf, where the Jag would be cool for the first time in its miserable life.

At the West Palm Airport corporate aviation ramp, I parked the Jag well out of view and walked to the interview that would launch my future. I passed by row after row of brand new, spit-shined bizjets that sat parked on spotless white concrete. They didn't do anything for me and never have. The little jets waited for their robber baron owners to finish playing in the sun before returning to do whatever it is robber barons do when they're not playing in the sun. I felt intimidated. In such an atmosphere of affluence, I was a Dickens' waif, well out of my league. I wished the doe-eyed lass had shined my shoes a little better.

I was to meet with a fellow named O.C. Sykes, the chief pilot, the *only* pilot for the company. Seems his copilot on the Learjet had quit without notice. A bad sign. On the other hand, he probably had to hire someone quickly. I planned on taking cold advantage of his dilemma.

O.C. Sykes didn't make it easy.

"So you're the guy with the pull, huh? Am I supposed to be impressed?" he said. He shook my hand. No chemistry passed between us, more like two stray bulldogs at a chance meeting in an alley. I immediately disliked the man and felt the feeling mutual. "Let's get this over with. I have other pilots to interview today. Ever fly corporate?"

"No, sir." I said, turning on the schmooze. "But I've always wanted to. I've dreamed of being a corporate pilot."

"That so? Where've you been flying? You're not one of those Corrosion Corner bums, are you?"

Until he said it, his voice full of disgust, I didn't realize how proud I was to be associated with the Corner. To my eternal shame, I denied it.

"Oh no, not Corrosion Corner. Never! I've been flying up north, mostly," I answered. "I've done a lot of charter and flew with Universal Air Transport, in C-46's, 'til I got laid off."

"C-46's? How quaint. This Universal Air Transport, it's a nonsked freight operation, isn't it?"

"Yes sir, it is," I said.

"I've always flown corporate myself," he said, searching my eyes for a sign of awe. He found none.

"I also have a little time in an Argosy," I said.

"An Argosy?" he said. The very name seemed to appall him. "What in God's name is that?"

"It's a four-engine turboprop."

"Never heard of it," he said.

Neither had most other people. For whatever reasons, in my early days I was drawn to many obscure, oddball airplanes. The Argosy certainly qualified. A four-engine, twin-boom design with a pod fuselage, the Argosy was the most incontestably ugly turboprop in the world. It was also the slowest. Needless to say, it had been designed and built in England.

I deftly changed the subject with a bit more schmooze. "Can we look at the Learjet?" I asked. "I'd sure love to see it."

I can be a hell of a salesman, even a conciliator, when I want. On the way over to the Learjet, I talked of my dedication to the safety of flight and high aviation ideals. Sykes started to soften. At least I thought.

"Well, here she is,"he said."A brand new Learjet. A 24, the latest model."

There wasn't so much as a scratch on the damn thing. The Lear lacked the character of the older airplanes I had been flying but I overlooked the shortcoming. I rubbed my hand on the gleaming surface of the wing.

"Unless you intend to re-wax that wing, I'd appreciate it if you'd take your hand off it," Sykes said.

I removed my hand and bit my tongue. It was not the time for one of my annihilating comebacks. Instead, it was time to put on the charm.

"I can't wait to fly this thing," I said. "Should be a lot of fun!"

"Fun?" he said. His tone suggested he had never thought of flying in that way. "What does 'fun' have to do with flying airplanes? And, just so there's no misunderstanding later, *I* will always fly the airplane when we have passengers aboard. *If* I hire you, you will only be allowed to fly when we're empty and the weather's nice."

I let it slide. I didn't want to, but I did. I opened the door on the Lear and started to enter.

"Take your shoes off!" he said. "This ain't no goddamn freighter!"

I almost didn't let that one slide; I wanted to punch him out but I restrained myself. I needed the job too much and I didn't want to let down the doe-eyed lass. No, it was time for even more charm. I had to reach deeply. Oh, what we do for love.

"Would be a pity indeed to dirty up that beautiful carpet," I said. I removed my shoes and set them down on the ground, like I was about to enter the palace of the emperor of Japan. "Assuming I get the job, what would my duties be, Mister Sykes?"

"I prefer *Captain* Sykes," he said.

How 'bout Captain Mutherfucker? Would that do?

"As for your duties, they'll be whatever I tell you to do. At the very minimum, you'll have to keep this airplane very clean. By that I mean wash and wax it at least every week and vacuum it each day."

I could do that.

"You'll load baggage and carry coats."

I could do that.

"Oh, and if you drink, you'll have to give it up since you'll be required to be available twenty-four hours a day seven days a week," Sykes said. "The people who own this airplane sometimes show up without warning. I'll expect you to be available with one hour's notice. Sober!"

We'll have to compromise on that one, pal. You could reach me at Bryson's 'bout anytime. I'll pick up some breath mints on the way out to the airport. And if I don't happen to be hooked up with some babe, I might even be able to make it to the airport in two or three hours.

"Speaking of drinks, you'll also have to cater the food and drinks and serve them in flight. The people who fly on this airplane are very particular. They are giants of industry and finance. Never allow anyone's drink to get low and never talk to the passengers, except to ask what else he or she would like. As with all proper servers, never look them directly in the eye."

My father raised me to look people in the eye. My fists tightened. I clamped my jaw till my teeth hurt.

You need this job, asshole. Keep your mouth shut. Just for once. Work a couple of months for this dickhead, get a few bucks ahead and then quit. Maybe strand him somewhere. Like in Africa, staked down on an anthill.

We made our way to the cockpit. I sat down in the copilot seat. The array of avionics was better than anything even the major airlines would install in their jets for fifteen more years. The Lear had an autopilot! I began playing with things. Captain Sykes pulled my hand from a knob.

"Don't ever touch anything in this aircraft unless I tell you to. On the ground or in the air!"

My teeth ground down about an eighth of an inch as the interview continued similarly for another fifteen minutes. Mostly, the interview consisted of Captain Jerk correcting my frequent breaches of corporate aviation protocol and lack of understanding about the finer things in life. Such as my not knowing the difference between peanuts.

"Which nuts do you serve before a meal with the drinks?" he asked.

It was an exam of some sort.

The same nuts I'll be serving all the while I work here.

"A peanut's a peanut isn't it?" I said.

"There will *never* be a peanut allowed on this airplane," Sykes said. "Peanuts are what you throw at monkeys in the zoo."

Damn, here we go with the monkeys again. Were monkeys somehow part of aviation, something I missed on one of the pilot exams? Perhaps I should have studied harder.

My future boss elaborated. "Among your many duties, you will have to purchase the selection of nuts you'll serve on this aircraft. Like everything else, they will be an assortment of only the finest and freshest nuts available. Like I said, the passengers we fly are very particular, extremely discriminating people. Nothing is too good for them. You could lose your job for boarding the wrong kind of nuts."

Now that'd be something to shoot for!

"And, if I hire you, get rid of that cheap suit. Our passengers would not approve of your suit. What the hell kind of material is that, anyway? You'll need two or three *good* suits to fly for this corporation."

There's no such thing as a good suit, Captain Prick.

"And that aftershave you're wearing, whew!" To make his point, Sykes took out a handkerchief and held it over his nose for the rest of the interview.

"It's *Old Spice*," I said. My bottle of *Old Spice*, which cost almost two bucks, was dear to me. I used it only on special occasions.

"*Old Spice?* Indeed!" Sykes said from under the handkerchief. "The passengers would gag if they ever got a whiff of that stuff."

I began to loathe my future passengers even before I met them—almost as much as I already loathed Captain Asshole. I struggled to remind myself that flying is a fun business. It was never meant for serious people like this. Why did idiots like Sykes ever become pilots in the first place? If he wanted to be so aloof and uptight, why didn't he become an NTSB investigator, or an infantry lieutenant, or an archbishop? I may be going out on a limb, but I think O.C Sykes was almost serious enough to fly for United Air Lines.

"You must understand that this isn't some kind of nonsked, dirt-bag operation," Sykes said.

Hold on a minute, you son of a bitch. I liked the pilots I flew with at the nonskeds. They're good guys, maybe the best pilots in the world. You couldn't carry Firecan's flight bag. Hell, you couldn't light his seven-cent cigars!

I caught my reflection in one of the instruments and disapproved. My subdued tie looked and felt like a noose; the starched shirt had become a body cast. I glanced around the inside of the airplane. At the plush leather seats and thick carpeting I was not allowed to walk on; at the individual television sets for the particular passengers I couldn't talk to; at the small polished galley in which I would slave; at Captain Dickhead.

This was going to be tough, almost like working for a living. But I had to do it. I smiled.

"*If* I hire you," Sykes began his next affront, "you'll get a type-rating in the Learjet at the finest facility in the world. You'll get all the time in the airplane you need before your type-rating ride. We don't rush our pilots through a half-ass training program like the nonskeds. Take all the time you want."

I had decided to put a full-court press on Sykes—tons of schmooze—when my big mouth tripped me up. As usual.

"It's nice that I'll get all the training I want," I said, "but frankly, Captain Sykes, if I couldn't get a type-rating in this Lear in five hours, I'd tear up my ticket. An asshole that weak shouldn't be flying airplanes." I thought my confidence would impress him.

Sykes' lower jaw vibrated with indignation. The handkerchief fluttered. For the first time since I met him, he was at a loss for words. I wasn't certain what I had done but I knew the interview, along with my job prospect, was over. I recognized the look.

"So, you say if you couldn't get the type-rating in five hours, you'd tear up your ticket, huh?"

"Sure, five hours, give or take an hour," I said, not quite as cocky as before.

"It might interest you to know," he said, "that I required *twenty-three* hours of training before I took the type-rating ride."

Even I couldn't blame this latest botched opportunity on the gods. Damn, I needed that job.

In retrospect, it was probably for the best. If Sykes had hired me, I wouldn't have lasted till noon the first day. I might even have stood trial for murder. In Florida they still used the chair in 1967.

Outside the airplane, I removed the subdued tie and draped it over the Learjet's pitot tube. The starched shirt served to patch a leak in the roof of the Jaguar. As for the suit, I never wore it again. I started the Jag and drove away from corporate aviation in a cloud of steam. I felt better knowing that I still had Trans Celestial Air Transport to look forward to—if I could get the thousand bucks together in time.

The doe-eyed lass didn't understand my failure to humor the corporate chief pilot and land the job. Her father, she reminded me, had gotten me the interview. He would be as disappointed as she. I tried to explain but she took O.C. Sykes' side on everything, even the peanut issue. It opened a gulf between us. Gulfs between men and women seldom grow narrower.

For the next few weeks I worked at any number of flying jobs in the Corner, including one for a character named Jim Peevis. Peevis, while a damn good pilot, was better known for getting thrown out of bars. To be a drinking pal of Peevis, which I remain to this day, meant being excluded by association from at least two-thirds of the bars in any city he had ever visited. Even at Bryson's, a joint known for its tolerance of troublemakers, Peevis was on lifelong probation.

"The bar hasn't been built yet that I can't get thrown out of," Peevis often bragged. He surely holds the record.

Peevis also claimed to be a minister. Most inspired to preach the Word when drunk, he had apparently skipped over the part about turning cheeks. According to Reverend Peevis, the highlight of the New Testament was when Jesus walked into the temple, offended everyone in sight and then mixed it up with the locals. He felt certain, although it wasn't written anywhere, that Jesus had been banned from that particular temple.

Reverend Peevis assured me that all we were bringing back from Peru in his Lockheed Lodestar, still in its World War Two olive drab, was a load of cheap native figurines. The stuff seemed innocent enough, just some old dirt-covered terra cotta pieces that ranged from simple bowls to statuettes of couples playing with each other. It looked like more useless Third World kitsch to me. Peevis even used one of the bowls for an ashtray in the Lodestar. I wouldn't have put one on a shelf.

Not that he offered me any of them.

I thought no more about the Peruvian haul until about twenty years later when, on an airline layover in New York City, the crew and I happened into the American Museum of Natural History. There, in a glass display case protected by alarms, was one of the very same statuettes that Peevis and I had hauled out of Peru. A small sign in the display case harangued the public:

"THIS IS AN EXAMPLE OF THE THOUSANDS OF PRE-COLUMBIAN ARTIFACTS BLATANTLY SMUGGLED OUT OF MEXICO, CENTRAL AND SOUTH AMERICA WITHOUT ANY RESPECT FOR ITS ARCHAEOLOGIC OR ANTHROPOLOGIC VALUE. THIS PRICELESS FIFTEEN-HUNDRED-YEAR-OLD REPRESENTATION OF A FERTILITY GOD AND GODDESS SYMBOLIZES THE SHAMELESS RAPE OF THE CULTURE OF OUR NEIGHBORS TO THE SOUTH. IT IS BELIEVED TO BE PANAMANIAN IN ORIGIN."

The looted object and the accompanying text dismayed me, a stark reminder of the gullibility and recklessness that marked my early years in aviation and seemed destined to shadow me forever. Nuts, more guilt, more tribal curses. I'd never live to retirement.

"It's not from Panama like the sign says," I told the crew without really meaning to.

"Oh really!" said one of the flight attendants. "So where's it from then, if you know so darn much?"

Flight attendants, by training and hard-won experience, are suspicious of pilots. The wiser ones believe almost nothing we say.

"Peru," I said softly out of the corner of my mouth in case anyone else might be listening. "It's from Peru."

"How do you know?" she asked. "I suppose you discovered King Tut's tomb too, huh?"

"No, I did not discover King Tut's tomb. But I know for certain that statue is from Peru," I said. "I just know. I shouldn't have said anything. Forget it."

She pressed the issue.

"I did a little…importing once," I admitted, nonchalantly backing away from the display case. "I guess you could say I was kind of an antiquities dealer."

"Whatever!" she said, in the inimitable way of flight attendants. They own the patent on the expression.

Not to minimize my own regrettable participation in sacking Peru of its magnificent past, but I couldn't help wonder why the museum people, so quick to cast guilt and censure, hadn't repatriated the artifact to Panama, if that's where they thought it came from.

Corner pilots could shed light on numerous archaeological riddles. Trust me on that one.

All said, I was still about four hundred dollars short and Three-fingered Hank's deadline was nearing. I checked the many bulletin boards in the Corner for job leads but found nothing worth pursuing. I stopped in the pool bar at the Traveler's Motel for a little change of pace and—voila—came across a promising lead in the men's room.

Written on a bar napkin and pinned over a urinal, it advertised: "Captain, copilot and professional flight engineer/mechanic needed to relocate one Bristol Britannia from Miami Int. to Guatemala City. Generous pay with full expenses and return ticket to Miami. MUST HAVE TIME IN BRISTOL BRITANNIA."

Perfect! The fact that I was only vaguely aware of the existence of such an airplane did not deter me. I had a hunch that the Bristol Britannia was a turboprop airliner built in England in the 1950s but I would not have bet on it.

As already mentioned, I had a little time in another English-built turboprop, a ship known as the "Argosy." I flew the Argosy about a year for a small freight airline until it filed bankruptcy. I knew enough about turboprops to talk my way into at least the copilot job on the Britannia. The captain they hired would have a type-rating in the ship. Even if he weren't real current, the professional flight engineer would know all about the airplane. Besides, an airplane's an airplane. Hell, I'd sleep all the way to Guatemala City.

I called the number on the note. The guy who answered turned out to be an aircraft broker, a stroke of luck since aircraft brokers are usually so desperate to deliver an aircraft they've sold that they seldom ask questions, check credentials or seek references. Airplanes would never get delivered if brokers were too particular. Nonetheless, I assured him that I had time in a Bristol Britannia just to make him feel better. Since this was the Corner in 1967, I was hired over the phone.

The broker told me to meet the captain and the professional flight engineer the next day at the airplane. Our airline reservations back to Miami were already booked. Copilot pay was two hundred dollars. I didn't mention it to the broker, but the job would also give me an opportunity to fly a Bristol Britannia and add one more loser to the rogue's gallery of aircraft that passed for my logbook.

Next morning I arrived at the designated location just in time to watch a ground crew tow the Britannia out of a hangar for the ferry flight to Guatemala City. It emerged foot-by-foot slowly, endlessly, like a giant moth from its cocoon. The sight of the Britannia in the full sun was staggering. It was gothic in size and assertiveness but at the same time as sleek as a throwing dagger. Four English-built Proteus motors, each the size of a school bus, hung from tapered wings that loomed imperiously over the ramp. It was easily the most majestic aircraft I had ever seen.

There seems to be no middle ground with the Brits, who build airplanes only two ways, either very beautiful or very grotesque. On a list of the three most fetching and three most ghastly airplanes ever built, all would be English. The Britannia was clearly one of that nation's masterpieces, the undisputed queen of all the four-engine turboprop airliners.

The Britannia failed to enjoy a long career as an airliner because, as beautiful as it was, ease and cost of maintenance were never considered. One has only to have owned a British automobile of the same era—a possessed, feverish 1953 Jaguar for instance—to appreciate the Brits' knack for wrapping a cursed and misbegotten engineering nightmare in the most lyrical of outer shells.

Complicated beyond all reason, the Britannia was the last hope of those who refused to admit jet power was the way of the future. Bristol had predicted, unpresciently, that passengers would never get on an airplane without propellers. But even if passengers had preferred props to jets, airplanes with big propellers driven by big gearboxes were mechanical money pits; they never had a fighting chance to compete with airplanes powered by jet engines, only a bit costlier to maintain than a blowtorch.

While I waited for the other two crew members with whom I would cast my lot in the Britannia that day, I took time to watch a nearby aircraft being scrapped. It was the Russian-built Shitski that I had seen my first day in the Corner. The ship apparently hadn't panned out for the new owner and had been condemned to the smelter.

As I watched the salvage crew cut the Shitski into little smelter-sized pieces, it confirmed what I suspected. The old airliners, however interesting, were not in the Corner to delight antique lovers. Aircraft that could not earn their keep were recycled with no more thought of their place in history than that of a junk refrigerator. As in the natural world, the extinction process was somewhat messy.

Oblivion for aircraft in the Corner was normally a four-stage process: First, the aircraft would stop flying on a regular basis. While the owner attempted to peddle the lemon, he would try to get it in the air once or twice a month, working from the back of a pick-up truck full of spare parts. The idea was that a flying derelict was worth more than a non-flying derelict. An aircraft could linger in this limbo stage for years, surviving a day at a time.

In the second stage, the airplane stopped flying altogether, though it remained intact. The ship seldom stayed in one place for more than a week at a time. Someone was always busily repositioning it, making room for more flyable wrecks. Nothing takes up more room or gets in the way as much as a lifeless Vickers Vanguard or Lockheed Constellation. Throughout stage two, there remained a slim chance of reprieve since someone with better resources—*two* pick-up trucks full of spare parts—might buy it and restore it to airworthiness.

During the third stage, the owner no longer bothered to move the airplane any longer. Tires went flat and the ship loitered in one place, all pretense of rehabilitation gone. At this stage, however, the owner still admitted to owning the aircraft but only because he wanted the right to sell parts off it. Radios and instruments were first removed in a kind of evisceration process. Next went the props, then the engines, usually one at a time. Hopes for an airplane's future dimmed significantly when the engines disappeared.

If the engineless airplane was a tricycle gear configuration, sometimes a couple 55-gallon drums filled with concrete were tied to the nose gear to keep it on its feet. Tail wheel types robbed of their tail wheels sunk into the ground ass first, as if being swallowed by the ramp.

In stage four, the airplane was simply abandoned. It became impossible to find the owner, who would go into hiding so that no one could annoy him to move the ship or pay ramp rent. The few salvageable parts left would mysteriously vanish in the middle of the night. Seagulls and *Cornerus Cockroachus,* a distinct variety of cockroach so big that one wondered but didn't really want to know what it ate, would take over. When the vermin were fully in charge, the end had arrived. No last appeals, no eleventh-hour phone calls to death row from the governor. The aircraft had a date with the scrappers.

Except for a large ground stain of oil and gull shit in the shape, say, of a Convair 240, no one would ever conclude that an aircraft had once occupied the spot.

I took some small consolation knowing that the Britannia was going to escape such a fate by the only way possible. It was going to get the hell out of Dodge. It pleased me knowing that I would be in on the escape.

I was again admiring the Britannia when the pilot hired as captain arrived. It was Morgan, my fellow *langosta* poacher. Funny, I thought, Morgan had never mentioned flying the Britannia in our drinking sessions. He mentioned everything *else* about himself. I became suspicious.

As did Morgan.

"Hey, Pete, where'd ya get your Britannia time?" Morgan asked. Cagily.

"I was about to ask you the same question," I said. Less cagily. "I never even *saw* one until about ten minutes ago."

"I don't have any time in a Britannia either, but I saw one once so that must make me captain," Morgan laughed. "Nobody asked to see a type-rating. I figured the other guys who showed up would know all about this thing. I don't suppose by any chance you know what a 'tiptoe' landing is all about, do you?"

"A what?"

"A 'tiptoe' landing," Morgan said. "The guy who hired me asked me if I was all checked out on 'tiptoe' landings. Naturally, I told him I was but I don't have any idea what the hell he was talking about."

"I would've tried to get the captain's job if I knew they weren't gonna ask to see a type-rating," I said. "I actually have some turboprop time."

"Good. It'll come in handy," Morgan said. "Anyway, shouldn't be a problem for two show dogs like us. The broker told me the oiler he hired is a limey, a professional flight engineer. He probably helped build the damned thing."

"I hope so," I said.

Morgan studied the big ship. "A beauty, ain't it? Be a shame to bend it up."

"Yeah, especially with us in it," I said.

A guy we assumed to be the Brit flight engineer arrived. He was of the old, dying breed of professional flight engineer, which meant he was a rated aircraft mechanic and not a pilot.

Professional flight engineers were considered a necessary evil on the complex four-engine propeller-driven airplanes of the 1950s. While PFE's operated in a pilot's world, they were invariably skeptical of pilots. They sat behind the pilots but were not afraid to speak their mind—oh boy, were they not afraid to speak their mind—and question a pilot's actions. The PFEs' forthrightness plus their working knowledge of airplane systems was invaluable.

Alas, a greedy pilot union wanted their seats. The union argued that the new jets were simple enough that even a new-hire pilot could be trusted at the flight engineer panel. The airlines saw it as a chance to save a few bucks. It was a mistake. A half-dozen airline crashes since the 1960s might have been prevented if there had been a professional flight engineer aboard. Those of us who know the difference miss the PFEs.

In the late 1980s the airlines and aircraft manufacturers took the concept one dangerous step further. Large aircraft built today no longer have *any* type of flight engineer, professional or otherwise. The bean-counters seem to think that an extra computer is better than an extra pilot. This is also a mistake. Three heads are better than two, at least until the avionic geeks come up with a computer that can ask, "Hey, what the hell are you guys doin' up there?"

The Brit took a long time doing his walk-around inspection of the Britannia. He stopped and poked at everything, especially the main landing gears which looked like stout jungle gyms. Each main gear had four tires on a cradle, which pivoted in the center and also swiveled. There must have been a million moving parts on those landing gears alone. The Brit studied the ship and shook his head over a suspect pool of hydraulic fluid that had formed under the right main gear.

"See, what I tell ya? Look at that limey check the airplane over," Morgan said.

The Brit finished his walk-around inspection. Morgan and I prepared for a Homeric-length debriefing of the problems he had found on the Britannia. PFEs could be boring as hell when it came to lecturing pilots on the workings of airplanes. Instead, the Brit ignored us and climbed the ladder leaning against the closed main cabin door.

"Good, he's goin' inside to finish his preflight," Morgan said. "A very good sign."

I felt a lot better. That is, until I watched the Brit struggle with the main cabin door handle. After a few minutes, he gave up and climbed back down the ladder. He walked over to us.

"You blokes the pilots?" he asked.

"Yeah, we sure are," I said.

"Got any idea 'ow you enter this bloody machine?"

Brits are known for their droll wit but neither Morgan nor I saw the humor.

"You mean you don't know how to get *in* the airplane?" Morgan asked.

"I 'aven't a clue, mate. That door mechanism's a son of a bitch," he said. "I was bettin' that I could query the lot of ya for info. You say you're the pilots they 'ired? Got a lot o' Britannia time, eh?"

Morgan and I looked at each other for help. We sidestepped the question for the moment and introduced ourselves to the Brit, whose name was Adrian. He admitted right away that he had never even been *inside* a Britannia, much less flown one. With no other choice, Morgan and I came clean. It didn't seem to bother Adrian.

"Well, she's just another machine," Adrian said. "Turboprops are all pretty much the same. We'll be fine, if we can ever figure out 'ow to get inside the bloody thing."

"Have you ever, just by chance, heard of a 'tiptoe' landing?" Morgan asked.

"Sure 'aven't, mate. That sounds like pilot stuff. I'm a flight engineer," Adrian answered. Proudly.

A line boy walked by, climbed the ladder to the Britannia door, opened what appeared to be a secret panel next to the door and held a switch. The door opened as if by magic.

"Might o' guessed the bloody thing was electric," Adrian said. "We Brits love our electrons, we do."

"Let's get in that airplane and get it the hell out of here before the feds show up and start asking questions," Morgan suggested.

A good idea. The FAA slipped in and out of a Corner pilot's life with the whimsy of gods in a Greek tragedy. Like the Greek gods, they were known on occasion to disguise themselves as mere mortals and appear on earth to vex pilots and ask questions for which only they had the answers.

The three of us quickly followed the line boy into the airplane.

"Hey, kid, you know anything about this airplane? Morgan asked.

"Jist how to fuel it. Need ta look at the fuel gauges in the cockpit," he said. "Some guys are gonna fly 'er out of here today. Are you them?"

"Yeah, as a matter of fact we are," Morgan said.

"How much fuel ya want?" he asked, looking at us warily. He had watched the door stymie Adrian.

"Uh...lots! Yeah, lots of fuel," Morgan answered.

It would have been the correct reply in any airplane.

The three of us quizzed the line boy for more information but, to our chagrin, all he knew how to do was fuel the thing—and open and close the main cabin door. He told us he would hook up the external air for starting when we were ready and then left.

The line boy closed the door from the outside. Morgan and I, sharing second thoughts about flying the Britannia, discussed jumping ship.

"You might as well scrap that idea, mates," Adrian said. "It'd be as easy to fly the bugger to Guatemala City as it'd be to get that door open again."

The cabin had been gutted of its seats in preparation for the Britannia's future dreary life as a freighter. The resulting empty tube was as long, high and awe-inspiring as a cathedral. I looked up, half-expecting a painting of a partly cloudy Heaven with angels blowing horns.

We made our way to the cockpit. I sat down in the copilot's seat and looked around. I was beset by the most baffling array of instruments and knobs I had ever seen, or ever will see. Nothing looked even remotely familiar. I had stumbled into a lost tomb full of the encrypted secrets of a vanished race, a bug inside a television set.

To add to my uneasiness, I noticed that many of the gauges and instruments were Lucas, the same English company that made those in my Jaguar, none of which worked. The joke in England is that beer is drunk warm because Lucas makes the refrigerators.

On the captain's control column was a list of "verbals," which are mechanical complaints about the airplane left behind by the last crew to fly it. There were no less than 106 meticulously numbered verbals.

Adrian studied the verbals list for a moment, crinkled it up and threw it out of the cockpit.

"Nothing serious, huh?" Morgan asked Adrian.

"Don't even know what most o' those items are," Adrian answered in a calm voice. "But she flew in 'ere, she'll fly out." Brits possess irrefutable logic.

The three of us went to work trying to demystify the cockpit. There were too many propeller mechanisms to count. Three separate devices looked as if they could qualify as the flap lever. Morgan and I enjoyed a good chuckle over four stubby red knobs labeled "high pressure cocks." Sometimes the Brits are funny without knowing it.

"Well, anyone got any ideas how we crank up this thing?" Morgan said, looking over his shoulder at Adrian, who was playing with the profusion of switches on the flight engineer panel and fighting the half-dozen adjustment levers on the flight engineer's seat.

"Well, can't be any great trick to it. Give 'er air, git them motors spinning an' throw fuel and fire to 'em. Why not open that window and 'ave that chap 'ook up our pneumatics? Then I'll see which gauges start moving back 'ere. That oughta give me a clue."

Morgan, unable to figure out how to open the window, pounded on the glass and waved until he had the line boy's attention. When the line boy at last looked up, Morgan blew into his fist, an impromptu signal to hook up the external air necessary for turning the engines. We had no way of knowing that the air was fed into the airplane from *under* the cockpit floor.

"WOOOSH!"

The sound of air rushing under the floor scared the hell out of Morgan and me, kind of like sitting on top of a wind tunnel.

The rushing air didn't faze Adrian. Nothing seemed to faze Adrian. Come to think of it, I never saw *anything* faze a professional flight engineer in the twenty years I worked with them.

"An English trick, puttin' the air in under the cockpit seats. I expected as much," Adrian said.

"Thanks for warning us," Morgan said. He looked at me. "We'll get even with him, won't we?"

"I hope not!" I said.

After trying a dozen or so switches, Adrian found one that made the number four propeller begin to turn. It then became a game of guessing which of the numerous levers supplied fuel and ignition. The line boy looked up at us impatiently. Ground crews are like that.

We finally got all four engines started, each by a different procedure. I called Miami ground control and got clearance out to runway nine left. Morgan cautiously pushed up what we all agreed were the throttles and the Britannia was underway. The Ferris wheel-sized props whistled and hummed as they passed through their pitch ranges. They sounded like four mammoth vacuum sweepers running in different directions.

Morgan positioned a lever that caused a faraway rasping sound. We assumed, and hoped, that it was the sound of the flaps lowering. A little gauge with an arrow-like needle seemed to confirm it.

"You guys ready?" I asked.

"If I think about this much more, I won't go," Morgan said. "What the hell! Call the tower, tell 'em we're ready."

"A less 'eroic crew would ask for the crash trucks to stand by, ya know," Adrian commented dryly.

"Yeah, like *that* wouldn't get the feds' attention," Morgan said. He looked at me. "You go ahead and make the takeoff and I'll make the landing. You get the first chance to kill us."

"You happy with everything back there, Adrian?" I asked, grasping the yoke.

"I'm not happy with *anything* back 'ere! I 'aven't identified all these gauges yet," he said. "Let's just go."

Each time a pilot climbs into an airplane, *any* airplane, he bets that his skills, experience and knowledge of the equipment are equal to the task. Normally, the odds are about even. That day the odds were far longer—in favor of the Bristol Britannia.

What the hell. I pushed the throttles forward. Dozens of gauges I hadn't noticed before came alive. Needles spun wildly, some clockwise, some counterclockwise. Lights of red, amber and green flashed from dark corners of the cockpit like the blinking eyes of skulking jungle creatures. The four unrestrained Proteus engines pulled the Britannia, the unfulfilled, ultimately discardable dream of another age and the last physical vestige of an empire in decline, down the runway. Britannia, England's mythical Queen of the Waves, could really haul ass!

The three passengers trapped inside her anxiously awaited the outcome. After rolling a couple thousand feet the ship longed to fly. I eased back on the "ram horns" yoke typical of British airplanes and the Britannia slipped into the air. The airplane had a solid feel. Like most airliners its performance when not loaded down with fuel, passengers and tons of baggage was pleasingly spirited. Oddly, the wheel itself did not turn to move the ailerons. Instead, the entire column pivoted at the floor and moved not only fore and aft, but left and right, giving the controls a motorcycle quality. A couple of miles later, over the posh hotels of Miami Beach, Morgan began searching for the landing gear lever.

"Anyone got any ideas how to get the gear up?" Morgan asked, "I don't see a fuckin' gear lever."

Incredibly, the Britannia seemed to have no landing gear lever. There was, however, a large guarded red switch where the gear lever should have been. Very tempting indeed but Morgan wisely resisted the urge. Impulsively thrown guarded red switches have been known to turn a bad situation into a crash.

"It won't be marked 'landing gear.' It'll be marked 'undercarriage.' And there won't be a big lever. There'll be a switch of some kind. Only you yanks need a gear lever the size of a cricket bat," Adrian said with undisguised condescension.

Adrian's cultural differences training did the trick. Morgan found the switch and retracted the gear and even managed to raise the flaps. The mysterious "tiptoe" landing was forgotten for the moment. Most pilots try not to think too far ahead. It interferes with the naps.

By some small miracle, Adrian got us pressurized and even broke the code on engaging the autopilot. We congratulated each other on our mastery of the Bristol Britannia's complicated systems. I took up a heading for Guatemala City, reclined my seat and dove into a crossword puzzle in the Miami *Herald*.

"What's a five-letter word for 'chance taker'?" I asked the rest of the crew.

"Idiot!" Adrian answered.

It fit.

I fell fast asleep during "11 across" on the puzzle. I dreamed of Trans Celestial Air Transport, especially the hot stewardesses that Three-fingered Hank promised W.W. and I could hire. For once, *I'd* be the guy asking the questions.

Morgan jostled me awake about forty miles from Guatemala City.

"Wake up, ace," Morgan said. "You don't wanna miss this smooth landing.

Guatemala City airport is built atop an ancient volcano, which is surrounded, like parapets on a castle, by other volcanoes of varying degree of activity. The runway is not only short and dangerously sloped—in both directions—but has abrupt drop-offs on both ends. The penalty for running off the runway at Guatemala City is worse than at most airports since it's just a short trip to the side of the mountain and the tin shacks full of local residents. I had heard stories of pilots who survived a crash in this part of the world only to be stoned to death for destroying a neighborhood.

The weather was clear and we spotted the airport at Guatemala City easily—it's the only volcano in the area with a runway. I called the tower, which cleared us to make a visual approach to the north.

Morgan entered a left base leg to land north.

"Gear down," he said. "Or should I say 'lower the undercarriage'?" He looked over his shoulder and grinned at Adrian.

At that point we were still having fun.

I flipped the gear switch and heard the gratifying dropping sound that is music to a pilot's ears, though in the case of the Britannia the sound was more like a ton of boulders being unloaded onto a steel truck bed. The airplane yawed disturbingly to the right. I looked for the three green lights that would tell us the gear was down and locked. The nose gear and left main gear showed steady green but both the green *and* the red lights on the right main gear flashed like a frenzied railroad crossing.

"What the hell do ya' suppose that means?" Morgan said.

Airplane malfunctions range from trivial to life threatening. An unsafe landing gear is somewhere in the middle. I recalled my experience with the shepherd's hook in the C-46, with which I manually lowered the tail wheel. The biggest shepherd's hook in the world wasn't going to help with the gear on the Bristol Britannia.

"Recycle that son of a bitch," Morgan said.

I retracted the gear, waited until all the lights had gone out, and lowered it once more. Again, we had two steady green lights and flashing green and red on the right main.

"Go have a look, will ya Adrian?" Morgan said. "Pete, tell the tower we're gonna turn back out on a downwind."

While I communicated the request to the tower, Adrian went to the back of the airplane to have a look at the problematic right landing gear out the cabin window. He returned to the cockpit perplexed.

"From what I can tell, the right gear is down, mate," he reported. "It appears to be locked but the front end of the bogey is 'anging down at a bloody sharp angle. I think I read something about it once..."

"Ah hah, so you *do* know something about the Britannia?" Morgan said.

"Not really. I read about it in a crash report."

"That crash report didn't say anything about a 'tiptoe' landing, did it?"

"Might 'ave. I don't exactly remember. I better 'ave a look at the port side, see what it looks like."

When in doubt, always compare one side of the airplane to the other.

Adrian disappeared to the cabin again for a few minutes. He returned to the cockpit even more perplexed.He said the front and rear tires on the left gear truck appeared level.

"What do you think, Adrian?" Morgan asked.

"I think one side's right and one side's wrong," Adrian said.

It was never easy to get a straight answer from a professional flight engineer. They tended to hedge their bets.

"I think this all has something to do with what that broker said about a 'tiptoe' landing and that puddle of hydraulic fluid under the right gear," Morgan said. "He knew that right gear was messed up. Probably knew this would happen, the son of a bitch."

"You don't 'spose you land the thing with the gear like that, do ya?" I asked. "Ya think that's why they call it a 'tiptoe' landing?"

"Do we have a choice?" Morgan turned to Adrian. "You sure the gear looks down and locked and that just the wheels are cockeyed?"

"Looks to be," he replied, calmly. "But we don't really 'ave enough fuel to discuss it much longer."

Despite our request to put plenty of fuel on, the line boy must have had orders from the broker to put just enough to get us to Guatemala City. Aircraft brokers are like that. The fuel-quantity gauges were moving toward empty, a normal process but one that seems to speed up considerably when something is amiss. None of us had bothered to measure how much fuel the jumbo Proteus engines had consumed per hour but we knew it was considerable. Compared to the prospects of running out of fuel and landing dead-stick in the mountains, a tiptoe landing—whatever the hell that was—seemed like child's play. If a pilot waits long enough, fuel quantity always makes his decision for him.

"Fuck it, let's just go ahead and land," Morgan said. "I'm gonna bet that you touch down on the screwed-up side first and then eeease it on down on the good side, kinda tiptoe like. You Brits build some goofy airplanes, Adrian."

"Just remember we probably won't git paid if ya botch this thing, mate," Adrian added to boost Morgan's confidence. "There's probably something about it in the emergency checklist—if we can find it."

I found the emergency checklist, a muddle of Brit doubletalk. Every possible contingency imaginable was thoroughly covered. Everything, that is, except the tiptoe landing. Not a word. The tiptoe landing apparently fell under the same catastrophic category as the loss of a wing, for which there is also no checklist.

"No problem for a Bryson's regular," Morgan said. "Here we go!"

Guatemala City tower cleared us to land. Morgan lowered some flaps until the airplane felt right. He set up a long shallow approach, hoping to touch down on the very first part of the runway for what promised to be a very thrilling two-stage landing.

The tower must have noticed that the gear didn't look right and started babbling in a mixture of Spanish and English. Foreign controllers know just enough English to cover the normal things. All bets are off when something unusual is involved. We already knew what they were saying. Morgan continued the approach.

Over the runway Morgan eased the right main gear, the side improperly extended, to the ground first. The tires thumped the pavement. So far so good. He then eased the yoke to the left while pulling off the power. The right side was a full four feet higher than the left and the airplane seemed to fall sideways forever. The airplane hit hard on the left side, bounced a couple of times, but finally stuck. We rolled along the runway with the right wingtip high in the air and the other only a few feet from the ground. Morgan fought with the controls to keep us on the runway while Adrian figured out how to bring the props into reverse.

The Bristol Britannia came to a stop in its new home. I looked down from my perch at Morgan, who was pressed against the left side of the cockpit, reaching for a cigarette.

"The next time somebody asks if you're checked out on tiptoe landings you won't have to lie to them, Morgan," I said.

"Suppose you can taxi the goddamn thing like this?" Morgan wondered out loud.

"I 'spect taxiing 'ill be the easy part after that landing, mate," Adrian said.

Like a giant bird with a broken wing, Morgan taxied to the cargo ramp where a small crowd waited on us. Someone brought a ladder over to the airplane and opened the door, which remained an enigma to us. Adrian was the first to reach the door. He almost fell out. Morgan and I carefully deplaned behind him.

On the ground I stepped back from the Britannia. It looked like a classy, if intoxicated, lady propped up on an elbow at the bar. Not too pretty, but all there.

"*Senor capitan*, that was the most beeeoootiful teeptoe landing I ever see," said one of the Guatemalan locals waiting for the airplane. "And never have I see anyone taxi like that. In fact, I never even hear of no one who taxi after the teeptoe landing! You good, *senor capitan*."

The crowd nodded in agreement, each face full of awe for Morgan's great skill.

"Well, when you've got as much time in the Bristol Britannia as I have, it's not that hard," Morgan said, laying it on like any pilot would have in his position.

We received our money for delivering the airplane, lopsided but intact. The impressed locals gave us a ride to the passenger terminal to catch our flight back to Miami. We left the Britannia behind to take her chances with the volcanoes and future "teeptoe" landings. I don't think I've ever been so happy to get away from an airplane.

The airline crew had watched our heroics from the ground and insisted on moving us up to first class. On the way back to Miami we drank heavily and threw food around. Morgan mixed it up a bit with one of the crew members who came back to settle us down. By the time we landed we had been moved to coach.

Like all other Wonders of the Ancient World, the Bristol Britannia in time will surely fade from reality to myth. Such aircraft are a decidedly unrenewable resource. And unless someone with a sense of humor and history, a ton of money and unlimited space has salted away a Britannia, future generations will doubt that it ever existed or that a "tiptoe" landing was once a certified maneuver.

I was now only about two hundred dollars short of the thousand bucks that would buy me a share in Trans Celestial Air Transport and a future of riches. The doe-eyed lass had forgiven me for disappointing her father and insisted on spotting me the money.

She was to prove as unwise in her choice of investments as she was in her choice of boyfriends.

I called W.W., who told me he also had his money. Seems he had spent a few nights flying rifles to a small airstrip outside Managua. The men who picked up the weapons told W.W. that they were to be used in a shooting gallery at a carnival of some sort. Back in Miami, W.W. had his doubts.

"Hey, Pete, didn't you tell me once that you worked in a carnival?" W.W. asked when I met him at Bryson's.

"Sure did. Gooding Brothers, Unit Number Five. Dart toss. We lived on the edge, absolutely no limit on teddy bears. A customer could win as many bears as he wanted. But after two, we slipped him the shaved darts. He'd be lucky to hit the back of the tent." I was set to launch into a good hour's worth of carny stories when W.W. interrupted me.

"Did the carnival have a shooting gallery?"

"Yeah," I said. "The rifle nearest the operator wasn't chained down, just in case one of us needed it to shoot a rube. I remember one hot night in Akron…"

"Never mind that shit. Do you remember what kind of rifles they used?" W.W. asked. He was not a gun man.

"Sure, Winchesters, twenty-two shorts," I said.

"Could you use something else?"

"Like what?"

"Like something called an AR-15? Ever heard of those?"

I looked at W.W. the way Jack's mother surely did when he announced his fateful trade for the family cow. The same way, in fact, that people would soon be looking at me when I related the Three-fingered Hank story.

"The carnival those guys talked about is the one they're going to have *after* the revolution you made possible with the AR-15s," I said.

W.W. took on a pained look as he put the pieces together—a seminal moment indeed for my old friend.

Paranoid marine colonels working unilaterally in the White House fruit cellar may have arranged the financing, but everyone in the Corner, except W.W., knew how the weapons got to revolutionaries or anyone else with cash south of the border.

At any rate, W.W. and I both had our money. We called Three-fingered Hank to set up a meeting. He arrived at Bryson's within ten minutes. He was a little too eager. It should have been a tip-off.

"This is the best thing you guys ever did in your life," Hank said, counting the money carefully. He bought a round of drinks with our money. He gave us stock certificates that had been run off on a mimeograph machine.

"Hey Hank, my girlfriend loaned me some money for this," I said. "How's 'bout I bring her around tomorrow to see the operation. That okay?"

"Sure," he said, walking away. "She'll be plenty proud of you."

Next day the doe-eyed lass and I, following a celebratory breakfast complete with champagne, drove to the future home of Trans Celestial Air Transport.

Hank wasn't there. For that matter, there was no sign of life anywhere, except for some gulls that circled over *Princess* like buzzards. The gate on the chain-link fence around the ramp was padlocked. There was a note wired to the fence. I thought it might be from Hank. Maybe he was eating breakfast or something. The note had a salutation that had become all too familiar to me in my aviation career:

"BY ORDER OF THE SHERIFF,..."

It was a bank lien, a lien against Douglas DC-7C registration number N10704, a lien against Trans Celestial Air Transport, a lien against my future.

"Must be some kind of mistake," I said, trying to minimize what was obviously a very bad situation.

The money was gone and we both knew it. To her credit, the doe-eyed lass didn't say a word. Good women never do when their men screw up; men seldom extend the same courtesy. After that morning, however, things were never quite the same between us. The romance, like my airline ownership dreams, was doomed. I'd never get a chance to meet her robber baron father. Just as well, I suppose.

I found W.W. at Bryson's and explained what I had seen.

"You think we got screwed?" W.W. said.

That comment remains the single greatest understatement I will ever likely hear in my life, aviation related or not.

W.W. and I searched every pilot bar on 36th Street in vain for Three-fingered Hank. We learned a little about him in the process.

Some Corner pilots we talked to condemned Hank as a crook but others said that Hank's intentions were honest and that he might have simply fallen victim to the biggest enemies of upstart airlines: overenthusiasm and underfunding. There were a lot of such unsettled character issues in the Corner.

Lingering guilt persists to this day concerning the doe-eyed lass. Today I have the money she loaned me and would gladly repay it with interest. I could even take care of that little matter about the cigarette burn on her antique Steinway. I just can't seem to remember her name. Identify yourself, doe-eyed trusting lady, and I'll put a check and an autographed copy of the book in the mail. One for your rich robber baron father, too.

After the doe-eyed lass threw me out, I slept a couple nights in the back seat of my car, ala Morgan the *langosta* runner and master of the tiptoe landing. I knew what kind of things had taken place on that back seat, none of which made for restful nights.

My career in the Corner was over. I had given it my best shot but once again aviation's brass ring had eluded my sweaty, grasping hand. I decided to return to Ohio where I could stay with my parents and maybe borrow a few bucks from my brother-in-law. I still owed him money for the long-gone DeSoto but he was a pretty good sport.

With barely enough cash for gas, beer and smokes, I packed up the old Jag and left Miami. Unable to resist one last look at *Princess*, I swung by the Corner again.

To my complete surprise and boundless joy, the padlock had been removed and the gate was wide open. There were a half-dozen mechanics working on the DC-7, climbing all over it. Hank had come through after all! I was ashamed of the way W.W. and I had talked about Hank the night before and the awful names we called him. To think I had doubted Three-fingered Hank's integrity, not to mention my own business acumen. I climbed out of the Jag, which was just getting up a good head of steam, and walked over to the airplane. Trans Celestial Air Transport was going to fly! I had arrived in aviation!

"Hey, you," a guy working on top of the wing yelled at me. "Get the fuck outta here!"

I didn't like the tone of his voice. I wondered if he knew that he was speaking to one of the founders, principle stockholders and soon-to-be line captains of Trans Celestial Air Transport. I'd make a point of getting his name. There's something about being involved in the upper management of an airline that turns a person into a petty, vindictive son of a bitch.

"Just who do you think you're addressing?" I asked in the stern tone of a top executive.

"You, fuckhead, that's who I'm addressing!" he said, spitting a dark brown wad of tobacco over the trailing edge of the wing. The wad sailed twenty yards in the coastal breeze. "Get out of here or go get a hard hat. No one's allowed in here without a hard hat."

Oh, how I had underestimated Three-fingered Hank, especially his approach to safety. Imagine that? I had never heard of a hard hat being required equipment in the vicinity of an airplane. Trans Celestial would surely break all kinds of new ground. Okay, I'd get a hard hat, but I'd still get the guy's name. I walked away to search for a hard hat.

"And put out that cigarette!" the soon-to-be ex-employee of Trans Celestial Air Transport yelled.

It seemed that Hank's safety-mindedness knew no bounds. In 1967, no bounty yet existed on smokers in America. With the exception of churches—never much of a problem for me—and movie houses, we were free to practice our vice openly. As a reluctant concession to safety, I flicked away my cigarette.

While looking for a hard hat, I heard a great resonating thud behind me. I turned around. The number one engine was no longer on the airplane; it was on the ground. I surveyed the situation more carefully. A guy with a torch was cutting through the motor mounts on the number two engine.

The men were not mechanics as I first thought. They were too rugged, too muscular, too destructive. They were salvage workers. They weren't fixing *Princess*.

They were *scrapping* her!

As if to punctuate my sudden revelation, number two engine crashed to the ground.

One by one, the four mighty Wright 3350s gave way to the cutting torch, shaking the earth as they hit. To keep *Princess* from falling backward, the salvage crew had attached a chain from a hefty truck to the nose gear, like a vestal virgin restrained for ritual sacrifice.

I walked back to my Jag. Its guts rumbled more than usual. The engine would have to cool before I could start it again. I was going to be there for a while, whether I wanted to or not. I figured I might as well stay and watch the show, a kind of gallows witness. I sure as hell had paid for the ticket. I grabbed a beer out of the ice chest and returned to *Princess*.

A stout, bull-browed workman appeared at the cabin door of the DC-7 with one of the pilot seats. He lifted it over his head and threw it from the airplane into a pile of scrap parts. I dragged the seat off to the sidelines, set it upright and sat down. I sipped my beer and savored what I might do to Three-fingered Hank if I ever saw him again. Maybe I'd dismember him, just like these goons were dismembering *Princess*. Three-fingered Hank? How about "No-fingered Hank?"

The salvage crew turned its full fury on the right wing. Ten minutes later, the wing separated and the fuselage keeled over. The left wing slammed to the ground in abdication. A seagull landed atop the rudder, surveyed the commotion for a few minutes, and shit.

I walked around *Princess* as the team of ax murderers truncated and disemboweled her. Like the Hindenburg burning on camera, she was quickly reduced to a pile of tangled, disassociated parts, deprived even of the usual four-stage Corner extinction process.

Oh, the inhumanity!

Truck after truck carried my aspirations away to smelter hell. *Princess* would reincarnate into beer cans or, worse yet, Jaguar parts. I felt profound sorrow for her. I knew I'd recover from the fiasco; I'd recovered from worse. But *Princess* would vanish without a trace—just like Three-fingered Hank and my money.

A couple hours later the scrappers loaded the last pieces of aluminum and steel that had been *Princess* onto a flatbed truck. As the truck drove off, a long aluminum stringer that draped over the tailgate swung up and down. The stringer seemed to be waving goodby to me. I'm not sure what made me do it but I waved back. I chugged the rest of my sixth beer and, with nothing left for me to do, laughed till I cried.

I'd been in the Corner for about seven weeks. In retrospect, maybe I didn't give it enough of a chance. Or maybe I wasn't tough enough. Hard to tell.

I filled five one-gallon jugs with water, enough to sooth the Jaguar's troubled intestines for about three or four hundred miles, and restarted my self-imposed exile to Ohio. Back to harsh winter, back to twin-Beeches, back to west side Cleveland babes. As usual, I left my latest aviation venture with nothing more than some hard lessons, a few good stories and increased doubts about my future.

The Jaguar overheated one last time on a highway outside Atlanta and caught fire, fulfilling its destiny. I managed to rescue only my beer and cigarettes. I watched the flames reduce the car to a charred carcass. All that remained were toasted seat springs and four cooked tires atop a smoldering black mass on the pavement. That Jag never looked better.

As a finale, the gas tank exploded and scattered the ashes. A small bit of fabric blew out of the fire and floated whimsically for a few seconds before landing at my feet. I picked it up. It was a hot pink hibiscus, all that remained of my snazzy Hawaiian shirt. I folded it carefully and put it in my pocket.

The wind also carried away bits of scorched cloth that I recognized as my despised cheap suit. No great loss.

My prized seven-dollar five-cell chromed flashlight was quite another matter. Heat-swollen batteries pushed out the burst end of the flashlight as if it were giving birth to quintuplet technomonsters. I loved that flashlight. It was the one thing in aviation I had thought inviolate and beyond the reach of ill fortune. I was never able to find another like it.

I became philosophical, a handy and mostly painless alternative to suicide. What is aviation, I asked myself, if not a burning, unreliable 1953 Jaguar that we stoke with our dreams, some more combustible than others. For six years I had fed my efforts to the flame and so far all I had to show for it were ashes: no money, no job, no prospects, no babe and, most recently, no transportation or prized flashlight. This latest outrage removed any doubts I might have had that the playful Gods of Aviation Misfortune had singled me out for their personal entertainment. And why not? I certainly never disappointed them. Folly loves a fool.

As I hitchhiked north I shook my fist at the skies and resolved to outlast the gods.

"You're bound to run out of lightning bolts sooner or later!" I shouted to the heavens. "I'll find a cushy berth in aviation yet! You'll see!"

Meanwhile, until the curse expired, I had no choice but to make the best of the diversions the gods tossed my way. Maybe I'd jot down a few notes. Someday I might even write a book. Yeah, sure.

The End

Made in the USA
San Bernardino, CA
14 December 2015